EMPIRES

ISBN:978-0-99794806-6 (Paperback)
ISBN: 978-0-99794807-3 (eBook)

Library of Congress Control Number: 2021920042

Any references to historical events, real people, or real places are used fictitiously. All characters, incidents, and dialogue are drawn from the author's imagination and are not to be construed as real.

New Rose Press

New York, NY

EMPIRES

C. J PASTORE

"Her name's Sanaz." A picture of a tall, dark-haired woman in Afghan army fatigues floods Buford's screen. "Sanaz is in the intelligence branch of the Afghan police force," he says, pointedly looking my way. Sammy and Mac's eyes remain glued to the screen.

"Two days ago, an explosive-laden Humvee penetrated their outpost and detonated." Another click, and the screen lights with strewn bodies and enough detached limbs to fill a hospital corridor. "All thirty guards were killed along with five American soldiers. Insurgents overran the unit. As the defenders fled, Taliban-linked militants picked them off one by one until the force of one hundred commandos, police, and militia fighters was eradicated. Sanaz was lucky to survive but was taken prisoner. A reliable source communicated she's being held just outside Lashkar Gah."

Stroking his Van Dyke, Sammy gives a low whistle. "That's Taliban turf." Sammy's been part of my team since our first tour in '06. We've seen enough death and suffering in this never-ending war to understand that it's best to carry out orders without getting caught up in the glory of the cause. I haven't been issued any orders yet, but already I know that entering this area is a risky operation. The province is home to poppy seed fields that produce more than three-quarters of the world's opium. Opium sales, plus Taliban, equal enough money to buy arsenals of sophisticated weaponry to attack American forces.

Buford works his way into what will be my final mission as part of a task force of military intelligence in the United States Marine Corps. On an overhead screen, the photo of a full-bearded Taliban bigwig emerges. He has the penetrating eyes of an assassin.

"This is Mullah Hamidi, referred to by his followers as *amir-ul-mumenin* or commander of the faithful," Buford says. "Hamidi first joined the jihadi war in the fight against the Soviets. Since then, he's led ruthlessly effective insurgencies against local governments, foreign soldiers, warlords, and basically anyone who stands in the way of his self-appointed military and religious authority. Currently, this includes Afghan military officials who, under his influence, have been known to switch sides."

No gray area in this mission. Trust no one except myself, Mac, and Sammy. On the screen, a map of the province appears with a circle drawn around a huge swath of territory. "Looks like our friend the mullah governs most of the province."

"He does." Buford stares hard at Sammy. "And his goal is to fight his way into each and every village until he controls the entire area's opium trade."

"So, the long and short of it is, this mullah is helping the Taliban seize back control of rural outposts one province at a time." Mac cracks his knuckles. "How does this Sanaz fit into the equation?"

I've known Mac since boot camp. His quick mind and nose for trouble have kept all three of us alive.

"Afghan intelligence indicates Sanaz is in possession of sensitive information concerning the whereabouts of a large arsenal of weaponry. It's essential that her release be negotiated before the mullah and his forces find out about the armory." Buford studies me with glacial determination. "Your orders are to slip into the region, negotiate and secure the release of the value item, and then deliver her back to the Afghan authorities." *Value item* is Buford's way of saying the kidnap victim is essential.

"How's she doing?" It's the first question I ask. I need to know how much time I have to recover her before she breaks and talks during an interrogation.

"For now, she's holding up, but who knows for how long before she lets on what she knows." Buford doesn't say it, but we know that there are always ways to break a prisoner to get the information you want. "If that happens, we run the risk of the information being sold to the mullah."

"What do I have to work with to negotiate her release?"

"Enough cash to guarantee that wells can be dug and water piped in to curtail the drought that's drying out the Helmand River."

"How does Chase get in and out of that heavily-guarded area?" Mac asks.

"A new militia under US leadership will make sure the surrounding area is cleared of enemy positions so Chase can slip in undetected and connect with his asset." Buford shifts his attention to me. "A trusted local has been assigned to navigate you to the village where we believe Sanaz is being held. Sammy and Mac will escort you to a deserted area where your asset will find you. After that, it will just be you and your guide looking for Sanaz. Once her location is discovered and proof of life is determined, you can begin negotiations. After Sanaz is released and returned to the Afghan police, your asset will contact Sammy and Mac, who'll pick you up at the designated safe zone." Buford pauses and brusquely adds, "Any questions?"

I confirm relevant locations and sketch a diagram of safe outposts. Buford adjourns the meeting with a swift, "Good luck out there."

As soon as I pack my gear, I FaceTime Alicia. Raking my eyes over my wife's face, I soak up the tug of her tender smile. We've been apart for several months and the need to reach out and feel her lips against mine is strong.

"Hey, you, how are you?" She dabs her mouth with a tissue and waits.

"I'm good."

"No problems?" she says, reaching for a cracker. Something's wrong, but I hold off asking what it might be. I can tell she's worried, so best to put her at ease first.

"No, everything is going smoothly. After I wrap up an assignment, I'll most likely be discharged."

"Yes!" Laughing and crying, she pumps her fist in the air. "When do you think you'll be coming home?"

"Soon. I have something to finish up first."

She pales and holds the tissue to her mouth again. "Is it dangerous?"

"Nothing I can't handle."

"Best we head out now," Mac shouts from the truck. Her eyes stay glued to mine.

"Communication will be tricky while I'm out on assignment, so you may not hear from me for a while." She reaches for another cracker, looking as if she's about to puke. That's when I figure it out. "Alicia, when was your last period?" She appears flustered, as if just becoming aware of something that shouldn't have gone unnoticed. "You might want to take a pregnancy test." She nods, and I kiss two fingers and press them to the screen. "Until later."

"Until later," she repeats and does the same. I slip a photo of her inside my shirt pocket, replacing the hollowness of not being with her with the logistics of the job ahead. The faster this mission is completed, the sooner we will be together again. The thought of seeing Alicia again coupled with the possibility of becoming a father is the optimistic boost I need to finish this assignment safely and efficiently.

I jump into the vehicle with Sammy at the wheel. Mac keeps watch from the backseat. It's not long before we're bumping along a thoroughfare that looks like it was constructed during biblical times. As we near the target area, a downpour saturates the road, making it difficult for our Humvee to navigate the rugged terrain. Finally reaching the location where we're to take our leave, I grab my pack and give Mac and Sammy a thumbs-up.

The rain has stopped but the usually dry sandy road is muddy and slick. Heading down a remote path, my eyes stay peeled for my asset. I don't have to wait long.

"Hello, my friend," he says, smiling and waving. He's young, too young to have grown a beard yet. In a place where long beards dominate among men, he stands out as an innocent. This will make it easier for him to slip in and out of hostile neighborhoods unnoticed.

"Mr. Chase," he hurriedly whispers. "Come with me now. It is not safe for you here." He nimbly leads me down a steep path while sweeping his eyes in front and in back of us. There's a caginess about him that's masked behind an affable, loose-limbed bearing. "My name is Ashraf." He extends his hand after our several-mile run slows to a brisk walk. By that time a desert wind has blown in from the south, wiping out any moisture from the previous rainstorm.

Traveling undercover inside villages that lead to where Sanaz is being held runs smoothly. Economics is universal, so with plenty of US dollars and Ashraf's linguistic help, Sanaz's location is quickly revealed. I slip Ashraf his payment, and like an actor stepping off a movie set, he meshes back into his life as a farmer.

The parley for release strums next. In Afghanistan, like everywhere else, presenting a deal so that the opposing side feels like the winner is paramount. I meet with a group from the Provincial Council, who directs me to a smaller village leadership association. Lots of American dollars with promises of water rights are exchanged and, *voilà*, Sanaz is released into my custody.

Sanaz strides toward me with the long-limbed gait of a gazelle and the blazing smile of a cabaret performer. "Let's not give them any opportunity to change their minds," I say, pointing my chin in the direction of the hut where she was being held. She deftly hops into my hired truck, securing her scarf around her head and neck. I slam my foot down on the accelerator, cut the wheel sharply, and in no time, we're bouncing off ruts and rocks to complete the first leg of our trip back to safety.

It's while we're at our second safe house that I learn how much Sanaz loves pigeons. Several locals keep pigeons in mud rooftop cages. Setting them free at various intervals then having them fly to meet other pigeons before returning home is a favorite pastime. Sanaz's piercing whistle calls some from the sky to her outstretched hand. She doesn't say much to me, but she's never at a loss of words with her birds. She even carries one with her during our treacherous trek to our final safe house. Holding it by the open window, she strokes its feathers before letting it fly free. "It's time," I tell her, walking toward the truck.

For several hours, we drive along a deserted road that leads to the Afghan outpost where she's expected. She looks at me and smiles, and for the first time since this mission started, I let myself relax.

"We'd best be careful how we approach the police checkpoints," she says, surveying the road ahead. "Your vehicle could become an easy target for terrorists. Let me off here and I'll walk toward it by myself. A woman is less likely to invite unwanted scrutiny from anyone who might be watching."

Another study of the outpost reveals only barren stretches of land snaking in all directions. I nod and she exits the truck.

"Thank you," she says, tapping the car door with the palm of her hand, then sashaying toward the guard post as if she hasn't a care in the world. When she's close enough to be recognized, I hit the accelerator.

It's dusk by the time I get to my pick-up point. I park the vehicle off the side of the road and behind a cluster of trees and bushes, where it will remain hidden until Ashraf picks it up later. Exiting the vehicle, I creep toward a collection of bushes, bending my head to avoid a tree. Where the hell are Sammy and Mac? There's no moon yet, which makes it better for hiding. Yet, in the blackening silence, I sense eyes. Mindful to keep away from the road, I step carefully into the shadows to wait.

I'm not sure exactly when I realize I'm not alone. Maybe it's the sound of the press of a boot against rocks and twigs. When I look ahead, a chill runs down the nape of my neck.

Heavily-armed soldiers in Russian-made night-vision goggles swarm in my direction. I don't see anything come at me as much as hear something swish across the air.

Blackness.

Next thing I know, I'm being dragged into a squat building in the middle of nowhere. My hands are tied behind my back and someone rifles through my pockets before I'm forced down a ladder and into a cellar where I'm thrust into a chair. The collar of my shirt is sticky against my neck. From the way my head pounds with pain, it's got to be blood. I'm not sure if I'm going to barf or pass out. Yet someone still thinks I'm alert enough to have a conversation, because directly across from me is none other than the mullah himself.

"You have been very active during your stay here." Mullah Hamidi's smooth, soft voice contrasts with the steel in his eyes. His English is quite good. The righteous mullah must have studied at an English-speaking school.

Sweat trickles into my eyes and blurs my focus, but if I'm going to get beaten anyway, I figure why not speak my mind while I still can. "I'm never too busy for you, Hamidi. In fact, now that I'm here, maybe we can swap kidnapping strategies over tea."

"Shut up!" One of his men slams the butt of a revolver against the side of my head, snapping my body sideways.

"Your teeth will not sink into us. We will break your teeth," he shouts, then stabs his fist into my face, forcing my neck back and leaving the taste of blood in my mouth as I hit the floor at his feet. This is not helping my headache, so I figure it's best to keep my mouth shut.

"Enough, Rashid," the mullah orders as Rashid readies his fist for round two. "Let's leave our guest conscious so he can adjust to his accommodations." His gentle, soft tone doesn't fool me. His type is generally the most sadistic in these situations.

He proves me right when he launches repeated kicks into my body, making it feel as if my ribs and stomach have been shoved against my backbone. He climbs the ladder to an opening in the ceiling, where Rashid waits to raise the ladder and bolt the hatch. It takes a while for my eyes to adjust to the darkness of the windowless bunker and discover that the only point of entry or exit is the opening in its ceiling, eight feet up.

Time marches on as it always does. If I had to gauge the days by the number of beatings, I'd say I've been here several months. The mullah is the worst of the lot. He has the habit of dropping in unexpectedly to shoot me up with some drug that turns my body and mind into mush. It's when I'm in one of these drug-induced sleeps that his smooth voice coaxes me awake. Forcing my eyes open, I see he's sitting in a chair opposite me, waiting for me to regain consciousness. For some reason, the respected mullah is choosing to linger in my sub-par accommodations. If it's to get me to talk, he's wasting his time. I've already disclosed all that I know about my assignment.

"We have something you'll be interested in seeing."

Thrusting a photograph in front of my eyes, he repeatedly kicks my sides to force me to focus on the image. I recognize the eyes first: two orbs of green smiling into the camera.

Alicia.

My hand automatically reaches for the pocket of my shirt, but there's only shreds of cloth remaining. "You bastard." I lunge and grab the photo with a strength I didn't think I had. For a brief moment, my thumb traces the corner of her mouth, and I swear her warm breath travels across my fingers. A fist that feels more like a cement block than knuckles slams into my jaw. The photo is pulled from my clutching hands as I topple backwards. I'm yanked up by my hair and forced to make eye contact.

"I will shed the blood of all infidels who come to my country," he says, spittle foaming the sides of his mouth. "She will know," he waves the photo of Alicia in my face, "what it is to suffer loss, as I have had to learn each time I bury those killed by your guns and bombs." He tosses me against the wall where, blindly reaching once more for the photograph, I collapse back into a heap of drugged stupor.

In and out of consciousness, minutes tick by, or maybe it's hours. It's hard to think past the drugs that cloud my mind. All I know is that one second there's stillness, and the next an ear-bursting explosion rocks the earth. My arms fold over my head as mud, bricks, and glass rain from above. Screams and moans puncture the air. Then, blanketed blackness.

When I come to, a whistling sound echoes in my battered eardrums and a layer of debris from the roof that once stood above me covers most of my body. I shift on the concrete floor from under the beam that saved my life, scraping the skin of my arms raw until I can tug my hands free. Wiping sand and grit from my eyes, I follow a stream of sunlight that peeks through mountains of debris. It's as if some higher power is shining a flashlight to guide me out of this hellhole. Above, the lintel and wooden door remain in place while the rest of the structure lies in scattered piles of rubble.

It's hard to breathe through my bomb-blasted lungs, but adrenaline keeps my body moving. Bit by torturous bit, I climb a mound of sliced rubble and surface into a day so drenched by sunlight, my unaccustomed eyes seem soldered shut. The stench of cooked flesh mingled with blood and dust sting my throat.

As I hug a well-shadowed wall of wreckage, a burnt, dismembered arm still clutching a rifle in its hand blocks my path. I slide the weapon free, hoping it's only the dead who keep me company on this scorched landscape. As soon as the thought pops into my head, the humming sound of a truck's engine vibrates in the distance and screeches to a halt just beyond the rubble. I drop to my stomach and crawl toward where the debris is piled higher. A heel scrapes against the ground. Voices approach. Clutching my weapon, I wait.

"We cannot stay here," an unknown, urgent voice says.

"Not until I find his body or return him alive to the mullah." No mistaking that voice. Sanaz's rapid, light footsteps advance, forcing me to slide deeper into the remains of the structure.

"*Mayne zamini,*" Sanaz says, her tone sharp. I can't understand what she's saying, but I do recognize that she's speaking Persian.

"No, no land mines here. This looks like an American drone strike," her companion answers, his English peppered with an Iranian accent. What the hell are two Iranians doing in an outback area of Afghanistan? No answer to that yet, but I have determined that Sanaz wouldn't shed any tears if my corpse was buried under this rubble.

Compromising my position is not an option unless I'm sure I can take out her partner. There's no way I'm being turned over to the mullah. I slowly raise myself into a crouching position, making sure not to disrupt any rocks. Fingering the rifle's trigger, I press my back against the wall of wreckage and stare ahead, my ears attuned to what my eyes can't see. Light, quick footsteps move closer.

"My cover's breached as long as he's alive and free to move about. I need to be sure this arms contract is finalized and the mullah collects his arms and bounty money for the kidnapping."

Arms contract? Bounty money? What the hell is she talking about? And then it hits. Sanaz must be brokering an arms deal with the Taliban, who, for some reason, were also paid to raid the outpost and then kidnap me. Amazing how the tangled conspiracy she's part of contradicts her packaging. She's fooled us into believing she's fighting on the side of the Afghan government when she's actually negotiating a weapons deal with the mullah and his forces. She had to have some kind of foreign government backing to carry out this operation.

More footsteps approach. Christ, how am I ever going to get out of here alive? The pain in my ribs from repeated beatings make it hard to breathe. The wounds on my stomach and back throb and my lungs feel as if they've been set on fire. I stay hidden. A Russian-accented voice rattles no more than fifteen meters away, and an icy ripple creeps up my neck.

"There is no way he survived this," he tuts. "And such a shame, too. I was starting to enjoy my little cat-and-mouse game with his comrades. What's done is done. Now is time to leave here and close our deal. That way your *great* country and mine," the Russian's words drip derision, "benefit from the chaos that follows, the *holy* mullah collects his money and weapons, and I satisfy my end of the deal and get my payment. Everybody happy." It's a voice I know all too well.

Dimitri Ostopenko. What is that psychopath doing here? He should be rotting inside an American jail for what he did.

The strange thing about fear is that it keeps adrenaline pumping, dampening pain and sharpening thinking. Sanaz is a double agent. On one hand she serves as a military operative for the Iranian intelligence agency, MOIS. On the other, she acts as an Afghan police officer. Both provide her with sensitive information about Afghan and American operations. With no political loyalties to Afghanistan, she passes sensitive intelligence to Taliban insurgents.

Her Iranian sidekick is some kind of senior commando sent to help her wreak havoc against Americans in this shadowy war we're having with Iran. And the Russian kingpin, Dimitri Ostopenko? Shaking my head, I mull over the implausibility of how a personal vendetta that began in my hometown when I was fourteen could stalk me fifteen years later in Afghanistan. Parts of this convoluted mishap make sense. Dimitri's notorious for appearing wherever there's money to be made from illegal enterprises. He's not afraid to insert himself into the political unrest of a country to do so. His being the man on the ground in conjunction with Iranian spies to supply the mullah with weapons is not surprising. That he's here at the same time I am is alarming. No one knows more than me how fate can be fucked up. But a coincidence that involves a direct encounter with an archenemy at a distance of over seven thousand miles from the original contact is no accident.

This is about you; a hard voice of truth talks inside my head. You *were the one who helped get Dimitri convicted for the rape of your friend.* You *were the one who offered the proof that crippled his power and took him out of commission, paving the way for the murder of his eldest son in a drug war. Now, he quenches his thirst for revenge by threatening and attacking* you *and* your family.

My final realization nearly brings me to my knees. What better way to satisfy his insatiable vengeance than to have Islamic militants kidnap an American soldier to sweeten a brokered arms deal? Dimitri could never have pulled this off alone. Even with the help of his army of thugs, it would be hard to take on the American military. He must have had the help of a Russian military intelligence unit who paid a sizeable bounty for my kidnapping and the deaths of American soldiers during the raid.

"Rashid don't look too good," Dimitri says. His footsteps stop and there's some rustling of paper before he's on the move again.

I'd love nothing more than to shoot a tunnel through his head for what he's done to me and my family, but that would mean turning myself into an easy target for the remaining two. Martyring myself to mete justice would only serve to satisfy this maniac's lust for vengeance.

"If we don't find his body here, we split up and search the countryside. He can't have gone far with his wounds." Sanaz is not accepting Dimitri's belief that I'm dead. She bridges our gap, but her steps are tentative. She must still be worried about buried IEDs. The crunch of their boots intensifies. Sanaz is so close, I hear her expelled breath with each footfall. Down the road Humvees rumble, and their footsteps freeze. "It's not safe to be here any longer," Sanaz's Iranian commando says, taking off in the opposite direction from the approaching vehicles.

"He's right. Is time to go now," Dimitri insists, moving away from where I'm hiding. It's no surprise that they can't get out of here fast enough. Two colluded to destabilize the Afghan government and another to amass huge profits selling illegal arms to fuel his nefarious underworld business. This unlikely trio does not want a run-in with the Afghan police or the American military. More footsteps approach and, crouching, I shift position and peer over the wall. Someone hollers from the distance. I duck back down.

"Sanaz, it is good to see you are well."

"Ashraf, my friend," she answers, "what brings you here where there is so much death and heartache?"

Ashraf sounds distracted. "I am looking for Mr. Chase," he whispers. "Maybe you find him?"

Why wouldn't Ashraf think Sanaz was also searching for me? As far as he knew, we were both operating on the same side, since I was hired to negotiate her release from the Taliban. Taking a chance, I gingerly raise my body for a glance at what I'm up against. Staring at their backs, I see Dimitri and Sanaz shifting closer to Ashraf. My finger inches toward the trigger. Two clean shots just waiting for the press of my finger. I turn to take aim when a thumping explosion kicks up rubble, sending debris rocketing through the air and me flying backwards. The stealth of warfare here is never-ending. It's as if explosive trip wires link one territory to the next.

I'm barely on my feet when Sanaz says, "Drop it, or I kill him." Her gaze never leaves mine while her hand holds a revolver to Ashraf's head. Ashraf, eyes scrunched closed, stands still as death. Several yards ahead, the Iranian commando—or what's left of him after triggering a land mine—lies crumpled on the ground. Standing next to Sanaz, mouth pulled into a wry grin, steely eyes oozing malevolence, is Dimitri.

"I'm amazed at life's little ironies," he chuckles as if we're in a classroom instead of a devastated death zone. I keep my weapon aimed at Sanaz, eyeing the best shot I have of killing her while sparing Ashraf's life.

"I don't know what you're talking about, Dimitri."

His reptilian tongue licks parched lips.

"One second your captors have you secured inside an underground prison," he says. "And then," his eyes widen and he snaps his fingers, "moments later you are free and they are entombed corpses."

"Well Professor D, sounds like your little tutorial applies

to you, too. What are the chances an incarcerated rapist can transform himself into an international arms dealer conducting business in Afghanistan? Talk about an irony that would interest the Pentagon."

Sanaz's eyes dart between us, then back to her hostage.

"You always were a cocky bastard. Even as a kid," Dimitri says.

"What can I say. I'm good with a camera and as determined as you are to settle a score." Dimitri's expression darkens with the reminder of the photos I secretly snapped of him raping my friend, Devie. Those photos I took when I was a fourteen-year-old kid helped convict and incarcerate a Russian mob king who had stymied the FBI for years. Talk about life's paradoxes.

"It's your sister who's the real photographer, if I recall." He hits back from my jab, tut-tutting and shaking his head with false concern. "So unfortunate that she is a drug addict."

I don't take his bait, but while I have his ear, and nobody's killing anyone yet, I push another one of his buttons.

"How's the wife and kids?" I know all too well that his oldest son Yuri was gunned down in a gang war in Moscow, and his wife and remaining children were tucked away in the witness protection program while he was rotting in a jail cell. He hasn't seen or heard from them since. Revenge sucks at his empty soul like a piglet to a teat.

"Far better than yours are going to be when I'm through with them," he snarls, reminding me of his ruthless attack on Alicia.

"Enough!" Sanaz shouts. Her searching eyes travel up

the contour of my body, and a slow smile spreads across her face. I watch her trigger finger, every muscle in my body alert. "I wondered where your hatred against one American soldier originated, Dimitri. For you men, it's all about getting even. I have no interest in your personal vendetta. The American knows too much to set free and is too valuable on the open market to kill. So, soldier," black eyes flash the icy gleam of a fanatic, "you've got until the count of three to drop your weapon, or I kill Ashraf." Her arm tightens around Ashraf's neck, her hand presses the gun muzzle to his head.

Something metallic juts from Dimitri's pocket, but he's not wielding a gun. He knows that if I decide Ashraf's life is not worth sparing, I can take out both him and Sanaz before he has the chance to reach for his weapon.

"Time's running out, Chase."

Sweat peppers my forehead. A fractured rib slices into my lung, making it hard to breathe, but my gun remains aimed at her face.

"One," she counts. Ashraf is so still, it's as if his soul has already left his body. My finger leans closer to the trigger. Hatred for what she did is so thick, my body roils with its weight.

Make the kill.

The venomous voice holds no doubt, no remorse, no foresight. It's all mine, and it can't be silenced.

A rapid movement of feathers flaps low in the sky. A clatter of wings whizzes above our heads. The pigeon aims for its familiar perch on Sanaz's shoulder.

Sanaz blinks.

Once.

Twice. That's all it takes.

My shot is a stem kill; a hit that paralyzes the victim until death seizes its grip. Sanaz's body folds into a mound of jellied bones and muscles, her mouth contorting into an open grimace of shock.

Ashraf springs free.

Relief frees a thought. The courier pigeon is how Sanaz communicates with her people. Simple, discreet, and efficient, just as I am when I fire a bullet into its side. It drops like a stone. Not missing a beat, my weapon swings toward Dimitri. Clouds of green smoke, thick as a tapestry, shroud the area.

"Killing you was never part of the plan," Dimitri calls out, his voice swallowed in rancid fog from the smoke grenade he detonated. "Death is easy but suffering . . . suffering is the hell our enemies thrust us into to even the score." Dimitri's emotionless voice travels through darkening smoke. "Every time Rashid beat you, he would say how much he hated your kind. Now, even in death he speaks to you."

I fire several shots, but the plume is too thick for me to hit my target.

"Mr. Chase, we leave now," Ashraf says, coughing and wheezing. He points at the approaching motorcade of Humvees. They look armored to American standards, but it's unlikely to be Americans this far into enemy territory. With so many factions struggling for power here, who knows who they are. The time to clear out is now, but something about Dimitri's final words echoes a threat.

"Wait!" I hustle toward Rashid's body. In the thick smoke I nearly trip over his remains. His blown-off head lies several inches from his tattered torso. Jutting from the blackened opening of what was once his mouth is a white piece of paper and a photograph. I fish both out, then feel my way toward Sanaz's body. I rifle through her pockets for her phone, then sprint with Ashraf over rocks and cracked, dry earth, anticipating gunshots or explosive devices to hit at any moment.

Spasms of pain wrack my body. My burnt and blistered hands throb. Dust and smoke from the explosion clog my lungs. When my breath seizes, Ashraf pours water past my lips, quenching my thirst so we can keep moving. It's dusk by the time we take shelter inside the engulfing blackness of a cave. I fight to catch my breath, but fear refuses to let my hand let go of the papers I took from Rashid's corpse. I unfold the photograph first. It's the one I carried of Alicia on our wedding day. I kiss it, then slowly smooth open the paper that was crumpled in my fist. If we were followed, any light could give us away, but I don't care. I need to see what it says. Using Sanaz's phone for light, I blink away sweat and grit and focus on the black scrawl. I live a lifetime in the few seconds it takes to process its message.

Alicia Cesare/Baby Reardon-765 Park Avenue New York, USA

From somewhere behind me there's a shuffling sound. I try to spin around with my gun raised, but the sharp pain in my ribs bends me double. "Who's there?" I mouth to Ashraf, lifting my head. He peers into the darkness and shakes his head. All is silent again, and I give a sigh of relief. I need to live. I need to get home NOW. Anything less means death to the person I love most.

There's a change in the dank air and new scraping

sounds get closer. I think I hear the faintest of whispers. My head spins and it's hard to breathe. I fall to my knees, clutching the kill list and my gun, as the floor of the cave looms closer. Footsteps approach, strange hands reach out, and then . . . blackness.

• • •

The shade of a tree umbrellas the heat as cool liquid moistens my lips and throat. "Drink easy now." My body sways with hands that raise my head and hold a cup to my mouth. Forcing my eyelids open, I realize I'm lying in a hammock in clean clothes, with my wounds dressed and my body washed. I look up into Ashraf's cagey, smiling eyes. "Good to see you are awake, my friend. You were gone long time. I try to find you, but very strong persons keep you. They search for you now."

What? My body shifts to flight mode, but my legs collapse when I try to stand.

"Do not worry," Ashraf places his arms under my shoulders and lowers me back to the hammock. "They not find you here. You okay in my family home for now. Your friends come get you soon."

I fall back asleep to the memory of Alicia smiling in her wedding dress.

• • •

Buford's not wearing his happy face during our post-mission meeting in Kabul City. After recuperating in hospital for three weeks, then being debriefed for several weeks after that, it's still hard for me to move without pain. Walking saps most of my energy, and I'm constantly thirsty. It's like the dust, grit, and stench from my captivity remain lodged in my throat. Yet all I can think about is getting home. Buford chooses to ignore my impatience. We sit at a small table. He glares. I remain silent. Finally, his lips flap. "New intel has come through, so a final debriefing has been scheduled for you tomorrow. Get some rest. The sooner we start the sooner you'll be back stateside."

Like hell I'm going to wait to be debriefed again. With Dimitri on the loose and my family on his hit list, all I can think about is getting home. I don't share these specifics because Buford doesn't give a shit. He'd just have some nitwit who didn't know his ass from his elbow assigned to sporadic security to watch over Alicia.

First thing Sammy and Mac let me know after we boarded a Black Hawk to safety was that Alicia could give birth at any time. They also informed me that there was no way they could reach me at our designated rendezvous point. Taliban had the area surrounded from the get-go, courtesy of Sanaz and her fucking pigeons.

"That's not possible," I tell Buford. "My wife's due to deliver any day, and I need the first transport back to the States. I know you have unanswered questions, and I assure you they'll all be addressed after I secure things at home."

Buford reddens from the scalp of his sharply-parted hair to the bottom of his clean-shaven face. "Counterterrorist specialists in National Security have more questions for you to answer."

I didn't believe it possible, but he flushes further while his eyes bulge like a frog's.

"She was a value target, for Christ's sake. Your orders

were to bring her in alive, not to kill her."

Now we get to what really matters, and it's not about my health and well-being. With Sanaz dead, valuable intelligence was lost.

"As I explained in my initial debriefing, I delivered Sanaz into the hands of Afghan authorities. What followed after that had to be done. She was an enemy militant working to arm insurgents to incite political unrest. With no way to make contact with you, I determined that as long as she was alive, US forces operating in unstable areas were in danger." *And, asshole, she was going to kill Ashraf.* I leave that out because Buford doesn't care. With Buford it's all about the greater good. He wanted Sanaz alive because he wanted her interrogated about the international network of foreign agents she was part of and dealing with.

"You say you brought her in. We never saw her."

"That's probably because your *value target* had other plans."

He bristles with frustration. "A more comprehensive debriefing is necessary ASAP. We have a volatile political and security environment, and we're heavily invested in the counterterrorism piece."

Translation: The Taliban are advancing and wreaking havoc with suicide bombs and rocket attacks in safe zones.

"You didn't seem concerned about my statement when that armed MQ-9 Reaper drone struck the location where I was held."

"We had eyes on you at all times. We knew you were in a basement cell. Just like we knew we were going to rescue you after the drone attack."

"Did those visuals show you who set the trap for my

capture?"

He stiffens. It doesn't take a genius to figure out Buford suspected Sanaz was part of that plot. US Intelligence officers must have assumed she was in tight with insurgents and wanted her corralled for an interrogation. Then there was the Russian connection. No way was Dimitri here acting alone. If I had to guess, that's the missing link Buford wants to learn more about.

"You survived like we thought you would, and we got you out as planned."

His mouthpiece is blowing out so much hot air, it sounds like he's talking out of his asshole. It was just a matter of time before the mullah and his army of soldiers discovered where Ashraf was hiding me. Buford and his team may have been monitoring my whereabouts, but there were little guarantees a rescue was secured.

"I gave an initial statement at headquarters, complete with Sanaz's cell phone. The tech staff unlocked it with information I secured from the time she and I spent together. It's all in my report. I'll be back for a final debriefing next month. In the meantime, it might be prudent to investigate the link between Russia's military intelligence agency and Taliban insurgents. My guess is Sanaz had their help brokering a half-billion-dollar weapons deal with the Taliban."

"We're searching for an endgame to this godforsaken never-ending war," Buford barks, "and missing weapons in the hands of a volatile enemy is not the way to go. We need to understand everything you know about the Russian mob link. We're concerned the strengthening association between enemy state structures and organized crime is destabilizing the area."

This argument is going nowhere. I'm out the door before he finishes. I love my country and plan to do my part, but they have enough to investigate for now. If I explain further about Dimitri, there's a good chance I'll be detained several more weeks to establish how far up the government chain the Russian link goes. Right now, I can't waste any more time. When a voracious cobra is slithering toward people you love, you have to be there to prepare for its strike.

CHAPTER 1

New York
After Chase's final debriefing
Alicia Cesare Reardon

"You're here." Wiping away tears, I face the man who, a short time ago, I thought was dead. Now, it's as if the candles I lit for his safe return provided a path for him to find me standing in the chapel in Summit where we were married just last year. My thumb nervously traces the smooth gold of my wedding band. Guilt and remorse clang inside my head with the force of a marching band. It's hard to forget what I did. It's going to be even harder for him to forget and to forgive. What an idiot I was.

You were scared, an internal voice whispers and, like a gnarled tree bent by betrayal and deceit, the past comes back to haunt me. I remember the jolt of loneliness I felt when, just two weeks after we were married, Chase left for his second deployment in Afghanistan. I knew Chase had completed one tour in Afghanistan, but never realized that he could be called to active duty again. When we started dating, he was a Yale graduate with a successful real estate development firm in New York City. Military intelligence missions, war, MIA, these were events that happened to those trained to fight and send loved ones off to battle. I was a fashion designer, clueless about what life as a deployed soldier's wife entailed.

Fear turned to panic when I learned that he went missing while on a mission. As days turned into weeks, then months, not even his superiors knew if he was still alive. It was as if he had vanished into the Afghan countryside. I was convinced he had been killed. When he was able to escape the clutches of the Taliban, I was ecstatic. It felt like I had returned from the dead, too. Once he was debriefed and returned home, we began piecing together the remnants of our former lives. Conceived shortly before Chase left for Afghanistan, Caroline was the surprise gift when I forgot to take my birth control pills during our weekend wedding festivities.

Chase had fought through the post-traumatic episodes resulting from the trauma of his capture with the same courage that propelled him through his difficult childhood.

I maintained my small fashion label while throwing myself into marriage and motherhood. I knew what I had done while he was away was wrong, and I damn well knew it was something we needed to talk about, preferably in a therapist's office. That chance evaporated when Chase dropped a piece of news that still reverberates in my mind.

"I have to leave for another debriefing in Afghanistan. It can't be helped . . . I'll be back soon. Wait for me . . ." he pleaded when he saw the shock and frustration that marred

my face.

I couldn't believe that after all the pain he suffered as a prisoner of war, he had to return yet again to Afghanistan. Would this be the third of a never-ending series of deployments? Furious, I felt as if I had been deceived.

"I married a businessman, not a soldier. Why should I wait? I didn't last time." I flung the ugly, hurtful words at him as he was readying to leave. What followed was a physical altercation I wish I could erase from the universe, but past events cannot be undone. Instead, they live on as regrets.

• • •

Light from the flickering candles of the church coax me back to the present. He's returned for good, I tell myself. Just as he said before he left last time, his return to Afghanistan was administrative. I bite my lip with worry. The possibility of yet another deployment remains a nightmare that lodges in my mind.

As if he hears my concern, he cups and raises my chin until our eyes lock. "I promise you it's over this time. My debriefings are complete. My superiors are satisfied."

I rest my palms along the sides of his cheeks, and my thumbs stroke his face before I pull his lips to mine. They're warm and gentle, not as hard and hungry for my touch as they had been before. When I deepen our kiss, he shifts his mouth to the side. I've scarred our relationship. I took something golden and turned it into lead.

Tell him how you feel, how you always felt even when you behaved like a deceitful fool.

"I'm glad your deployment is over, but it's no matter. I'll love you forever."

I want to jump into his arms, cry, cheer, laugh, and hold him to me to show him how happy I am that he's back, but shame gnaws into me, its teeth sinking so deep, I'm a prisoner to its hold. Eyes the shade of the Mediterranean at high noon stare into mine, prompting me to finish telling him what I have thought of every day since he left four weeks ago for his final debriefing.

"I need you to know that I'll wait even if you're ordered to leave again."

My eyes fix on his lips that I want so badly to kiss again, but it's too soon. I lock my hands to my sides and look down, so I don't have to see the disappointment on his face.

"When did you get back?"

"I just arrived in Summit," he says. "Once my work was finished, my discharge orders came so fast, I didn't have a chance to phone before leaving. As soon as I flew into the country, I tried calling but couldn't get through. I phoned Sammy and Mac and they mentioned you were hosting Thanksgiving dinner at our country house, so my buddy flew me into Albany. Sammy and Mac picked me up at the airport, and we drove straight here. They tried phoning and texting you several times to let you know I was on my way home, but service is so spotty here, they couldn't get through either." It's hard to overestimate the value of the friendship and business connections Sammy and Mac share with Chase. The three formed an indestructible bond of brotherhood during their deployments in Afghanistan. Even now, each would risk his life to protect the other, including any or all loved ones.

"I wouldn't have planned this Thanksgiving dinner if I knew you were coming home and . . ." I'm finding it hard to finish so I stop, stand on my toes and kiss him lightly on the lips, letting my finger trace the stubble on his chin. I can't help myself. The urge is too strong. He doesn't quite pull away this time, but he doesn't lean in either.

"Chase, we need to talk. There's so much I have to explain . . ."

"Not now with everyone at the house. C'mon, I noticed you have Mae tethered to the tree outside the chapel. We'll ride back to the house together. I haven't seen Caroline, and I hear your family is here and mine is on the way."

He's in charge again, indicating in no uncertain terms that he's not ready to talk yet, but I'm bursting. I want to tell him how sorry I am, how he's all that matters, but his mind is made up and with a houseful of guests waiting, there's no time to explain all that needs to be said. How do I just blurt out that the terrible choice I made was my inept way of trying to escape a dire situation? Even to my ears, the excuse sounds lame.

Chase takes my hand in a warm, firm hold. This simple touch, after all we've been through, makes it seem as if I'm floating inside a slice of heaven instead of wrapped in the harsh reality of what I know is yet to come.

Straddling the saddle behind him, I wrap my arms around his chest and rest my cheek against the soft fabric of his shirt. The hardness of his back presses into my skin. "Mmm." I close my eyes. "You smell good."

He doesn't answer, but I feel his smile.

"You won't believe how big Caroline is," I tell him. "She makes these ooh and ahh sounds, and well, she's such a happy baby."

"That's good. I missed her." He pauses, his back

tightening under my grip. "Any problems while I was gone?"

I'd prefer not to have to talk about Dimitri, the vengeful, murderous fiend hellbent on destroying us since Chase and I first began our relationship, but after all he's been through, I want to put him at ease. "No, it's been quiet." I shrug. "Maybe Dimitri fled the country."

His back stiffens again, but he doesn't say anything. He's holding something back, that's for sure, but now is not the time to press for details.

My fingers itch for a cigarette. Instead, I stare at the path ahead, waiting to be soothed by the majestic maple and oak trees that line the driveway to our ranch.

Purchased by Chase while he was growing his real estate empire after his first deployment, our country home in Summit sits atop a mountain surrounded by one hundred fifty acres of prime forested land. Blanketed by pine needles, the stone path leading to the entrance paves a warm welcome. Terracotta pots bursting with chrysanthemums and marigolds sit atop each of the four steps leading to the veranda. Planting them was the salve that soothed my soul while Chase was gone. Likewise, for the two wreaths woven with crimson-colored leaves and flowers that hang on the oak double doors.

"I think my sister's car just pulled into the driveway," Chase says.

He helps me dismount, then leads Mae into the barn. Chase's sister Fiona walks up the long path with his nephew Liam skipping at her side. Fiona, Liam, and I formed a tight bond here while hiding from Dimitri and his murderous thugs, who were trying to kill my unborn baby.

Liam is clutching his stuffed giraffe, Pepi, and the Dr. Seuss book, *Oh, the Places You'll Go*. I remember reading that book to him here when I was pregnant with Caroline and didn't know if Chase was alive or dead.

And when you're alone, there's a very good chance you'll meet things that scare you right out of your pants. The urge for a cigarette heightens with the memory of the words that scrape my insides raw.

I'm ashamed to admit that while Chase was away, I started smoking. Continued even though I was pregnant. Each night I escaped to our rooftop terrace where, wrapped in Chase's coat, I lit up and stared at the stretch of tall buildings and city lights. Each time I promised myself it was going to be my last cigarette, until the next lonely night rolled around and the need for one urged me back onto the terrace. It was during one of these nights that it happened. God, how I regret that I let sadness and fear drive me to hurt the only man I've ever loved.

Waving to Fiona and Liam, Chase walks up the path and pulls me into his shoulder. "You're shivering. Are you cold?"

I inhale. Mmm, sandalwood and soap and inside those, his own human smell, warm and musky. I missed those scents.

"A little bit."

His arm tightens around me, releasing it only when Liam reaches up to give him a kiss hello. "Hey there, little guy." He lifts a squealing Liam onto his shoulders, then gives a quick scan ahead. "Where's Dad?"

Fiona pauses, her smile tight.

"He's feeling a bit under the weather. Said he'd drive up tonight or early tomorrow morning in time to join us for Thanksgiving dinner."

Chase lowers Liam onto the porch, wincing a bit in pain when he bends to scoop up Liam's dropped book and stuffed animal. Although it's been several months since his release, jarring pain in his ribs and back still linger from the repeated beatings he suffered during his captivity.

"What's wrong with Dad?"

"Nothing serious. Some indigestion and a headache." The features on Fiona's elfin face remain smooth; even her smile is level. I'm not surprised. I've known Fiona for years and have seen firsthand how any discernible tension is hidden in her stillness. It's a quiet that makes you forget she's present. It's what helps her discreetly disappear for weeks without anyone knowing where she's been or why she left. And after she resurfaces, bruised, beaten, and hooked on drugs, her vague explanations are peppered with calm assurances that it won't happen again. Fiona is an enigma that defies logic. On one hand she's a devoted mother and loyal family member, and on the other, a drug addict plagued by poor decisions and low self-esteem.

When I think back to before Chase and I married, it's impossible to forget Fiona or her ring. The very ring that played a part in my abduction by Dimitri. The one that I knew by heart: the flawless luster of its turquoise stone, the elegant filigree of its white gold setting, the perfect lift and angle of the stone. Imagine my surprise when it showed up on a severed finger in a package sent to me by that monster, Dimitri. It wasn't Fiona's finger, but it damn well was her ring.

At the time, Fiona flatly denied it was her ring in that package. She only admitted her ring had been missing after it was confiscated from the apartment of one of Dimitri's thugs during a police raid. Without batting an eye, she told the police that it must have slipped off her finger and gotten lost. How it had showed up in that apartment, she claimed she had no idea.

I scan her hand quickly and there it is, the ring that belonged to her deceased mother. My relief is so immediate, I want to take her in a hug and cry. I know it's silly, but that ring on her finger gives me some assurances that Dimitri is not winning.

"Enough about Dad. Let me give you a big welcome-home hug." Fiona hands me wrapped platters of food that a sneak peek shows are her signature cinnamon rolls and spinach quiche. She throws her arms around her brother and stands on tiptoes to kiss him on the cheek.

"We missed you." Her eyes closed, the relief on her face runs deep. "We couldn't believe it when Alicia said you were called back after all you'd been through." She breaks contact, then strides over with wide-open arms and takes me in a warm embrace. "Hey sister-in-law, it's great to see you, too."

"Same here." I pull her close, the solace and optimism she provided while Chase was missing still fresh in my mind.

She holds me at arms' length. "This is the happiest I've seen you in a while. You're relieved, I can tell."

"I am." I smile and take hold of Chase's hand, giving it a squeeze. He even lets me kiss his palm, but I stop there. Another kiss might be pushing it too far. All in good time.

"We have some serious pie baking planned, but we've got lots of help." She sweeps wisps of auburn hair away from her forehead and tilts her head, mischievously widening her eyes. "Why don't the two of you go inside for some alone time, to catch up and all."

Chase stares stonily ahead. "You all go ahead and do what you planned. I'm going to check on Caroline."

A fissure widens in my heart, but I can't blame him for the way he's acting. His rejection is all my fault.

"Oh my goodness, look who's back," my mother calls out. Face flushed from baking, she envelops Chase in a hug and kisses his cheek. People jostle through the door to welcome him home. There's some backslapping from my brother Antonio and my father, hugs from our friend Devie, and another round of kisses from Fiona and Liam. And then there's me . . . standing in the background, smiling relief on the outside while crying regrets inside.

Returning everyone's hugs and kisses, Chase stretches his thumb in the direction of the nursery to indicate that he's going to check on Caroline. If anyone senses Chase's apathy toward me, they're too polite to comment. I know there are no alternative pasts where reality can be undone, so I grasp a positive I can savor. *He came to the chapel to find me first.* For now, it will have to be enough.

The kitchen whips back into a flurry of activity. My mother is up to her elbows in flour. Antonio, in crazy patterned pants with the rim of a Mets cap backwards on his head, mixes pastry dough for pie crusts. Mac and Sammy carry in bushels of fresh apples and jars of preserved peaches for pie fillings. Devie, head bent, hair angled into a sleek bob to conceal the scar Dimitri carved into her left cheek when she refused his orders to hurt my unborn baby, cores and slices apples pulled from a basket resting on the counter.

Emotionally and physically scarred by Dimitri, Devie unwittingly sealed Chase's fate with Dimitri when she and Chase were teenagers, growing up in the same south shore community of Long Island. Chase provided photos to the authorities that showed Dimitri raping her when she was only thirteen. My god, even then he was brave, putting his life on the line to ensure that a good friend found justice.

But that is a truth that paves the past. Now, everyone's laughing and talking at once, happy that Chase is safely back. I try to look busy, setting aside some apples to slice, but above the din, Antonio shouts, "Hey sis, what are you doing hanging out here? We got this. Go be with your man." He wiggles his brows. "And leave the baby monitor here. We'll take care of Caroline when she wakes from her nap."

I brace my shoulders, draw in a shaky breath, and step into the nursery. Chase studies Caroline, who's asleep on her back, arms thrust back, hair curling onto her forehead. He passes a finger over her soft cheek and watches her sleep.

Tiptoeing from behind, I wrap my arms around his chest and rest my cheek on his back. I will away the tears burning my throat, but they fall anyway. "I missed you," I whisper.

"Did you?"

His sarcasm cuts into the silence that follows. When I don't let go, he turns and breaks my hold. Face to face, we lock eyes, mine imploring, his skeptical. He leans forward until I feel his breath caressing my lips. Then just as quickly, he pulls away. "I've been having some flash-backs that keep me tossing at night. I'm going to sleep in the guest house. No need to wake Caroline. She looks so peaceful." He gently strokes her auburn tufts of hair with his finger. Refusing to look at me, he grabs his packed bag, steps toward the windows, and pokes his finger under one slat of the horizontal blinds to peer outside. Satisfied, he tugs at each window to ensure they're locked.

When he heads toward the bedroom door, anxiety shoots through me for two reasons: One is the obvious. He's leaving our bed, which means he's refusing to have sex, and two, the one that shatters me in several places, is that he hasn't unpacked his bag. A part of me—the rational part—says he is planning to unpack it in the guesthouse, but the other part, the part that harbors my deepest fears, shouts that he's keeping it packed because he has to report back. It's what happened last time, so why not again.

Feelings of loss, loneliness, and fear that haunted me when he went missing pummel my gut now. What if . . .? I don't let myself complete the thought. Instead, I buck up and share what I know is a steadfast truth for him to carry with him wherever he might go.

"Only you. It will always only be you." The words, choked by tears, crack and when my voice trails off, he turns back to peck me on the cheek before leaving.

It's more than I deserve.

CHAPTER 2

"Is Chase going somewhere?" Devie says, after he nearly takes off my nose when I try to walk him out the back door. Devie knows what happened that day. She happened to be coming into the apartment to babysit Caroline just as Chase stormed out to report back for his final debriefing. It takes me a few seconds to realize the kitchen clan has stopped working and is waiting in silence for an answer. I force a smile.

"Chase thinks it'll be better if he sleeps in the guesthouse. He's exhausted and it's quieter."

Their continued silence speaks volumes about this turn of events. Our behavior is markedly different from last year, when we couldn't take our hands and mouths off each other.

Devie brushes her hair from her forehead with the back of her hand and lifts her chin in the direction of the closed door. "Good idea for him to rest up. He'll need it for later. No?" Her glib tone adds levity to an otherwise awkward situation. Everyone returns to baking pies.

Catching Devie's eye, I point in the direction of the

living room where we can talk in private. She picks up the cue and, wiping her hands on a dishtowel, slips out of the kitchen. By now, my façade has crumbled.

"He's leaving me, Dev," I blurt, not giving her a chance to disagree. "I just know it, and all I keep telling myself is that I have no right to expect anything less. I'm not the kind of woman a man like him deserves, a man who'd give his life for his country, who lives for his family, who's loyal . . ." I throw my arms around her, allowing myself to break down for the first time since Chase returned.

She wraps me in a hug. "I don't think he's leaving you, and what's with all this talk that you're not good enough for him? You're special person who deserves to be loved."

"I'm a terrible person."

Devie's Russian accent is more pronounced with each point she makes in my favor. "You are not bad person. Would terrible person risk their life to save me like you did?"

I study her through tear-streaked eyes.

"You were the one who drove me here after Dimitri sliced my face and beat me to a pulp, even though Detective Wilson told you to leave me at the hospital. Before that, you suffered under Dimitri's knife too when he sexually attacked and tried to maim you in your building. He wouldn't have been able to do that without my help. Yet you refused to leave me alone in the hospital. If anyone is a terrible person, it's me. My cowardice nearly got you killed."

"But you didn't hear the horrible things I said to him before he left. I was so angry and scared." It's hard to say the words that haunt my conscience out loud. "Oh God,

Devie. How could I have cheated on him with another man while he was missing in Afghanistan?" By now, I'm sobbing into my palms. Not only did I betray my husband, I did it while he was risking his life to serve his country. As if that wasn't bad enough, I blurted it all out in an angry tirade right before he had to report again. There is no end to my shame.

"I'm not saying you didn't make a mistake, but you were afraid; you thought he was dead; you were pregnant and alone. I know what it's like to be so trapped by fear and loneliness that you would do anything to run from the pain." She hands me a tissue from her pocket. "Sometimes we have to get lost before we can find ourselves. Besides," her face brightens before memories from an ugly past resurface. "It only happened once, and you ended it."

"Yeah, one time and before Chase, none." Her eyes widen, then relax when I continue. "He was my first and only lover until . . ." I can't bring myself to say his name. "And now that one time may impact my life more than the countless others with Chase that meant so much more." Being with Chase is what I wanted at the time. It's what I still want, but I may not have a choice in the matter. Watching our relationship slide through my fingers like scooped water might be the painful punishment I deserve. "I'm beginning to understand that this whole business of growing up and learning lessons is unending; and it's exacting too. You don't get it right the first time around, it slaps you down until you learn it the next time."

"What are you talking about? You are most reliable person I know. You have a family who loves you. You're a dedicated mother. You always choose the right path to take."

"Not really." Twisting my lips into a wry grimace, I count off successive wrongdoings: "Arrested for smoking pot in Monaco, sexually assaulted and beaten by Dimitri after I didn't heed Chase's warning to stay put in my apartment . . . and no, I don't blame you for that attack. Your life was threatened by a madman who had hurt you so many times in the past. Just like me, you were a victim, too. Now I have this major blunder to reckon with. I'd throw in forgetting to take my birth control pills right before my wedding, but that would mean clumping Caroline into the mistake category. She may have been an accident, but she's cherished and adored, and I can't imagine life without her."

Self-loathing and remorse rocket through me once again.

"Yeah, I get what you mean," Devie says. "I had so many scuffles with life, I was like boxer who fights rounds in ring just to fight one more the next day. You think you are only one with mistake list? Running away from home, quitting school, experimenting with drugs, sleeping around with men who abused me. I did it all to try to escape my past."

I close my eyes and nod. Her childhood, like Chase's, was fraught with hardships. Her mother still abuses drugs, taking up with all kinds of men to feed her habit. Dimitri was her live-in boyfriend when he raped Devie. As bad as that is, if that was the worst of it, we'd all be moving on with our lives. But as luck would have it, Dimitri turned out to be a Russian mob boss. He wasn't happy about being convicted of statutory rape, thanks to Chase's evidence and eyewitness testimony. He was even less happy when his eldest son was killed by a rival gang, and his wife and remaining children entered the witness protection program while he was incarcerated. Mounting rage turned to ruthless vengeance against Chase.

After Dimitri's conviction, things just got worse for Chase. He lost his mother to cancer. His father drank himself into a perpetual alcoholic stupor, and the police lost interest in protecting two teenagers from Dimitri's vengeful thugs. They had their man locked behind bars. The case was closed. Chase was on his own.

She squeezes my hand. "I've known Chase since we were kids. He's stubborn pain in the ass and won't be easy to deal with, but he loves you. He'll forgive what you've done." She lowers her head, crestfallen. "He forgave me after your attack."

"Don't go there, Devie. You can't blame yourself. Dimitri gave you no choice but to help him. You grew up with Chase and his sister. They were a big part of your past. Once you knew Dimitri had Liam's schedule and that he threatened to kidnap him if you didn't cooperate, you felt a need to protect him and Fiona. In the end, it all worked out. I survived, Liam stayed safe, and you," here my voice cracks again with tears, "you went on to save Caroline from that butcher even though you knew what that meant." I move strands of her dark hair from the scar that mars her left cheek. Even with the carved mark, her angled cheekbones and otherwise flawless apricot-tinted skin present an alluring sophistication.

"Go face him, and the sooner the better. Hear what he has to say and be strong. He's not going to go easy on you," Devie advises.

I wipe my tears with my sleeve. Waves of nausea hit my stomach.

"You can do this."

I nod, because what choice do I have? More than anything, I want to repair our relationship. I want to be his wife. I want Caroline to have a father in her life. None of that is going to happen if we don't talk about what happened.

"Dev?"

"Yeah."

"Do you ever think about life's cruel twists?"

She studies me, waiting.

"I couldn't wait to embrace adulthood. I wanted nothing more than to be able to go out into the world, make my own decisions, and to pursue my dreams. When Chase proposed, I knew without a doubt that I wanted to spend the rest of my life with him. I figured, once he returned from his tour in Afghanistan, we'd start up again exactly where we left off, madly in love and blissfully growing businesses."

She's listening, but she has this skeptical look that's a cross between pity and disbelief. Life has slapped her around so many times that understanding my conviction must be tantamount to believing that a fairy godmother is real.

"I know you're thinking, *how can anyone be so naïve*, but I was." I shake my head and look down. "Now that I'm bearing all the burdens of the mistakes I've made, I crave the simplicity of my youth, but it's too late to ever get that innocence back. I can't undo what I've done."

My heart feels like it's collapsing into the smallest pieces possible, taking my self-worth with it. Devie throws her arm around my shoulder and guides me toward the kitchen.

"You're twenty-three but talk like you are old woman. Let's think positively. Chase is back and even though he acts like stubborn pain in the ass, he's staying. No? You have a whole happy life ahead of you."

"Only if he forgives me." I dab my eyes with the tissue, but tears continue to fall.

"Talk to him. Find a quiet place here where just the two of you can meet." She hands me another tissue and kisses me on the cheek.

• • •

"Well, don't just stand there looking confused," Fiona calls out, a smear of flour dusting her cheek. "Grab rolling pins and start smoothing out these crusts."

My brother Antonio locks her in an embrace and playfully nibbles her neck. "I love it when you act all bossy."

It's weird hearing my brother act that way with Chase's sister. It's like extending your family with the inverse of another family, but they've known each other for a while now so I've had time to adjust.

Falling into step with the others, I throw myself into pie baking, using the press and roll of the wooden cylinder to help me pull out and smooth through the thoughts I plan to share with Chase. If he'll let me.

Once done, I grab my coat and head to the porch for some alone time to think. Pulling a cigarette from my pocket, I light it and take a long drag. Ahead, several hundred acres of land, cross-stitched with trees, brambles, bushes, and ivy, climb a summit that has at its base a stretch of lake as smooth as glass. Flakes of snow move in the air like pieces of lint blown this way and that. Crisp, chilled air smelling of baking and woodsmoke mingle with an aftertaste of regret.

Through the pine needles of tall trees, slivers of filtered sun elongate a shadow. Blinking through the smoke, my gaze shifts toward the window of Caroline's nursery where a large shape, hidden by a cluster of trees, skulks through the brush. I stub out my cigarette and step from the porch for a closer look. The moaning wind shakes leaves to the ground and whips them across the path ahead.

To my left, a doe and her fawn stop along a worn deer path to feed. The grace of their munching steals my attention away from the shadowed form that, when I finally do look back, has disappeared. Seems like my preoccupation with my marriage is stirring my imagination to see monsters when the real beast lies inside of me.

Placing one foot gingerly in front of the other, I head down the long slope toward the trees where a herd of female deer feed with their young.

"Hey there," I whisper to the closest fawn. "Look at you, eating your fill with your mamma." Through the filter of trees, I admire the sheen of the fawn's spotted coat.

Caroline loves to watch the deer. Her creased legs kick and her arms whirl with fascinated excitement when she sees one. Staring at the luster of the fawn's fur, my mind conjures a jacket in the same hue that I'll sketch later. Hope and creativity are stimulating companions. One uplifts the spirit. The other stokes the imagination. Chase is safely home. All else will fall into place.

Looking into the silence of towering trees, I inhale a

lungful of pine-scented air. The closest doe's head jerks up, its dark eyes peering from the trees. There's a snap of twigs, then another. A loud crack sends me reeling back. Something warm and wet splatters my face, assaulting me with the sickening metallic odor of blood. A suddenness that gives me no time to process what's happening thrusts me back in time.

• • •

A large envelope with my name scrawled on the outside sits on a table in the mailroom of my building. Inside, the bloody pulp of a severed finger wearing Fiona's ring glares back. A hand snakes around my mouth and drags me down the steps to the basement. I want to shout, to run, to push my captor away, but the knife Dimitri Ostopenko presses to my throat freezes me in place. His fetid breath dampens my neck.

• • •

A scream carried in waves by the wind plunges me back from then to now. A second, more piercing cry sends flocks of crows cawing from treetops, their wildly flapping wings moving in tandem against the gray sky. It's then that I realize the screams are mine. My legs lock in fear, and a cold prickly sweat peppers my neck. Nausea hits my stomach. Blood gushes from the fawn's side. Felled, its eyes watch with death's unseeing gaze.

Someone tackles me from the side. We hit the ground hard. His body covers mine. His extended arm swivels a rifle in an arc like it's part of his hand. I don't recognize this person who's more soldier than lover, but I do smell his sandalwood and soap. It's amazing how different smells can cause an involuntary familiar flooding of both safe and horrific memories.

The heat of Chase's body, his face framed in falling snow, lulls my terror to a dulled fear. Shouts in the distance call out an all-clear. Chase springs to his feet, takes my hand, and hoists me to my feet. My heart races, my legs wobble. All I can think about is where I first saw that ominous shadow. "Caroline," I shriek and make a mad dash for the nursery.

"Wait," Chase tugs me back. "Caroline is fine." He pulls me toward his chest. My spiked adrenaline slows. No longer do I feel like I ran a sprint. My eyes linger on the once-vibrant fawn that lies in a crumpled heap of tan coat and long legs. "It's cold and you're shivering. Let's head back to the house. There's nothing more we can do for the deer."

CHAPTER 3

S ome internal force seals my mind to the scene of the senseless kill I just witnessed. The fallen fawn carries a gruesome message.

Caroline. Dimitri is after Caroline.

His stink is all over this incident. I've learned a lot about Dimitri in the two years I've been with Chase. Maim, murder, terrorize, sexually assault, kidnap. It doesn't matter. No ploy is too dirty or callous to be off limits. It doesn't matter who's destroyed so long as the retribution war is won. We are all targets for him to use to punish Chase.

Gazing at the fire, sipping spiked, hot cider, the playback of the dead fawn dims. Chase hasn't left me or Caroline alone for a moment. Sitting on the sofa, my feet folded under me, his arm wrapped around my shoulder, the other holding Caroline in the crook of his arm, I watch him narrow one eye, while a muscle throbs in his jaw. Chase knows as well as I do that Dimitri purposely left me alive even though I was in his crosshairs. The dead fawn is a dress rehearsal for his real intent. My flesh creeps when I think his attention is now riveted on Caroline.

I take another sip of cider and the hot, sweet liquid spreads through my chest, warming my body and relaxing my limbs. I lean into Chase's arm, savoring this closeness, while Caroline, her pacifier drawn in and out of her mouth in soothing sucking motions, studies his face. My parents, along with Fiona, Liam, and Antonio, have hit their beds for naps. The long drive here, hours of baking, my bloodcurdling screams, and a murdered fawn have left them exhausted.

Chase pulls me closer to help quiet my trembling and bits of what we once shared fall into place. It's foolish to think that fear for another's safety excuses a betrayal. For our relationship to survive, he's going to have to accept me as his wife because he feels the full depth of my love for him and understands that what I did was a mistake I won't repeat. His loyalty to our marriage can't hinge on the blame he heaps on himself for Dimitri's attacks and threats.

He loosens his arm from around my shoulder and turns to meet my gaze. "We have to talk about what just happened and the sooner the better. I need to know what you saw and heard while it's still fresh in your mind."

Outside, the wind whistles, rattling the windowpanes, making me want to stay nestled under the blanket, nuzzled in his arm. Caroline only wants to stay cuddled, too, because she starts crying when I strap her into her seat so we can have our discussion. Putting her pacifier back into her mouth soothes her cries, but she studies me with teary green eyes that tell me the quiet won't last long.

Thank heavens Sunny arrives. Who would have expected a former Pakistani army medic would become part of Chase's tight band of combat brothers who keep our home ordered and our lives safe? It just goes to show that the frenzied force of war can cement strong relationships as powerfully as it destroys lives. Chase saved Sunny from a roadside bomb during his first tour of duty in Afghanistan, and when Sunny showed up at his doorstep offering his loyalty and services to pay Chase back for saving his life, Chase didn't have to think twice. He renovated the apartment to include a room and private bathroom for Sunny and invited him to stay.

With calm self-assurance, Sunny sweeps into the room, nods a formal hello to us, then lifts Caroline from her seat. She kicks her feet and smiles, dropping the pacifier from her mouth when he holds her up and gives a sniff. He wrinkles his nose, and both disappear into the nursery where Caroline will be bathed, fed, and pampered so we can take care of business.

I walk into the study first. Chase follows. The crackling fire in the large stone fireplace radiates a warmth that I hope will ease my shivering. I always did like the serenity of this high-ceilinged room with its expansive views of lake and woods.

Mac, already at the desk, clicks a key on the computer. There must be a glitch because the same photo freezes. It's a stretch of barren desert with narrow curving indentations that seem to go nowhere. In the right corner of the screen is the location, Lashkar Gah. My eyes follow a path of arrows flagging names I don't recognize. One catches my attention because the words KILL LIST are written next to a chalked image of a body labeled, *Sanaz*. From where I'm standing, I can't make out the complete text without enlarging the font.

Chase clears his throat. When I turn to face him, he's pulled up two leatherback buttoned chairs for us to sit in. Now the screen shows images of the perimeter of our house flanked by different sections of the woods and lake.

The door opens and Clyde, who manages our property, enters, Devie on his heels. While growing up, Devie was often forced to trawl the underbelly of Dimitri's nefarious strongholds. Any clarity she can provide about where he might be operating from is valuable.

"Why don't you start by telling us what you saw." Chase's voice is business brusque. He wants answers, but I know his tone is heavy from the weight of the hurt he carries. There's no room for regret in this dangerous arena so I plunge ahead, amazed at how steady my voice is.

"I stepped outside for a bit of fresh air." I leave out the part about smoking, although I'd like nothing more than to light up right now. "At first, nothing out of the ordinary happened. But then I thought I saw a shadow—"

Sammy interrupts, turning the screen in my direction, "Can you recognize in these photos where you first saw this shadow?" He hits an arrow that highlights different shots from various angles outside the house. It's hard to determine where I was standing in relation to the different locations shown in the photographs of the house.

"You'd have been standing in this area." Chase points to the image on the feed. "The woods are to the north," he slides his finger to an area not seen, "and the house," he hits a key to highlight another photo, "is situated here with the bedrooms looking out in this direction."

Looking closer, I locate the angle and source of the

shadow. "This is where it was, because I remember thinking how it slanted toward the window of Caroline's nursery."

No one says a word.

Sammy strokes his Van Dyke goatee, his gaze fixed on the screen. "What did this shadow look like?"

"I can't be sure, but it seemed to be the shape of a man with a large, square-like head and a broad torso."

More silence.

"Then, what happened?" Chase asks.

"I walked in that direction to see who was there."

He bristles, and I know he's annoyed at what he sees as a foolhardy decision on my part given our problems with Dimitri. I also know that the only reason he's not holding me accountable is because he wants me to continue explaining what happened without the messy constraints of an argument.

"The doe and fawn caught my attention and when I looked back, the shadow had disappeared."

"Did you notice any reflection of light nearby or a laser dot centered on the fawn?"

"No, but I did hear a snapping noise right before the loud crack of gunfire."

The memory of the blood from the shot fawn and the flashback it triggered jars my mind. I put my shaking hands in my lap and take a deep breath to quiet my racing heart. Dimitri's attack remains an emotional scar that I have no choice but to live with.

"The shot could have been fired by a hunter looking for an easy kill, unaware that hunting is prohibited in this area," Mac suggests. He pours me a glass of water and only a bit topples from my trembling hand when I take a sip.

I take another swallow, then meet everyone's gaze head-on. Even I know the shadow I saw was too close to the house to be a hunter. Now is the time for me to speak frankly about what I believe. This can't be about protecting me, keeping me from knowing what is happening because I'll get upset if I know the truth. I understand alright. My family is trapped in a life-death situation that leaves no time to spare for coddling.

"This wasn't the result of some rogue, overenthusiastic hunter who doesn't abide by the laws because he wants," I wave my hand in frustrated anger, "to score a trophy to mount over the fireplace. The fawn was too small to provide bragging rights or meat for the table. No," I shake my head. "This was a calculated hit meant to serve as a threat of what's to come. It's . . ." my voice quivers, and I swallow back what feels like a stone caught in my throat. "It's Caroline he's targeting. He doesn't want Chase to have a family. That's why he tried to have Devie push me in front of a moving car when I was pregnant with Caroline. That's why someone was hovering outside her nursery window today, and that's why the fawn was killed." Anger defeats fear and my determination strengthens. "That maniac has to be stopped."

It's the first time I've ever wished someone dead.

Surprise widens Chase's eyes as they watch mine. He's shocked by my grasp of the scope of Dimitri's grisly cravings to hurt us, but I'm a quick study and Dimitri's a ruthless teacher.

"I hate to say it, but Alicia's right," Clyde says, his craggy face forcing a smile, as he bends his lanky body to offer me a cup of espresso. "When I inspected the area, there were human tracks angled toward Caroline's bedroom. I also found this." He holds out what looks like a hollow metal cylinder.

"That's a bullet casing from a Russian sv-98 sniper rifle," Devie announces matter-of-factly. How she knows this is anybody's guess. Could be when, as a child, she was forced to live with Dimitri when he and her mother were lovers. I'm guessing she witnessed the small arsenal that maniac must have owned even then. I'm about to ask if she has any idea where he might be now, but any further thoughts hit the brakes after one sip of the coffee has me covering my mouth with my hand and running to the bathroom. The retching is so sudden and intense that it takes me a while to realize it's Chase holding my hair back while I purge into the toilet. Crouching beside me, he helps me up and hands me a tissue.

"I'm sorry," I croak, shaking my head. "This has me rattled."

With a cool cloth, he sweeps back strands of hair that perspiration seals to my forehead. I melt into his touch, and my unsettled stomach calms.

"Are you feeling better now?" The back of his hand strokes my cheek, and I think I hear his breath catch when I cover it with mine. The moment passes when he slides it free and drops it to his side. My betrayal separates us like barricades in battle, only I'm not fighting. I want to surrender my regret with offered assurances that I'll love him forever. But most of all, I want to earn back his trust. I want him to look at me with that same blend of tenderness and excitement that drew us together before he left.

He lingers while I brush my teeth and smooth a comb through my hair.

"Let's get back so we can pick up where we left off. We need to formulate a plan." I'm already through the bathroom door when he takes my hand and tugs me back.

"Are you sure you're alright?"

My mouth curves into a soft smile. He still cares.

"I'm fine."

He looks skeptical, but I'm firm. I refuse to play the damsel in distress for sympathy when it's forgiveness I'm looking for.

Beams of relief greet me once I return to the study. They remind me of the bond that emboldens us to do whatever it takes to protect the other. It's almost enough to make me relax. In between our connection and Dimitri's vengeance lies the fact that Dimitri could win.

Chase jolts me back to reality with a cracker, a glass of water, and a familiar, no-nonsense tone. "It's obvious Dimitri is active and out to harm my family, but it's not only Caroline he wants to hurt." His voice cracks when he mentions her name, but he collects himself and continues. "That shot came very close to you. We have to assume it's both of you he's after."

He's partially right. Dimitri's menace hangs over us like canisters of poisonous gas ready to be released at any time, but I know that if Dimitri wanted me dead, that sniper had an easy enough shot to see that it happened.

"I don't think he wanted to kill me."

Chase stiffens when I disagree but doesn't take his eyes from my face.

"At least not this time. If I was the target, I'd be dead

now. The shot that killed the fawn was a clean, direct hit. I was in close enough range to be next. That shot was a warning of what could happen or will happen later on."

"That's a good point," Devie interjects. "Dimtri's hired killers rarely miss their targets." Chase swivels his head in her direction. "Don't look so surprised. The maniac once shared the statistics of his successful hits at the kitchen table. My mother was so high it barely registered, but he wasn't sharing for her benefit. He wanted me to know how he operated. The bastard needed me living in fear so I would be his pawn." Devie's revelation comes as no surprise. Dimitri banks on our suffering from the fear and anxiety his threats conjure in our imaginations. Dimitri's happiness, even his very existence, depend upon our anguish.

I reach out my arm and give her a hug. Devie is tough, but everyone has their limits of endurance. Being raped, beaten, and disfigured over the course of many years are hefty tolls to pay for unwittingly crossing Dimitri's path and then trying to escape from his tight hold. After all the times he successfully used her as bait to catch and harm us, he wasn't about to let her go without sending dire messages about what he was capable of doing next time.

"I don't doubt the validity of what you're saying about his targets, but we have to take Dimitri's actions seriously. He may not have wanted you dead today," Chase looks in my direction and then quickly away, "but tomorrow might be a different story."

"I'll do whatever you need me to so we can all stay safe."

Gone is the girl who resisted moving back home after Chase's initial deployment, the girl who believed independence meant not needing or accepting the help of others, the ignorant and untried innocent who thought that unwavering individualism was the only acceptable way to achieve independence and success.

Sammy knocks back his espresso in one gulp, then turns his attention to me and Chase. "It'll be easier when you're all back in the city. You're on the penthouse level, there's basically one way in and out of the building, and your doormen are vigilant. I will need to know when either of you leave the apartment no matter who you're with."

"Yeah, sure."

Logistics are put into place, schedules discussed, and recommendations made with the emphasis that nothing out of the ordinary should be ignored, no matter how trivial it may seem.

"Whenever you see, hear, or even think something's suspicious, tell one of us," Mac insists.

Gathering the coffee cups, Devie looks up and shoots me a nervous glance. "Are you okay?"

"I'm fine. Just had some passing nausea."

She quirks her brows and looks at my stomach.

"Impossible. He's been away and when he was home, we were careful." Regret fires up the thought that he refuses to lie with me now.

"Give him time," she whispers, while the others file out of the room. "He'll come around."

I walk with her until a voice pins me in my place. "Can I have a word."

Chase ushers the rest out and shuts the door. Oh boy, that expression, that tone can only mean one thing. I'm in trouble. I just can't fathom how it can get any worse than it already is. I don't have to wait long to find out.

"So now you're a smoker?" He nods his head in the direction of the ashtray I must have left on the porch.

All we have to deal with, and *this* is what he reams me out for. He studies me, head tilted, one eye squinting, as if searching for something he once held close but now seems to have lost. I want to tell him that he doesn't have to search for the person he loves. I'm here. I just let sadness cut me adrift. I never lost my love for him. I don't say any of this because he needs time before he believes in me again, and I need time to show him that my loyalty is sealed.

"I'm not proud of my actions or my habit." I close my eyes to shut out the shame. "I've been trying to quit."

"Oh yeah, and how's that going for you?" His skepticism hangs heavy between us. Having dealt with his father's alcoholism and Fiona's drug dependency, Chase is no stranger to what's involved with breaking addictions.

I don't avert my gaze. I've shrunk enough in his estimation of who I am. "Not good."

He whips out his phone, taps in a name, and waits. "Hello, Dr. Alexander, this is Chase Reardon." His voice is clipped and businesslike, his message brief. "I'd like to schedule an appointment for my wife, Alicia. Please call back at 917-868-3902 so we can schedule a session. Thank you." He hits 'end' and fixes me with a stare. "As soon as you can, text me days and times that work for you," he says in a mechanical, cold voice.

I've no time to ask who this person is I'm to see or what his or her specialty is, before Chase's expression hardens. Standing tall and stiff, he searches my face.

"Who was he?" he demands.

CHAPTER 4

All night, I think about that dead fawn. As soon as I shut my eyes, its bullet-shattered body and lifeless eyes spring into view. I imagine its carcass on the floor next to my bed with its mother circling in grief.

I tried answering Chase's question by explaining how I was feeling when he was missing. "Not knowing if you were dead or alive was terrible. I felt removed from the world, invisible." The words, trapped in my throat by my tears, continued in a painful whisper. "I would have done anything to free myself from that pain."

He listened in deafening silence.

When I paused to place my hand over his heart, he became still, his eyes mirroring angst and confusion as if he couldn't understand how he could be so wrong about my loyalty and love.

"I'm sorry. It was once and meant nothing. It will never happen again." Empty words that sank in quicksand when I stopped short of telling him who I slept with.

He waited. I hedged, holding my breath for some response, something that showed he understood why I'd done what I had, or even that he needed time to think over what I'd said, but these never came.

"You're protecting him," he finally spat. Then, angrier than before, he stomped off to bunk with Clyde in the guest house. I dropped my head in my hands and sobbed. I felt just as vulnerable, naked, and alone as I had when he was missing.

It's still hard for me to believe that I slept with Thomas. Thomas, who I'd known since third grade, climbed trees with, accompanied to weddings, proms, and birthday parties. Thomas, who stood by my side during my mother's depressive bouts and coaxed me back to life when I blamed myself. Our friendship strengthened as we got older, but there were no sexual overtures. At least not on my part. I wasn't interested. Thomas was a good friend. Period. End of story.

The act itself is an insignificant blur. One minute Thomas and I were talking and the next he leaned in and kissed me. At first, I pulled back, but then I relented. I barely remember the rest. Now, I'm afraid if Chase knows it was Thomas, this one-time act, committed under dire circumstances, will seem more significant than it actually was. Chase knows our friendship has deep roots.

Shame spearheads into insomnia. I toss. I turn. Then thrash about in my empty bed. Sheet and blanket coil around my legs and perspiration dampens my neck. I become angry at Chase for leaving and going missing, then turn that fury against myself for cheating while he was gone. Wrath wars with fear. Both take me into an unsettled sleep that churns with one nightmare after another. Dimitri holds a knife to Caroline. I seize a gun to save her only to realize it's jammed and won't fire. Again and again, I squeeze the trigger but nothing happens. Dimitri sneers with contempt, "She belongs to me now." I try to slam into Dimitri with the force of my body, but my legs are paralyzed along with my scream.

"Shh, shh." Firm arms cradle me against a muscled chest. A hand strokes my hair. The touch quiets the demons in my nightmare. Chase has come back to our bed.

"Don't leave me," I murmur. Vulnerable and stripped raw by fear and guilt, I allow myself to need him, and like countless times since we first met, he shows me that I can.

It's early dawn when I finally wake, spooned by Chase, his leg covering mine, his arm cast around my shoulder, where he softly brushes a kiss. One kiss and a flood of relief runs through my core. I'm not being totally rejected. I edge my backside closer to his warm body. "I'm here," he says. "You're safe. Go back to sleep."

And I do.

• • •

Gold slivers of sun slide through the blinds, and groggy from last night's unsettled sleep, I slip on my jeans and a hooded sweatshirt to fight the morning chill and see to Caroline's crying. Chase's side of the bed is empty, but I'm reassured when I hear the shower running.

Caroline refuses to stop crying and, squeezing her quacking duck to distract her, I quickly change her diaper then put her to my breast. She quiets, but it's just a matter of seconds before she's squirming and crying again. When after several attempts, she still doesn't respond, I hit the fridge to warm a bottle of formula. It's on my list to speak to the pediatrician about why she's rejecting breast milk. Maybe it's from all this stress. Deep breathing and yoga exercises are added to my to-do list. I would have fit in more of each, but my few free moments have been taken up with sketching. So many different designs envelop my mind and one in particular, a cream-colored silk taffeta dress cinched with a black patent leather belt, is begging to be drawn.

A screeching wail whips me back to reality as Caroline, red faced and squirming, demands to be fed. Bottle held to her mouth, I hug her to me and stretch out on the sofa. Dressed in a crisp white Nehru jacket and black pants, Sunny is already peeling potatoes. My mother rattles around the kitchen, preparing the turkey to roast.

"Good morning!" She brings me a sparkling water with lime and kisses Caroline's forehead. One long look at me, and her brow furrows. "Are you feeling alright?"

"I'm fine."

She pauses, prompting me to add, "I didn't sleep very well last night."

"Once we get this turkey going," my father hollers from the other side of the kitchen where he's mixing a chestnut and cornbread stuffing, "we'll take Caroline so you can get more rest."

Antonio saunters in and moves to the stove to start preparing mushroom and spinach omelets for breakfast. Owning a family restaurant and vineyard provides us with lots of cooking know-how, and Antonio, a graduate from the Culinary Institute, is an amazing chef.

"You look like you can use a cup of coffee," he calls out from the kitchen.

"No, thanks. I'm trying to stick to a pristine diet for Caroline. I'll take a cup of herbal tea, if it's not too much trouble."

"Coming right up."

The back door clicks open and Mac, standing where only I can see him, unloads and secures a rifle back into the lockbox. He's obviously been combing the perimeter of our property for anything suspect. His expression is warm, but he wears worried eyes. "Hey Alicia, how are you feeling?"

That's three asking if I'm well. It's certifiable. I look awful.

Shifting Caroline over my shoulder and rubbing her back to help her digest, I shoot him a toothy smile. "I'm good."

"No problems out there today," he adds, a rare grin tugging up one side of his mouth. I know it's to put me at ease. Mac must suspect that there's something wrong between me and Chase, but he'll never ask. The pact that seals them is grounded in privacy and respect.

"I invited Virgil to Thanksgiving dinner here. I hope that's okay."

"Virgil, my former boss at Estelle Designs?"

"Yeah, we ran into each other at Penrose and got to talking . . . as friends." I prick up my ears at the last two words. "He didn't have specific plans for Thanksgiving, so I figured why not ask him, since you and Chase know him and he often speaks highly of you and your talents."

"I'd love to see Virgil and catch up."

Virgil took a chance and hired me as a design fledgling right out of Parsons. Under his tutelage, I worked my way up from assistant to lead designer. When he and Charlotte, another Estelle Designs executive, left to create their own fashion design house, they invited me to join them as an equal partner. I raised the money needed and had the necessary documents drawn up by our attorney. Then, Chase went missing, I found out I was pregnant, and Chase's nemesis Dimitri went on the prowl to hurt Chase by setting out to kill me and my unborn child. I had no choice but to abandon my career and flee to Summit with Devie, Fiona, and Liam, certain that Dimitri was out to hurt or kill any or all of us.

Propped by pillows, my attention pivots from Mac to my fervent hope for a reconciliation with Chase, especially since he slept in our bed last night. I must doze for a bit, because next thing I know, Caroline is scooped from my arms.

"Why don't you get a bit more shuteye and then take some time for yourself to shower and get ready for our guests. I'll take care of Caroline. Hey, little pumpkin." Chase tickles her cheek. She gives him a smile.

"Speaking of added guests," Antonio interjects, putting a cup of coffee on the table for Chase, "thought you'd enjoy seeing some old friends to celebrate Chase's return, so I asked Thomas and Beth to dinner."

Dread jumpstarts my heart.

All I can think about is fleeing the room to figure out what to do next. Growing up, Thomas, Beth, and I were a tight threesome, so it stands to reason that Antonio would think I'd want to spend time with two childhood friends. I'd love to see Beth, but Thomas? There's no way he can come. Facing Chase, I force a smile.

"I'm going to take your advice, rest for a bit, then shower so I can help out later with dinner." I lock myself in the bathroom and, with shaking hands, splash cold water on my face. I don't want to phone Thomas or make any contact. I could call Beth and ask her to call Thomas and tell him that he can't be here, but then she'd want to know why. I don't want to provide an explanation about what happened over the phone, especially since Chase doesn't know that it was Thomas. I can't have Thomas upset any chances Chase and I have of reconciling. I'm just going to have to . . .

There's a light knock on the bathroom door.

"The market is open this morning," Chase tells me through the closed door. I hear Caroline cooing in his arms. "I'm going to take a ride into town with Caroline for some last-minute supplies. Do you want anything?"

Deep breath. Take a deep breath.

"No. Thanks. I'll see you later."

Footsteps drift down the hallway. I plop on top of the lidded toilet and rub my temples to ease the cluster migraine that's starting. I look into the mirror. Dark hollows stare back from a pale, pinched face. The deception . . . the regret . . . the fear of losing the love I once had . . . flash and roar, shredding any integrity I thought I possessed.

In the shower, the first spray of warm water eases the tension from my shoulders. I rest my forehead against the tiled stall, and steamy water spills over my back, rinsing away soap, shampoo, and stress but not guilt or shame. There's a fine line between human frailty in a time of need and open, in-your-face deceit. Teetering between the two and absolutely wanting to avoid the latter helps me decide what has to happen, and the sooner the better. Wounds like this fester if avoided and Chase's emotional biography is already fraught with family trauma. I'm going to have to sink through time and surrender my guilt with all the details intact, hoping our relationship won't crumble under the weight of what I reveal.

Mind made up, I wind a soft bathrobe around my body and blow dry my hair. I apply under-eye concealer—God knows I need it—mascara, and tinted lip gloss. I slip on a charcoal-colored cashmere dress and black heeled Jimmy Choo boots—nothing like beautiful footwear to help boost your confidence—then vigorously brush my shampooed hair until it falls past my shoulders in soft waves. Time to find a place where Chase and I can talk privately, with full disclosure this time. No holding back the who, the what, or anything else related to my infidelity.

"Well, you're looking better." Antonio quickly prepares me an omelet and, famished, I dig in, stopping between mouthfuls to wipe my mouth and ask if anyone's seen Clyde.

"Last I heard he went for a ride to watch the sunrise."

That's civilian-speak for *Clyde went to check for any criminal activity on our property*. I keep my fingers crossed that either all is quiet, or some culprit is caught and handed over to the authorities. Dimitri rarely does his own dirty work, but capturing one of his thugs would bring us one step closer to finding him and having him thrown back into prison where he belongs.

"He just got back. I saw him head to the cottage," Devie answers, flashing me a relieved grin.

I pull my attention back to the sink and start washing my plate and utensils, but my mind's not on the task and the plate crashes into the sink, breaking into several pieces. Sunny takes the sponge from my hand and shoos me away from the mess, insisting he'll clean up. I can't compete with Sunny's regimented kitchen skills and orderliness under the best of circumstances, never mind when I'm trying to collect my thoughts to figure out how I'm going to save my marriage.

Clyde's surprise when he answers my knock rapidly turns to concern after he ushers me inside. "Is everything alright at the house?"

"Everything's fine," I lie. Nerves have me quaking with cold. I head toward the fire that crackles in the pebble-stoned fireplace. There's a patterned Afghan carpet spread across the polished oak floor, gifted by Chase to Clyde as a thank-you for helping take care of me and our unborn baby while Chase was held prisoner in Afghanistan. In the corner sits a Cabana Yeti chair upholstered in soft sheepskin. Along the wall is a hutch with lively patterned red-and-yellow dishware. No doubt about it. Clyde is a caretaker with decorating talent. Best of all, though, is Chase's bag opened and emptied.

He's staying.

The knotted thread of worry strangling my heart loosens. Clyde answers my relief with a smile that stretches beyond the handles of his white mustache. I skim through reasons for asking to use the cottage, then just plunge ahead with my request. "I don't want to inconvenience you in your home, but I thought Chase and I could have a bit of time alone to talk . . ." He doesn't let me finish.

"It's all yours. I was just on my way to the house to bake bread for dinner."

He grabs a wool plaid jacket off a peg. Black brows that contrast with a heavy mop of white hair perk when he meets my nervous gaze with a thumbs-up. "I think I just heard him pull into the driveway. I'll let him know you're waiting for him here."

"Thanks."

I try to look relaxed, forcing my shoulders to loosen and my lips to pull into a smile. Once he leaves, I crumble. My legs feel like they're about to collapse. My palms are sweating and that ever-present nausea worsens. I remove any armor I may have put on in anticipation of this conversation. This way, when Chase brandishes his words like weapons—that's if I'm lucky enough to merit anger and not just cold detachment—my defense will be naked truth, not pathetic pleas for forgiveness.

Be fearless, I tell myself, while pacing and swiping sweaty palms against the sides of my coat. I slip off my coat and place it over the back of the sofa, so as not to appear that I want to rush the conversation, then rev up my nervous pacing, stopping to peer out the window to see if I can spot him coming up the walkway. It's empty. Biting the side of my mouth, I worry that he might not come, but after a few minutes there's the click of the lock. He stands staring straight at me, his eyes pinpoints of anger.

"Thanks for meeting me here. I wanted to talk to you alone to pick up where we left off the other day."

He stays quiet, takes off his coat, and unwinds his scarf. Walking to the sofa, I sit and invite him to do the same. He doesn't. I know it's a power play. He wants as much control as possible over a situation that he was unable to monitor while he was away. So, okay. I'm willing to have to look up to him while I talk. I already feel like a rodent at his feet. Words spill softly. "I realize that keeping parts of the truth from you, when you were asking for more, was continuing my deceit. I want the chance to start again." My voice catches as I delve for the right words. Motionless and expressionless, he waits, keeping his eyes rooted toward mine.

"When it happened . . ." I stop and take in a breath. "It had been a particularly bad day. I couldn't relax, I couldn't sit. I kept seeing you lying dead in a place where you'd never be found. My strained nerves were stretched further when I heard on the news that two servicemen had been killed in Kandahar. The names of the fallen were being withheld until their next of kin were notified. You had been missing for several weeks. I became frantic, dreading that the phone would ring with bad news. Anxiety escalated until I felt I was going mad. Fear, doubt, dread . . . everything negative ripped through my mind. It was like I was trapped in some deep, dark cave of unhappiness with no way out. I started to believe that the reason no trace of you could be found was because you were dead. That's when the buzzer rang."

He looks at me hard.

"It was Thomas."

He stills. It's a quiet filled with distaste because now he knows. To his credit, he doesn't interrupt or storm away.

"I let him in. We had dinner, then went into the den to chat. For the first time since you went missing, I felt myself relaxing, like I do when one of my brothers visits. He joked,

I laughed, and when he leaned in and kissed me, I was startled and pulled away. But then the next time," here my face heats as shame threatens to steal my courage.

"Go on," he snaps, startling me back to my omission.

"I just wanted to escape my loneliness, feel some spark of life again. It was as if my heart had been torn from my body, making me want to do anything to fill the empty space."

I look into his eyes with a stripped soul. "But afterwards, I felt worse than before. He left and we haven't seen each other since. I promise you I will never see him again. It's you I want. Only you."

I know it's selfishness, but the relief of unburdening the weight of guilt is liberating, until I see fresh pain and resentment lining his face.

"You said you were in the den. Is that why you purchased a new sofa for the room and tossed out a perfectly good one?"

A hot flush creeps from my neck and flames across my dampened cheeks when I think of that offending piece of furniture. "Yes."

Sardonic laughter spiked with anger follows. "You think removing a couch takes away the fact that you fucked another man while married to me."

I swipe away tears and shake my head. "Nothing will change that. I'm only asking for a second chance."

"And how do I know that you won't do it again the next time you feel the need to unload a piece of your misery."

I stop crying. I won't let tears disrupt the momentum of this conversation. Now, I'm firm.

"Because I've promised you I won't, because I'm not a

liar . . ."

"Yeah, but cheating's not beneath you," he mutters.

I wince, take the hit, and continue.

"Because I'll do anything to preserve our relationship, because I've said repeatedly since then that you are my one and only love. I can't change what happened, but I can offer myself to you with the hope that we can put this behind us and start again." I don't move, stutter, or cry.

Silence. Then, more silence.

Finally, he nods. "I need some time and space to think about all this."

The iron band of fear around my heart loosens. He's willing to consider the notion of a life together.

"Take all the time you need. I'll be waiting."

He processes that with the same look he gets when he's unsure about someone, and if that person is someone he cares about, you can see the pain swing through his eyes. It's the expression he wore when Fiona told him she was fine and then disappeared. It's the same look he wore when Detective Wilson told him Dimitri had Devie's help with my attack.

It nearly levels me that now he feels I can't be trusted. Full disclosure, I chastise myself.

"Uh . . . one more thing." I jump right in with another explanation. "Not knowing the situation, Antonio invited Thomas to dinner today. I wanted you to know that I plan on texting him that it's out of the question, if that's okay?"

"He's that stupid that he needs to see it in writing to realize he's not welcome here?"

"I don't think he'll come, but I don't want to take any chances."

"It's up to you if you want to make contact, but I better not see him anywhere near you or our home."

He starts to leave, then hesitates, head bent in contemplation as if a sudden thought locks him in place. When he does look up, it's with a gaze so penetrating, it peels away layers of my essence, exposing with raw clarity who I am and what I stand for.

"You need to figure out how to be content and confident inside your own skin so that when the going gets tough, you can dig deeper to find the courage to go on, instead of searching in all the wrong places to fill the gap. Being an adult means having principles so that you can navigate through hard times with integrity and stamina. Learn that, for god's sake, so you can grow up."

He's saying I have no honor, that I'm still a child, and he's right. Our separation required maturity, courage, and perseverance. I lacked all three and caved into my weaknesses, making a ruinous choice. I have never thought less of myself than now. Why would he ever want me again?

I am not an honorable person.

I am still a child.

His thoughts about who I am slice into me like barbed wire. My hope for a quick reconciliation crumbles and, through choking tears, I answer with what I think he'll understand. "Even nations reconcile after the atrocities of war."

His reply is quick and sure. "Not the one I fought in."

It's hard to see the old, hardened mask slide back into place, the one that replaces unbridled passion with cynicism and apathy. I hate that I'm the reason it's there again. When he clicks the door shut, it's hard to know if my tears are from disappointment that he's left or relief that at least he listened to what I had to say.

When I leave, he's waiting at the end of the path, a solitary figure, coat opened, scarf undone, tough demeanor shouting he's oblivious to the cold. It reminds me of the Chase from the past, the resilient son of the town drunk who was able to even unequal social and economic class scores using nothing more than sharp intellect and relentless hard work. Unlike me, he overcame his obstacles with bravery, honor, and reliability.

He became an adult.

He watches me approach and when our eyes meet, my heart flips. I want to put my arms around him, brush his eyelids with kisses, and lock my mouth onto his. I want to, but I don't. I do sidle close, making sure to keep my hands at my sides. I wonder if it's always going to be like this: him waiting and me struggling to keep up. The thought stalks me into the house, a fiery brand of judgment scorched into my consciousness when I turn and lock the door.

CHAPTER 5

"You ought to consider Virgil's proposal to come on board his and Charlotte's fashion start-up. It's a steppingstone toward growing your original brand and then continuing on your own. How have your jackets been selling?"

I take a bite of pretzel, suck the salt off, chew, and swallow. Traffic is moving well and if it continues this way, our car ride from Summit to the city should take no more than three hours.

The only sounds in the car are my munching and Miles Davis's trumpet playing "When I Fall in Love" on one of the smooth jazz radio stations. Family members are pooling their efforts to allow me and Chase quality time alone. My parents took Caroline to spend the night with them on Long Island. After that, Fiona is going to pick her up to stay with her, Liam, and Grandpa Bill. Bill eventually did show up for Thanksgiving dinner, looking a bit peaked from the lingering effects of a stomach bug. No signs of an alcohol relapse were evident. Traffic is light, and that's how I plan to keep the conversation.

"Sales of my jackets are solid. Those that have hand-painted logos are commanding unbelievable prices. Even so, I agree that I can learn from experienced players in the business, like Virgil and Charlotte. I'm considering Virgil's proposition. I don't particularly like Charlotte but . . ." I bite into another pretzel and when Chase reaches out for one, I take it from the bag and place it inside his mouth. Warm lips hug my fingers. My breath hitches when I slide them out.

"You were saying . . .?"

"Oh, right." I bob my head in a manner that pretends his question is all that's on my mind. "Charlotte's complex. On one hand, she's a brilliant technician. Her work demonstrates a lot about precision and shaping contours. Then, there's this twisted side of her personality. She's driven to seize success from a person just for the sheer pleasure of owning what belongs to someone else. Charlotte wants access to a piece of my jacket label. She even made some lowball offer for it when you were . . ." I stop to gather strength just to say the word, "Missing."

I reach for his hand and give it a squeeze. It's a relief to be discussing career opportunities instead of murderous gangsters, life-threatening deployments, and spousal betrayals.

"I know I said it before, but I think it's important enough to tell you again. It's not in your best interest, at this stage of your career, to share your label in a partnership. You developed it from your sketches before you began working at Estelle Designs. That label is exclusively yours to maintain." He extends his thumb and gently swipes a pretzel crumb from my lip.

"I won't, but I thought you were against the idea of me signing on with Virgil and Charlotte."

I steal a sideways glance while he chews, admiring his chiseled chin and sweeping eyelashes.

"As a partnership, I still am opposed. As a short-term opportunity, it's a good idea for several reasons." Reaching for another pretzel, his arm grazes my breast, making me want to plant small kisses down the side of his neck. Instead, I crack the window, turn my face into the brisk breeze that rushes in, and wait for him to continue.

"For starters, you'll be stepping back into the business after a lengthy absence. With your work ethic, you'll quickly build up your confidence and business acumen while gaining experience dealing with new contacts. Both Virgil and Charlotte respect you enough to give you free rein to exercise your creativity."

I raise a skeptical brow. "Not Charlotte. She'll criticize me and my work any chance she gets. People like her don't change."

"True, but she's not stupid. This is her business. It's different from when she was your boss at Estelle Designs, and you all functioned under the umbrella of a large corporation. You've got talent and your designs are profitable. You started with doing one thing very well: your jackets, and they continue to sell. She knows that now you're going to add another item and another with the same perfection of style and detail. Believe me, she'll let you flex your creative muscle unencumbered. Her pocketbook depends on fresh ideas. Just don't give her access to your sketchpad or your former named designs."

This is spot on. After I used the money from the

planned partnership with Charlotte and Virgil to help secure Chase's release, I added different designs to the jackets, pairing them with silk blouses, dresses, and flared pants. My latest is a free-flowing frock balanced with the cropped jacket that continues to be a solid seller. I know Chase has great business know-how, but the fact that he can apply it to fashion, an industry he knows little to nothing about, speaks volumes about his skills.

Cars whish by, their sound hypnotic, and for the first time since Chase got home, I notice his fatigue. We never discussed how his final debriefing went and I know better than to ask. Most of it is classified information.

"If you're tired, pull over, and I'll drive."

Shifting seamlessly into fourth gear, he shoots me a have-you-lost-your-mind look that reminds me of the time I drove him to the car rental garage in Monaco. I had used my own wits and what I gleaned from watching my brother maneuver the clutch in his Porsche to drive a standard rental car through the south of France. Needless to say, I hadn't quite mastered the shifting part. For the entire trip, which took no more than fifteen minutes, Chase white-knuckled the dashboard, moving his feet as if there were control pedals on the passenger side.

"Oh c'mon," I needle, knowing we're thinking about the same time. "We only stalled twice, and I got us to where we needed to be, safe and sound."

"Tell that to the cat that leapt into the air when you side-swiped the curb."

"I hit the curb to avoid a swerving car and . . . what cat?"

"I rest my case." He's smiling. I'm smiling. Life is good. Then in typical Chase fashion, his mind shifts gears.

"The safety plan we've put in place for when we get home has to be strictly followed."

"I know."

He's not convinced because he repeats the logistics. "Sammy will remain on Long Island to watch over Caroline while she's at your parents' house and then when she's with Fiona. Mac is here to help you get around. Just give him a heads-up if you plan to leave the house or if you see anything suspicious."

"Does Mac really need to be on call if I'm staying at home? He can . . ."

His head whips around, eyes burrowing into mine. If I had to gauge the atmosphere of his mood, I'd say stormy with the likelihood of heavy winds. "Do not even think about giving me a hard time about this."

So, this is how it's going to be. He speaks, and I listen, no questions asked. Since I'm trying to reclaim his trust, I really have no choice but to back down. What was it he said earlier? Oh yeah, that I needed to dig deep to deal with problems on my own. I'll be digging moon-sized craters to find the patience to manage him and his edicts during this acclimation period.

Without so much as a single humph at his highhandedness—and believe me, I am thinking a lot of them—I acquiesce. "Sure. I understand."

When confronted with Dimitri, Chase's irascible demands leave no room for disagreement. He wants orders followed when they are issued, especially now that Caroline has been threatened. But—and this is a big but—he's going to have to learn to trust my judgment and understand that I'd never do anything to jeopardize myself or our family.

Well, maybe one thing. My fingers itch for a cigarette. Good time to change the subject.

"Who's this therapist I'm supposed to see? I don't indicate what it relates to because I don't want to admit my problem out loud. One more addition to my tower of shame and culpability might just topple me over.

"What do you mean?"

I'm not getting off the hook. He's going to force me to say it. "The doctor I need to see about my smoking habit." There. I said it. Smoking, habit, and need, all in one sentence. Nobody's perfect, and a glimmer of anger surfaces at the unfairness of life. Gangsters, war, long separations, threats . . . so many challenges. It's exhausting. Who wouldn't screw up?

He mellows his tone. "Her name is Dr. Alexander. She's a hypnotherapist."

Awesome. Just awesome. I'll be put into a trance, so I can babble and drool over myself while some stranger delves into the root of my smoking.

"Maybe I can try chewing Nicorette or wearing a patch?"

"Haven't you tried those? Packets of gum spilled out of your purse back in Summit, and you were wearing a patch under your arm during our meeting after that poor fawn was killed."

Oh, for heaven's sake, Sherlock Holmes has been reincarnated to profile the noncompliant smoker. ARGH. He's right. I tried both the gum and the patches many times. Neither worked.

I stare at the cars whooshing by on I-87, then back at him, and smile weakly, resigned to seeing this sage woman but eager for some more information.

"A hypnotist. That sounds . . . interesting."

Now I know why Sammy referred to her as "one helluva healer" when he added her name to the schedule. In fact, when I think back on it, Sunny respectfully referred to her as "the *medium*" as if she were somebody who could conjure up spirits to help me kick my American Spirits habit. Normally I would have taken note of these peculiar comments, but I was so wrapped up with Dimitri's toying threat to Caroline, I figured they pointed to the doctor's matchless know-how in dealing with nicotine addiction.

"You'll like her. She has a kind demeanor and her home office overlooks the ocean in Belle Harbor."

Mm, I can stare at the sea while I slip in and out of consciousness.

Realizing that much of our conversation has been about me, I ask about his upcoming work schedule. Chase's voracious mind for details doesn't need much prompting to start churning out information about the string of properties he's purchased on the Upper East Side.

"I've been bullish on the more remote Upper East Side tenement buildings for the last several years and we just broke ground on a large plot there."

"In Yorkville?"

"Yeah. The closing condo prices there have been rising since . . . I'd say . . . around 2012. Now they average about two thousand dollars a square foot." My mind doesn't have to struggle long to do the math before he adds, "That means a two-bedroom can fetch over two million. Compound that even more for new-development condos."

Chase's accomplishments since he graduated from

Yale are staggering. Starting with the purchase of a parking garage in Brooklyn using his savings and investments from his father, Sammy, and Mac, he's increased his property developments to over ten sites scattered throughout Manhattan and Brooklyn.

A bit of unease gnaws inside when I consider what's happened to me since graduating Parsons. If I take away getting arrested, beaten up by a thug, and cheating, I'm left with an award-winning jacket that continues to sell well under my label. Not bad, but could be better. I've big shoes to fill and they better be fast if I want to keep up with Chase.

He reaches past my silence and, with the pad of his thumb, gently rubs the worry creases from between my brows. It's a tender touch that leaves me wanting more. He says he needs time, so I'll wait for him to reach out for more first. I'd even consider seeing a couple's therapist to help us reconcile. I've held off mentioning it because he just got home and I figure he needs some space to acclimate to civilian life, now that it appears he's completed the administrative requirements of his deployment.

We make good time, taking only a bit more than three hours to drive back to our apartment. Boris, the evening doorman, greets us with a grin as broad as his frame. He hops to the trunk to unload our bags. "Mr. and Mrs. Reardon, welcome home."

Then to Chase, "It's good to see you back again, Mr. Reardon." He peeks over our shoulders. "Where's the little one?"

"She's visiting her grandparents," I share, gathering the remnants of our snacks and beverages. Boris immediately puts down our suitcases and takes the trash from my hands, then hustles over to the rubbish bin and tosses them out.

The lobby's snappy marble checkerboard floor is waxed to a shine you can almost see yourself in. Blush-colored sofas made from leather as soft as a baby's bottom rest on either side of an oblong glass table. On top, crimson- and ginger-colored roses spill from an antique brass vase that I admire no matter the number of times I walk through the revolving doors.

I would have thought Chase was more of a downtown loft kind of guy, but he says he was able to secure the best transaction here on the Upper East Side. Sammy and Mac call him the deal whisperer. When it comes to locating a property and brokering a transaction, Chase's sharp eye and surefire negotiating skills are second to none.

Lori, from the eighth floor, pops out of the elevator sporting athletic wear that costs more than it would to feed a drought-ravaged village. I can't criticize paying the bucks to dress in designer clothing. It is the business I'm in, but I can take issue with the entitlement worn with the garb. Two Pekingese poodles yap alongside her Nike trainers as she scrolls through her phone. Lori gives me a watery smile, glances at Boris with a sulky pull to her mouth, and issues her orders. "Boris, work your magic and get me a taxi. I'm late for my yoga class." There's an emphasis on yoga as if it's scheduled brain surgery.

Chase gives her a tight nod. "I got this, Boris."

Chase lifts our remaining suitcases onto the cart and wheels it toward the service elevator. "No need to run up with our packages, either. I'll pick them up later."

Chase understands what it means to work hard and

overcome adversity. The sins of the father should never be passed onto his children, but that's exactly what kids in our community did, mocking and jeering him while he hauled his inebriated father home after a night of binge drinking. Chase navigates prominent social circles with ease, but he rarely steps out of the shoes of the young outsider who, with a critical and knowing eye, saw how the entitled judged those with less money and power.

"No rush, Mr. Reardon. I'll keep them secure in the back, and again, welcome home." Boris doesn't say alive and well, but when someone is deployed to a war, it's usually first on their minds.

"Why don't you head up to wait for the suitcases while I stay here and get our packages from Boris." As soon as the words are out of my mouth, I realize this seemingly reasonable division of labor is a mistake. Chase's gaze clouds. He holds the elevator and politely repeats that he and Boris have it covered.

Even being in the lobby alone is going to be a problem. Burying a frustrated sigh, I step into the elevator, no questions asked. It's important to tread carefully on this new tightrope of trust. No need to sever it with an argument when he's only been home a few days, and we've already had an incident with Dimitri. At some point, this will have to change. It can't only be about what he wants me to do and where he thinks I should be. I understand we need to protect ourselves and Caroline, but it has to be a joint effort, with my ideas and views about our safety considered as valuable and trustworthy as his.

We step into the darkened apartment, heavy with the weight of what our aloneness holds. Chase takes the suitcases from the cart and then tips the maintenance serviceman who brought them up. I slip off my coat and, flicking on the light in the hall closet, reach for a hanger. Behind me, Chase's arm grazes my shoulder when he leans forward to clasp another for his coat. A wisp of his breath heats my neck. His extended arm and taut torso lock me in place. His mouth, when I turn, is a hairsbreadth from mine. I watch the curve of his lip. Then, like so many times in the past when I couldn't resist, I kiss his mouth with all the yearning and need stored inside. He returns my kiss and it's as if I'm the one soaring home after an agonizing absence. All the times I longed for his touch, hoped for his well-being, and lived for his return, are satisfied by the feel of his lips against mine. My roving hands burrow into his hair.

He scoops his hands under my backside and carries me to the sofa. Then he stretches out on top of me. His lips singe a path down my neck and across my collarbone while his hand slides up my stomach and lifts my sweater. Sneaking it under my bra, he teases my nipple with his thumb and forefinger. It puckers. My breath quickens. My body arches under his weight, craving more touching, more feeling, more momentum of what could be forgiveness.

He reaches to remove the tag of a new pillow that presses into my neck. That's when we realize that where we are is different. The fire of our momentum is doused by the stark reality of why we're lying on top of a new sofa. He's on his feet in no time, leaving me lying breathless, breast exposed, emotions raw. His chilled gaze bores into my soul.

"I can't do this right now." He grips his suitcase and heads toward the guest bedroom.

I tug down my bra and sweater, attempting to hide his rejection, but the rebuff bares my heart. Ignoring the scraping of the pillow label against my cheek, I curl into a ball and sob into the stuffed cushion of my betrayal.

It's an hour or two later when I finally lift myself from the sofa. The mind has a way of muddling misery. Gravitating toward my packed bags, I reach for my sketchpad and pencils and head toward the kitchen to make an espresso. Designing allows my imagination to escape the constraints of heartache. Freed images with form, detail, and color merge onto a blank page. Whoever said haute couture is dead mustn't know what it feels like to yearn for a lover's body inside yours.

My mind fashions a tapered knitted silk top, offset with a flowing, hand-painted organza skirt in shades of plum and deep violet. The blend of sharp tailoring on top and soft ruffling speaks of how life is a blend of softness and severity, delight and dejection. My next is a silk georgette gown in soft tones of tangerine with gold embroidery along the plunging neckline. Somewhere during the several hours of work, exhaustion takes over because one minute I'm working and the next my head is lolling onto a muscled arm that scoops me from the chair. I'm placed onto our king-sized bed, that seems to be my bed now because when I sleepily stretch out my arm and leg to the other side, it's empty. Exhaustion surpasses worry, with the latter surfacing only when the first hint of light peeks in from the window.

CHAPTER 6

It's a quiet morning: no feedings, soiled diapers to change, laundry, cooing, cajoling, rocking, or wrapping, just eons of time to wonder how long Chase is going to exile me from his life. Who could blame him for not wanting to build a life with someone who was so unformed as an adult, so unsure of herself as a human being, that she let her insecurities take that gift of love and toss it into the wind? Words I think I have yet to use to explain my behavior scatter through my mind.

I'm sorry . . . I barely remember what happened. I felt nothing. I'll work harder at being honorable. I will never let this happen again.

It's when I'm trying to shut out this endless litany of excuses that I realize each one revolves around my feelings, my thoughts, my worries: *I* didn't have the integrity needed to endure the kind of separation thrust my way. *I* was so lonely and scared. *I* behaved like an impulsive adolescent. It's really his feelings that take priority. The decision to resume our relationship as husband and wife is *his* to make. *He* is the one grappling with the painful memories of being tortured and facing death. It's painful coming to grips with the possibility that a lack of character might make one unworthy of love. But . . . however this turns out, I will continue to assume full accountability for my actions.

My phone rings. On the other end, my mother's chirpy voice is welcomed. Slicing up your character until its tattered remains hang sullied in your mind is exhausting.

"We're all having a good time," she prattles. I hang on each word, grateful for the distraction. "Caroline slept well. Your papa put off his paperwork and is getting ready to feed her now. If it's not too cold later, we're taking her to the park." She stops talking, and in a sing-song voice says, "Look at that little monkey-face smile." My father laughs in the background.

"Thanks again. It sounds like Caroline is having a great time. Let me know if there are any problems," I add after a brief pause, knowing that my mother will understand what I'm referring to.

"Don't worry. Sammy's here and Fiona will give you a call after she picks Caroline up later this afternoon."

The conversation ends. Cloying silence saturates the kitchen. My wrung-out mind is void of any more self-deprecating thoughts. It's time to move away from mistakes I can't undo. Chase hasn't eaten since last night. I'm famished. What better way to invite a good conversation than over a hot breakfast? If eating crow would gain me forgiveness, I'd add it to the menu.

The fridge is stocked thanks to the ever-efficient Sunny, who was thrilled to stay and help Clyde with fall clean-up on the ranch. It takes me all of fifteen minutes to get breakfast going. Near-perfect rings of pancake batter bubble on the grill, strips of bacon sizzle in a skillet, and scrambled eggs fluff in a hot pan. The only chilled addition is the stare I get from Chase when he enters the kitchen. Fully dressed for his first day in the office, his navy vested suit hugs his body in a way that stirs mine. Suit jacket fitted across broad shoulders, pants belted against tight abs, and a crisp white shirt, open at the collar to invite kisses from chin to collarbone.

"You shouldn't have gone through this trouble." He says it like he's speaking to someone he just met and wishes would leave.

"It's no bother at all," I say, smiling. "I have time before my appointment with Virgil and Charlotte." I look at him for a sign, a gesture, anything that would show a crack in his iceberg manner, but all I see is an inflexible countenance that barely registers I exist.

I made a promise that I'd wait for his forgiveness, and I'm going to keep my word.

"Will Mac be driving me to midtown at ten o'clock?" We're short-staffed here with Sammy on Long Island watching after Caroline and Sunny in Summit, but still my voice is tentative, unsure of the reaction it could unwittingly trigger.

"Yeah."

He's refusing to speak to me, making me worry that he's continuing his relentless anger toward me with no end in sight. There's too much to do to dwell on the same issue all over again, so shoving it aside for the time being, a newfound determination shifts into place. I'm meeting with Virgil and Charlotte to continue my career after it was abruptly halted when Chase needed to be rescued. There's nothing more I can do or say at this moment that will change his truculent mood. Making a mental note to remember my updated sketchpad, I get up to put it near my purse and pour us some coffee.

One sniff of the dark brew has my stomach roiling like bilge rising in the bottom of a ship. I barely make it to the toilet where, retching and heaving, I lose last night's dinner. From the doorway, Chase watches me with a strange combination of exasperation and concern. When I get unsteadily to my feet, he takes my hand and guides me out of the bathroom and back to the kitchen chair, handing me a moistened napkin to wipe my mouth.

"I'm fine now. It's just a bit of a stomach upset from all that's happening." Sipping some water and nibbling on a cracker, I'm engulfed in his incensed muteness. "Please. Don't cut me out of your life? Speak to me so we can try and work through this." My words are soft, but what I really want to do is shout how I'm not only the sum of my worst moments.

I watch in shocked silence as his mood swings from disquiet to bewilderment.

"Why, Alicia? That's what I keep asking myself. In that fucking dungeon, you kept me alive. Wanting to see you again got me through the worst of my time away." His tone assumes a tender lilt that shreds my heart with each word that follows. "How come I wasn't enough for you?"

I've asked myself that question hundreds of times. How could I have betrayed him like this when he is the only man I've ever desired or wanted?

"All I can say is I was drowning in sadness and loneliness.

I was weak. I wasn't thinking, but I never stopped loving you." I reach out my hand to grasp his in a plea for understanding, but he keeps his at his side until I'm forced to drop mine in defeat.

He raises his chin in my direction. "That's the problem with you, Alicia," and I know by his squinting eye and pointed finger that he's going in for the kill.

"You have no idea who you are as a person, and even worse . . ." he twists his mouth cynically before hurling at me more truths I don't want to hear, "instead of trying to figure it out, you anchor yourself to someone, hoping he's going to make you feel better. That's what disgruntled teenagers do."

I recoil as if I've been punched. He's rubbed my doubts about myself raw, and he's not done.

"How do I know you're not still meeting this lover?"

Fury clings to his words, widening the gap between us. He's wiped clean what he knows about me and replaced it with a blemished etching. How unfair. I was pregnant and alone and trying to survive the possibility of his death and a maniac in pursuit. The constancy of this argument is wearing me down. A slow-seeping annoyance surfaces.

"Lover? Strong label for one time. And . . ." I choke back tears, needing my voice to make my point, "you know I'm not meeting him or anyone else for that matter because I'm telling you I'm not. It's called trust. At some point you're going to have to start believing what I say."

"I suggest you take a pregnancy test," he says, contempt clenching his jaw. "And if you are pregnant, I'd be curious to know who the father is. I had a vasectomy shortly before I left for my debriefing." He shakes his head at my shocked, widened eyes. "Don't look so stunned. We discussed it several times after your difficult delivery, and you agreed."

"I know, but then you seemed to have doubts. Where did you . . . I mean how . . ." I sputter before regaining my flow of words. "I had no idea you had it done. When was that?"

"Ten days before I left. It was all last minute. I bumped into my marine buddy Doc Sanders, told him what I wanted. He suggested I show up the next morning for the procedure, and I did. I planned on telling you, but you were visiting your parents for a few days with Caroline. Then I found out I had to leave for my debriefing, and you blasted me with what you'd done."

"I know and I'm sorry." If I expected some positive response to my umpteenth apology, I'm disappointed because once again he wears a flat stare. Will I ever have to stop apologizing for my actions? And who the hell shows up for a life-changing procedure after he just happens to bump into a battlefield doctor buddy on the street? My anger kicks up another notch.

"What about you, Mr. Perfect? How come you don't feel the need to admit you can be wrong? You should have told me beforehand that you might have to leave again for a debriefing, and you sure as hell should have mentioned you had a vasectomy."

He closes his eyes to block me out, leaving me on my own to fill in the blanks. He's right that we had discussed his having a vasectomy many times, especially since I hemorrhaged while giving birth to Caroline. The doctor called it a placental abruption. All I remember is that one minute everything was fine and the next I was bleeding profusely.

It was terrifying. In the end it worked out, but the OB-GYN shared that the possibility of it happening again was greater for me than with other women who hadn't had that particular problem.

Chase, who had just returned from Afghanistan, insisted he'd seen enough blood and death in war without having to worry about it at home. At first, I was opposed. A vasectomy seemed extreme, but then after several debates, I agreed for his sake as well as mine. I wanted to put him at ease after all the suffering he went through, but there was a selfish motive to my acquiescence. I planned to resume my career and was concerned about the time constraints of having more children. I grew up watching the sacrifices my mother made to raise four children with a loving, but mostly absent husband, who worked around the clock running a restaurant and vineyard. It swayed her away from building a career in fashion design, even though she had the talent and a good job offer. I love my mother and appreciate all she did for us, but I know that's not how I want to live my life.

My eyes stay fixed on his. The air is thick with tension. Brusquely, he says he has to leave. He's being interviewed by a journalist for an op ed in the business section of *The New York Times*. In an irritated tone, he reminds me I should be sure to call Mac to confirm when I'm leaving.

My first thought is, *Wow,* The New York Times *is interested in an interview. How fantastic is that,* but before I can comment or offer congratulations, he slams the door on his way out. It is the biggest fuck-you shutout of my life.

Wiping my eyes with the back of my hands, I realize that no matter what I say to the contrary, he still thinks

I'm deceitful. He's so blinded by pride that he's doomed me to the "once a cheater always a cheater" category. With time he will see that it's ludicrous to believe I'm pregnant with another man's child. I said I'd give him time to figure out if he still wants to be with me, and I will. If I don't pull myself together, my interview with Virgil and Charlotte will be wasted.

For the next hour, I meticulously dress for my meeting, opting for an emerald-and-black print silk dress, coupled with a cropped matching jacket. Sliding on stockings and Christian Louboutin black leather pumps, I complete the outfit with a Givenchy black pebbled shoulder bag.

There's an impression to be made with Charlotte that shows my purse strings are as lavish as my wardrobe. When Charlotte sought to buy—no, actually steal—my label for next to nothing, she knew I was abandoning our partnership because I was desperate for money. She didn't know it was to secure Chase's release, but she knew the funds were needed for something.

Who could forget those sharpened red enameled fingertips tapping, against the surface of her desk, her lips pulled up like some benevolent despot mulling over a generous handout to an underling? Of course I refused. If I hadn't, my small but thriving brand as well as my name would have become hers to do with as she pleased and for a fraction of their worth. Chase warned me about that kind of offer during our last FaceTime chat before his capture. Even when he knew he was facing danger, he insisted on discussing how my decisions impacted my life.

Tears spill for the countless times Chase helped me pick up the shattered pieces of my mistakes. He assisted with my release after I was arrested in Monaco and drove me out of the country when the authorities ordered me to leave. He moved me into his apartment after I didn't stay put as instructed and was assaulted by Dimitri. Now, he's set up an appointment to help me beat my smoking habit. Fuckups that contributed to Chase's assessment of my rash behavior.

Well, that about covers it. I've gone another round of pummeling. Time to go face Virgil and the talented, but snarky, Charlotte. I call Mac, put on my coat, sling my leather satchel and purse across my shoulder, and exit the building. Mac immediately pulls up. I slide into the passenger seat and give him the once-over. Leather jacket, gold aviator glasses, black Wu-Tang cap. All give him a bad-boy biker persona that contrasts with his even-tempered and reserved bearing. That's not to say I haven't seen him level somebody who was up to no good—but even then, his punches were delivered with just the right amount of force so as to stop the offense without brutalizing the perpetrator.

"Nice look."

"Hey Alicia. You're headed toward the Fashion District, right?"

"Mm hmm. On the corner of Seventh and Thirty-sixth. Do you mind?" I don't wait for an answer before cracking the window and lighting up a cigarette. I had quit in Summit. Or had sort of quit.

"When's your appointment with the smoking guru?"

I smirk at yet another euphemism for who I'll be seeing. "Thursday at six." I take a final drag, stub it out in the ashtray, then spray my mouth with mouthwash. "Will you be driving that night?"

"No, Chase indicated on the schedule that he'll be taking you."

Well, there goes any chance of lighting up on the way there—or the way back for that matter, if the *doctor* is not all she's cracked up to be.

An incoming call lights up the monitor. It's Chase. "Have you dropped off Alicia yet?"

Even though he's not addressing me, I answer, "We're on our way there now."

"Don't bother. Virgil was in a car accident. He's at Lenox Hill Hospital."

Color drains from Mac's face. The news hits like an unexpected blow.

"Is he okay?" I ask.

"I have no idea. Charlotte says she tried texting you but there was no response."

I fish around in my bag for a phone that's not there. Swirling in mental loops of self-loathing make it easy to forget the basics.

"I think I left my phone back at the apartment."

"Chase, I'm going to the hospital to see how things are," Mac says. He shoots me a quick glance. "You mind coming? My guess is your meeting is called off for today."

I shake my head.

"Alicia's coming too. I'll keep you posted."

"Bye," I say, then quickly add, "love you." I'm relieved Mac ends the call before Chase has a chance to answer. The lack of a response would be too painful.

CHAPTER 7

On Seventy-seventh, off Lexington, we pull up to the gray canopied entrance of Lenox Hill Hospital. Mac gives the valet a hefty tip to park our car, then heads with me through the automated doors. At the front desk, an employee searches through the list of patient names for Robin Virgil May.

"Room 910," he says, handing us visitor passes. We hustle to the elevator, hit nine, then have to wait while it stops at every floor to pick up visitors and hospital personnel. Once on the ninth floor, an arrow indicates that even-numbered rooms are to the right. Mac, walking by my side, scans the perimeter of the hallway. Unease does not replace sharp surveillance skills.

Inside the private room, Virgil's brown face peeks out from a swath of white sheets and bandages. His left leg is imprisoned, knee to ankle, in a teal-and-black striped cast that resembles a colorful sock. His right wrist rests inside a plastic support that's held in place by wide black straps.

"I'm about as mobile as a flounder on a slab of marble, but the doctors say I'll live."

Mac's relief is palpable. They lock eyes. Mac clears his throat and breaks the silence first.

"Have the doctors given you a thorough report on the extent of your injuries?" Mac's former fluster is gone, replaced by the firm tone of someone concerned and in charge. I recognize it well.

"Let's not get tedious about my condition. The doctors say my leg and arm will heal and it appears my head's too hard to be permanently damaged. I think I'm being released tomorrow but . . ." he looks at me and shakes his head. "I'm sorry to report that the car you loaned me is totaled." I didn't know that Virgil was driving one of our cars. He must have borrowed it to drive back from Summit.

"Not to worry. That's what insurance companies are for."

"How'd it happen?" Mac asks.

"All I remember is that one minute I'm driving down Park Avenue and the next some car shoots through a red light and barrels into the driver's side of my car."

Mac stiffens but says nothing.

I'm trying to get past the fact that Virgil's being released tomorrow. "How do you plan on getting home when you're discharged?"

"I'll probably hire a car. If that's not possible on short notice, I'll Uber it. I've already arranged for a private nurse to help me once I'm home."

Mac and I look at his casts, then dubiously at each other. "I think I can save you the trouble of having to get yourself home. Mac, why don't you pick Virgil up tomorrow."

Mac's eyes meet mine in that way that says, *okay, you have my attention*, but he says nothing.

"As it happens," I go on to put him at ease, "I'm planning to stay at home and sketch while I wait for Sammy to bring Caroline home." I let my simple and efficient idea percolate, but Mac doesn't answer. It doesn't take me long to figure out that Mac won't commit to anything until he clears it with Chase first.

Virgil reaches out his good hand and struggles to grasp the cup of water from his tray. Wordlessly, Mac takes the cup and lifts it to Virgil's lips. For the briefest moment, their fingers touch. I watch with a tender smile as Mac grazes the back of Virgil's hand with his thumb. Their faces express the love that their voices have yet to share with others.

It's not that I never considered Mac's sexual preferences before. For as long as I've known him, I never met a girlfriend, or a boyfriend for that matter. I simply concluded that Mac kept his private life, well . . . private, as was his right to do. I don't know if it's relief that Virgil's going to be alright after an accident that could have had far worse consequences or trust in me that prompts Mac to open up.

"Virgil and I want you to know we're together. I'm gay." Mac's tone is matter-of-fact, his manner so relaxed and sure, it's like he's floating weightless. "I didn't plan on explaining anything today, but Virgil has been wanting me to say something and right now just feels right. Are you surprised?"

Mac's frank question is unexpected. It's true that I had no idea Virgil and Mac were seeing each other or even that Mac was gay, but what does that matter?

"What I think isn't important, but for the record." I get up and give them hugs. "I'm thrilled for both of you."

Mac wears a smile. Virgil flashes that sideways grin he sports when he's pleased.

"When did you start dating?" I know Virgil and Mac crossed paths several times. Mac worked with us, and Virgil was my former boss, but I never thought they had the opportunity to get to know each other.

"I think the first time we met was when Chase and Mac came barreling into the office of Estelle Designs looking for you." Virgil watches me, smiling. "It appears you had ditched Mac and decided to take the subway to work."

"I remember." Chase and I had just started dating. I had reluctantly agreed to drive to work with either Mac or Sammy. Then decided my independence was more important than my safety.

"I'm sure you do. Chase was furious."

"You've been together since then?

"More or less. Virgil asked if I wanted to meet him for a drink. I said yes. We went to the Camp exhibit at the MET, had a great time, and continued seeing each other."

"I was sure he was going to hate that museum trip because of its emphasis on design, but he actually enjoyed our time together. Said the expressive artistry was fascinating. He even read Sontag's essay on the subject." Virgil tilts his face toward Mac. "My man is a tattooed, gun-toting fashionisto."

Mac rolls his eyes.

The scene with two such different people in love is uplifting. "Now that you're together, I'd like to invite you as a couple to our Christmas celebration."

Our celebration.

It is a bold statement, given what transpired between

me and Chase this morning. It has me reminiscing about last year's party, right after Chase and I were married, when all I thought about was succeeding at work, building a brand, and living happily ever after once Chase returned from his deployment. My egotistical naiveté was staggering. Now, an intimate Christmas celebration with close friends who are in love seems like a festive start to a new chapter in our lives. A little optimism in a hellish multitude of doubt can't hurt.

"We'd love to have you . . . that is, if you're okay sharing your relationship with others."

"Of course we'll come," Virgil says, "and why wouldn't Alicia be surprised? Have you ever told anyone?"

Mac seems rattled, as if he's only just learning how to flex his feelings' muscles instead of a combat fist. "Once," he says. His eyes shut. I'm not sure if it's to capture the memory or try and shut it out. "My father asked if I had a girlfriend. I told him I did not and probably never would."

"And how did he take that bombshell?" Virgil asks.

"He said, 'That's what I thought.' We never spoke about it again." Mac shrugs. "He didn't treat me any differently, and I never offered any details."

"It couldn't have been easy hiding in the shadows like that," Virgil says. "Were you afraid of offering more?"

Oh boy, Virgil has a lot to learn about what it means to label a Special Forces Officer fearful. Mac's words escape from their buried prison.

"I wasn't afraid, but I'd say I was emotionally stalled when it came to accepting my whole self. I kept a part of me so hidden, I forgot it existed."

"It went on for too long and at your expense," Virgil said.

Rubbing the side of his clean-shaven chin, Mac studies the wall ahead. "For a while it wasn't bad. The discipline of the military made it easy to starve myself romantically, but after my deployments ended, I wanted something more. I'd seen enough death and fighting to last a lifetime."

He looks at me and smiles. "Seeing how in love Chase and Alicia were made me realize I wanted to know what it felt like to really care for someone else. After we met," he strokes Virgil's hand, "I knew you were that person."

My throat tightens as I'm reminded of the sparks of passion ignited when Chase and I were together. Now, he barely looks me in the face. Who can blame him? I have a problem looking at myself in the mirror. I swipe back tears, then discreetly fish through my purse for a tissue to dab my nose.

"He'll come around," Mac says. The comment takes me by surprise. I didn't think our marital problems were obvious, but when a cluster of buddies who are like brothers live and work in close proximity, it's hard to mask discord.

I don't even try to deny what appears obvious. "When?" The one-word question comes out in a crushed hush that speaks volumes about how upset I am.

"When you see your goodness and forgive yourself for whatever it is that happened that you think is all your fault," Mac says quietly.

"*Tout comprendre, c'est tout pardoner,*" Virgil answers.

"To understand everything is to forgive everything. Voltaire, right?" Mac adds. Their eyes lock and Virgil nods.

Their unison makes the mountain of conflict that separates me from Chase feel even taller. I've apologized to Chase countless times, explaining that what I did had nothing to do with not loving him and everything to do with the web of loss and grief that trapped me while he was missing. If he would just let himself feel my love, he might start to forgive what I did. I can't be the only one who epitomizes what it means to be human during a dark time.

It's not that I'm trying to excuse my despicable behavior. It's just that when life puts so many obstacles in your way, it's easy to trip and fall. Problem is, I didn't just fall. I sank to new lows. Tears leak and leak some more until it becomes impossible to swipe them away with my crumpled tissue. Virgil clears his throat and waves a large white hankie for me to take.

Any self-recriminating thoughts are interrupted by a jangle of wheels and a rapid click of stilettos echoing from the corridor. A glum-looking hospital server parks a food cart near Virgil's bed. Pudgy fingers lift a tray of covered plates onto Virgil's food table. That's when I think I hear Virgil greeting Charlotte. I can't be sure, because a combination of what smells like cabbage soup and stale coffee grips my stomach the second it hits my nostrils. I bolt for the bathroom, but my foot catches on the leg of the cart that reels into Virgil's bed. There's a crash, some hollering, and raining coffee. Arms outstretched, my body launches like an out-of-control plane veering for the runway.

The brakes are slammed when my head hits the doorway, and I'm knocked onto all fours. A split second later, my stomach lurches, and I vomit over a pair of Manolo Blahnik black suede pumps. When I raise my head, Charlotte is glaring down, looking as if her toes have been hammered instead of barfed on. Someone grips me from under my shoulders and helps me to my chair. I squint up and see Mac. He passes me his handkerchief and a cup of ice water, then studies my shaking hands when I put the cup to my lips.

"I'm fine, really," I say between sips.

Some muscled male nurse who must have heard my crash landing appears to check me out. "What happened?" he asks.

I stare into kind coffee-colored eyes that scrutinize my face. "I just tripped. I'm okay now."

Given the severity of Virgil's injuries, it's embarrassing that there's all this fuss because of my clumsiness. I try to stand to make sure Virgil is alright and to apologize to Charlotte for ruining a gorgeous pair of shoes, but Mac and the overzealous nurse reach out and grasp me by my arms to keep me seated. It's when I happen to catch a glimpse of my thumb that I understand why. Protruding from the side of my left hand is a purplish lump the size of a golf ball. Wincing pain tells my probing fingers that its big brother just popped out on my forehead.

"I'm getting the doctor on call to take a look at that wrist and your head," the nurse informs me before fetching an ice bag and turning his back on my protests.

Awesome. Just awesome. A hospital visit has spun into a fifteen-hundred-dollar designer-shoe wipeout, a head and wrist bang up, and a coffee spill onto what I can only hope is a waterproof cast.

Charlotte disappears, no doubt to try and clean her shoes, and Virgil studies me from his propped pillows with a wicked grin.

"Trouble follows you like a bridal train."

I dismiss his remark and ask him if he's alright.

"I'm okay but . . ." he appraises me with a calculated look, "are you pregnant?" He's courteous enough not to add *again* but the implication hangs in the room like some pesky fly that can't be swatted away. Mac studies me with questioning concern.

"Absolutely not," I say, shaking my head for emphasis. Both he and Mac look unconvinced. I sit and take deep breaths to fight the ever-present nausea.

A janitor and a doctor walk in, followed by Chase, who takes one look at me and asks what happened. He must have decided to come straight to the hospital after his interview to make sure Virgil was okay.

"It's nothing really. I stumbled over the food cart." I look toward the doctor. "I really don't need to see you. I'm fine, thank you."

"Stumbled?" Virgil pipes from his sickbed. "More like bolted from a chair, tripped, tumbled, crashed, and then puked."

His leg may be screwed up, but his mouth sure still works.

As if the crowd isn't large enough, out pops Charlotte, smiling as if her life depends on it once she spots Chase. Now it's my turn to curl my lip in disgust.

"Chase, how nice to see you," she gushes, the pink tip of her tongue licking glossy red lips. Chase smiles a quick hello, then turns to the doctor.

"Alicia will see you now," he commands, standing as erect as a general waiting for a private to snap to attention and salute. I'm tempted to follow through, except he keeps scrutinizing my head and hand with this worried pull to his face.

"It's fine," I whisper in his ear, relishing the closeness he's allowing because he's concerned. What purpose would it serve to refuse to see the doctor and trigger an argument when he's uneasy, and I'm banged up?

"Another injury to your hand," the doctor comments, gently lifting my wrist. I recognize Dr. Argant, who was the emergency room's resident on duty when I was brought there after Dimitri's attack. The palm of my hand suffered a deep cut from the shard of glass I used to slice Dimitri's arm. At the time, I was worried that I might have killed him. Now, I wish I had.

Dr. Argant moves my wrist one way, then the other. He tells me to wiggle my fingers which I do. "I think it's just bruised, but we should take an X-ray to be sure." He shifts his attention to my head, shines a light into each eye, and asks if I lost consciousness after my fall.

"No," I answer, wishing that I had blacked out instead of having to face Charlotte's flirting, Chase's scowl, and Virgil's probing eyes.

Glancing around the crowded room, Dr. Argant suggests I step out into the hallway. Chase follows and once we're in the corridor, the doctor holds a pen to a papered clipboard and asks me the date of my last period.

"I haven't had any periods since giving birth a little more than five months ago. I doubt I'm pregnant, if that's what you're thinking. I'm nursing, and my husband has had a vasectomy." I look at Chase who nods assent.

"I'd like to be sure in case further tests are needed. Bathroom's right through those doors. There are cups with lids inside."

I look heavenward for strength, then disappear into the

bathroom to provide a urine sample. That done, I wash my hands, rinse out my mouth, spray it with mouthwash, and pop in a mint to erase any residual sour taste and smell from my earlier upchuck. Sample handed over, I walk back into the room where I'm greeted by Charlotte perched on the wide arm of Chase's chair, butt crushed against his shoulder, back erect, and chin thrust out like a queen waiting to be crowned. This day just keeps getting better and better.

"Are you sure you don't want to sit," Chase asks her, leaning forward to dislodge his arm from the press of her ass.

"Absolutely not," Charlotte insists. She shifts her attention to Virgil and tut-tuts, "You could have been killed."

"Don't be melodramatic, Charlotte. I sustained some injuries, but I'll live."

Her look shifts to indifference.

"Yes, I know, but how long will you be out of commission?"

Now we get to the crux of the matter. She's worried about how Virgil's absence will affect their business.

"No more than a week. I'm hiring a driver once I get the all-clear from the doctor that I can be up and about on crutches."

Charlotte turns her attention to me, making sure the move allows her to park her butt once again close to Chase's arm.

"You said you were bringing your portfolio. Why don't you leave it for me to review? If it's up to par . . ." she pauses to unsheathe her claws, "and not too clichéd, we can discuss the necessary details about moving forward."

I start to think about how gratifying it would feel to wipe that smug look off her face with my fist.

"Charlotte," Virgil's annoyance strums through the room. "I'm half crippled and Alicia just took a fall that nearly knocked her out. We are not conducting business now. Besides, it's Alicia we're talking about. We both know from experience that her work and her talent are anything but conventional." Leaning forward, he winces, then puts up his hand to suggest he's okay. "Charlotte is going to need help launching our new line now that I'll have to slow down for a bit. So, the sooner you can let us know if and when you can start, the better."

Holding Virgil under his arms, Mac eases him back against his pillows. Once Virgil is comfortable, he takes hold of his good hand.

Charlotte lifts a perfectly-plucked brow.

I start to toss around the idea of what it would be like to leave Caroline. I was hoping to wait until she was at least eight months before returning to work full time. But . . . my mind ricochets to the positives. She has taken to feeding from a bottle, even seems to prefer it. She's comfortable with Sunny. He loves her and is an excellent caretaker. I'll be close by and probably could work from home on Fridays.

I'll have to discuss it with Chase who, like me, seems to be lost in thought about what this all means. He gives me a look that says, *let's talk about it later when we're home*, then discreetly wrests his arm free once again from Charlotte's rear end.

"This is up to Alicia but I'm thinking she . . ." He's interrupted when a pink-cheeked, meaty-bodied nurse bubbles into the room clutching a chart.

"Mrs. Reardon?" she asks, mistaking Charlotte for me. Charlotte forces a stiff smile and points in my direction. The enthusiastic nurse waves me, with Chase following, out of the room and into the corridor where we confer in a huddle. I introduce Chase, and once she hears he's my husband, her broad smile coincides with a bellow that renders stepping into the corridor for privacy meaningless.

"CONGRATULATIONS, you two. You're pregnant!"

Now there are several reasons why I have a problem with what she just said. First and foremost, I'm the one who's going to carry and give birth to a baby so *we're* not pregnant. Next, there is no baby because Chase had a vasectomy. I zoom in, read her name tag, then patiently tell *Zoey* that she's mistaken, that neither of us are having a baby because one, I point to Chase and smile, he's a man and can't have a baby and second, he's had a vasectomy so both of us are not going to be giving birth any time soon, if ever. She looks at me, then at Chase, then back to me and chortles.

"You almost had me with that one." Still chuckling, she hands me a sheet with some instructions on how to treat a sprained wrist and a bump on the head. It's amazing how deep denial stretches when the truth carries guilt and insecurity.

"Wait. There's been a mistake," I call out. She circles back, looking confused. "You must have mixed up the readings. It's impossible, I can't be. My husband had a . . ."

The more I sputter, the longer Chase's silence intensifies until shaking his head in disgust, he strides back into Virgil's room. I soon follow, and the chill wind of a marital storm blows in with us. When I try to take his arm to quietly explain that we should talk later, he jerks it away.

"I have to leave for an appointment," he says.

Charlotte leaps from her seat like she's going for a jump shot. She gives him a hug goodbye. Her behavior is expected. His catches me by surprise. Placing his hand on the small of her back, he leans in for a kiss that allows their mouths to meet for a fraction of a moment. The deliberateness of his move unleashes a shadow of doubt that whispers, *your marriage is over.*

Tears cloud my eyes, then dry with my resolve to say nothing. This retaliatory tactic of his will not incite a flare of jealousy. After all, doesn't envy originate from insecurity and the belief that a person's not good enough? I dug deep for that one, thank you very much, Mr. Perfect. Yet . . . her ass against his shoulder, his hand on her back, and *the kiss* called for some kind of a reaction. And just like that, sadness flips to indignation.

I slide between them, making sure to step on only one of Charlotte's toes where I get the added bonus of seeing a smidgen of my breakfast staining her left shoe. "Sorry." My apology is fake, but what follows is anything but. I pull Chase toward me by his shirt collar until we're so close, I can feel the heat generating from his body. The kiss I give him is so blistering, so full of yearning, that it drowns me in mounting desire. I know from the hard press I feel against my belly that he's feeling the same way. When we separate, we're breathless, Charlotte's peeved, Mac's stoic, and Virgil's grinning. There's a couple of beats of silence before Chase regains his composure.

"See that she gets home," he says to Mac before turning

to me with glacial eyes. "Either head straight back or make sure Mac takes you where you're going." There's a quick but genuine, "Hope-you-feel-better" goodbye to Virgil before he strides from the room.

I stand stock-still, numbed by his cold tone. He's treating me like some nitwit who needs to be issued orders to function in the real world. *And* he did it in front of prospective employers. Well, I can't control his behavior, but there's no way they have to know how hurt I feel. I shoot to my feet, determined to get in the last word.

Leaning into the doorway, I call out sweetly, "I'll see you at home, honey. Mind those double doors don't swing into that beautiful ass on your way out."

His head tilts so I know he's only just pretending he hasn't heard me when he yanks them open and storms out.

I swallow hard and lean back into Virgil's room. My face hurts from my forced smile. I gather my coat, hug Virgil, and wave goodbye to Charlotte. "If it's alright, I'd like to take some time to consider your offer." Virgil nods. Charlotte's face remains noncommittal. "I'll let you both know in the next day or two, at the very latest."

Having said his good-byes, Mac is already through the door. Charlotte's condescending voice brings me up short once I'm out of view. "She must have given that vaginal thermometer a workout as soon as the vows were exchanged so she could keep him latched to her."

"Now you're being daft. Didn't you see her face? This was an accident, pure and simple." My ears perk up as Virgil's voice lowers. "The man's black ops. They don't shoot blanks or miss targets. She never stood a chance." He pauses, then mischievously adds, "How I wish I could be a fly on their wall tonight."

My face heats from neck to head. Two births in a little over a year is like being caught fucking. It's also a sure bet that if your husband's had a vasectomy and knows that you've cheated, he's going to wonder who the father is no matter how many times you tell him it was just once, that it happened when he was missing, and you were blanketed by so much dread and loneliness you thought you were suffocating. I don't let myself break down until I'm in the car, and even then, I sob silently into my hands.

CHAPTER 8

Staring at the ceiling of our bedroom in the dark, I'm too wound up to sleep and too weary to get up.

Get a grip, my mind shouts through my sobs, but every time I stretch out my arm and feel empty space, I fall apart. I think that maybe I should get up and go the guest bedroom to talk to him, but I don't have the energy to explain myself again.

Charlotte's accusation that I plotted pregnancies to keep Chase trapped couldn't be further from the truth. I never wanted to need Chase more than he needed me. I was determined to build a fashion house with the same growth prospects as his rising real estate empire. And then he was deployed . . . and disappeared . . . and I slept with someone else while he was a prisoner of war. Deflated, I conjure what the newspaper headline would read if I was the one interviewed instead of Chase. *Downwardly mobile fashion designer betrays self-made mogul* comes to mind. I am a spinning kaleidoscope of confusion. Independent woman? Wife? Mother? Fashion Designer? Divorcée? The last has me sobbing into my pillow.

Get a grip. Get a grip.

Focusing on deep breaths, I repeat the mantra until my body stops trembling. Curled into a ball, I slide into sleep.

In my dream there is no sky nor is there a sun. All that exists is a black wall of water that barrels toward the window I'm looking through. Mesmerized, I watch a giant wave climb and advance, until dread drives my legs toward Chase. In the next room, he gazes somewhere else. "Don't you see what's happening?" I shout. "We've got to get away from here." But he's too preoccupied to acknowledge what I'm saying. The floor buckles, filling with brackish water and the windows rattle with the water's impending force. I reach for his hand, but he keeps it at his side, his eyes looking away from me and the wave. Sobbing, I extend my hand for his again, shooting one last look at the monster tsunami that's about to strike.

Something tender and moist nips my earlobe and, fluttering my eyes, I snuggle closer to its warmth.

"Shh." The hush of the sound tingles my awakening senses. A deep voice so close to my ear it sends shock waves through my body whispers, "I can't bear to hear you sobbing anymore." I hadn't realized I was still crying, but when I turn to face Chase, the pillow feels damp under my cheek.

Hair mussed, eyes groggy with sleep, Chase slides under the sheets and lies facing me wearing nothing more than briefs and a T-shirt. He puts his hand on my cheek. "It's all going to work out."

The heat of his breath hugs my neck. Nestling into his warm body with his hand stroking back my hair, I feast my eyes on his face. "How can you be sure?" Tracing my index finger across the lovely curve of his lips, I drink in his presence.

"Because even after I left you with a mess to deal with when I went missing, you held everything together. You gave up your partnership with Virgil and Charlotte to raise the money for my release. You waited after I was called back for another debriefing when you were still traumatized by the first. You're still here in my arms even though I walked out on you at the hospital after your pregnancy test."

"I swear," my voice cracks, "I don't know how this happened."

His eyebrows slide up his forehead, "You don't?"

"I get the how," my smile twists into a crooked grin. "It's the when that's confusing. If I am pregnant, and I still think it's a big if, it had to have happened that last time, right before you left, when we . . . when I . . ." I can't bring myself to finish. I may not want to revisit the hurtful things I said, but it looks like I might not be allowed to forget what followed.

Fresh from a terrible row after I told him what I had done, we made love like it was going to be our last time ever. It was angry, punishing sex. He didn't use a condom. I was nursing Caroline and off the pill. Both provided the perfect backdrop for him, once again, to leave behind his calling card before going away to fulfill his duty to his country. Still, the elephant in the room has to be addressed before we can move on. "You said you had a vasectomy. How can I possibly be pregnant? If I am, no one else but you can be the father."

He swipes my tears away with his thumbs. "I believe

you. No more crying. We'll sort it all out. You'll see a doctor to confirm that you're pregnant. I'll visit my buddy Doc Sanders to find out what might have gone wrong with the procedure. Besides, who am I to be the judge and jury of your actions." His eyes darken. "I've done things I never thought I would or could." He stares ahead, and it's as if he's watching a movie of a past he wants to forget, only his mind won't stop it from streaming.

"I killed someone during my deployment, shot her at close range and watched her body fold to the ground like a puppet with its strings cut. Only she was real. She was a human being who I had spoken to and traveled with for weeks before. I was supposed to bring her in alive, but now, because of me, she's nothing more than a rotting mass of flesh and bones in desert sand."

I stay quiet and slide my hand under his T-shirt to trace the scars that map a journey through his suffering.

"I can't believe you would do anything rash or harmful to anyone without good reason."

"I never thought I could. Now, I'm not so sure. I don't know what came over me that day. I could have shot to wound and then turned her over to the proper authorities. Let them deal with her and her duplicity. Instead, I let go of my better judgment and shot to kill, telling myself I did what I had to do to survive and protect my . . ." There's an abrupt pause like he's putting the brakes on a speeding vehicle he's maneuvering through an obstacle course. "Countrymen," he adds, but I don't think that was what he originally planned to say. "I needed to be sure," his words drive onward, "that she wasn't going to do more harm. She was embroiled with powerful people capable of carrying out lethal actions."

I put my finger to his lips. "No more regrets. Maybe it's time we both start fresh."

"Yeah," he blinks long and slow. "The way I see it is, you did what you felt you had to in order to survive a terrible situation. I know the loneliness you describe. It's a heaviness that presses at your insides until your chest aches into your stomach. After my mom died, I couldn't lift that weight no matter how hard I tried. I started drinking to numb the pain. Got drunk every night and picked fights for no good reason other than I needed a release from the rage I buried. A bloodied lip, a broken nose, stitches, all of that physical pain was a hell of a lot easier to deal with than the grief I carried inside."

His eyes flash with tears that don't fall. Even with me, it's hard for him to let his control slip. Inside, though, I know he's shredded by regrets and sadness. I stroke back his hair and kiss the furrowed lines of worry that crease his forehead.

"I never did thank you," he says, kissing the palm of my hand.

"Thank *me*? For what?"

"For keeping yourself and our baby alive while I was away. For helping Devie after that maniac had her face cut, for insisting that Fiona and Liam come with you to Summit in case Dimitri was planning another strike. You have an instinctual empathy and goodness that make me feel loved like I've never felt before."

His mouth is so close it tingles my lips.

"Kiss me," I murmur, hungry for the intimacy more than anything else. He captures my mouth with his lips, sliding his tongue inside until it melts with mine. The coiled spring of tension buried inside me loosens. "I'm happy you're home," I murmur, letting my mouth caresses his neck with soft nibbles. He moves his hand up my thigh and nestles it under my bottom. That little ache tugs inside, and it's not only me wanting. His groan vibrates on my lips.

Opening the top of my nightgown, he lowers his mouth to my breast and sucks. I arch toward his touch, and my fingers lace through his hair. I tug him closer. My libido's at the helm, gunning for gratification, but there's a part of me that needs him to know how grateful I am that he is here, that he is alive and unharmed, that he still wants me after what I did.

My palms rest on both sides of his face. I pull his lips back toward mine. This kiss, peppered with tickling bites and dancing tongues, has his penis pressing into my belly and me wet with need. He slowly lifts the hem of my nightgown, his fingertips grazing my thighs, then my waist. He stretches his thumbs to tickle the nipples of my breasts before tugging the gown over my head. Charged with passion, his gaze travels down my body as if he's seeing me for the first time.

"I missed you, baby." His deep voice resonates with desire. He lowers his head and grazes his lips across the scar from my C-section. Then, when our eyes meet, he kisses my eyelids, my cheek, then my ear, where he nips the lobe.

I help him lift his shirt over his head. My eyes feast on the chute of his taut abs and muscled biceps. I finger scars that sear his chest, placing my lips to each, hoping to kiss away the pain they inflict on his memory. My mouth travels lower, making sure to stop just short of the stiff pennant that pricks the air with a length that begs for release.

I slide off the bed and stand, tugging his hand to stand too. Our eyes meet and, holding his gaze, I shove down his briefs and sink to my knees where I cup his backside with both hands. Taking his cock inside my mouth, I enclose it in moist, rocking embraces. His hiss of pleasure has me pulling stronger, each time taking in more of its hardened length. I massage his balls with one hand and give his ass a playful squeeze with the other while my mouth continues its momentum.

There's a growl low in his throat. "I'm going to come," he warns, finishing with a tight, "So now's the time to pull away." I strengthen my pull and lengthen my intake. His body shudders. A forceful burst fills my mouth. This is not a comfortable sensation, but giving such passionate pleasure is consoling and uplifting, sort of like making a peace offering that says *I recognize your generosity, and I want to be as giving as you are.*

Taking a minute to catch his breath, he looks down at me through lidded eyes, bedroom eyes that signal his need for love and intimacy. "Your turn," he says. Everything below my waist jolts in anticipation. "But first," he takes me by the hand and leads me into the bathroom. "How are you feeling?"

I'm wondering why the heck he's asking if I'm alright. It was just a blow job, for heaven's sake. Then I remember my persistent vomiting and the positive reading from the pregnancy test, add my fall and our argument, and you have the perfect storm to raise his level of concern.

He hands me a cup of water with minty mouthwash

added. I rinse out my mouth. "I'm fine," I say and give him a kiss. He opens my mouth with his tongue and lifts my ass to bring me closer. When we break, my legs are unsteady and my head's in a fog. He scoops me up under my knees and carries me, giggling, to the bed, where he lowers me onto my back.

"It's good to hear you laughing." He rains slow kisses down my arm. My pulse lurches when he traces his lips from my armpit down my side and leg to my toes, where he latches his mouth on the big one and sucks before moving his mouth to gently bite the arch of my foot. When he stops, I open one eye and prop myself up on my elbows. He quirks his lips.

"Tell me," he says, his mouth trailing kisses up my leg. Just as I'm ready to fall back onto the pillow, he pauses.

"Tell you what?" I murmur, my voice thick with passion.

"Do you," small nibbles travel past my knee. He raises my leg. "Still," lazy, moist kisses trail my inner thigh, "really think I have a beautiful ass or did you just say that to be a wise-ass?"

"I knew you heard me, and yes, Mr. Perfect, you have a beautiful ass. Don't let it go to your head. It's big enough already." His answer is to gently suck my inner thigh, causing my head to drop back onto the bed.

The first swirl of his tongue parts my swollen folds. When it teases its wet warmth into the sensitive flesh of bundled nerves, my pulsing ache turns into a throbbing tension.

He stops.

I reach down to push his head lower. "What are you—"

He interrupts my dazed words, "Is this what you want

from me, Alicia?"

"Yes," I gasp, hardly recognizing my whimpering when he pulls my clit into his mouth again. I'm breathing hard now, hovering on the brink of peaking. He raises his head. Teasing, feathery kisses trickle across my navel.

Nooo.

My vagina relaxes, sending a shiver through me that says my pleasure hangs incomplete. I worry my bottom lip. I want to show that I have what it takes to endure the pleasurable agony his withholding produces, but it's been too long. The sexual energy he sparks in me is wild with a need to ignite.

"Please," I murmur, reaching to lower his head again. He does, sucking my clit into his mouth and rolling the sensitive skin against his tongue. The sweet agony of the sensation takes me to a precarious peak where I totter on the brink of a strong, strumming need that begs for release. He stops. *Fuck me two ways from tomorrow.* How long is he going to let this go on?

"Who do you want this from?" he finally asks, his eyes droopy with desire. When nothing more happens, the fog in my head clears enough for me to realize he's deliberately stifling my orgasm until he's satisfied I've had enough. Seems my goodness and love extend only so far on his scorecard. I brace myself, remembering he's the master of this technique.

"You," I answer, not even hesitating because it's the truth.

He returns to teasing with his tongue, slowly at first, then quicker, then back to slow, until the mounting tension rises in brutal waves to just the point of fulfilment before lowering again when he raises his head. I squirm pressing my thighs together to relieve the ache. He spreads them apart.

"I want you to remember," he says, returning to circle his mouth around the outer folds of my vagina, then stopping to lightly pinch my nipple, "this is mine alone." He moves his tongue back into all the right places with all the right momentum until my body strums like a struck tuning fork. When he stops again, I bite my lip to keep from crying. "Let me hear you say it, Alicia."

"I'm yours. Only yours." The words spill out of me in a rushed whisper. He starts again, his tongue brushing hidden spots that stimulate divine sensations. It doesn't take him long to find just the right rhythm and pressure that has me pulsing and rocking against his mouth.

I gasp, letting out choked cries, as rising crests surge into a giant tide that sends me hurling through an orgasm. I ride out the waves of vibrating ecstasy until, panting and drained, I sag back into the sheets.

His mouth leaves my sex, and he cocks his head. "I'd forgotten how beautiful you are when you come."

My mouth's not operational yet, so a satiated, "Mmm" is all I answer. He eyes the bump on my head and hand, then looks at my stomach before rifling his hand through his hair. How like him to act like a bastard and then worry about the consequences. But who am I to judge? After what I did, it's a small miracle that he's still here.

"I'm fine," I smile. "That was fantastic."

He shoots me one of his drop-down-dead gorgeous smiles.

"It's good to see you happy."

I sit up and put my arms around his waist, surprised when a certain part of his anatomy presses into my stomach demanding another round. "And . . ." I reach below to give it a firm tug. "I think I have a way to make you even happier."

He eyes my naked body, then pulls away. "Why don't we shower first," he says.

"Sure." My eyes light with an idea. "How about a bath?" Thoughts of lathering each other in our freestanding tub while performing naughty water sports has my libido surfacing again.

"I prefer we shower." He walks me into the bathroom, turns on the shower faucets, then repeatedly tests the water temperature before letting me step inside. Even for him, that's weird. He rinses out his mouth at the sink, then steps inside the shower stall. But . . . and this is a big but, all he does is gently lather my body with scented soap, beginning with my arms, then bending and lowering his hands to my legs and my feet, raising one clean while making sure I balance myself with my hand against the wall before he starts on the other.

"Lean back your head." When I do, he squirts shampoo into his hand, rubbing it into my hair while being careful to avoid the bruise on my head. Firm fingers massage my scalp, loosening my neck and shoulder muscles and sending currents of calm through my body. I do the same for him, and when we step from the shower squeaky clean but minus any dirty business, I begin piecing together what's happening. No bath, no sexual penetration, worries about the shower water being too hot.

"Chase."

He stops brushing his teeth and looks at me as I wrap myself into my robe. "Have you been googling pregnancy dos and don'ts?"

He wipes his mouth. "Yeah, and the research shows that taking hot baths should be avoided. It could overheat your body and cause complications for you and the baby. You didn't learn that when you were carrying Caroline?"

That last comment sounds a tad testy, but remembering who I'm dealing with and our recent reconciliation, I let it slide.

"I do remember that it was on a list of things to avoid, but I didn't think it would matter because I haven't seen the doctor yet for confirmation." *And Mr. Perfect, I wasn't going to soak in a hot bath for hours, just long enough for us to have mad passionate sex.*

"Well, it's a good thing I've been thinking and doing some research." Hit number two. I close my eyes and silently count to ten. Our peace pact has been validated, but my crime still stands. If he can accept me and my flaws, I can go along with his overly-cautious behavior.

"Why are you making that face?" he says.

"What face?"

"That scowl you wear when you're aggravated." Seems like my face got the message my mind was attempting to hide. I let out a loud sigh.

"I'm trying to digest everything. I'm thrilled with the job offer but then, instead of just having to consider that, there's a positive pregnancy result that has to be dealt with despite your vasectomy. It's all overwhelming."

"Let's take it one step at a time. Tomorrow you'll make an appointment to see the doctor. I'll follow up with the urologist. Afterwards, we'll discuss everything and make a plan on how best to move forward."

"That's just it. I was forming a plan. I thought I could return to work and jumpstart my career again. My agenda never included doctors and . . ."

When realization hits, it's like being swept onto a plummeting rollercoaster. Sudden bursts of vomiting, Caroline rejecting my breast milk, a positive pregnancy reading. "Oh god, I *am* pregnant." I drop my head in my hands and burst into tears, heaping mood swings onto the pile of mounting evidence.

He waits until my crying shifts to sniffling, then hands me a tissue and pulls out the vanity stool. "Sit, while you have your moment."

Once I'm settled, he takes a comb to my tangled wet hair, ends first. After a bit, he switches to a brush, stroking its bristles from the top of my head to the ends of my hair. Closing my eyes, I succumb to the rhythmic motions of the brush. I lean my cheek into his hand.

"Chase?"

"Yeah."

"Thanks for giving me a second chance."

"Baby, without second chances we'd never be more than what we were yesterday." He clamps his hands on either side of my face and firmly pulls my head back to meet his eyes. "Just don't make the same mistake twice."

I shake my head, never breaking eye contact.

In bed, he wraps his hand around my ribcage and spoons me into the curve of his body. My naked backside nestles into his hardened penis and the sensation tantalizes my urge for him inside my body. It's obvious he's feeling the same, but when I try to make a move, he locks me in place. "Let's hear what the doctor has to say about having sex before we do anything feisty."

Feisty? I'm hankering for a hearty, give me your worst, bang-up tussle after all the time he's been away, and he won't even consider feisty.

"You're giving me that face again," he says into my back. I bite his finger playfully and nuzzle closer. Something tells me I'm going to be flashing lots of that look during the next nine months.

Within minutes he's asleep. I close my eyes and drift off to the lullaby of his even breathing.

CHAPTER 9

"Hello, mamma's little sweet pea." I lift Caroline above my head and nuzzle her tummy with kisses. She smiles, kicks her feet, and mushes her hands in my hair. Inside the kitchen, Sunny's rattling a myriad of pots and pans needed to prepare a four-course breakfast. This tells me he's been told about my possible pregnancy.

"How are you feeling?" Sammy smiles, lugging all of Caroline's baby paraphernalia into the apartment before heading in the direction of the coffee pot. Obviously, he's been told as well. I'm not surprised. Sammy and Chase's military bond is bolstered by an unspoken oath that anything and everything will be done to ensure the safety of the other. With Dimitri out to destroy Chase's family, babies and pregnancies just strengthen their determination to protect the family unit.

"I feel good."

Sunny shakes his head no and points a spatula toward the far end of the kitchen, indicating where Sammy must go if he wants to enjoy a fresh cup of coffee without me running to the toilet to throw up. I give Caroline more kisses, savoring her sweet baby smell.

"Before I forget," I force my attention toward Sammy, "I'm wondering if you could fill in here for a bit so Mac can be on hand to drive Virgil home from the hospital. Virgil thinks he's being discharged today."

Stilted silence follows. I've known Sammy for a while now. We've been through several life-death situations where he's rescued me from a speeding boat and the pursuit by a masked madman. He was also on hand to take me to the hospital after Dimitri's attack. So, I know that when his face flattens and he turns inward as if the moment holds nothing more than ordinary happenstances, he's holding something back. My alert button flashes red. "What's wrong?"

"Have you spoken to Chase this morning?"

"No, he left early for the office saying he had a lot to catch up on." The warning signal shifts to panic. "Is he alright?"

"He's fine. There's no need to worry. Everyone is okay."

That has the sound of *don't worry your pretty little head,* which doesn't lessen my concern or help me hold my temper.

"Sammy, I want to know what's going on, and I want to know now."

My phone jingles and, too afraid not to answer in lieu of what's happening, I raise my finger and ask if he could please hold that thought.

"Hello."

A frantic-sounding Virgil spews a stream of panicked words that are hard to decipher. "Virgil, what was that you just said?"

"Mac's been ordered to report back for some kind of interview. Why he has to travel into a war zone to answer a few questions is beyond me," he says.

"Calm down, Virgil. Do you know for a fact that Mac's been deployed back to Afghanistan?"

"No, he hasn't given me any specifics, but it's somewhere overseas because he took his passport."

Remaining in the dark about these missions is something I'm familiar with. During both times Chase had to report, I had little to no idea where he was stationed.

I'm shaking, but I make every attempt to ease Virgil's frazzled nerves. "The same thing happened to Chase. It's called a debriefing. It's administrative and takes much less time than a deployment." I don't have to dig deep to remember it took four weeks, six days, and eighteen hours for Chase to return home. I could probably state the minutes and seconds if asked, but why share all of this with Virgil, who's clearly beside himself with worry.

"That's comforting to hear."

"Good. Are you still being discharged from the hospital today?"

"Yes, I'm just waiting to see the doctor, who I'm told should be here any minute."

"I'm thinking Sammy can pick you up." I glare at Sammy, daring him to disagree. He doesn't. Last thing he needs is a pregnant woman with a baby in her arms all over his case. "Call as soon as you see the doctor and Sammy will head your way."

"Thanks, Alicia."

"No problem."

When I disconnect, I'm quick to offer Sammy

reassurances. "Sunny is here. All I have planned is spending time with Caroline and sketching once she goes down for a nap."

He looks skeptical but before he has a chance to complain, I'm onto another topic, one I don't want to address but want answers to.

"How long have you all known that Mac has to report back?"

Sammy hems and haws.

I glower and frown.

He looks at his shoes.

I stare him down.

He capitulates. "About three or four days."

That familiar stab of dread seizes my stomach. What if Chase is called back too? That same voice of lurking fear tells me that this time he may never come home. Color leaches from my face. Nausea crawls through my stomach.

Sammy raises both hands in a calming surrender. "Take it easy, Alicia. I swear, I've heard nothing about Chase having to report back. As far as we all know, he's served his time and is home for good."

All I have time to do is hand Caroline over to him before fleeing to the bathroom to vomit whatever little food remains there. It's become so routine that Sunny is waiting for me with crackers and a cup of tea after I emerge from the bathroom, depleted and exhausted.

"I'm better now." I slide onto the sofa and nibble on the cracker and sip some tea, hoping both will soak up the ever-present nausea. Eating has become a chore I dread. Nothing stays down, and it's getting worse with each passing day.

Tears threaten when Sunny takes Caroline from Sammy to change and feed her because it's a reminder that I'm too busy getting sick to hold her and give her the time she deserves. I'm noticing that guilt is a big part of being a mother. And now there'll be more responsibility heaped onto what's already spiking. I'm not looking forward to having another baby, which triggers more guilt, making me feel worse.

Snuggled into the couch, I must nod off because when my eyes open next, the sun has slid into late afternoon. There are no calls or messages on my phone, so I assume Sammy drove Virgil home from the hospital and is settling him in as planned. A quick peek into Caroline's room shows she's serenely napping. Sunny's bedroom door is closed, which means he's either resting or listening to music on his headphones. He often does both before dinner. I think about calling Chase, but he was so concerned about catching up on work that accumulated while he was gone, I don't want to interrupt his momentum. Maybe I should reach out anyway, make sure he's working on new proposals and not getting everything in order because he's leaving for active duty. I press his number. It goes straight to voice mail. Before I can leave a message, I get an immediate text response.

In a meeting call u soon. And because he's Chase he adds, *phone if there's a problem.*

All good, I text. Then, because I am who I am, I head into our bedroom to check the bottom of our walk-in closet. I spot his empty duffel bag squished beneath another suitcase and exhale a breath of relief.

I consider getting back to Virgil and Charlotte about

helping out their fledgling business but then remember Chase's suggestion that I wait until I hear what the doctor has to say. Sketching is a possibility. It's what I planned to do today, but my creative juices have been dissipated by nagging nausea and lingering lethargy.

It's when I'm contemplating all these buts that I hear the doorbell. That's strange. No one buzzed from the lobby that someone was on their way up. I edge toward the door and rest my right eye against the peephole. The passageway is empty.

"Who is it?" I call from behind the locked door.

No answer.

I grasp the doorknob, hesitate, then shift my hand away, pressing my ear against the door instead. The only sound I hear is my breathing and the rumbling of my unsettled stomach.

I peer through the peephole again. An empty corridor stares back. I'm just about to turn away when a high-pitched yelp that sounds like the cry of a child catches me up short. Someone is definitely slinking around our entryway.

Sunny materializes, holding his finger to his lips with one hand and brandishing a semi-automatic pistol with the other. He mimes that I should head to the nursery and lock the door. I slide a large carving knife from its holder in the kitchen, then slip into the nursery. Caroline's blissfully asleep so I'm careful when I wedge the rocking chair under the doorknob. Clutching the knife in my fist, I flatten my body against the wall adjacent to the door and wait. My pulse races and a nervous sweat beads my neck. The only sound is the rhythm of the clock ticking in the foyer, a jeering reminder that no matter how much time passes, the possibility of an attack by Dimitri still threatens our lives.

A hurried, harried voice carries from outside the apartment. My grip on the knife tightens.

"I tried to stop him, but he was fast, slipped into the service elevator carrying something that he said he was delivering to the penthouse."

It's Boris. I remove the chair from under the doorknob and go see what's happening, making sure to first return the knife to its wooden sheath on the kitchen counter. Boris, winded and perspiring, swabs his forehead with a handkerchief. Sunny steps outside and inspects both ends of the corridor and the stairwells.

"I watched what floor he got off on, then had to take the stairs when both elevators weren't returning to the lobby. By the time I got to your floor, he was gone. I found this outside your door."

I recoil. My hand flies to my mouth to stifle a scream when I see what's resting on the carpet directly outside our door. Sunny takes my arm and tries to usher me inside, but my legs won't budge. I can't shift my eyes from the mangled car seat that sits on the hallway carpet. The flattened carrier handle has crushed the sun visor into the headrest, making it clear that no infant would have survived this hit. What really makes my flesh crawl is the doll compressed under the disjointed parts, its neck twisted so its head hangs to the side while its eyes stare unblinkingly ahead.

Sunny's gaze assumes a chill I've never seen before when he recognizes Caroline's car seat. For a moment, we all stare at the battered seat, Boris still gasping from his run up fifteen flights of stairs and Sunny keeping his hand near his jacket pocket where I assume he's hidden the gun.

Just as I've seen Chase and Sammy and Mac do many times when confronted with trouble, Sunny levels any shock from his face and calmly addresses Boris. "Thank you for your effort to alert us that someone was heading here without being announced. A friend of the Reardons had an accident while driving one of their vehicles and must have made arrangements to have the contents of the damaged car returned."

"Is Caroline okay?"

"She's fine. She wasn't in the car."

A very relieved Boris smiles and nods his head. "Do you want me to cart this to the basement for the garbage disposal?"

I'm too shaky to answer but Sunny is quick to add, "That won't be necessary. We'll take care of it." Sunny knows that Chase and Sammy will want to study the seat to determine whether the police need to be informed.

"Let me know if you change your mind." Boris backs toward the elevator, his gaze fixed on the battered car seat. "I hope your friend is okay."

"He's on the mend. Thanks for your concern, Boris." I answer breathlessly, stifling a sob that's surfaced from the terrifying implication of what this all means.

As soon as Boris disappears into the service elevator, Sunny shifts the car seat into the stairwell, then double-bolts the door, insisting I sit so he can bring me a cup of tea. Sinking into the sofa, I draw in heavy breaths.

For the next several minutes, I feel numb. Curling my legs under me, I stare ahead. My attention is jostled when Sunny places a hot mug of tea on the end table.

"It's fresh peppermint and ginger with a touch of honey."

I force a smile, take a sip, then place it on the table to grab my phone and call Chase.

"I phoned Chase with an update while your tea was steeping."

"Thanks, Sunny. Does he want me to phone as well?"

"I filled him in. He's ending his meeting and told me to tell you he'll be home within the hour. Drink your tea and try to relax. No one is going to hurt you or Caroline." Sunny's mouth curves into a smile but his eyes stay hard.

"Thanks again, Sunny. For everything."

He pats my hand. "You just take care of yourself."

The first thing I think once my mind starts functioning again is that Virgil's accident was no accident. The car targeted is one we usually leave in Summit. The last time that car was used by us was when Chase went to the market with Caroline on Thanksgiving morning. That explains why the car seat we keep in the vehicle in Summit was in the back seat of the borrowed car.

This has to be Dimitri's doing. Adding the mangled doll is his cold-blooded way of making sure we understand what could have happened had he wanted it to. At Virgil's expense, Dimitri's threatening us much like a cat paws a mouse, then lets it go, but never stays more than a breath away from eventually killing it. There's no doubt that, when Dimitri tires of this game, he will slice into us with his claws for the kill. The images of the battered car seat and the doll's broken neck race through my mind until I can't bear to think about them a moment longer.

What I do next is like answering a call that won't quiet unless obeyed. Sliding on Chase's coat, I slip onto the terrace and light up a cigarette, just like I did countless times when he was missing. The brisk chill of early winter clears my head but doesn't remove my apprehension. I consider what it signals that Mac has been called back. I recognize there's a good chance Chase will never be deployed again. He's told me countless times that having served twice and been a prisoner of war eliminate him as a viable candidate to be summoned again. Intellectually, I understand this reasoning. It's processing it emotionally that's a challenge. Just thinking about the possibility of having to face Dimitri alone while fretting about Chase's safety sends streaks of fear racing through my body.

I take a drag, then another, with slow deliberation. My thoughts wander to where Dimitri might be now. He's a wanted man, yet remains at large with an uncanny ability to maneuver freely. His threats creep closer and closer, first in Summit and now here. That has to mean his underworld network is broadening and strengthening.

I sense eyes stitched to my back and go for one last pull. The cigarette is snagged from my fingers and flicked to the ground before I can get it to my mouth. I had forgotten how quick Chase's reflexes are but not how cutting his words can be when he's angry.

"How can you even think of smoking when you might be pregnant? Are you that set on harming yourself as well as our baby to satisfy a craving?" *Set, harm, baby*, three words that slam truths into my mind, that are so heavy with regret and guilt, I feel crushed under their weight.

Before I can admit my fault, he shouts, "Across the board, your actions are deplorable." The *across the board* part of his comment cuts even more into my core because I know what he's referring to. I also know that if we stand any chance of moving forward, these references can't be used against me whenever I make a mistake or he's annoyed at something I've done.

"I know you're angry, but it's unfair to jab at me about what happened when you were away. What I did was inexcusable, but like I told you countless times before, I was grief-stricken, I felt alone. Any coping mechanisms I thought I had crumbled, so I cheated . . . once, and started smoking. The first, I swear to you will never happen again and the second . . . not so sure. I'm trying."

"Yeah, well, *you* are *trying* to deal with." He slams his hand onto the terrace wall and snatches my nearly-empty pack of American Spirits, then spots the unopened pack on the table and confiscates it, too. "I've a good mind to throttle you for being so reckless." He stops shouting long enough to eye me up and down. "Why are you wearing my coat?"

"I find it oddly comforting."

This seems to catch him off guard. In the silence that follows, I search for some shred of understanding, but all I see is disappointment. I'm not surprised. It's what I'd see in myself if I had a mirror. All at once, the emotional load of Mac's recent deployment, Dimitri's ghoulish threat, and my poor coping mechanisms plunge me into a sea of sadness. "I never meant to hurt you like I did, and now, like some damn wrecking ball, I'm continuing to sabotage myself. You have every right to reject me . . . to hate me, but you could never dislike me more than I already despise myself."

I stare at the ground. My hand brushes his when I use it to shade my moistened eyes. It's then that I realize that ordinary tears prickle, but tears of shame burn. "I don't want to live my life believing I've lost your trust." The words are squeezed through choked tears.

For several suspended seconds, my face stays buried in my palms, until I feel his hand on mine prying it, finger by finger, away from my face. With a tender touch, he raises my hand to his lips and places soft kisses on the pads of each finger, then rocks me in his embrace until I stop sobbing and can take regular breaths.

"A warrior has no time for self-loathing."

"A warrior?"

"Yeah, that's what you are. You're a soldier who'll do whatever it takes to defend what you believe in and who you love. I meant what I said last night about your strength and courage. Even today you held strong."

"All I did was try not to barf and hide in Caroline's nursery. How is that brave?"

"You didn't pick up something along the way?"

"I may have taken a knife with me. But that was just in case I needed to defend Caroline."

"More like a saber, if Sunny has anything to say about it." He kisses the top of my head. "I was out of line with that criticism about your behavior. I said I wasn't going to keep passing judgment, and I will stick to my promise. It won't happen again."

Did Mr. Perfect just apologize?

I nod, fishing through the pockets of his coat for the tissues I know I kept there. "I was so upset about everything that happened today." I swallow a dollop of raw emotion, because, yet again, fear drove me to make the wrong choice. I dab my tears with the tissue, holding it crushed in the palm of my hand when I'm done.

His breath is warm when he kisses my temple. "I don't want you to worry that we're not safe. The highest level of surveillance is going to be implemented. There'll be two cameras installed on either side of our hallway along with visual monitors and motion detectors inside our apartment. No one will be able to travel to our floor or into our apartment without being photographed and seen on the screens mounted inside. It's a powerful deterrent." His switch from a subtle attack on my fidelity to concern about my safety shows how conflicted he remains about the best way to maneuver through what's happened. Forgiveness might take time, but we don't have time to compromise our safety. The dead cannot repair relationships.

A frosty gust of wind penetrates the loose sleeves of his oversized coat. He rubs his hands up and down my arms to help keep me warm.

"Dr. Alexander called to say she had a cancellation tonight. I said we'd take it, knowing that Thursday you have an appointment with the OB-GYN in the afternoon. It lessens the load for you that day."

It's hard shifting gears from a murderous thug to a hypnotist's session, but that's just the way life works. No matter how grave one facet is, ordinary components like appointments, work, and meetings mundanely move forward.

"When do we need to leave?"

He checks his phone. "Now. If we're going to make it by six." He studies me for a bit. "Have you eaten anything today?"

"Some light snacks."

He's not fooled by my evasive answer. "How many times have you vomited?"

I debate shaving a bit from the actual tally so he doesn't worry, but since honesty has been in the forefront of our relationship, I go with the truth.

"Four or five times."

I hear his intake of breath. "I think you should eat something before we leave or at the very least take something with you in the car."

The thought of eating in a moving car has me nearly spewing in anticipation. "I'll bring along some crackers and a bottled water, but I don't think I'll eat anything until after my appointment and—"

"And what?"

"I don't want to leave Caroline tonight. I wasn't able to give her much attention today and now this . . ." My voice trails off.

"So, we'll take her along on our drive to Belle Harbor. You can sit in the back seat and play with her while I'm driving. Then, when you're meeting with the doctor, Caroline and I will have our long-overdue discussion in the waiting room."

"Is that so." I smooth down his jacket collar that's lifted with the wind. "And what is so pressing that you both need to talk about tonight?"

"Just the usual father-daughter stuff." He presses a feathery kiss on my lips, then, keeping his mouth a hairsbreadth from mine, whispers, "I'll explain how I had to leave her mamma for a time even though I didn't want to." He kisses the tip of my nose. "Then I'll tell her how, instead of one beautiful gift waiting for me when I got home, there were two." He kisses my eyelid. "I figure by that time I'll have to address some of her more salient questions about safety. I'll assure her that she and her mamma are safe because I won't ever be going away like that again."

I put my arms around his neck and look up into his eyes. "You think she'll believe what you say?"

He kisses my other eyelid. "I know she will, because she'll sense the love and truth that's here." He presses my hand to his heart and holds it there until it absorbs the heat of his body. He's being open and honest, but it's not enough to quell the panic that surfaces when I'm forced to probe and then piece together threadbare shreds of information to find out what's happening in our lives.

Keeping my arms locked around his neck, I lean my head back. "Why didn't you tell me Mac was ordered to report again?"

"I didn't think it was necessary to explain what simply amounted to Mac having to return for routine administrative purposes for two weeks at most." His tone is casual, as if stepping into a war zone is part of most people's daily job description.

"I suppose it works for you and Mac and Sammy to be unbothered by what you refer to as *routine*, but to the civilian population, it's alarming."

"I'm sorry I didn't prepare you and that now you're worried."

"It's not just me. Virgil called all upset and confused. He has no idea what this entails and . . . did you know they're a couple now?" I'm hopping through topics but only because I know he'll never share the details of Mac's mission.

"Mac told me several days ago, and before you become angry that I didn't share that information too, you should know that he asked me not to say anything. He wanted to tell you himself, and I respected his right to have it that way."

"I understand his need to decide who and when anyone is told about his personal life, but from what I saw at the hospital, they're so in love, they're oblivious to who knows or what they might think. Mac was really showing his tender side."

"I saw it, too. We'll invite them for dinner once Virgil is able to get around. Now, c'mon," he takes my hand and steers me toward the terrace doors. "Let's get you some crackers and hit the road or I'll be late for my meeting with Caroline."

CHAPTER 10

I notice Dr. Alexander's smile first. Wide, warm, and welcoming, it puts me at ease. Sliding into the cushioned chair in a dimly-lit corner of her home office, I peer out two large windows and imagine the expanse of ocean that stretches beneath the night sky. Dr. Alexander slips into a hard-core office chair, one of those ergonomic ones that is contoured to keep your back straight and your neck at the perfect angle. Leaning back, she watches me through soft hazel eyes.

"I understand you're here to address a smoking habit?" Her voice is smooth and mellow.

"Yes, that's right."

"Do you mind sharing when you smoked your first cigarette?"

"Not at all. I pilfered one from one of my older brothers when I was fifteen and smoked it while taking a bath, making sure to crack open the bathroom window before lighting up."

"How did smoking that cigarette make you feel?"

"I didn't like it. I remember putting it out after a few

puffs because it burned my throat and chest."

"You didn't like it. So, what made you decide to smoke again?"

"When my husband was called back to active duty in Afghanistan and then went missing, I started smoking more often. I don't know exactly why. I guess it took my mind off my jitteriness."

"And the burning sensation?"

"It was less but still there."

"You didn't like the burning, but you did like the internal good feeling smoking provided. It afforded you a temporary release from fear and worry."

Well, she nailed that in the first three minutes of the session.

"Yes, I suppose so."

"And now that he's back, why do you think the urge to smoke is still there?"

The question unleashes a flood of worry I've been wallowing in, and my answer comes out in a stream of hurried words. "That's just it. I don't know if he's back for good. He didn't tell me the last time he had to leave. I think that may have been because he had orders not to say anything. In either case, I was blindsided and now our friend, who served with Chase, has been called back for a debriefing."

"This obviously has you upset." She hands me a box of tissues.

I gratefully take one and wipe my eyes.

"Have you told him how you feel?"

"Yes." I briefly blow my nose. "He says I shouldn't worry, that his tour of duty is over, and he's home for good."

"I see." She pauses to give me some time to get a handle on my emotions, then proceeds in the same melodic tone.

"Let me try to clarify to you what's happening so you have a clearer understanding of how the mind works. There's a part of your brain that understands your husband is back and that he is safe. There is also a part of your brain that remembers the pain you felt when he was gone and what you did to ease it when he was missing. Now, when you experience negative feelings, that part asks, *what can I do to feel good again*? Learning that your husband's friend has to report back unleashed thoughts about what this could mean for your husband. These fears triggered your brain's need to make you feel better. My guess is you had a cigarette."

"Yes." I admit.

"But that's not the only trigger. If there were only one, smoking would be easy to cure, and it's not. It is a dangerous, persistent dependency that poisons the body. You need your body to survive so you must protect it from harm."

There is nothing disapproving in the delivery of this frank assessment. Yet, each word is a dart to my heart. Staring out the bay window and onto the lighted boardwalk, I watch Chase, with Caroline tucked into her pouch sling, head back toward Dr. Alexander's office after what must have been a brisk walk to calm her restlessness. My eyes cloud with tears but my ears remain open to what Dr. Alexander has to say.

"Nicotine addiction is rooted in the subconscious, so we have to determine what thoughts are keeping the habit in place."

I give her a cautious, tight smile, not sure I want to expose unconscious thoughts even if they might be driving me to smoke. Letting someone peek at personal thoughts I'm unaware of seems like relinquishing control of my mind.

She must sense my unease because she clarifies, "All we're going to do is reframe your subconscious thoughts, so you think negatively about smoking. Perhaps allow you to think that cigarette smoke smells like burning garbage or exhaust from an old truck. Then, when your mind receives a stress signal, your tendency to reach for a cigarette will be lessened or eliminated."

That all sounds optimistically sound. It's the method of achieving that goal that has me concerned.

"How is that done?" A quick scan of the room shows there are no swaying watches or spinning wheels.

"I'd like you to take a seat here," she points to a tan leather recliner. Once I'm settled, she adds smoothly, "We're going to do some relaxation and breathing exercises. You'll be aware, but you might feel like your mind is daydreaming."

I nod assent. What do I have to lose? I want to kick this habit. I focus as directed. She speaks. I listen. Musical chimes ring in the distance. My eyes flutter, then shut. My mind floats in darkness, and as I listen to her suggestions, a tingling takes hold of my body. While the light ringing floats in my brain, I breathe as directed and listen to her soothing voice. At the end, she counts to five. I open my eyes, and poof, with the snap of a finger, it's over. She smiles in her fashionable seat. I relax in my comfy recliner, relieved that our mindful session was so effortless.

"So, who is Matteo?" she asks, piercing my relief with the intensity of a sword. She waits for me to take the time to collect myself and answer.

"Did I mention that name?"

"You said you were sorry for what happened."

Oh boy, I must have rambled while in that hypnotic state. I feel my chin for spittle, but my fingers come away dry. "He was my twin brother who died at birth. He was too underdeveloped to survive."

"But you were normal weight?"

I nod.

"What was it like growing up knowing that?"

"I didn't find out I had a twin until I overheard it from my aunt when I was twelve. She was visiting to help care for my mother. My mother suffered through bouts of depression and would take to her bed for long stretches of time." Taking a deep breath, I try to bide time so I can continue without crying. "That particular day, my mother was inconsolable. She cried for hours. I was worried. I waited outside the closed door for her to stop. That's when I heard my aunt explain that it wasn't my mother's fault, that often one twin doesn't thrive in the womb because the stronger one absorbs all of the sustenance. I think my aunt was trying to make my mother feel less guilty about the stillbirth."

"So, you found out about the loss of a twin while trying to cope with a parent whose depression made her disappear into her room for weeks at a time. How did all that make you feel?"

She hands me the tissue box again to help me mop up the tears that continue to fall.

"At first, I was in denial. I didn't believe what I heard. It seemed impossible that I had another sibling, a twin, that no one mentioned before. But then it started to make sense. This despondency she had usually swirled around me, the distracted expression and forced smiles she wore during graduations or other milestones in my life, how she missed my school plays or sporting events because she was too depressed to get out of bed. It was like she had this sad, untold story that had been buried with the baby. During those times, I felt enormous guilt, like I was the one who stole this missing piece of her happiness. I started to think I left my twin ravenous and too weak to survive. I know it seems ridiculous and unrealistic because I was only an infant, but the weight of the guilt and responsibility is anything but."

"I think your feelings are very real, and now you're still struggling to reconcile your current personal self with your mother's past grieving. Were you able to share with anyone in your family how guilty and sad you were feeling?"

"Not really."

"Why was that?"

Memories of everyone tiptoeing around my mother's depressions spring to mind along with my father's over-protectiveness, like at any given moment I could become depressed too or worse, die as my brother had.

"I don't think I ever felt free enough to let my parents know I was unhappy or sad, especially about my dead brother. Obviously, I couldn't talk to my mother about the problem while she was depressed and then when she was feeling better, I was afraid it would make her depressed again."

"What about speaking to your father?"

"He was so concerned about my welfare that giving him more cause for worry didn't seem to be an option. He also kept such long work hours, splitting his time between the restaurant on Long Island and the family vineyard in Tuscany, I felt he had enough burdens. The first person I shared my guilt and grief with was Chase."

"Seems like speaking about the death of your twin was prohibited. I now see why fears of loss fuel sadness and discontent in your mind. With no healthy outlets or coping mechanisms modeled earlier in life, these negative feelings prompted you to search for relief in ways that harm your body and sabotage your happiness."

Amen to that. Before Chase's deployment, dealing with the death of a spouse was something I only considered in the abstract. It was a sad event that happened to people in movies or to those much older in real life. After he went missing, there were no words to express the raw emotional impact of the shock and grief I felt. Smoking became the easiest outlet, the crutch that helped me relax and sort through my thoughts.

"We'll work more on developing strategies to deal with this trigger and any others that may come up."

I hear Caroline crying in the waiting room, then a gentle knock on the door.

"Come in," Dr. Alexander cheerfully announces.

Chase lifts Caroline out of the pouch and slides her pacifier back in her mouth. He eyes the tissues and my swollen eyes but says nothing.

"We're just about done here." Dr. Alexander gets up and presents Caroline with her enormous, infectious grin. Caroline smiles back through her shifting pacifier.

Giving Chase's hand a squeeze to signal all went well, I take Caroline, who's now squirming and reaching for me.

"Thank you, doctor. I appreciate your help."

"Shall I book another appointment for next week?"

"Yes, please."

She opens a large daily planner with a foamy sea and bursting sunrise on its cover and records our agreed-upon day and time within its narrow lines. I like that she's old-school, depending on a paper calendar and a fountain pen to keep her schedule. There's something comforting in the meticulous way she prints my name in the designated time slot. In fact, just about everything to do with this session has had a calming effect, as if I just woke from a deep meditation.

Chase helps me slip on my coat and we're on our way back to the city, with Caroline asleep as soon as she hits her car seat. "So, how did it go," he finally asks, handing me some crackers and an apple.

"Seems like I'm the poster child for finding destructive ways to deal with loss."

Instead of laughing, he lifts and kisses the palm of my hand.

"I promise you my deployment is over. I'm here to stay."

"I know that. I just don't feel it yet."

"What was your impression of the *healer*?" He widens his eyes and *ooohs* spookily.

"Professional, thorough, and on target."

I realize that even though I'm talking about my fear of Chase leaving, there's no urge for a cigarette. "Once again, Mr. Perfect, you were right."

"Mr. Perfect, eh? Even when you think I'm being overly cautious?"

"When you fly that hallmark of your personality, I'd

have to say you become Mr. Pita."

"So, you're saying I'm either perfect or a pain in the ass."

"Yep, and sometimes both at the same time."

"Fair enough," he laughs, then turns serious. "I'm glad you think it was worthwhile enough to make another appointment."

"Yeah, she said I can kick this smoking habit, but it takes time. I'm determined to give it my all."

"I know it's hard and I'm sorry I got angry before. I want to help in any way I can."

Two apologies in one night. Definitely a record.

"I know you do. Tonight was a good start." Resting my head against his shoulder, it hits me that rehashing unpleasant memories makes you feel like you've experienced them all over again. My eyes close and only open again when we reach the garage to our building.

I want to say that I sit down to dinner with Chase to enjoy the scrumptious meal Sunny prepared, but I'm too busy throwing up the apple, five crackers, and one bottled water I consumed in the car. When I come out of the bathroom, I catch Chase rubbing his hands across his face, as if he can't think past what he's planning next. I slide under the blankets too depleted and too scared I'll vomit again to think about anything else. I hear Chase on the phone demanding an appointment with the OB-GYN for first thing tomorrow morning. I know we'll be going because he won't back down until he makes it happen.

The first thing I notice when I wake is Caroline's incessant crying. The next is that my pants hang loose on my waist when I scurry into them so I can go see what's wrong. Red-faced and hot to my touch, Caroline fusses in Sunny's arms. I take her while he goes to fetch the thermometer even though we both know she has a fever.

"Chase, Caroline is sick and I'm going to have to take her to the pediatrician. We might have to postpone my appointment," I shout from the kitchen."

He's out of the shower in a flash with a towel wrapped around a body that, even under these trying conditions, makes me want him. I nearly slap myself silly. *That's how you got yourself in this predicament,* an inner voice reprimands.

Sunny appears with the thermometer, takes Caroline's temperature, and announces she has a fever of 101. While I rock and soothe her, he phones the pediatrician and schedules an appointment for early afternoon. He assures me he'll take care of Caroline and that once I'm finished, we can all meet at the pediatrician's office.

I don't want to leave her, but Chase is insistent I see the doctor this morning. I reluctantly agree, realizing there's not much more I can do that Sunny, who was an army medic, can't do as well if not better. I kiss Caroline's warm forehead and head out with Chase for my scheduled appointment.

CHAPTER 11

Did you ever step into a room and get the feeling that something's about to happen that will send pounding waves of change into your life? That's the impression I have lying on the examination table, waiting for the technician to set up the internal sonogram after—SHOCKER—my pregnancy is confirmed. Relaxing as much as possible with the device in place, Chase and I stare at the monitor, waiting to see our tiny sign of new life.

Talking to us but looking at the screen, the specialist asks us to be patient because she thinks she can locate the heartbeat. It's like waiting for the climax of a mystery to unfold.

"And here we go," she says again, peering closely at what appears to be swirling circles. We all stare at the screen. "Right here," she points to a moving part, is the embryo's heartbeat, and here," she points at another location, "is the other heartbeat."

Surprise flaws Chase's usually impeccable ability to collect, analyze, and correlate information. "Are you saying our baby has two hearts?" he says.

"The image indicates you're having twins, Mr. Reardon."

Now, it's not like I haven't seen Chase stressed before. I've watched him rifle his hand through his hair until it spiked in all directions. I've just never seen his hair stand on end of its own accord. Staring wide-eyed at the monitor, he looks like he's been struck by a high-voltage current. I shift my body to peer closer. Yep. Definitely two pulsing pinpoints. It's like some higher power is toying with us, chanting, "You don't want any more children, well I'll show you, here's two more for you to raise."

After I dress, we sit side by side, in the consultation room, waiting to speak to the doctor. Chase's phone jingles. He declines the call without bothering to see who it is.

"You know what this means, don't you?" I ask, my eyes boring into his.

"Yeah, we're going to have three kids under the age of two. Talk about unbelievable odds. We should buy a lottery ticket."

"Want to hear some more crazy probabilities?" I don't give him a chance to answer before adding, "How about only two accidents," I raise two fingers, "and three," I add another one, "babies."

"It's all going to be—"

"Here's another absurd unlikelihood," I cut him off. "My mother once had to make three different trips." I raise three fingers for effect. "To the emergency room over the course of the same afternoon because one or another of my brothers needed stitches or a broken bone set."

"Are you done?"

I ignore the question. "This is going to send us right off the social grid. Forget travel, going out with friends. I might as well delete my contacts."

Rubbing his chin with the palm of his hand, a twinkle of humor flirts through his gaze. "Oh c'mon, it's not all bad."

I challenge him with silence and a raised brow.

"I'm thinking we can cut a deal with the doctor," he adds.

"What do you mean?"

"A twofer, you know, a buy one, get one free offer. We pay to have one kid but take home two."

"You're the mediator. I'll leave that negotiation in your capable hands. Do you wanna know what else I think?"

"Maybe." He eyes me warily. "You still have that vinegar tone."

"I think you should go for another vasectomy so next time we can have triplets. Make it a clean half-dozen kids, buy a minivan and . . . and . . ." I rapidly wave my hand, "scramble them all inside like a stuffed omelet." I stare at him for a bit, trying to gather my thoughts, but it's hard to focus past my mind's whirling shock. "I don't understand how we can be having twins. I read somewhere that multiple births in families skip a generation."

He leans his head toward mine. "Our two mustn't have gotten that memo."

"Funny, very funny."

Before I can ramble further, he takes my hand to his warm lips and kisses it. "We'll get through this."

The doctor appears, nods a quick hello, then bends to lift the bundle of manila folders piled on his desk chair. He searches for a home for them in the crowded room, deciding finally to drop them on an overstuffed shelf where they cling precariously to the edge.

Satisfied with this filing system, he sits, peering at us from half-moon glasses with a practiced smile. "Congratulations, Mr. and Mrs. Reardon, the ultrasound indicates there are twins on the way."

Stupefied silence is our response. It seems the double-hauling stork has rendered us mute again. It has me torn between wanting to protect those two beating parts of both of us and feeling like they're two erasers poised to remove parts of who I thought I was becoming. I had made up my mind to tell Virgil I was ready to return to fashion design full time. Now I'm going to be responsible for the lives of three dependents. The worrying ramifications cling to my silence while my mind shouts, *you're following the same path your mother traveled.*

He glances through a folder containing my medical history. "You saw my associate, Dr. Diamond for one visit during your former pregnancy." He looks up expectantly, and I'm assuming it's for an explanation as to why I never kept my scheduled appointments or bothered to call to cancel. How do I explain that fleeing from a cold-blooded crime boss out to kill your unborn baby makes it challenging to keep appointments or call to cancel?

"Yes, that's right. When my husband left to serve overseas, I moved to our country house and delivered our daughter in Albany. I had their office transfer my files here. Were they received?"

"We have them." He moves to a computer monitor, flicks a bit here and there, studies the screen, then reverts back to the page inside the folder.

I try to decipher what he's reading, but it's impossible

to see anything beyond his bent head.

He finally looks at both of us and beams. "The ultra-sound shows you're about six-and-a-half weeks pregnant and so far, all looks good." He hands over a copy of the image and once again, the two pumping pinpoints beginning their life's journey inside my body trigger a slew of emotions. Excitement, fear, joy, and resentment all hit at once, inciting my mind to eliminate the last reaction when my conscience heaves guilt in my face.

"Usually when there are multiple births, we monitor their development and the mother's well-being more often and with extra caution than if there's a single fetus. How have you been feeling?" His mouth curves into a smile but his eyes remain impenetrable.

"For the most part, I feel fine."

Chase interrupts, ignoring the pleading look I shoot his way to keep quiet. I want more time to see how my body adjusts to this pregnancy before I start complaining about problems. I'm thinking a better diet and absolutely no smoking will curb the vomiting.

In typical Chase fashion, he speaks his mind anyway. "I don't know how normal this is, having not been here when Alicia was pregnant with our daughter, but she doesn't seem to be able to hold anything down."

The doctor trains his gaze at both of us, and I move toward the edge of my seat, not wanting to miss anything he has to say.

"Normally some vomiting is expected by the fifth and sixth week, but my records indicate that you're seven pounds less than you were at the time of your first visit during your first pregnancy. How many times are you vomiting and urinating a day?" His pen is poised to record my response.

After my subconscious tête-à-tête with Dr. Alexander last night, a photographed internal exam earlier, and now questions about excretions, my body has become an open book for others to study. It slips further from my control when I hear terms like Hyperemesis Gravidarum, ketosis, electrolyte disturbances and body breaking down fat for energy. Obviously, my numbers didn't meet the going rate for the correct number of times you should pee and vomit when pregnant.

My head snaps up when he suggests I check into the hospital for hydration and monitoring. Ignoring the bands of tension squeezing my temples into a throbbing headache, my answer is firm. "That will have to wait. My baby is sick and I need to go to the pediatrician's office to see what's wrong. Then I have a business phone call . . ."

Chase takes my hand, his touch soothing only some of my panic. "What I hear the doctor saying is that you need to be examined in the hospital, maybe have an IV or two, and then possibly be released within twenty-four hours. Don't you think that's reasonable?" His question holds unspoken authority, but he watches me expectantly for some sign of understanding. Rationality is not what's foremost in my mind right now. I haven't had time to process the cyclone-paced changes invading my life.

"Couldn't I go as an outpatient? The IV can be attached, and I can leave . . ."

Chase squeezes my hand. "Let's do as the doctor suggests. Caroline is in good hands with Sunny. Sammy is also on hand to help, and we can call to make sure all is okay with Caroline on our way to the hospital."

My voice quavers, accepting the futility of any further arguing. "Alright. If there's no other choice . . ." I recognize the importance of maintaining my health and the health of the babies I'm carrying. But it's hard not to feel like I'm hurtling through life on a rocket I can't direct or stop. Even worse is the realization that the ride is leaving the professional part of myself behind.

It takes several hours for the paperwork to be completed and a private room to become available. Although it's the middle of the afternoon, the private corridor leading to my room is free from the regular bustle of hospital personnel we passed on the hallway adjacent to the nurses' station. The quiet at this end of the hallway further calms my frazzled nerves.

I've already phoned home twice, once to find out the pediatrician's diagnosis and the second to make sure Sunny and Caroline were home and that Caroline's fever dropped. *No infection, stuffy nose, slight cough, temperature normal* are answers that put me at ease. I have to admit it feels good not to have to worry about eating and then throwing up. Propped up in the hospital bed, I take out the photo and rub my finger across the two beating dots.

"They're beautiful, don't you think?" Chase asks.

I look again at the printed copy. "Yes, it's a miracle, a VERY unexpected miracle."

"That's for sure." He takes the photo from me, studies it again, and shakes his head. "I still don't understand how this happened. When Doc Sanders returned my call, he said there may have been some swimmers that stayed active."

"Swimmers? That's how he explained what happened?"

"I think he referred to them as Olympians racing for the gold."

This sets off all measures of aggravation. How could a doctor remain so cavalier about a life-changing event? "I don't want to hear the word vasectomy again. Just do what you have to do to clip the fins of those swimmers."

"It will be taken care of. All you need to do is lie back and rest."

My head sinks into the pillow. My eyes close, but my mind shifts into high gear, like I have an axe to grind against myself. At least Chase tried to prevent another pregnancy. All I did after he was called back to duty was shout dreadful accusations. Then, when my anger shifted to passion, had sex without precautions.

"Alicia," Chase says softly, "I want to introduce you to Eleanor. She's a private nurse I hired to help; they seem a bit short-staffed here."

Stocky and sure-footed, with a moon-shaped face and short, dark hair, Eleanor strides toward me with a sense of purpose a bulldozer couldn't stop. Chase is not taking any chances ensuring I stay safe.

"Just lie back now." She places a green ball into my palm to pump while gently tracing the crook of my arm with the tip of her finger to search of a vein. "This will only take a minute." She painlessly inserts the needle, then props my arm onto a pillow to ensure I'm comfortable.

With not much else to do, I stare at the ceiling, then the white walls ahead and the black screen of the mounted TV, before asking Chase, "Do you think you could bring me my bathrobe and cosmetic bag from home? Also, the book

I was reading that's on my nightstand."

"You got it. Do you want to watch some TV?"

"Not right now. I think I'll just lie back and relax." My lids become heavy, and my former edginess dissipates into a floating feeling of ease. Whatever is in that IV bag calms me into relinquishing cognizance. The last sentence I register is Chase telling me he's waiting for Sammy to come. Then he's going home to check on Caroline and get the items I asked for. The rest is a blur of distant beeping, nurses and doctors moving through rounds, and Eleanor explaining she's getting me some ice chips to suck on to quench my parched throat. Free from nausea, my muscles, nerves, and joints feel weightless. I drift into darkness until . . .

There's a presence. Someone breathing and pressing against the side of my bed. I try to open my eyes, but my lashes feel glued to my face. I groggily reach for Chase's hand. He's not there, so I let it drop onto the covers. Even through this haze of sleep, I know someone is there. Wheezy breaths tickle my arm, and a squelching sound of cushioned soles travel the length of my bed. Through lidded eyes, I watch someone with a head the size of a bucket and a jaw that looks like it was chiseled in cement fiddle with a device near my IV bag. Thick neck rolls fold over his shirt collar and a hospital jacket stretches tautly across his barreled chest. With brows knitted in concentration, he fingers the tubing of my IV bag.

I sit up with a start. "What are you doing?" I croak.

His lips curl into the veneer of a smile, exposing teeth splayed like mismatched rail tracks. "Theez good medicine. Will make you feel better," he says. Then with calm efficiency, he attaches a fluid-filled spike to the tube leading to the suspended IV bag.

Fear escalates to terror when I realize he is neither a doctor nor a nurse. Grasping for the syringe, I force out a scream that changes to a shocked gasp when five monster-sized fingers splay against my face and thrust me back down. Kicking and bucking, I try to pry his fingers away from my nose and mouth.

He presses tighter until it feels as if the breath has been knocked out of me.

I watch his free hand finish attaching the device to the tubing. Making one last attempt to fight back, I thrash my hands and kick my legs, resisting the press of his hand, but he's too powerful. My lungs scream for oxygen. Tears dampen the sides of my cheeks when I think of what poison he might be adding to my IV.

There's a strangled grumble. Some scuffling. Then more. Five leaden fingers lift from my nose and mouth. Sucking in air in heavy gasps, I strain my eyes to focus on what's happening while groping for the nurses call button. The first person I can make out is Chase, his arm snaked around the brute's fat neck. Fighting Chase's tightening grip, the monster's cold eyes travel the length of the tubing the syringe is screwed into. All that remains to complete his job is to press the pump. Stretching out a butcher-sized hand, he waves his meaty fingers until they're less than a fraction of an inch from the lever. Chase wrenches him back with his arm, forcing his face down with the palm of his other hand.

I start to pull the taped needle from my arm. My fingers freeze once I recognize Eleanor's white, thick-soled shoes.

Confident fingers push the bed tray aside and remove the pike from the tubing in one swift tug.

She turns in fury toward my assailant. "Who do you think you are, coming in here and terrorizing my patient?" Her knee slams into his groin.

He groans and lurches forward to ease the pain, but Chase's chokehold keeps him upright and pressed against Chase's chest. Red-faced, his feet twitch. Air gurgles from his throat.

Eleanor pats my shoulder and smiles as if there isn't a fight to the death happening right before our eyes. "You just lie back and relax. I'm going to remove the catheter insertion just in case it's been contaminated. Then, I'll go fetch some help."

Eleanor must be another one of Chase's hires who comes from stock that follows the *see no evil, hear no evil, speak no evil* creed because she asks no questions and doesn't seem the least bit ruffled. I'm beginning to think Eleanor is a former army medic that's seen battle. It wouldn't be the first time Chase hired from the veterans' association.

When she slides out the needle, I hardly notice. I'm too busy watching Bucket Head break free from Chase's grasp.

Blinking away blood that drizzles from the side of his head, Chase dodges a punch. His eyes dart in my direction. "Baby, don't you worry. I'm neutralizing the complication."

Complication. Is he serious? Black spots of panic dance before my eyes. Finger held to the nurse's call button, I holler for help again, swinging my legs over the side of the bed, ready to run into the main corridor to flag down help. We could all be dead by the time anyone responds to this useless button. It doesn't help that we are in a single room at the end of a long, private corridor.

Bucket Head winds back a fist that could punch holes in cast iron.

"You have gotten on my last nerve." Eleanor has returned, brandishing a syringe the size of a jackhammer. With a firm set to her jaw, she jabs it into Bucket Head's thigh. For a few suspended seconds, nothing happens. But then, Bucket Head's jaw slackens. His hands drop to his sides and, whirling several times, he hits the floor face-first like a block of granite.

There's a flurry of movement and some shouting as Sammy darts into the room, pistol drawn, arms shifting left to right.

"What the hell kind of hospital are you running here?" Chase growls into the corridor. "Didn't anyone bother to see what was going on in my wife's room?" Chin jutting, hands gesturing, hair spiked, he's a man brimming with resolve to keep his family safe, thwarted whichever way he turns. Smoothing my hair from my eyes, he kisses my forehead, then pulls me to his chest.

"It's over. He's not going to hurt you again." Then, to prove his point, he kicks the thug back onto the floor when he tries to stand. The drugged giant barely registers the blow.

"You're hurt." I go to wipe away the blood from his head, but he just continues rocking me in his arms. When my trembling lessens, he lowers me against the propped pillows.

"It's all good. You just lie back and relax."

Hospital staff run this way and that. A red-lit alarm buzzes and flashes in the hallway.

Bucket Head moans on the floor.

Sammy has a gun aimed at his head should he decide to go another round, and Eleanor is stealthily disposing of a syringe filled with enough barbiturates to level an elephant.

Despite the fact that I'm shaking and worn out with fear, a laugh bubbles from inside.

"Relax? I'd get more rest in a combat trench."

Chase puckers his lower lip in contemplation. Sammy strokes the underside of his chin with his fingers. And, without exchanging a word, they reach a consensus.

"Eleanor," Chase screeches, making her wince. "Can we wrap all this up?" He sweeps his finger in circles around my IV stand and drip like it's Chinese takeout. "Alicia's right. This is no place for her to relax. She's safer at home." His voice is urgent and clipped.

I want to remind him that getting treatment at home was my original idea, but instead I take his hands and hold them reassuringly.

"I'm fine. He never got to push the lever."

Chase blinks slowly and his features relax, but not for long. A second later, the commander returns. He looks toward Eleanor, waiting for an answer.

With compressed lips, her eyes shift to the side, following Bucket Head being handcuffed and dragged off by hospital security.

"I don't see why we can't. I can arrange for the hospital to release the supplies and medications we need, then get Alicia settled in at home with the IV."

Everything happens quickly after Bucket Head is carted away by the authorities. If you ask me, the hospital cannot get rid of me fast enough. The doctor shows up from nowhere, papers are signed, medical supplies bundled, and a wheelchair procured. Hand gently on my back, Chase guides me into the chair where the impact of all that's happened hits. My palms start to sweat, my stomach churns, and my heart races. I would say I was having a king-sized panic attack except for the sour bile stinging my throat.

Eleanor's critical eye scans my face.

"Wait," I screech.

Chase stops short, bringing my wheelchair to a sudden halt. Pulled forward by the sudden contraction of my stomach, I vomit into the basin Eleanor is already holding under my chin. She hands me a moist towel.

As I wipe my mouth, my direction is short. "Okay, now we can go."

CHAPTER 12

You'd think I'd be beyond desire.

I've a Mafia maniac in pursuit, two tiny beating hearts growing inside my body, and an urge to upchuck every other minute. There's no doubt in my mind that the person who attacked me in the hospital was one of Dimitri's underworld gang members. The contents of the fluid-filled device haven't been determined yet. If I had to guess, it was something to make me abort this pregnancy. Dimitri tried the same tactic when I was carrying Caroline. That time Devie foiled his attack and paid for it with a ruthless beating. Add that to the car accident, mangled car seat, and gunned-down deer, and you have Dimitri in active pursuit.

Chase knows it, too. I think he suspected that Dimitri's attacks would intensify after he returned from his deployment. Coming to the church to find me even though he was furious, constantly checking to see that Caroline's nursery windows are locked, not letting me remain in the apartment lobby to help Boris. All extreme measures even for him to take. How he would know anything about

Dimitri's cold-blooded plans after having spent so much time in Afghanistan remains a mystery.

Brushing my teeth and rinsing any sour taste out my mouth, I toss around what I need to say to get Chase to talk about this escalating problem. I want to know what he knows about Dimitri's plans, and I refuse to be waylaid by ambiguous answers. For now, though, all I want to do is wash away the stench of the brute's hand pressing against my nose and mouth before Eleanor reinserts the IV needle.

"I'm going to jump into the shower," I say over the whir of my electric toothbrush. Chase appears in a flash.

"There's no way you're getting into the shower alone. You've been dizzy since we got home."

Quickly removing my jeans and sweater, I'm too weary to argue.

He strips and steps into the stall with me. I watch his hand reach for the scented bath wash while another part of his anatomy waves a big hello. Like I mentioned, you would think I'd be beyond desire, but something in my belly heats to melting with his touch. I give him the faintest glimmer of a smile when the circular sweep of the soft cloth soaps my skin.

His touch is gentle, almost platonic.

My spent body relaxes with each massage of his hand on my neck and arms. I lean against his shoulders when he bends to wash my legs, then rub my hand gently over the red welt on the side of his head.

"Does it hurt?" Foolish question to ask. He'd never admit to any pain from an attack, especially one that put me in jeopardy.

"No, I'm fine. I should have known better than to leave you with only Sammy in charge. It made it too easy for a sneak attack."

"Is Sammy okay? He looked a little dazed when he ran into the hospital room."

"He's fine now. He thinks he may have been struck by some sort of drugged dart."

• • •

When I think back to this attack, I'm seized by a rage so intense and concentrated, it takes me by surprise. Dimitri wants to hurt us to get back at Chase. Caroline and I, and now these two new babies, are nothing more than blank sheets of paper for him to scribble a merciless message to Chase. Dimitri thrives on being in total control. Like a puppet master pulling a marionette's strings, he wants Chase dancing to his tune of terror while he attempts to kill one or the other of us.

I will see Dimitri dead before I let him hurt my family. That includes killing him myself if I have to. My neutral acceptance of this grisly thought steals my balance.

• • •

Chase catches me under my shoulders, watching me warily, afraid that after I have been sick so many times, I might be too weak to stand. He waits with his arms wrapped around me until my feet are steady. "I think we should put a stool in here. Even if you don't use it to sit on when you're showering, it's something for you to grasp if you get dizzy."

With our faces inches away and our eyes locked, any thoughts about pregnancy or dizziness or morning, afternoon, and evening sickness vanish. All I want is to put any distress behind me and lose myself in his embrace.

"I love you." My voice is as warm and sultry as the water cascading over our bodies.

When his lips reach mine, I come to life. Our kiss deepens. His fingers slowly massage soapy swirls around my nipple. When it tightens, he runs his tongue over my earlobe, nibbling a bit before his mouth trails kisses down my neck. A wave of heat ripples through my body.

"Are you sure you're up for this?" he says.

"Yes."

Moist fingertips brush across my vulva in slow circles. A whimper escapes my throat. I lean into his groin and extend my hand toward his lengthened penis.

He presses me against the shower wall and, with one hand burrowed in my wet hair, he lets the other work its magic below.

I melt into his touch and together we give and take pleasure, hitting points we know the other craves.

He rains burning kisses across my pebbled nipples.

I stroke and pull his cock and he nudges it against my pulsing folds.

"This is going to go slow and easy," he reminds me, turning me to face the shower wall.

I reach back to continue my stroking, but he removes my hands from his body and flattens my palms against the wet tiles. I forget everything when his thick shaft enters from behind. His thrusts are easy . . . tentative.

My craving pulsates, deep and strong. "Harder," I say.

He presses deeper, and my body yields to the penetration.

Desire thrums through me with each thrust,

accelerating my need to climax.

His groan is low when I gyrate my backside into his movements, deepening our union.

Shudders rock my body when his rhythm takes me to my peak. While I quiver with aftershocks, he gets his release, prolonging my orgasm.

Finally spent, we remain flattened against the tiled wall, stomach to back, with a warm spray of water raining on us.

Chase extends his hand and turns off the faucet. Bending one arm under my knees and the other across my back, he effortlessly scoops me off my feet and out of the shower. "Let's get the three of you toweled and back into bed for your treatment."

I smile into his neck. "First, I need to get ready," I tell him. Last thing I want is to get into bed with washed hair that dries into serious bedhead. He lets me down onto the thickly-cottoned mat, then wraps a towel around his muscled body and scrubs his wet hair with another.

I can watch him do this all day, but I've other things on my agenda, procedures that involve needles and medicines and nurses and doctors.

"Once you're settled into bed, we need to discuss something."

I stop creaming my body. "Whatever it is, you can tell me now."

He doesn't mess with my determination. "Detective Wilson called and asked if he could get a statement from you about what happened at the hospital."

"I'd like some answers myself. Like what it was that monster was trying to drug me with."

"The forensics report hasn't been finalized. Detective

Wilson also indicated your attacker is refusing to talk except to ask for a lawyer. No surprise there. Dimitri's network is trained to remain silent and take the hit when caught."

"So, what do we do now?"

"You give your statement. Then we get on with our lives. We stay vigilant and work together to keep our family safe. We have a network too." He kisses the tip of my nose.

He's right. I have the lives of three innocents to protect, one asleep in the next room and the other two nestled in my womb. Nothing to do now but hunker down and carry out what needs to be done to keep them safe and healthy.

I blow-dry my hair into soft waves and slip into a champagne-colored silk negligee with matching bath-robe. Why let fear and pregnancy keep me from looking and feeling alluring? Giving birth to twins does make me pause. At twenty-four, I will have had three kids in two years with no established career in place and the Russian Mafia in pursuit. Go figure.

Chase does a double take when I step out of the bath-room, then reminds me what's next by pointing to the IV that's been set up adjacent to the bed.

"I know. Just one more thing." I tiptoe into Caroline's room and stand by her crib. Her cheeks are flushed with sleep. When I reach out my hand, she's cool to the touch. I stroke the soft skin of her forehead and brush away her fine auburn curls. Watching the small up-and-down movements of her chest, I see a thriving life force that won't be stopped, just like the two thumping hearts I carry inside me now. More than ever, I'm determined to see that Dimitri does not win this war.

Stepping out of her nursery, I grab my sketchpad and pencils, and when I reach out my arm for Eleanor to inject, I make sure it's my left so my right hand can draw unencumbered. There's no need for me to stop producing just because I'm reproducing.

CHAPTER 13

"Aliii!" I finish the loose tumble of a French braid I'm weaving into my hair and turn with a surprised smile to face my old friend, Beth.

"Hey there. I haven't seen you in forever." She pauses, eyes wide. "Oh my god, you're huge." Only Beth can get away with saying that now. Everyone else sidesteps my sharp tongue and grouchy grumbling.

Not that I don't have reason to be. I went from being attached to an IV because I was losing too much weight to developing a ravenous appetite when the vomiting finally abated. Then, somewhere during my sixth month, the doctor relegated me back to bed rest for the remainder of my pregnancy. Now, in my ninth month, I wallow from bed to sofa to armchair to bathroom then back to bed. Grouchy is an understatement. Bitchy is more like it.

"You've just spent half an hour complaining about wasting time," Chase had said after I repeated how useless I felt.

I'd studied him, pregnant stare intact, and he withered, fear crossing his widened eyes. I've been seeing a lot of that look lately and not just from Chase. Devie threw it my way just before scurrying out to get me mint chocolate chip ice cream after I nearly chopped off her head when she suggested a freshly-chopped salad to satisfy my hunger pangs. And when Fiona asked how I was feeling the other day, I saw that same expression of alarm when I snapped that I felt like one of the elephant seals we saw wallowing along the shore of Santa Barbara. She tried to escape before I could finish, but my glare held her in place.

Worry is what makes me restless and irritable. What if one or both of my babies don't make it? This is not the type of angst that creeps in when you're headed to a job interview or to an appointment with the gynecologist. This unease pounds and stamps until I don't know if I want to stop to catch my breath or flee to escape its clutches. I don't share this with anyone. Talking about it might make it real.

Chase knows, though. He's the only one I share my terror with, the only one I let look into my strained soul. He lets me talk however many times I need to share the same concerns, and he listens without offering assurances about the unknown, like it's all going to be alright or how foolish I am to be so worried. He just strokes my hair and murmurs how much he loves me and Caroline. He brings home my favorite dishes and desserts from all the restaurants I love and takes the time from his busy schedule to enjoy them with me at the end of his long day. He helps drive my panic into a corner where it quiets for a bit so I can rest and relax.

Everything with this pregnancy is going as planned so far. The doctor remains optimistic, but with my history of placenta previa when I had Caroline, he has stressed the added risk of complications when delivering multiple births. Now, thinking about living with the loss of one or both babies fills me with a dread that is rooted in my past. My life began with the death of another.

What if the same happens to one of my babies?

I close my eyes to these thoughts and don't open them until I hear Beth's voice.

"It's amazing." She places her hands on my shoulders and turns me around to study my back. "From behind you look the same as always and then . . ." She turns me back, laughing good-naturedly when my stomach bumps against hers. "There's the front of you. Are you sure there's only two in there?" She throws up her hands to protect her face. "Please don't hit me."

It's better to focus on the amusing aspects of my pregnancy. Humor muffles the monsters that haunt me with fears for my babies' lives.

"I would throat-kick you for that comment," I smirk, "if my body didn't already feel like a war zone. I'm telling you Beth, if these babies can hear from inside the belly, their first words might be, 'fuck this.'" I whisper the last two words in her ear just in case Caroline's nearby. Caroline has started to mimic everything she hears. Her new word is tute. It must mean something to her because she's always saying it, but we have no idea what she means.

"It's like I've been boarded by two little hijackers," I say, happy to let humor muffle the worry that stokes my fears. "The little invaders are already telling me what I can and can't do, and they're not even here yet."

I lower my voice and check the vicinity for Chase. When I see that he's nowhere in sight, I say what's been on my mind for most of the day. "I'd give anything for a cigarette right now."

She looks surprised. "Hasn't that shaman helped you quit?"

"She is helping, but every now and again there's still the urge. We've had to have FaceTime sessions these past several months. They're not as effective as seeing her in person."

Beth nods sympathetically. "It's hard for me to identify with your general vibe because it's not my reality, but I hear your frustration." Her face illuminates into a broad smile. "That's why I arranged something special for you today."

"What?" I shake my head. "There's not much I can do these days."

"Not telling. It's a surprise. And speaking of surprises, don't couples today have those gender reveal parties where everyone gets together to find out the sex of the baby? How come you still don't know what you're having?"

"You mean those cake parties where everyone assembles and when it's cut the color of the inside tells you if it's a boy or girl."

She shrugs. "I guess that's how it works."

"Not for me," I shake my head. "I don't hold with the baker knowing what I'm having before I do. We do have the information in a sealed envelope that we can open at any time. Since we had no idea of Caroline's sex before she was born, we decided to follow the same protocol this time around."

"Got it. Enough baby talk. I just heard from a blast from our past."

"Oh yeah. Who?"

"Marcel called asking about you. He's living in Paris. I think he still likes you and admit it," she widens her eyes, "you had a thing for him too, before Mr. Black Ops Hot Shot showed up like some dark knight to rescue you from prison and scoop you into his lair."

"I never had a thing for Marcel. You were the one that set us up on a blind date. You worried that I didn't socialize enough." I survey the sofa in the den that has become the center of my universe since being confined to bed rest. "That seems like a lifetime ago."

"It's only been two years and you're twenty-four, not eighty-four, so stop talking like your youth is over."

I'm about to say that's how it feels sometimes, but she interrupts with a question that cuts me to the core. "What happened between you and Thomas? He never mentions you, says you haven't seen each other in almost a year, and every time I try to arrange for the three of us to get together, he changes the subject. Did you two have an argument?"

I must look stricken because she studies me hard.

"It's complicated," I say, unable to look her in the eye.

"Oh. My. God. You didn't." I don't answer, but my cheeks heat fire-red. I can't keep the tears from forming. She's at my side in one quick stride. "It's okay."

"It is not okay. What I did was terrible."

"This had to have happened when Chase was missing. I would have known if it happened before then."

My response is to sob quietly into the tissue she places in my outstretched hand.

"Shh." Her arms wrap me in a soothing hug. "Thomas should have known better." Her lips firm into a scowl that tells me she's going to give him a piece of her mind.

"Please," I plead. "Don't mention this to Thomas. It's over and done with. I don't plan on seeing him again."

"Does Chase know?"

"Yes. I told him everything." I close my eyes and try not to remember his shattered look when I admitted all that happened. "It was hard at first. I thought our marriage was over, but then he said he understood and well . . . here we are."

"I'm impressed. I wouldn't have thought he was the type to forgive that kind of transgression. I always knew he loved you, but this really shows how much he cares, and you know why?"

I shake my head. Trapped tears clog my throat.

"Because you're worth that forgiveness." She hugs me tightly while my shoulders shake with quiet sobs. Reaching out an arm, she fishes through her purse for another tissue. "Here, sit down and relax. What I have planned is going to be the perfect fix for how you're feeling."

Through tear-filled eyes, I study the friend I've known since grade school. She has always been there for me and now, looking sharp and professional in her Dior dress and Gucci pumps, she's taken the time from her executive position to be here for my benefit.

There's a loud buzz from the intercom and Beth excitedly gives a throaty chuckle. "You're going to love this."

"We have someone on the way down to escort them up," Sunny tells Boris through the speaker. He's obviously aware of what's happening, because he comes into the vestibule pulling the same face Beth just sported.

Within minutes, clusters of beauty experts are ushered

in by Sammy, who scrutinizes each with the look of a bare-fisted fighter.

Two white-jacketed women, one with short, spiked hair and the other with long, straight hair dyed black at the roots and platinum at the ends, spew off spa services that sound like a combination of recipe ingredients and jewelry components.

"Mrs. Reardon," Spike Hair says, smiling affably, "Would you prefer an avocado mask, a sugar scrub, or a fruit facial?"

Before I can answer, Ms. Platinum suggests I try a diamond file or 24K gold facial. An array of different semi-precious stones that I imagine in rings or pendants, are proudly listed as exfoliating tools.

A nail technician, at least that's what her name tag indicates is her title, carries in stacked trays of at least one hundred different colors. She's followed by a hair stylist, who extends his hand and introduces himself as Roman from Frederic Fekkai. Roman frowns, shakes his head, and tut-tuts as he lifts my messy braid.

Chase walks in from his study, greets Beth with a hug, then promptly asks if all the products are allowed during pregnancy.

Beth's retort doesn't skip a beat. "All checked and certified to be non-toxic and pregnancy-safe, including the nail enamels."

I'm not surprised at her ability to pull this off. In the span of just two years, she's been promoted from assistant to social media specialist at Edelman, one of the largest PR firms in the city. Her phone is an ever-expanding Rolodex of the best professionals in just about any field.

My back gives a jolting spasm. Beth considers me rubbing my hand across the pressing pain and swivels her neck to Chase. "The only thing you need to be concerned about, dude, are those swim—"

He raises his hand, not letting her finish. "I know. I know. The swimmers will be taken care of."

"It's good to see you smile. The past is done," Beth whispers in my ear, making room for Chase who, noticing my blotchy, tear-stained face, tucks a stray lock of hair behind my ear.

"The hospital called. Your C-section is confirmed for Monday morning at eight. Just two more days, and this will be over."

Letting out a weary sigh, I lean into the warmth of his hand. I had wanted a VBAC, but the doctor indicated that a vaginal birth, after having had a Cesarean with my first baby, would involve too much risk given that I'm having twins, and there was such a short interval between pregnancies. My prior delivery complications also called for a planned delivery. Three strikes and you're out. So, a C-section it is.

"I'm taking Caroline to the park while you relax and have some fun with Beth." Chase picks up Caroline, who's been toddling around studying all our guests and their wares. As they head out the door, Caroline stiffens her body and kicks her feet, shaking her head no. Chase rocks her, tells her they're going to the park, makes funny faces, waves her quacking duck. Nothing works. The crying is now a red-faced, full-blown tantrum, peppered with screams of *Ma Ma Ma Ma*. She knows something is up. Babies have this sixth sense that tells them their lives are about to change.

"Okay, okay," Beth interrupts the loud wails, blowing strands of wavy hair away from her face. "No one is going to be unhappy during my watch today. Hand her over."

Chase gives her Caroline. Grasped under her arms, Caroline completely stills when Beth pulls a toothy grin. "How about a haircut?" she asks Caroline.

"Tute," Caroline answers. Beth shoots me a questioning glance.

I shrug my shoulders. "No idea."

"Hmm, whatever that means, I can tell you it will be a hoot." She gives Caroline a kiss on her forehead, then puts her down to toddle over to me, where I lift her onto my lap on the sofa for some cuddling.

The guilt that there'll be two more babies soon to keep our attention from her prickles my already seesawing emotions.

"Everyone," Roman claps his hands for attention. "Who's up for some styling." He eyes me, then Caroline, who claps her hands too.

"Caroline," Beth suggests, studying my face. "This way Ali can get a relaxation facial first and," she peers closer, "an eyebrow waxing."

"What? No pregnant *glow* yet?" Beth catches the sarcasm etched in my deadpan expression but has learned during her short time here that my mood swings make it best to let it go.

She scoops Caroline into her arms while Roman pulls a black leather pouch from the pocket of his tailored jacket and extracts a small pair of scissors.

"C'mon sweet Caroline," she tickles her belly. "Let's

have a bath and shampoo. Then you can get your first haircut."

Sunny follows her into the bathroom, to supervise and explain where the baby soaps and creams can be found. I'm helped onto a padded table that's been wheeled into the den. The closed door and shuttered blinds bathe the room in dim silence. I close my eyes and give in to what begins as a head massage, then moves into the most soothing facial I have ever experienced.

It's early evening by the time the troupe leaves. Ensconced on the sofa, with hair trimmed and styled, nails done and skin glowing, I feel better than I've felt in a long time.

When Chase steps into the den with Caroline giggling on top of his shoulders, I do a double take. Laughter erupts from deep inside until I can't stop. Over athletic shorts, Chase wears a pink tutu that he snagged from one of my design racks. If that was it, I wouldn't still be doubled over laughing. Bulging biceps extend from a sleeveless t-shirt with two iridescent pink wings pinned to its back, I had been storing them after they were used as part of a catwalk during fashion week. Caroline is dressed in a pink leotard with a drawing of a large tooth pinned to her shirt.

"Whatever are you wearing?"

"Meet the tute." Grasping her by her legs, he looks up at Caroline, who's clapping and laughing, "and . . ." he takes a short bow, "the tute-fairy."

"You figured out she was saying tooth," I gasp between hard laughter. As if on cue, Caroline opens her mouth wide and points to a tooth.

Chase wiggles his brows and tracks his mouth to one

side. "After dress-up is over and the kid's asleep, you and me, babe, are going to have some dinner, then break into those containers of ice cream and whipped cream."

He sits down at the edge of the sofa, grinning, and lifts Caroline off his shoulders and onto my lap, where I cocoon her against the pillows at my side.

"Tute."

"Yes, my love. You have a new tooth." I rub my nose with hers, then stretch back against the pillows.

"You got yourself a date, but . . ." I purse my lips, "there had better be enough ice cream for all of us." I circle my hand around my protruding stomach. "Or my tutes are liable to bite off your hand to get our fair share."

He bends and gives my neck tiny nibbles . . .

It's when he raises his head that it happens. Fast and without warning, my stomach tenses with pain. I feel an oozing wetness. At first, I think my water's broken, but then I notice red liquid oozing onto the coverlet I'm lying on top of.

"Chase?" He traces his eyes to where I'm staring and pales.

"I think I need to go to the hospital now." I sound calm but the more seeping blood I see, the more frightened I become. Doubled over, I expel a head-clearing, lung cleansing inhale and exhale to help mediate the stab of pain that's now taking my breath away.

Chase puts his arm under my legs and gathers me up with the coverlet wrapped around my bent body.

"Sunny!" he shouts. Sunny scrambles out of his room, takes one look at me, and sweeps the baby off the sofa. "Go, go, I have Caroline." He thumbs through his phone with his free hand. "It's time. Bring around the car and make it quick," he tells Sammy.

City blocks speed by as Sammy runs red lights and swerves past double parked trucks.

Chase phones the doctor and relays what just happened. When we pull into the large, curved drive of New York Presbyterian Hospital, Chase barely waits for Sammy to brake before jumping out and bending to scoop me into his arms. It's good he has the strength to carry me because I'm wracked by tightening spasms in my stomach and back that make it hard to think, let alone walk.

Not bothering to check me in through the maternity ward, Chase enters the emergency room, shouting, "My wife is pregnant and hemorrhaging. She needs to see a doctor now."

The room springs into action. A gurney spills through automatic doors at the hands of a tall, lean, and very agile hospital attendant who lifts me under my arms and places me onto the wheeled bed. There is a sense of urgency as I'm stripped of my clothing, slipped into a surgical gown, and attached to several monitors. A nurse asks the time of my last meal and what it was I ate.

A doctor appears and studies the monitors. His face remains composed, but his voice emits immediacy. "Mrs. Reardon, we're going to have to deliver your babies now. One is experiencing distress, and you're still bleeding."

Clutching Chase's hand, I'm wheeled through a long corridor and into the delivery room. My OB-GYN walks in and gives me a concerned smile.

All at once, I'm overtaken by a primal need to deliver these two babies safely. The urge vacillates between intense fear for what might be happening to me and a deep yearning for the survival of both my babies. I need to snip the ties to my past, not relive the loss that carved a hole into my being for so long. "I want to go home with two babies. Do you hear, Chase?" I bend my head and grip the sheet in my fists, willing away the pain before continuing. "You be sure to explain to the doctor in case I can't that I want him to do whatever it takes to see that both survive."

Chase nods, but I need to be sure he understands.

"You be sure to tell the doctor that," I repeat. "Do you hear?" The thought of reliving the death of a small being before it breathes life fills me with the same intolerable fear and loneliness I suffered when Chase was missing. It's the same feelings that chased me through my childhood. These types of deaths have no closures. They haunt like coffins in unfilled graves.

Chase nods, kisses my hand, and then my forehead. The plunger of a needle is depressed into my arm. "Do whatever you must to save my wife," Chase tells the doctor.

They are the last words I hear.

CHAPTER 14

Staring at the sparse stage, the ballet performance unfolds before my eyes. A spinning, tutu-wearing ballerina locks arms with another dancer in a swirl of intensifying strength and stamina. The lack of balletic grace of this poorly-choreographed performance confuses my notion of what it is I'm actually seeing. Dimly aware of the commotion, my eyes close once, twice, then flash open with the scraping of loud, angry shoes against the floor. I blink several more times to try and clear my blurred vision, but still can't recognize who's there or what's happening.

"You bastard, I want to know how this happened," a lean but muscular performer grits out between clenched teeth.

The shorter of the two dancers, who's dressed in a suit and tie of all things, raises his arms in a plea for understanding. "I may have created less of a blockage than recommended. There was a remote chance . . . You seemed unsure."

"She could have died." The taller one lands a punch to the other one's chin. He doesn't go down.

"C'mon. Cut it out," the suited performer says. "It's not completely my fault. Sometimes spliced ends rejoin. Besides, you should have waited at least thirty days to make sure there weren't any live sperm." He dodges a punch, then chooses the reprieve to wiggle his eyebrows suggestively. "I don't blame you, though. Even now, she's a real looker." The next punch connects, and he goes down.

I finally make out that it's Doc Sanders, Chase's former battle buddy and current urologist, who's sprawled on the floor next to my bed. Doc Sanders bounces up and charges Chase, who I recognize now as the one wearing the tutu and wings. It's then that I realize I've just given birth. A panicked glance to my right shows there are two cribs standing side by side in the corner of my room. My body relaxes until whispered cussing and locked tussling revs up around me. Yep, Chase and his Marine buddy, Doc Sanders, are brawling in my hospital room over what I assume is Chase's failed vasectomy. What is it with him and fights in hospital rooms?

"You call yourself a doctor?" Chase mouths hoarsely, placing a punch to Doc Sanders' gut that doubles him over.

"I did you a favor. Look, you have beautiful twins," he gasps, clutching his stomach before winding back and landing a left hook into Chase's jaw.

"Hey!" I shout, having seen enough of their shenanigans. They spring apart like smiling bobbleheads. Doc Sanders straightens his jacket.

"I wanted to be sure to congratulate you both on the birth of your babies," he smiles, as he does a Michael Jackson moonwalk toward the door. No way is he going to turn his back on Chase. I shoot the good doctor the stink eye, letting him know I know they've been brawling in my hospital room, for heaven's sake.

He seems guilty when he adds, "Hey bud, stop by my office at the hospital, and I'll take care of . . ." he pauses, looking at Chase, "your situation."

Chase turns toward him, clenching his fist, then looks at me and relaxes it, allowing Dr. Sanders to escape without further mishap.

"What was that all about?"

"Nothing that can't be fixed later. How are you feeling?" He kisses my hand, his brow furrowed with concern.

"I'm okay." Shifting my eyes toward the two cribs, I make a feeble attempt to get up.

"Wait, easy now." He gently lowers me, securing the back of my head with one hand while propping several pillows beneath me with the other so I'm in a sitting position. Once I'm settled, he jerks his chin toward the two cribs. "We have a new son and daughter."

Reflexively, my eyes close, and gripping his hand, my cheeks dampen and my shoulders rock with sobs of relief. All the months of unspoken panic that one or both wouldn't survive are washed away with my tears.

"Shh," he gently kisses my temple and holds his warm lips there until my weeping quiets. "It's all good. I'll bring them to you." He hands me a tissue, then walks to the cribs. "Okay you two," he whispers, "which one of you wants to be first." He cups the baby's head and hands our daughter into my waiting arms.

"Aren't you just magnificent," I tell her, stroking the side of her cheek. She rewards me by opening her eyes and pursing her tiny pink lips as if getting ready to suck. The next bundle leaves me no free hands, so I hold him close and gently kiss the top of his forehead. He turns his head to root to my breast, feels that it's covered, and opens his small mouth into a yawn. He resembles his sister, with the same soft sweep of dark hair, but his lips are a bit fuller, and his face is longer.

Chase beams a smile that shines through his eyes.

"You may want to slip off the tulle skirt and unpin the wings," I suggest.

"Oh yeah, right." He glances at his costume as if seeing it for the first time and sheepishly slides it off. Reaching back to detach the wings, he asks, "Any ideas for names?"

We had discussed some possibilities, but most times I was too worried that there'd be problems to decide. I study our daughter's delicate features. "How about Juliette?" I suggest.

"Juliette," he repeats it a few times, rolling the name over his tongue, measuring the sound of the syllables. "I like it. Did you want to add your mother's name as a middle name? With Caroline named after my mom, it seems like a good idea." He looks sad at the mention of his mom, but it passes when one of the twins lets out a cry. I rock him gently, and he quiets.

"Juliette Elvira is a bit of a mouthful. What do you think of the simple name, Elle? My mother's sisters often call her that."

"Juliette Elle Reardon has a nice ring to it." He pauses, "and for our son, my mind is made up. We have ourselves a little Matteo."

My eyes fill and too choked to speak, I nod, smiling and crying at the same time.

"Matteo Daniel," he finishes. "Do you like it?"

"Yeah, I do. It's good."

It's hard to let go of them, but I'm exhausted, and this sharp pain in my gut tells me whatever they gave me for pain is wearing off.

Chase takes one, then the other, and places them back in their cribs. "Okay Juliette and Tayo, back you go. You need to let your mamma get some rest."

"Tayo?"

"Yeah, T.A.Y.O. It's short for Matteo. Don't you think he looks like a Tayo?"

"I have to give it some thought, and it should be spelled T.E.O," I clarify through eyes too heavy with fatigue to stay open. I lie back and don't wake until several hours later, when I hear Fiona's voice.

"They are just beautiful," she oohs and ahhs, peering into Juliette and Matteo's cribs. As soon as she moves to my bedside, I notice purple crescents under her eyes that make her look like she hasn't slept in days.

"Congratulations," she says cheerily, kissing my cheek, then glancing behind her. Liam steps forward, smiling while holding two stuffed teddy bears in his outstretched hands.

"They're for the new babies," he tells me curiously, peering at their tiny, swathed forms.

"How cute. Thank you, Liam." I tousle his auburn mop of hair and give him a kiss as Chase takes the stuffed animals and adds them to the pile of flowers and gifts that keep coming.

"Where's Caroline, Uncle Chase?" Liam asks, looking around the room.

"She'll be coming in a little bit." Chase lifts him up and gives him a kiss.

"He was so excited to see the babies and Caroline. I hope it's okay that he's here. He's healthy and all caught up with his vaccinations." She blinks and a shadow crosses her face before she counters it with a weak smile when she sees Chase dodging fake punches from Liam.

"Of course, it's fine." I'm thinking, at this point, what's one more kid added to the mounting pile. "Sammy's bringing Caroline by in a few minutes, and Mac's stopping by, too." Our whole family is here, so it stands to reason that they will be here too, mostly to enjoy the moment with us but also to make sure Dimitri and his hatchet-men stay away. Turns out the contents of the pump Egor Petrov, aka Bucket Head, was prepared to infuse into my IV tubing were a combination of mifepristone and misoprostol, drugs used in tandem for medical abortions.

Most likely Egor was the shadowed intruder lurking outside Caroline's nursery in Summit, and the one who shot the fawn. It hasn't been substantiated because he refused to talk without a lawyer present, but we all know he was following Dimitri's orders. Chase says he is bound by a loyalty oath to his boss. He would never capitulate to police questioning. He knows the horrific death waiting for him if he does. So, the long and short of it is that Dimitri still has the opportunity to carve ruinous retaliations into our family.

Fiona expels a measured exhale of breath. Her eyes warily follow Liam when he goes to sit on the chair and read the book he's brought.

I feel her fear but have no idea what she's frightened of.

I've just given birth to twins after a complicated delivery. I should be thinking about how I'm going to fire on all cylinders to handle the child-rearing feats that lie ahead, but memory of Fiona's ring on a severed finger makes me hypervigilant as to how she fits into Dimitri's schemes.

"Are you okay?" I inquire when everyone's attention seems riveted on the twins.

"I'm fine. Just a bit of a stomach upset. Must have enjoyed too much of Liam's birthday cake." She throws me a wry smirk. "Shouldn't I be asking *you* that?"

"I'm relieved, ecstatic, over the moon that it all worked out. Chase tells me the pediatrician said that, while both have lower birth weights than average—I think Juliette is five pounds and Matteo, five pounds two ounces—they are both healthy with normal lung development."

Fiona kisses me on the cheek. "It's over. Now you can rest. You did beautifully."

"Not really. I'm terrible at the whole delivery process. Seems there's nothing natural about it for my body."

Fiona pats my arm, color leaching from her face when she discreetly catches a glimpse of her watch.

There's no time for us to discuss anything further because Juliette starts crying. It starts with a soft sound that escalates to a piercing wail within a few seconds, and because there's two of them, Matteo picks up the crescendo with his own brand of moaning that moves even faster into a howling cry. A nurse comes in to help, carrying Juliette to me to nurse, then handing a bottle of formula to Chase.

As if on cue, in walks Sammy holding Caroline. She takes one look at me with Juliette in my arms and another at Chase holding Teo and becomes perfectly still. We beam smiles and hellos while Caroline quietly and seriously studies the scene. I know exactly when her little mind tells her that she now shares her place with two others because she protests this new station in life by stiffening her body, holding out her arms to us and wailing. All three sound like a deafening crescendo of howls that beg for muzzles.

I hold Juliette to my breast, Chase puts the bottle in Teo's mouth, and Sammy places Caroline on the bed next to my free arm, where she nuzzles and finally quiets.

Blissful silence.

This allows me to ponder how important military organizational expertise is going to be in this situation. This three-at-once neediness requires perseverance, agility, and speed. Proving my point, Chase's arm shoots out like a first baseman diving for a line drive when Caroline's little hands try to forcibly pry her sister's head from my breast. Gently tugging each away from Juliette, he kisses them and shakes his head no.

"This is your new baby sister, Juliette," I tell her softly. "If you want, you can kiss her like this," and I gently kiss Caroline's forehead to demonstrate. She's not having any of it and moves closer to snuggle into my shoulder.

Shifting his attention back to Teo, Chase says in his most serious tone, "Okay little guy, here's how it's going to go down. Since all of us are clamoring for the same thing," he eyes my chest as I shift Juliette under a light cover to keep her rooted to my breast and away from her sister's impulsive hands. "We're going to have to learn how to share. Your turn will be next and as for me . . . well, I should be the one complaining. I won't get any part of your mamma for five or six weeks at least." He considers me, Juliette, and Caroline, then shifts back to Teo, ruefully shaking his head. "If even then."

I bite my lip to stifle a laugh, too afraid of the pain it would trigger if I let it out. Right now, any thoughts about sex or even feeling sexy are buried inside the KEEP OUT/ UNDER CONSTRUCTION sites of my body.

The clamor just starts to settle when in strides the doctor. One look at our bustling bundles, and his mouth curves into an emoji beam, teeth and all. "I see you have your hands full, so I won't be long. How are you feeling?"

Everyone except Chase clears the room so I can chat privately with my doctor. Sammy tries to take Caroline with him, but as soon as he stretches out his arms, she grabs onto me with a hold that would take a crowbar to loosen.

"Thanks, Sammy, but it's probably best if Caroline just stays here for now." I kiss her on the top of her head, and she gives me a what's- this-all-about pout before diving deeper into my arm.

"I feel good." I say even though my stomach feels as if it's being poked with pinching knives. I don't much care for the lingering effects of painkillers and, remembering the healing process after giving birth to Caroline, I'm thinking I can tolerate it for a bit longer.

"Any heavy bleeding?" He studies me with eyes trained to cut through bullshit when evaluating his patients.

"No, just the usual."

"Good. Tomorrow morning we'll remove your catheter, and you can start walking. Some light exercise will help you heal. Just no lifting or climbing stairs." He studies me again.

I flash him my best grin, but a sudden tight pain when Caroline accidentally presses on my stomach makes me wince.

"I think it's best we continue with pain medication for the next two days."

"Could there be more hemorrhaging?" Chase asks, removing the bottle from Teo and picking up Caroline with his free hand. He sits Caroline on his chair and standing, continues to feed Teo.

"That is unlikely to happen." Adjusting his wire-framed glasses on his nose, he eyes us with a proud twinkle. "You will be happy to know that everything went smoothly after we got the bleeding under control. You should have no problem conceiving again. That's not always the case in these situations." Pleased with himself and his handiwork, he exits the room whistling.

"He's about as funny as a rainstorm after a tsunami," Chase grumbles, sitting down on the edge of the hospital chair with Teo feeding in his arms and Caroline's arms wrapped around his waist.

CHAPTER 15

"Where's Mommy?" Liam asks, hugging Pepi, his stuffed giraffe, close to his chest. Hearing the footsteps of more visitors approach my room, my attention is distracted from Liam to my parents and brother Antonio. A flurry of kisses and congratulations follow with more gifts to add to the pile. It's only when Liam repeats his question fifteen minutes later and ten decibels louder that we all take notice.

Chase is the first to look alarmed, the first to recall that Liam celebrated his sixth birthday not too long ago and that somehow or another, Liam's birthdays are triggers for Fiona's drug abuse lapses. She's known to disappear for days. When she finally does resurface, she's either strung out on drugs or marred by bruises and cuts, struck by a mystery person's fist. Her only explanation is that she had a moment of weakness and relapsed.

The weariness I'd been feeling shifts to apprehension, but I figure we should at least start by checking the obvious. "Maybe she's in the restroom? Mamma, do you want to check it out?"

My mother passes Caroline to my father and is out of her chair and in the hallway before another word is spoken. My brothers have been friends with Chase since grade school; we all grew up in the same community. My mother is no stranger to Fiona's disappearances.

Head down, tears drop from Liam's eyes. "I want Mommy."

"Hey, buddy," Antonio kneels in front of him, a smile masking his concern. "We're going to find Mommy."

"Where is she?"

"I don't know. Maybe she's in the coffee shop buying snacks." That quiets him for a bit.

"Liam," I reach out and pull him closer, giving him a kiss on the cheek. "Why don't you go read your book to Caroline and her grandpa."

Wiping his tears with his sleeve, he looks toward my father and smiles shyly.

"Come, Liam," my father waves his hand, "Caroline wants to hear your story."

Liam scoots over and climbs onto his lap and opens his book.

"She's not there," my mother mouths once she returns. "And when I asked at the nurses' station," she whispers, "one said he thought he saw her get into the elevator."

Antonio and Chase melt into the corridor, where I'm sure they're discussing options of where to begin searching. Devie, who arrived a half hour ago and is cradling Teo, immediately hands him to my mother and slips out to join them, along with Mac and Sammy.

In the thick of all these visitors Eleanor strides into the room, assuming a take-charge attitude that would challenge the maneuvers of a general. She looks at all the people, presses her lips into a terse line, then strides toward me carrying a thermometer, IV bag replacement, and blood pressure monitor. Chase must have hired her to help, and I couldn't be more relieved. I also know that whatever is in that new bag is going to put me out before the pain escalates further. The room clears except for Chase, and of course the twins, who are tucked back into their cribs, sleeping.

My parents take Caroline and Liam with them to the snack bar. Sammy follows while Mac, Antonio, and Devie confer in a terse knot in the corridor.

Eleanor wraps the blood pressure band around my arm. It puffs, we wait, and when it's done, she frowns. "It's a bit high."

Chase is at my side, holding my hand a second after Eleanor speaks. "I don't think it's anything to worry about. Now that the room is quieter, I'm going to wait a bit and then retake it."

I look toward Chase. "Go do what you need to do to help find Fiona. I'm fine with all this help."

He shakes his head.

"There's plenty of people searching. This is typical behavior for Fiona around Liam's birthday. If she isn't found soon, my guess is she's going to relapse. We've already contacted her sponsor."

"Isn't that information private?"

"Usually, it is, but Fiona left her phone behind and we located it in her contacts."

"Why wouldn't she take her phone?" My mind spins lots of scenarios, none of them good.

"Liam had it tucked inside his pocket. He must have been playing a game on it when she left, and then when she didn't come back, he stuffed it there. That's where Antonio found it, and since Liam knows her password, we have access to any emails or texts she initiated before she disappeared."

"Should we alert the police? Detective Wilson knows her history. Maybe he'd be able—" Chase doesn't let me finish.

"We're going to see what we uncover first. Usually, the police wait twenty-four to forty-eight hours with a missing adult before they start an investigation. With Fiona's drug history, they'll just assume she relapsed."

I open my mouth to retort, but there's nothing more I can offer. Chase is right. Even if we did inform the police, they'd probably suggest we wait to see if Fiona voluntarily shows up as she has so many times in the past. Other than her ring gracing a severed finger, there has never been any evidence that implicates Dimitri to Fiona. Fiona insists she has never been threatened or attacked by Dimitri or anyone in his criminal network.

"For now, I'm going to stay with you and the twins. Your mom and dad are taking Caroline."

My next words leave no room for disagreement. "No, I want her home where there's tight security and Sunny is in charge."

"Don't worry," he strokes my cheek. "Your parents are taking her to our apartment and staying there for a bit to help Sunny. Devie and Antonio have already left to search for Fiona. And Sammy is staying here with me while you rest. It's all decided, so not another word."

I lie back, feeling relaxed, but then my head pops back when I remember it that Dimitri threatened to kidnap Liam if Devie didn't help him with my attack. I don't care what Chase says about Fiona being spared Dimitri's wrath. Liam and Fiona can be just as easily targeted as we have been. "Where is Liam going to stay?"

"My dad is picking him up here and taking him to his house."

"No, don't do that." I have to restrain myself from appearing too agitated, but I'm convinced Liam is not safe with only Grandpa Bill watching over him. "Have Liam stay at our apartment. That way your dad can stay at home just in case Fiona shows up and needs help." Since all three live in the same two-family beach house on Long Island, it makes sense that Fiona might return there.

"Sounds like a good plan. I'll let him know."

It's only when I see him firing off a text to his father that I finally relax. I've learned it's the element of surprise that gives Dimitri the upper hand and right now with all of us here and on guard, he's lost the ability to wield the same level of vindictiveness and vengeance as when Chase, Mac, and Sammy were away. For the time being it will have to be enough to give me some solace.

Eleanor retakes my blood pressure and seems satisfied.

This helps Chase unwind, too. He leans back in the chair next to me and his eyelids slowly close. He hasn't slept in over twenty-four hours. It's not long before I follow, knowing that Eleanor is on hand, Sammy is standing watch in the corridor, and Caroline is safe at home with Sunny and Mac. Before the drugs take hold of my mind and body, I imagine Dimitri dead in a ditch somewhere. I know that when all is said and done, none of us will be safe until he is either captured or killed.

Chase clasps my hand, holding it tightly even as his breathing becomes slow and heavy, and I slip into the serenity of sleep.

• • •

It's Juliette who cries for the breast the most, rejecting any attempts to bottle feed. And me? I seem to be living in a world where the sameness of NOW has erased any ideas about a future that doesn't include babies, bottles, diapers, feedings, swaddling, rocking, bathing, burping . . . the list seems endless. The only pastime that isn't repetitive is sleep. Sleep has all but disappeared, except for catnaps snatched here and there during the twenty-four hours a day, seven days a week job of caring for three babies. My life is so tightly focused on those little lives that I think if only I could blur its sharpness for a few hours, I'd find myself inside it.

Instead, I walk around like some zombie coasting on an energy reserve that I seem to pull from the air. I can't even enjoy a pick-me-up espresso to keep functional, although I admit I snuck one the other night. Everyone lived, so it's all good. I'm so wrapped up in the sameness of my NOW, the only variance I recognize is our concern over Fiona's disappearance.

"It's been three weeks. Where the hell can she be?" Antonio places his empty coffee cup on the kitchen counter and rubs the palms of his hand across his eyes in a vain attempt to rid himself of the fatigue he's been fighting since our search for Fiona started.

"She's done this before and always resurfaced," Devie interjects, putting her arm around him. "Let's stay confident that it will be the same this time."

I nod agreement, but the truth is, the more time that passes with no word from her, the more worried I get. She would never leave Liam for this length of time. Even Chase says this is the longest she's been gone. Worried beyond belief, he works all day, assists with the search in the evening, then helps with the twins' feeding in the middle of the night. I've no idea when he sleeps either.

Fiona's phone is kept charged and in sight in the hopes that she or someone she knows will call with information about her whereabouts. My nervous hands pick it up again. I rifle through its contents, thinking I may have missed some relevant clue the hundred or so times I've looked through it before. I jump when it jingles in my hand. Antonio and Devie look alarmed.

"Hello," I answer.

Silence.

"Hello, Fiona? Are you there?" I hear heavy breathing, but no one speaks.

"Is it Fiona?" Antonio asks.

I shrug and continue listening. Finally, in a strained, hoarse whisper, Fiona slurs, "I need you to come now. I can't stay here long."

A tenseness clamps my heart. "Where do you need me to go? Where are you?" I repeat, trying to keep panic from clinging to my words.

Antonio pinches his lower lip thoughtfully, hanging on my every word. For a long time, there's silence, so much silence that I wonder if she's still there. I hear her weary sigh.

"Roosevelt Island, the . . ." her voice trails off, and it almost sounds as if she's sleeping, her breathing is that heavy.

"Fiona!" My tone is sharp. "Tell me where in the park you want me to meet you, and I'll be there within the hour."

"The south side of the park, near the wall in the Four Freesum . . ." She stretches a pause then corrects herself. "Freedoms, Four Freedoms Park, and no Mac, or Sammy, or my brother." She stops then continues with a catch in her throat, "Or Antonio. None of them are to come or I'll disappear again." She laughs. It's a chilling sound, high pitched, rapid, almost hysterical, as if she's just seen something that no one but her thinks funny. "He says the fourth one is overrated." Her laughter turns to sobbing before she hangs up.

This is the voice of someone who is so shattered, she speaks a stream of consciousness that ping-pongs through grisly events while trying to hold onto reality.

"She's in trouble. I've got to find her and bring her home."

A heavy silence descends on the room.

"Where is she?" Antonio asks.

"Roosevelt Island. At The Four Freedoms Park."

I grab my purse and stop only to think about who has been fed and when. Juliette just nursed, so she should be okay for about the next two hours or so. Eleanor can give Teo a bottle when he wakes in about an hour. Sunny can feed Caroline in case they overlap, and Antonio will keep an eye on Liam, who is busy playing with his Legos in the playroom. I'm good to go.

Antonio cuts into my hurry. "This sounds problematic. Fiona could be a handful to get home if she is even where she claims to be. You haven't fully recuperated from giving birth, and the twins need you. I'll go get her."

"No. She explicitly said that if you came, she'd disappear again."

"Chase is not going to like this," Antonio responds.

I shoot him a sharp look. "Keep this to yourself. No need to involve Sammy or Mac. They're like a direct line to Chase. If Chase knows, he'll insist one of them follow me to the park. If that happens, we might not ever find Fiona."

"Did she say I wasn't to come either?" Devie asks. When I hesitate, she gets the answer she's looking for and reaches for her crossbody purse. "Let's go." She stops just before stepping into the hallway and raises her chin toward the nursery. "Is everyone fed?" She visits often to help out and knows what is involved in the day-to-day care of three babies.

"Yeah. I just hope Juliette doesn't wake earlier than usual."

"If she does, I'm sure we'll hear her wails from Queens." She eyes my breasts. "Isn't it about time you hang a closed sign on that twenty-four-hour-a-day food factory?

I give her an incredulous stare. "They're three weeks old."

"Seems to me that's two weeks too long for that kind of service."

There's no time to debate the benefits of nursing with Devie, who's been on her own since she was a child. As far as Chase goes, I'll deal with him later. Right now, finding Fiona is the priority.

The hot, humid August afternoon wraps around us like a wet cloth. We hail a cab to Fifty-Ninth and Second, and, with only a three-minute wait for the overhead tram to Roosevelt Island, we make record time.

Heading south, we leave behind the former mental health and smallpox facilities, which some believe to be haunted by those who perished there over a century ago. The walk from the tram to FDR's Four Freedoms Park should take no more than ten minutes, but I have trouble keeping up with Devie's brisk trot. My stomach muscles ache, and my leaden legs drag with fatigue. Bent double, I struggle to catch my breath. "Go ahead and try to find her. I'll catch up," I shout at Devie's retreating back. She nods and takes off.

When the pain subsides, I lengthen my stride through the tree-lined path that leads to the FDR memorial. My feet pound against the white stone of modernist architecture that resembles an open-air temple kissed by the sun. Walking toward a platform, or *room* as this section is referred to, I spot Devie striding, among three or four onlookers, toward a stone bench. When my eyes trace the length of her movement, I flinch in shock. Sitting on a polished ivory granite platform, studying the wall inscribed with quotes from Franklin D. Roosevelt's eighth State of the Union address, is Fiona. Except it's not the Fiona I know. This person is shrunken with grief. Droplets of sweat cling to her brow, sealing her limp hair to her forehead. The same clothes she wore to visit me in the hospital hang soiled and loose from her wasted body. Devie hovers above her, looking more shocked than I am.

"Where is Alicia?" Fiona looks up through eyes open no

more than slits.

"Let me handle this," I tell Devie, who now nervously eyes the perimeter of the platform.

"I'll be standing there," Devie points to an elevated section that provides a view of the expanse of the park.

I sit next to Fiona and place my arm around her shoulder. "It's going to be alright. You're safe now," I say, then shut my eyes to block out the horror of the red needle marks that trace the inside of her arms.

"How's Liam?" she asks, blinking away tears.

"He's fine." I pull her closer and she cries into my arm.

"Where is he?" she sputters between sobs.

"He's staying with us." Her shoulders relax and she inhales a deep breath.

"Where does he think I am?"

"We told him you took something that made you sick and that you were staying at a special hospital to get better."

Liam may have understood that something was wrong but at six years old, he was still willing to trust what adults told him without asking too many probing questions.

Fiona expels a small sigh, and tears drip onto her cheek. I hesitate for a bit, rubbing her back, waiting for her to collect herself, before plunging ahead with the question that's been worrying all of us for the past three weeks. "Where have you been?"

Instead of answering my question, she reaches out and grabs my hand. Her words, marked by tears and shame, come out hurriedly. "I don't want Liam to see me like this."

"We won't let that happen until you're better." I try to calm her, but she's not listening.

Her gaze becomes preoccupied; her eyes shift to the

side as if there's someone there who only she can see. Every muscle in her body goes rigid and she quakes with fear. "We have to leave now. Penko said *he* might be coming back."

"Who might be coming back?" I ask, my eyes mirroring her terror. I wait for her answer, but it's as if those last words cost her the little bit of coherence she was clinging onto.

She forces herself to stand but instead collapses, her body folding into itself like a rag doll. Devie runs over and clutches her under one arm. I grab the other and together we sit her back onto the granite block before she falls to her face. Devie gives her cheeks light taps, and her eyes flutter open. She peers ahead at the stark white wall as if we're not there.

"What's she staring at?"

Fiona stretches her finger toward the wall in answer to Devie's question. I follow its line and realize she's pointing to the fourth freedom.

"I think she's pointing to the freedom that states people should live free from fear. When she phoned, she told me someone told her this particular freedom is overrated."

Devie whitens. "Whoever she's been with wants her scared, or why else mention this particular freedom?"

My mind stumbles over a muddle of options about what could have happened.

"Maybe she owes her dealer money. She mentioned someone called Peko or Piko. I can't remember exactly."

"I have no idea who that is. This may sound terrible, but she could have slept with people for drugs and some pimp is after her. We've no idea where she has been or who she has been with."

"We have to get her away from here now."

"Agreed."

Half carrying her, half encouraging her to walk, we head toward the tram station. We don't have to walk far before I spot our Range Rover with a stone-faced Chase sitting in the driver's seat. Damn Antonio's loose lips. He never could keep things to himself.

Chase gets out of the car. His eyes pinion mine like the prongs of a pitchfork, then shift toward Fiona. Adeptly, he lifts and slides Fiona onto the back seat. Devie gets in next and takes Fiona's hand.

"It's okay. You're going to be alright," she says when Fiona begins to moan and cry.

Wordlessly, Chase helps me into the passenger seat. He doesn't get back into the car until he sees that Fiona is breathing and conscious. I'm sure he's considering whether we need to call 911 to save her from a lethal overdose from whatever she's flying high on. Fiona flutters her eyelids and gives Chase a loose wave. Assured that she is somewhat coherent, Chase gets behind the wheel and hits the accelerator.

Gingerly shifting in my seat, the aches and fatigue from my surgery grab my body. Eyeing me from the corner of his eye, he reaches into the cupholder and hands me a small bottle of apple juice. I reach for two more and hand them back to Devie. Lately, we've taken to stocking the car with water and fruit juices. It's important to keep hydrated when nursing.

Sipping silently, I realize how concerned he must have been to leave a string of meetings to come find us. I also know that now that he has found us, that worry will flash into anger like a lit match. I take another swallow of apple juice and wait for it to unfurl. He lets out a gust of breath and . . . here it comes.

"What were you thinking to just leave the house to go search for Fiona? You just gave birth for Christ's sake."

My gaze remains even. "I know. I'm sorry I worried you. When Fiona phoned, she specifically asked me to come. What else could I do?"

"What else could you do?" he repeats, his lips pressed into a tight line. "I can think of dozens of different possibilities. For starters, you should have shared this information with me or Sammy or Mac or even Sunny. We've had this conversation before." He lowers his voice but not the conviction of his tone. "We spoke about having enough trust in each other to share problems openly. You asked for mine, and I gave it. Why can't you do the same?"

I don't have a ready answer, so I mumble another apology. He's right though. I was so worried about finding Fiona, I never thought that he could have offered another viable solution. One we could have discussed and mutually decided upon.

Wait a minute.

Who am I kidding with that line of thinking? If I had told him, he would have gone in search of Fiona himself, without listening to any of my suggestions. And that is our problem. He issues orders for me to obey, and when I don't, he rolls out a guilt-saturated argument like some yellow brick road I have no choice but to agree to follow.

I lie my head back, sipping juice and trying to will away the pain in my stomach. All this is fodder for another discussion once Fiona is taken care of. Now is not the time, and I do not have the strength.

I may be perseverating on his last accusation, but in typical Chase fashion, he's whipsawed onto another. "Where did she even get a phone to call from?

Fiona rouses herself enough to come to my defense. "I told Alicia if you or your buddies showed up, I would leave and . . ." she pushes the words through her white, parched lips, "some good Samaritan let me use her phone." Her head falls back, and Devie gently pushes it forward and holds the small bottle of juice to her mouth.

Chase shifts his glare to Devie. "You should have known better, too. God knows where Fiona has been and who she may owe money to. All your lives could have been in danger." He rubs the back of his neck with his hand.

Fiona moans then slurs before rolling back into unconsciousness, "He didn't come back. Izz okay for now." I feel another dull prick of fear with the reminder of her panic when she thought someone might be returning. There's time enough to find out who this person is after she has gotten the help she needs. She is in no condition to answer questions now.

Chase's voice drops to a low timbre. "I have no idea who she's rambling on about, but now is not the time to try and find out. She's barely conscious. We're going to have to clean her up and get her to rehab. Best that happens tonight."

"I know. I'll help bathe her and pack a bag with some of my clothes for her to take until we can go get hers."

"You'll lie down and rest. You could barely stand before you got into the car."

And that's just the kind of ordering about I'm referring to. I'd let him know about it too if I didn't have such searing pains attacking my stomach. Helping lift and carry Fiona were not things I should have been doing so soon after surgery.

"I'll help Fiona get ready," Devie offers, covering Fiona's now-shivering shoulders with a blanket from Caroline's car seat. "Who knows when she had her last hit or how much she took." Devie studies Fiona, then adds, "If I had to guess, I'd say she's been shooting up heroin and lots of it. She should be seen by a doctor as soon as possible."

Chase takes hold of my hand. "I'm glad you're okay," he says. "You too, Devie. Thanks for going so Alicia wasn't by herself, because if I had to guess," he looks at me and shakes his head, "Alicia was ready to head out alone." Neither Devie nor I answer, which is tantamount to admitting that's what would have happened, but it's hard to argue with silence. Rifling back his hair, he looks at me, then gives a quick glance toward Devie. "You both helped save her life."

I pull his hand to my lips and kiss it. "Fiona's family. I'd do it again if I had to." The words just slip out, probably because it's the truth, but I see his face souring, so before he becomes unhinged, I correct myself, "I mean we'd work together," I point my finger at him then myself then back and forth again with just enough sincerity to drive my point home. "And have a discussion where we reach a mutually agreed upon decision and—"

Devie's raucous laughter interrupts my babbling. When I turn around, even Fiona wears a small smile.

"C'mon, Chase, what you said earlier is bullshit, and

you know it. If Alicia had told you Fiona phoned and needed help, she would not be in this car right now. You would have assumed your usual control and—"

"Don't start with me, Devie. And to finish your sentence, I would have gotten the job done, and Alicia would have been resting at home instead of being here and in pain."

"What's done is done," I interrupt. "I'm fine. Stop talking about me as if I'm a pane of glass."

"Well, Chase is right. You're not looking well. I don't know how much rest you'd be getting at home with that flock of fledglings in the nest waiting to be fed. Who can keep count of the number of butts that need to be wiped in any given hour? Forget thinking about getting any sleep or thinking about anything, for that matter." Devie's comments are delivered with her usual tour de force of candor that even a crisis doesn't silence. She shakes her head and offers Fiona more liquid.

In the garage, it's a struggle to get out of the car. As soon as the elevator reaches our floor, I hear Juliette's cries. I follow the screeching into the nursery, where Eleanor is feebly trying to feed her a bottle that, red-faced and squirming, Juliette refuses to take. I quickly grab a cleansing wipe for my hands and, opening my blouse, I sweep her into my arms and hold her to my breast.

Blissful. Silence.

Eleanor switches her gaze to me and frowns, pointing to the rocking chair and insisting that I sit on top of a down pillow. "I'll be right back with the heating pad. You can rest it on your stomach while you nurse."

"Thanks, Eleanor. You're the best." I collapse into the

padded chair and close my eyes, rocking slowly. "Mamma's here, my sweet angel. I'm here."

CHAPTER 16

"Mommy is better now?" Liam asks for the umpteenth time.

The city disappears behind us as we cross the bridge and head toward the treatment center where Fiona has been recuperating for the past five weeks.

"Your mommy is feeling much better," Chase assures Liam. "She can't wait to see you."

Liam smiles and looks at Juliette, who's asleep in her car seat. "Mommy is going to be so happy to see Juliette." He reaches out from his car seat and gently strokes Juliette's tiny hand with his finger. Children know when something is wrong, no matter how hard you try to shield them from the harsh reality of what's going on.

Mommy took medicines that made her sick. She's away because she has to see special doctors to make her well again.

We repeat these and other placating comments, like parroting optimists who want to believe that this time will be different. This time Fiona won't be sucked back into the mysteriously hellish zone she visits when compelled to relinquish control of her body and mind to drugs.

After Fiona disappeared, everything unfolded quickly. Liam moved in with us even though Bill was initially reluctant, insisting that Liam could stay with him at the beach house. He thought adding another child to our three was too much for us to handle. He agreed when we explained that Eleanor was remaining to provide an added layer of protection for the children and that, with Sunny also on board, we had the help needed to manage two infants, a toddler, and a six-year-old child.

Yeah, right.

There are times when I think an army would not be enough to get through the day, but I've learned that when life deals you a problem, you can either rise to the challenge or get swept away with it. So, when the school year approached, I made several calls and was able to schedule an appointment for Liam to take the ISEE for private school admittance. His scores were high and with excellent references from Chase's contacts, Liam was given a coveted first-grade slot at a private school on Ninety-First and Park. During our initial interview, Chase and I explained to the director of admissions that Liam's mother was ill and receiving treatment in the hospital. She didn't ask any questions and we didn't add much more information except to say that she was expected to make a full recovery and we were Liam's guardians until then.

The roads that lead to this expanding patch of ocean vistas are quiet. Families powered with Wall Street money have already plucked their children and staff of servants from their Hamptons beach mansions and returned to the city for the start of the new school year. The three-storied structure where Fiona waits for us sits on a four-acre private estate, with sprawling gardens and expansive views of the sea. The facility presents more like a well-appointed villa than a rudimentary brick-and-mortar rehab institution. When we found Fiona, we had to think fast. Chase called several contacts in the medical profession. One specialist recommended a facility in East Hampton that was known for its high relapse prevention rate. We figured this had a lot to do with the amount and quality of help offered there. With a three-to-one staff-to-patient ratio and its holistic approach to recovery, it seemed best suited for Fiona.

I have Juliette snuggled to my chest in a baby pack, with Chase holding her empty car seat by the handle in one hand and Liam's hand in the other. Juliette has become part of me, like an extended limb or an extra hand, because she stubbornly refuses to suck from a bottle. Since the doctor had some concerns that she wasn't gaining sufficient weight, I can't bear to watch her fuss or cry when it's offered for her to try again.

With Chase holding the door open for us, we step into a wide vestibule. Ahead, a long staircase with a polished wooden handrail leads to what I assume are bedrooms. To the right is a sitting area with honey-colored parquet floors covered by a plush carpet. There are overstuffed sofas, several checkered wing-back chairs, and an oak paneled wall with built-in shelves holding hundreds of books. A backdrop of floor-to-ceiling windows look out at sand dunes, wild grasses, and a vast spread of ocean and sky. Toward the rear of the room, a high-back leather chair is pulled back from a mahogany desk and a tall, elegantly dressed receptionist greets us with a smile.

"How can I help you today?" Her voice is smooth and

soft, with a lilt of an Australian accent. She shoots me a polite smile, then does a double take when she sees Chase. He returns the look with an impersonal smile, providing all the required information for us to sign in. We're escorted through French doors that lead to a manicured garden. Once she walks away, I clasp my hands under my chin and bat my eyes at Chase. He shakes his head, laughing, then pulls me to him to knuckle the top of my head. Whoever said romance is dead after having children is wrong. It doesn't die so much as go into hiding so that sleep, rather than sex, can be snatched in between caretaking chores.

We catch sight of Fiona sitting in a chair on a flagstone terrace, surrounded by flowerbeds of purple sweet alyssum and yellow aster. Clutching a stuffed elephant and a box of Legos, she wistfully studies the ocean as if its breakers have something to say.

"Mommy, Mommy." Liam breaks into a run and heads toward the door leading to the terrace.

Pleasure settles into Fiona's scrunched eyes and upturned mouth as she wraps Liam in her arms. My eyes moisten and Chase takes my hand and gives it a squeeze. Allowing them some private time, we settle for watching their bent heads pressed together through the large wall of sitting-room windows. Every now and again, Fiona ruffles Liam's hair and kisses his cheek, then hands him another Lego from the box he tore open to begin building a robot. Occasionally, he reaches out to touch her hand as if to make sure she's really there.

After about fifteen minutes, Fiona points to us and whispers something in Liam's ear. Nodding, he pops off the garden bench and sprints our way.

"Uncle Chase, Aunt Alicia," he calls out, swinging open the door and popping his head inside. "Mommy says to come outside so we can show Juliette the ocean."

Fiona's face brightens when she spots us heading in her direction. The stark and sunken look of a skeleton has been replaced by rosy cheeks and clear, sharp eyes, the eyes of a photographer who can capture a piece of the world with the press of a finger. It is good to have her back.

She embraces us in tight hugs. "Thanks for coming and for bringing Liam. I . . ." Her eyes fill with tears. She shakes her head to fight them off and find her voice again.

Chase looks as if sadness is cracking him open inside, too.

Dashing away tears with her fingers, Fiona studies Juliette burrowed in her baby sling. "Look at how big she is."

"You've just said the magic words to help Alicia relax. She's been worrying about Juliette gaining enough weight," Chase says, wrapping his arm around me and kissing my cheek.

"Is everything alright?"

"It's all good now. As long as she can nurse, she's content and growing."

Fiona watches her with a tender smile so when Juliette starts to stir, I ask if she'd like to hold her.

"Yeah, let me see the little gem up close."

I lift Juliette out of the carrier and place her in Fiona's open arms. Fiona tickles her cheek and coaxes a smile. Rocking the baby, she starts to speak, compresses her lips, then opens them again. "I want tell you both how sorry I am that I let all this happen."

I start to interrupt, to indicate all is well, but the waifish fragility of her face hardens into a rock of resolve.

She reaches out her free hand to grab hold of mine. "No, please, it's important that I say this . . ." She pauses again, working past tears before continuing, "That I make amends for how my behavior hurt the people I love most. I should never have left Liam at the hospital, and I should not have asked you to come alone to fetch me when I was in such a state." Her next words come out crisp and clear. "I would never forgive myself if either of you were hurt because of my actions."

"We're fine, Fiona. It's you we're worried about."

She ignores her brother's comment, her gaze skittering away as if the only thing that matters is finding the right words to express how she feels. "I can never thank you enough for all you've done for me and Liam." She looks at him and smiles. "He looks so happy and content. Without you, this all could have turned out far worse."

Chase pulls her to him in a hug and kisses her cheek. "What matters most now is that you get well and stay well."

"Yes, I know. I'm working on it."

"I'd like to talk to you about something before we leave. I'd have called you sooner but thought it best if we could speak face to face," Chase says.

We settle comfortably at a picnic table while Liam constructs his robot on the bench behind us. Positioning Juliette's seat onto the table, I strap her in and place a pacifier in her mouth. She becomes very still and soon her eyes close.

"I've been doing a lot of thinking about everything

that's happened." Chase leans forward on the bench and stares across at Fiona. "I've even discussed it with Dad, and we thought some changes might be good."

"What exactly is it that you've both decided?" She chews on the side of her thumb.

"Liam has made a great adjustment to Colton. It's a good school, with good teachers and a competitive curriculum. So . . ." Chase pauses for a beat then plows ahead, "I took the liberty of buying a two-bedroom apartment in our building that recently came on the market for you and Liam to live in."

Fiona expels a loud breath of relief, and the tears start flowing again. "It's too generous. I . . . I . . ."

"We insist," I add. "You'll love the building. The staff is courteous and hardworking. The apartment is spacious with lots of light . . ."

Fiona throws her arms around my neck and then her brother's.

"It all sounds . . ." She doesn't get to finish because when her head shifts toward where Liam was sitting, there's only empty space.

A breath of wind stirs her bangs as she puts her hand to the base of her throat and gasps. Under normal conditions we'd simply be worried that Liam wandered off and would be found nearby, but these are not normal circumstances. Dimitri has threatened to kidnap Liam in the past and with Dimitri at large, it's hard to discriminate between a normal occurrence and a deadly pursuit. I jump up and begin to take Juliette from her seat. Fiona runs to where Liam's sneaker prints press into the sand in a path toward the ocean.

"No!" Chase sharp tone stops us in our tracks. "Leave Juliette in her seat." Grabbing hold of Fiona's arm, he holds her in place and does a quick scan of the vicinity. Liam is nowhere in sight. Chase grabs Juliette's seat opens the door, and ushers me and Fiona into the facility.

Choked by sobs, Fiona tears at Chase's chest to try to move him away from the doors. "I need to find out what's happened," she cries out. But Chase is adamant, and when he is that serious, you listen.

"I need you both to remain inside. Stay close to the receptionist's desk and the other visitors, but away from the windows." His eyes meet mine. "Make sure you keep Juliette in your immediate line of vision and her seat no more than an arm's reach away."

My heart beats into my throat with the realization that this might be a ploy to hurt Juliette.

Fiona looks as if she's ready to tear through the property to try and find Liam.

"Fiona," Chase puts his arm around her and speaks in a cajoling tone, "Liam probably took a walk to the beach to see the ocean. Let me handle this."

He slips through the door in one silent, fluid motion. Hunkering low in the wild grasses, he pulls a Sig Sauer compact semi-automatic pistol from inside the back waistband of his pants. I recognize the weapon but not the man holding it. The business executive has transformed into a combatant ready to take on an enemy who may have taken his nephew. I knew we had at least that one firearm at home, but I had no idea Chase carried it with him today. This tells me he anticipated trouble, and in typical Chase fashion, didn't share the details. Now, he's heading out to find his nephew, hoping for the best but anticipating the worst.

It's at this moment that I decide I need to learn how to fire a gun. Dimitri's unwavering notion that he has a right to seek revenge against Chase without impunity has gone on for too long. He needs to be stopped and he needs to be stopped now even if it means bloodying my hands to make it happen. I might not feel good about doing it, but our lives are too important to me to have any one of us end with his treachery.

Fiona and I huddle around Juliette, wordlessly watching each other's stricken expressions. She sits on the edge of the armchair, legs crossed, her free foot shaking, her eyes nervously combing our space.

"Someone has taken Liam. I just know it." A split second later she's up and striding toward the door. "I'm going to the beach to help Chase find him."

"Wait!" I reach out and take her arm in a tight hold. "What are you saying? Who do you think has Liam?"

She's reluctant to answer, so I take a gamble and fill in the blanks with the name I heard her mention after Devie and I found her drugged and choked with fear on Roosevelt Island.

"Do you think it could be this Peko person you mentioned at the Four Freedoms Park?"

For the first time, a crack appears in Fiona's armored expression. She stares ahead, muttering more to herself than to me, "It might be Penko." The name hangs between us like a stench.

"Is *Penko* someone you owe money to?" I remember Fiona's disturbed state when I first found her after her disappearance. She was disheveled, broke, and half-starved. "From when you were using?" I add. I need answers about these disappearances she falls prey to, and I need them now.

A ghost of a smile parts her lips, but she shakes her head as if she doesn't want to discuss it. Only this time, I'm not letting it go. We don't need more danger in our lives. "Well, do you or don't you owe someone money?"

She slumps back into her chair. "Yeah, I owed him. But I paid it back and then some."

"I don't understand. You have been here since I found you. How were you able to get money to anyone?"

"I . . ." She doesn't get a chance to explain, because walking up toward the French doors is Chase, a smiling Liam by his side.

Like so many times before when danger lurked, adrenaline leaves my body, and relief seeps in.

"Seems Liam wanted a closer look at the ocean and decided to take a stroll to the beach." Chase coolly tosses out. His nonchalant attitude is probably why Liam is oblivious to our panic.

Fiona grabs him in a fierce hug, then holds him at arm's length. "Next time, tell Mommy when you're leaving to go play or take a walk. Okay?"

He nods his head yes. "When are you coming home?" he asks, staring at his mother, teary-eyed.

"Very soon. In fact, I think I'll be back next week." She looks at me and Chase. "My doctors feel I am well enough to be released, as long as I attend local meetings and meet with my sponsor. Will the apartment be ready for us by then?" She smiles her gratitude.

"How many more days is next week?" Liam interrupts, his lower lip quivering.

Fiona holds up seven fingers. "This many," she tells him.

He counts her fingers. "Seven sleeps?"

"That's right." She taps the tip of his nose with her finger, then looks toward Chase for his answer.

"Everything's ready for you, Fiona," he says.

"I hope you don't mind that I purchased some pieces of furniture and had them delivered to help you and Liam settle comfortably into the apartment." I hold my hand up when she starts to protest. "It's just the basics, beds for the two of you, a table and chairs and a sofa. When you're ready, you can add other pieces to your liking or even return the ones I bought if you want. I left the tags attached."

"Mind? Are you kidding? I don't know where to begin to show how grateful I am."

"You don't have to say anything. We love you and want to help as long as you continue to help yourself," Chase says.

For the briefest moment, Fiona's pastel-blue eyes spark fury. "I swear. This will not happen again, and I insist on paying you back. There's a gallery in Soho that has expressed an interest in showcasing my photographs, especially the ones I took of the beach here."

I gather her in a congratulatory hug, feeling how thin she is even with the current healthy diet and weight gain. "That's great."

"Mommy, Mommy, Mommy," Liam repeats in that demanding way children have when they want your immediate attention. "I brought you a surprise. Wanna see?" He fishes into the pockets of his jeans, pulls out two fistfuls of sandy shells, and places them on the coffee table we are seated around. Fiona gently fingers a few and holds a transparent one up to the light to show Liam its luster.

Wiggling his body in excitement, Liam grasps one to hold up to the light, too. Smiling, he looks back at Fiona. "He told me you would like that one."

The comment ices our bones.

Fiona slides off her chair and kneels on the carpet next to where Liam stands. They meet eye-to-eye.

"Who told you I would like them?" she casually asks.

"The man at the beach who helped me find these shells."

Chase stands and casually moves closer to the door. He watches the path that leads to the beach, his right hand staying near his pocket.

Chilling "what-ifs" pop into my mind. What if this was one of Dimitri's goons stalking Liam on the beach to get at us? What if Dimitri has a foolproof plan of attack that outsmarts us? Worst of all, what if next time he succeeds, and one or more of us are killed? The limbo is like watching a poisonous vapor drift closer.

"Look, Aunt Alicia. Do you like them?"

I lean forward with a smile to admire his shells.

"They are beautiful."

Liam rifles through the pile and selects a light-gray stone the color of a kitten's fur.

"I like this one. He said it was his favorite too because it looked like the color of my eyes." Liam goes back to looking through his stash of sea treasures.

"Did this person know your name?"

Not lifting his head, Liam shrugs.

Fiona looks at us, perplexed, waiting a bit to allow Liam

time to play before asking more questions.

We stay still and wait with her, wanting to learn more from Liam without pressuring him for answers that might frighten him into saying something he thinks we want to hear.

"What else did the man on the beach say?" Fiona finally asks.

Liam stays quiet for a bit, too busy studying random shells with surprised wonder, to answer. "He said he had to go back to work."

Chase shifts to a corner of the room that offers a clear view of the entrance to our sitting area as well the patio doors, in case the man is someone posing as a hospital employee. We've been on our guard for so long now, I recognize the moves. Not wanting to badger Liam, we continue to give him time to play with his shells, hoping he'll reveal enough information to tell us who this stranger was or what, if anything, he wanted.

"Look at the color of this one, Mommy." He holds up a mini conch shell and places it in Fiona's open palm.

"That one is lovely." She gently rubs the contour of its surface with her finger before adding it back to the pile.

"I like this one too," he pipes up, holding out a small, patterned shell. "Don't you, Aunt Alicia?" He lifts it up near my face so I can study the swirls of its reddish hue.

"It's very pretty, Liam."

"That color is a stunning red for a dress," Fiona tells me, reaching out her hand to pull Liam closer, her demeanor relaxing now that she has him close.

"I was actually thinking it's the perfect shade for an evening gown, a cross somewhere between ruby and claret."

The mundane conversation about fashion mellows the menace felt a few minutes ago.

Holding a remaining shell apart from the others, Liam places the crimson shell back into the palm of Fiona's hand. "This is for you to keep, Mommy." Liam's face lights up. "The man said this shell was best of all because it matched the color of our hair and Caroline's."

All at once, I'm sick with fear again.

Chase stiffens. When he addresses Fiona, his tone has a hard edge.

"Do you have any idea who this guy might be?" The powerful silence that follows does not go unnoticed.

Fiona's expression remains blank. Finally, she answers. "I have an idea who he might be. It may not be as bad as you think."

Chase and I have a dim view of her evasive answer. Experience has shown us the *it's not as bad as it looks* outlook generally translates into, *it's actually worse.*

"It's possible he is an employee here. I have seen firsthand how friendly the staff can be with children who visit, and . . ." her eyes brighten, "I have a photo of all of us pinned up on the bulletin board in my room. I may have mentioned Liam and Caroline's resemblance in group meetings."

Chase looks doubtful. For the first time since I've known him, he's not accepting Fiona's explanation. I swallow back the thought that there is a veiled threat buried in the verbal exchange between Liam and this person.

"I don't like how he got so personal, especially with a kid." He gives Fiona that look of his that slices apart a conversational thread that doesn't add up.

Fiona's placid expression slips back into place. "I don't

want to discuss it in front of Liam but," she drops her voice to a whisper, "it's possible I was tracked here to pay a debt owed from before."

"What do you mean, Fiona? You said earlier it was paid," I remind her.

"It was settled, but this last relapse unearthed someone I owe from a while ago."

I start to lose patience with her tap dance around the truth. First, it's someone she owes money to, then it's an employee from the facility, now it could be another person she borrowed from in the past. Her story has more moth holes than a vintage Versace scarf.

"That doesn't explain how he would know so much about our family. When you last disappeared, Caroline wasn't even born yet and when you were found and tested there were no drugs in your system."

"I know, but I still had a running debt going, so when I ran into him this time around, I paid back some of what I owed and, and . . ." She pauses, taking her voice several notches lower. "We got high together a lot. It is possible I shared stories about family and friends. The details are fuzzy. I was out of it most of the time."

"What do you owe?" The question shoots from Chase's clenched teeth like a dart aiming for a bull's-eye.

"About a thousand dollars. I was planning to get it to him as soon as I returned."

"How?"

"I know his hangouts. I thought I'd send a messenger who can be trusted with the cash."

Chase cocks his head and squints, still doubting the plausibility of her explanation. It crosses my mind that this person she's had a rekindled relationship with could be Liam's father. That might explain why he tracked Fiona here, then had a personal conversation with Liam. I don't say anything because I know it won't lead to any new revelations. Fiona vehemently refuses to discuss anything about Liam's father except to admit that it happened during a time when she was high and sleeping around a lot, and that it's best Liam not know any of the details.

"Look, Chase, Liam wasn't hurt. When you found him, he was obviously alone or you would have said something. We are all fine. I really think it was an employee making friendly chitchat while taking a walk on the beach during his break." Fiona's eyes plead for understanding. At this point, there is not much we can do but allow her to pay back what she owes and hope, under our watchful eyes, she goes to meetings—every day if necessary—to stay clean.

Chase must realize this too, because he backs off. "We don't want anything upending your recovery this time. Pay whoever this person is the money you owe without going anywhere near him. If needed, Sammy or Mac can deliver it, no questions asked."

She stares at her brother, pretending to hear his suggestion, but I can tell her mind is made up.

"That's not necessary. I have a PO box number to send it to if the messenger proves too risky."

"I recommend that. The further you stay away from anyone linked to your problem, the better."

Nodding grimly, Fiona brushes hair off her forehead.

It's pushing four o'clock when we wrap up our visit. Chase scoops up Juliette's seat with her nuzzled inside asleep, and I put Liam's gifts in my carry bag.

Fiona reminds him that she'll be coming home soon and helps repack his shells into his pockets. Before we leave, Fiona explains that Antonio is picking her up when she's discharged.

"Alright. Sammy will drive him here and then take you both back to the city."

Chase is not taking any chances with her safety. A whole lot about this visit crowds my mind with problems, too. It almost keeps me from missing the strange exchange.

Almost, but not quite.

Behind a large potted fern in the corner of the vestibule, a tall, tanned, flaxen-haired man leans with his shoulder bumped up against the wall. Sporting white trousers, an open-collared striped shirt, and a navy blazer with some club's coat of arms over its front pocket, he looks as if he's waiting for a staff of hired underlings to service his yacht. An employee identification card with the name of the facility in bold, block letters dangles from his neck. When he raises his hand to give Liam a friendly wave, my eyes widen. On his wrist is an 18K Rolex Yacht-Master II watch that whistles to the sum of at least thirty-eight thousand dollars. Casually fingering back his floppy hair, his mouth curls into a grin when he sees me staring. I cannot get past the implausibility of how a facility employee can embody such wealth.

"That's the man who gave me the shells." Liam points and waves back in his direction.

Chase reacts quickly when my face pales. "Here." He hands me Juliette's seat. "Stay inside and wait by the other visitors."

I clutch his arm. "Be careful. There's something strange about that guy." It's not only the watch that leaves me wondering who he is. His snide, studied look tells me he was deliberately watching us leave.

Chase vanishes behind the potted plant, but I can already see that the space is empty.

An uneasy silence follows us home.

CHAPTER 17

Autumn leaves drop once, then twice. Intervals pass rapidly from when Fiona left rehab to now, where family responsibilities press upon me with more urgency than jumpstarting my career.

Winter snowfalls have us marching to the park with sleds to enjoy their white splendor. Frosty nights leap into spring daffodils that transform into wrapped sunflowers that stand tall in the sunshine of deli stands. A year, then two speed by in a whirl of new milestones: first steps, first words, weaning, toilet training, preschool for Caroline, toddler programs for the twins.

My sketchpad morphs into a receptacle of my creativity, but the designs remain dreams captured on paper that wait to be brought to life. That starts to change with a phone call from Virgil. He has a business proposition he wants to discuss that seems too interesting for me to dismiss. It's been three years since I met Virgil and Charlotte on that day of Virgil's car accident. And now here I am, in my living room, sitting across from Virgil, anticipating a shift in my life that I tried to make several times before.

"Nice," his appraising gaze travels the length of my dress. "Spry, sophisticated with just enough edge in the plunging neckline to make the proportions unique. One of yours?"

I nod. I dressed with care for our meeting, choosing a blue silk sheath dress that just nudges black. I completed the outfit with the same color suede pumps. I know what a fastidious dresser Virgil is and he doesn't disappoint. Clad in a gray flannel blazer with matching slacks and burnished leather Gucci loafers, he looks like he just stepped from the cover of *L'Umo Vogue.*

"And what is *that*?" He lifts my finger to take a closer look at the emerald ring I'm wearing. "The transparency and clarity of the stone is magnificent. Is it Columbian?"

"Yes. It was a gift from Chase after the twins were born."

"The Chaser knows how to do things in a big way. I'm assuming he still has no idea you posed nude for *Vogue*?"

I close my eyes at the thought of discussing those details with Chase. When I open them, I give Virgil my coolest stare. "I wasn't *completely* nude, only from the waist up, *and* it was taken to show the beauty of nursing." I shrug at his doubtful look. "Don't be such a prude. The photo is more a tribute to mothers than a titillating exposure of female flesh. Besides, it was all unplanned and last-minute. I happened to be visiting their office with Juliette to approve a draft of one of my jackets for their fall issue. Juliette was fussing, so I slipped into a quiet area to nurse her. One of the photographers spotted me and asked if he could photograph us, insisting he would not publish anything without my approval. I saw the artistry of his work and agreed it could appear in an Italian *Vogue* issue that was paying tribute to designers who were mothers. That photograph will never appear here."

"I'll take that as a no."

I definitely did not tell Chase. It was my body, and I made a quick decision based on the quality of the photographer's work. End of story.

Virgil finally gets back to the point of his visit. "Will you at least consider coming back into the industry full time? I've drawn up a plan of action for the development of a new business and informed just about everyone I know in the field to help market its launch. The industry needs your creativity."

Virgil's offer fuels the hunger for success I crave. "Why don't you grab your coat, and we'll continue this conversation on the terrace."

Clutching an ashtray, I make sure to close the blinds and fasten the outside top lock to keep small, curious eyes and nimble fingers away from opening doorknobs and stepping onto the terrace. We make our way to the pillowed sofa and sit near an electrical outdoor heat lamp that offers warmth from the autumn chill.

"Do you mind?" I ask, flipping the wheel of my lighter and cupping my hand to light a cigarette without waiting for an answer.

"I thought some maharishi helped you quit."

I raise my head and blow out a bit of smoke, allowing myself time to consider the offer he presented earlier.

"Let's just say I'm a loosely lapsed ex-smoker who likes lighting up every now and again."

"In that case . . ." He fishes through the inside pocket of his jacket and lifts out a pipe and small packet of tobacco.

I've learned from watching my father countless times

that smoking a pipe requires a modicum of work and lots of fidgeting to get to the point of actually smoking the contraption. Virgil removes a pouch of tobacco from his jacket pocket, pinches a bit into the bowl of his pipe, leans back to study it, then puffs the gadget to life. He smokes a pipe with the same patient accuracy he uses to craft designs.

"You've had your modest start with your new label. Now is the time to honor the creative fire inside. Haven't you put your life on hold long enough?" He puffs out ruminative clouds of pipe smoke and waits for an answer to a question I have asked myself countless times. The same answer comes back.

Life put you on hold, it says. And it's so true. Life hurled a series of disruptions at me that had to be dealt with right then and there. Teo's chronic ear infections, Juliette's refusal to bottle-feed, Caroline's erratic sleep patterns, any one of them or all three simultaneously coming down with the flu, sore throats, colds, ear infections, coughs.

I have to admit that even with help, those in charge, including me and Chase, are threatened by mutiny when the crew gets rambunctious. It's like having to manage triplets, except one of the three has a bigger vocabulary to complain and longer legs to run faster from those in charge.

Despite all this, there's a predictability to my life that's reassuring. I'm lucky to have a solid support network to help with childrearing. Accepting a generous salary offer from Chase, complete with hefty health benefits and a 401K package, Eleanor has stayed on as a no-nonsense nanny and nurse doling out love and discipline that they all need. Coupled with Sunny, who takes little to no guff, the team runs a tight ship. My children show me how to enjoy the everyday marvels of life. Watching them study a butterfly on the terrace, their bodies so still it's like they've been frozen in time, is life affirming. When I listen to their surprised giggles from the same stuffed animal's squeak yet again, it's like I'm hearing it for the first time, too. Ordinary happenings transform into priceless pieces of time. I can honestly say, without hyperbole, that these moments will remain etched in my mind for the rest of my life.

Yet, I can't help but feel like I've morphed into someone who thrives off her family's well-being, someone who measures happiness by their bliss and sadness by their downturns. Maybe I always was that person or maybe that's how my parents unwittingly raised me to be. Fears about how events in my life triggered bouts of my mother's depression kept me from differentiating a right to desire something from a selfish demand of wanting too much. Now, I continue to search for pieces of myself that have been buried under one compromise after another.

Don't get me wrong, there is lots of love permeating this cloud of confusion, and I'm grateful for it each and every day. But what if this life has thrust me into an anonymity where nothing remains that is mine alone? Chase has his business, his acquisitions and development projects, the children their pre-K, art, and gym programs, and me? Am I to be just another bourgeois mom shuffling off to fundraisers and baking brownies for school bake sales?

Tapping my forehead with my palm, I make a mental note to pick up ingredients for the cake I volunteered to make for Caroline's school bake sale. I take a last drag, put the cigarette out, and fight the urge to light another.

There is an obstacle that keeps me from branching out into the fashion world. The underlying fear that Dimitri could strike at any moment is the paramount problem that roots me at home. It's been quiet for a while, with no threats, attacks, or sightings from him, but the ever-present shadows of past threats make it difficult to consider much more than the safety of my children. It's good to know that Egor Petrov remains incarcerated for attempting to poison my hospital IV bag when I was carrying the twins. As expected, he refused to implicate Dimitri, said he never heard the name before, and that he just felt the urge to abort babies to limit the world's overpopulation. Smart and shrewd, he pled insanity. In between incoherent ramblings, he denied he was the intruder on our property who shot the fawn, even though he was captured on a surveillance camera buying groceries at the general store in Summit. If I had to guess, he also carried the mangled car seat up to our hallway.

I know Dimitri initiated these terror tactics. Internet research and conversations with Detective Wilson after my hospital attack helped me piece together information about the Ostopenko Gang. An international crime circle of musclemen with Dimitri as their leader, it operates out of St. Petersburg with links to countries that span several continents. Sex and drug trafficking and money laundering are just a few of their specialties. Chase refuses to provide the facts about how all of this affects Dimitri's vendetta against us, except to say that he is a wanted man who is running out of options, and it is just a matter of time before he's apprehended.

Sammy, Mac, and Sunny form a solid support network that protect us round the clock, but when someone is as determined as Dimitri, an attack can come at any time. Preventing this involves an uncanny ability to predict when and where he might strike next. Every day I ask myself what that maniac might be plotting. Then, I try to avoid it. None of us leave the apartment without Sammy or Mac accompanying us and that includes walks to the park, the local ice cream shop, or even a stroll around the block.

"This is a chance for you to reenter your profession." Virgil cuts into my dark thoughts.

I listen as he switches from now's-the-time-to-make-your-move talk to flattery to make his argument more convincing.

"I'm telling you that for you it's a vocation. You're not just good. You excel on a level not seen before. Your small brand begs for more merchandise. I would bet that you're finding it difficult to meet your clients' demands on your own. Let's be a team, combine our talents to create a sure-fire brand of our own."

"And Charlotte? How will she fit into this new venture?"

He leans back and points his pipe in my direction. "Charlotte has been devoured by her quest to come in first in both fashion design and entrepreneurship. I don't know if you heard but after she bought me out, she started opening shops in countless locations: Manhattan, Brooklyn, Long Island City. Now she's considering Chicago. Definitely overextending herself. She doesn't even have the foresight to integrate e-commerce in her step-by-step expansion plan."

"That's too bad."

Inwardly, I'm glad the conniving opportunist won't be involved. I figured her ultimate goal was personal gain and that it was just a matter of time before she used Virgil's health as a chance to seize control of their joint enterprise.

"How are you feeling? Is your leg giving you any more trouble?" I eye the antique ebony walking stick leaning against his chair, its ivory handle carved into the shape of a lion's head watching the world through a slanted eye of amber.

"The bone fusion seems to have taken, and the infection is gone. My knee still feels a little rusty every now and again, but overall it's worked out."

After Virgil's leg wasn't healing properly, there was mention that he could lose it if the infection was not arrested. Mac was beside himself with worry. He finally convinced Virgil to accept Charlotte's offer and put all his attention toward his recovery.

"Fashion week kicks off in Paris in February with the top echelon of the industry attending. We can start preparing for that event by showcasing our original designs to see what feedback and press we glean from meaningful players. It's a good time to cultivate our former connections. I think our work is good enough to reel them in."

He must be aware of my doubt. It's a skepticism rooted more in the intricacies of my current life than the quality of my work. How do I leave three children, three years and younger, for a business trip to Paris and the round-the-clock work required to expand a fashion line and grow a brand?

"Look, I know you don't need to work. God knows you

have oodles of money. I read the article in *The Real Deal* about Chase's development projects that he seems to be closing at breakneck speed. How did they refer to him?"

Tongue in my cheek, I sweep my hand in an arc in front of my face. "The Little Startup Who Could: Sizing up NYC's Development Giant Chase Reardon."

It's hard to keep from laughing out loud when remembering Chase's comments during our celebratory lovemaking that night. "How's that for the Little Engine that Could?" he asked while I struggled to catch my breath. "Assholes," he mumbled under his breath, as I tried, between gasps and giggles, to tell him that it was meant as a compliment.

"So, the *little* startup purchased six more low-rise tenement buildings on the Upper East Side at the cost of forty-four million," Virgil says. "The article indicated he is going to construct a thirty-floor, seventy-two-unit condominium development complete with basketball court, gym, pool, yoga studio, and nine-thousand-square-foot commercial space." At this point Virgil's mouth hangs open.

"I believe that is the plan."

"What about if the real estate market depreciates?"

"Chase doesn't think it will sink, just that it will drop, then plateau when it reaches a well-needed correction and potential buyers adjust to the new tax laws."

"Sounds like you have deep pockets to wait it out if they're not sold or rented quickly. Still, it might be time for you to come back on board."

He meets my gaze. We both know the angst on the other's mind. He's first to poke at my ongoing fear. "It seems all has been quiet. No threats or attacks?" He states it more as a question than a comment, in case he may have missed something. Mac, like Chase, is close-mouthed and finding out what both may know about Dimitri's current exploits is like trying to break into a Fort Knox vault.

"No sightings or problems for a while now. Why? Have you heard something?

"No. Not really." He hesitates. His mouth opens then shuts.

"Don't even think of holding back something that might be relevant to my life. I want to know what it is now, even if you think I shouldn't."

"Okay, but not a word to Chase. Mac will have my head if it gets back that I said something to worry you. As it is, Chase is not going to be happy about my coming here to recruit you again."

My look must spell confusion because he adds, "He has you right where he wants you now, at home, with three children in three years under the supervision of a horde of vets who are all tough, pig-headed, and loyal to him."

"Two years," I clarify.

"What?"

"Three children in two years, but who's counting. You make it sound like I'm nothing more than an emotionally fragile homemaker who lives and breathes under the thumb of her man. That is far from the truth. I've dealt with life-death problems and survived very well on my own. I'm tougher than I look, thank you very much."

Virgil's words smart, but I want to know about the pending problem more than I care about any hurt feelings, even if the comment holds a snippet of truth. I have replaced my former career ambitions with my role as wife and mother, letting my heart control my life and my fears dictate my decisions. I've let a vicious maniac consume my peace of mind like it's nothing more than a piece of meat on his dinner plate ready for him to devour whenever he wants. Virgil seems to have unleashed anger I hadn't realized I'd harbored. There's no way it's going to fade any time soon, especially since he knows something concerning my life that I don't.

My attention rivets back to him and I let out a deep sigh of frustration. "Stop changing the subject and tell me what's happened."

"I've no idea how relevant this is . . ." There's a pregnant pause while he mulls over if he should reveal what is on his mind. Then, convinced I'd never let him rest otherwise, he blurts out, "Does the name Buford sound familiar?"

"Buford?" I repeat it out loud, letting the name permeate for a bit before coming up empty. "Never heard it before. Why?"

"Mac was having a phone conversation with someone by that name, and a few minutes into their discussion, he mentioned Dimitri's name. Then, later on that day, he said he might have to leave for a week or so to report for a military meeting."

My eyes widen, and I move to the edge of my seat. "Again? Why?"

"He assured me," Virgil continues, accentuating the word *assured* when he notices my alarm, "that I shouldn't worry because it's in a safe zone of Afghanistan that sees no action. I couldn't get any more details out of him, so I told him not to worry, I have my morgue info to keep me busy while he's gone."

There's something so raw about the fear and uncertainty of a loved one dying in combat that it is impossible to ignore the possibility, no matter how much optimism and hope everyone expresses and clings onto. Virgil and Mac realized this early on in their relationship and opted for morbid humor as a coping mechanism. Tired of panicked episodes after accidentally discovering that Mac was called on a military assignment, Virgil subscribed to several mortuary magazines, hoping to nudge Mac into confiding more information. Another time, he hung a framed photo of the embalming process complete with a depiction of a corpse and labeled diagram so Mac could know the extent of the worry he had for his safety. It worked. Virgil now has far more information about what's happening and who may have to report than I do.

Chase and I . . . we play a tug-of-war game with him using all his force to yank complete control of the distressing situation and me wrenching back, demanding he share information. My way of thinking is that Mac's and Virgil's way works better. Although Virgil has moments of panic, they are short-lived and laced with optimism.

Military lingo conceals more than it reveals, so when I hear *report, safe zone, and no action*, I eliminate the *no* and replace *safe* with *war*. A new ache rolls over in my heart, and a noisy chaos of unanswered questions rattles inside my head. What does Dimitri have to do with military concerns in Afghanistan? Possible answers jumpstart frightening conclusions. Dimitri must be active there, or why would Mac have to report to discuss him with military intelligence?

There is no doubt in my mind that Buford must be part of that particular branch of the armed forces. Chase must still be part of military intelligence, so he must know how Dimitri is involved in Afghanistan. He says Dimitri's wanted by the CIA and is digging deep to hide. Seems as head of a Russian crime syndicate, he has morphed into an international mega force. We've had run-ins with him in the US as well as in Europe and now he and his nefarious undertakings have surfaced in the Middle East. He's a wanted man here for violating parole and is on a list of wanted men in other countries, but without more detailed information, I can only speculate how this impacts Chase's role in Afghanistan and the danger it presents for our family.

The seeds of more disturbing thoughts plant themselves in the fertile ground of worries that already spread in my mind. What if Dimitri's acquired power from his role in Russia and Afghanistan is so great, it becomes impossible to thwart him from having any one or more of us killed?

I am cold. The sudden chill in the air, compounded by agitation, make it impossible to sit still. Grabbing the ashtray, I invite Virgil back inside. Once he eases himself into the living room sofa with me sitting in one of the armchairs across from him, he continues with his original topic. "If you think you may not be ready to come on board full time, at least dip your toe into the water and come to Paris with me to see what is involved."

"Let me see what I can find out about this Buford person first, then I'll—" I don't get a chance to consider committing to going to Paris or even think any rational thoughts a moment longer because thumps of little legs pumping to get to the door are followed by peals of giggles and excited screeches.

"Daddy's home. Daddy's home."

Chase's presence fills the room. Teo climbs onto his shoulders, Juliette jumps into his arms, and Caroline hangs onto his back.

"I demand to know where all these little people came from." He catches my eye and winks, then struts over to Virgil and hands him Juliette.

"Here, have a kid."

Virgil's eyes flare. He has no idea what to do with the squirming bundle of energy on his lap. Juliette saves him from any awkwardness when she scoots onto her knees, stares him in the face, and plants a kiss on the cheek.

"Hi, Wergil," she says, wiggling off his lap and running toward the others. Virgil watches her quick retreat.

"As a mother, maybe you can tell me why children are always a tad sweaty and a bit sticky." His face is deadpan, but there's a pleased glimmer in his eyes.

"Sorry. She just ate some apple slices for dessert, and the sweaty part? Has to be because they are all in constant motion."

"We live here, Daddy, 'member?" Teo bends his head forward from Chase's shoulders, his hands clasped on each side of Chase's face.

"Oh yeah." Chase snaps his fingers as if he just remembered something important. "That's right, little man." Lifting him off, he lets Caroline slide from his back. He gives them all kisses, then strides toward where I'm sitting.

"You look beautiful," he whispers in my ear, lingering

to give my lobe a discreet nibble.

I blink my eyes, note my quick intake of breath, and cross my legs. It may or may not have been in that order. It's hard to tell because the room becomes warm, and the nerves in my body smolder. If Virgil notices anything he's not talking, but I do spot a knowing smirk. Now that he's been seeing Mac, his humor and temperament have ticked up a notch, so he seems enthused and relaxed all at the same time. I know the feeling well.

I uncross my legs and shoot Chase a small smile. *Later,* his eyes say.

"Hey Virgil. Good to see you. Mac told me you were both free for dinner tonight, so I took the liberty of making dinner reservations for the four of us at Daniels."

"Sounds great."

He looks toward me for my thoughts.

"Sure. The food is phenomenal." My mouth waters when I think of the Scottish Langoustine and the vanilla-infused tropical fruits. The foie gras is amazing, too. After chasing down three children today, sitting down to an adult meal in a quiet setting is a gift. I discreetly wave Eleanor inside to help with the end of the day roundup of all three.

"Good. Let's help get the troops into their pajamas and ready for bed," Chase says.

I freeze.

Chase freezes.

But it is too late. The dreaded words of pajamas and bed have been spoken out loud. Bedtime bedlam begins. Caroline runs screaming in one direction, Juliette the other, and Teo stands his ground and stamps his foot.

"Damn it, Miss Elnor, no jammies!" he shouts.

"Matteo!" Chase reprimands. Now it's Teo's turn to freeze. "You are not to speak to Miss Eleanor that way." He looks at me and shakes his head. "Where is he learning these words?" He reaches for Teo but is interrupted when his phone jingles.

"Chase Reardon." His tone is clipped. Clearly annoyed by what he's hearing, he exclaims, "Damn it, Lena. We needed that contract signed today. What additional changes does she want now?" He must sense my annoyance boring into his back because he claps his hand to his mouth and corrects himself with a loud, slow enunciation, "Darn it, Lena." Then he leaves in long, quick strides so he can use more colorful language without being heard.

I scoop up Teo. "Those are not polite words for you to use . . . or for Daddy. Now go tell Miss Eleanor you're sorry."

He snuggles his round baby cheek into my shoulder and plugs his thumb into his mouth. Letting him slide down, I give him a stern look and point toward Eleanor to remind him what he has to say. "I sorry," he says.

Eleanor nods at his apology and takes him by the hand while bending to coax Caroline out from under the table where she's run to hide from bedtime. She wraps her arm around Caroline's middle and scoops her up.

And then there was one.

Juliette looks at me and raises her pointer finger. "Just one more time, Mamma."

We both know that means she wants to nurse, and that her 'one more time' shows no sign of ending any time soon. Looking down at her beseeching face, I brush a lock of hair from her eyes and take her outstretched hand. Guilt has me thinking about that cigarette I just smoked. I am determined to make it my last.

"This will only take a minute," I tell Virgil, guiding Juliette toward the rocking chair in the nursery. She seems to just want this closeness, because it happens only before bedtime and lasts no more than a minute or two.

"Juliette's a mamma's girl," Caroline swivels her head and sings out as she's being led to the bathroom for her bath.

"Caroline, that's enough. Name-calling hurts feelings," I chastise, even though Juliette has yet to understand it as an insult.

Caroline nods like she knows it's wrong, but it's just a matter of time before she says it again. It must make her feel more grownup. Either that, or she's jealous of this attention Juliette is getting. Who can figure all this psychological stuff out? They're like little warriors armed with battle strategies to help them gain what it is they want or don't want.

I can't fault them, though. At least they know what they want. And me? It seems I can create a design that perfectly fits my body but cannot figure out how I fit into myself. If I haven't worked out how I want to live my life, how am I ever going to teach my children how to carve their way through life?

CHAPTER 18

"You're very quiet tonight. Is everything alright?" His measured gaze, from eyes so shockingly blue they mirror a cloudless sky, is intoxicating. Thoughts stretch in my mind. Beginning with Virgil's invitation to partner with him, they move right along to his notion that Chase has me right where he wants, at home with three children. They don't stop there, though. Unanswered questions about who the hell Buford is and how he relates to Dimitri's sordid plots march right in there with the rest.

A red haze of anger surfaces when I think of how I have to scuttle around for information about what's happening in our lives instead of getting it straight from Chase. The man is infuriating. No matter what I do or say, I cannot convince him that not knowing jacks up my fear and frustration until my blood boils with each new discovery I'm forced to uncover on my own.

My functional childhood reinforces his already-established notion that he has to man-up and insulate me from the consequences of his devastating one. I did experience a caring childhood. Three older brothers all looking out for me. Suffocating at times, but definitely protective. I never even had to deal with a pushy date.

Once, at a family barbecue, Beth offhandedly said, "Ali was forbidden fruit for Chase, but I'd say they felt something for each other ever since she was fifteen." That would have made Chase twenty-one at the time, but Beth was unbothered, since Chase and I had been married for over a year when she made the claim. Did not matter. My brothers glared, and Chase went into duck, dodge, and punch mode: eyes shifting, neck limber, fists flexing. Any attempt at a physical altercation by my brothers would have been foolish. I mean, what chance do a medical resident, a lawyer, and a chef stand against a trained black ops officer?

"No, not like that," Beth interrupted, when the tension mounted. "Innocent and sweet, like a first crush. Well, for Ali anyway."

So, Chase feels he has stiff competition when it comes to keeping me safe, and he's going to make sure everyone understands he has it under control. There's another factor too. I hate to admit it, but I think he resents me for my easy past and compensates for the guilt it produces by being overprotective. Yes, even Mr. Perfect has human shortcomings. He once angrily accused me of being born with a silver spoon in my mouth. That about says it all for how he feels about my past, so why should I bother trying to deny what is basically true? I never had to worry about money or alcoholism or a terminally ill mother. Aside from my mother's depression—which, I might add, did impact my happiness—I had a supportive and loving family.

I sweep my hair to the side and turn to let him unzip me while I toss around ideas about how to approach what's on my mind. I start simply. "Virgil has given me a lot to think about and . . ."

He wraps his arms around me as I slip out of my dress and pulls me close, breathing through my hair. The move resonates playful provocation. "Let's talk later . . ." his lips hover just above my ear. The warm rush of his breath brushes against my neck. The outside world evaporates, and reflexively, I stretch to the side to give his mouth easier access. He finishes his thought in between nibbles on my neck, "After we've had some alone time."

A moan escapes my throat, stifling the words I want to say, the words that signal my career ambitions and what could happen to us if I pursue those goals. His lips travel lower across my collarbone, and I weave my hands through his hair to pull him closer. Thoughts scatter, one for each nip and lick that sweeps across my breasts, until my mind empties of all except the feel of his roving mouth and hands.

His phone's jingle interrupts playtime. The name Buford looms on the screen in bold letters, snapping me back to reality. He dismisses the call and returns a smoking-hot gaze my way, but the fire is extinguished. This is no time to let bedtime games replace sensibility. I pull my wits together and try to sound casual. It doesn't work. The words slip out like a breached dam.

"Who is Buford, and why is he calling you at this hour?" Maybe I purposely want to take him by surprise. See how he likes being caught off guard for once.

"Just business. No one you know."

"Obviously I don't know who he is, or I wouldn't be asking."

His silence carries a typical MI stubborn stance: straight back, blank eyes, tight mouth. Must be illustrated in some spy manual as the standard face to pull when asked for information that should not be revealed. I've seen the same look on Mac and Sammy countless times.

This time, I refuse to back down.

"Well . . . who is he?"

"Why do you want to know so badly? Have you heard the name before?"

I've learned in my dealings with Chase that his response to a question with another question is a masterful way of avoiding a direct answer. It gives him time to figure out what I might know so he can measure his response with nondescript answers that fall just short of being outright lies. Next, he'll shift around the topic, offering vague details that are structured to conceal the terrifying specifics of the problem. This is how Chase's world works. Create a life, surround it with heavily-protected loved ones, and do not worry them about the dangerous possibilities that loom each and every day. It's not working this time.

"What makes you think I heard his name before?" Two can play this game.

"I did not say you heard it before. I only want to understand what is motivating your interest. Why, all of a sudden, are you concerned about one phone call?"

At this rate, we'll be swapping unanswered questions all night. So, as the civilian in these exchanges, I crack first.

"I heard Buford's name from Virgil who thought I might know who he is and how he might be connected to our problems with Dimitri." Ignoring the hard set of his jaw, I add, "Now Mac is leaving for Afghanistan on military business. Are these occurrences linked?"

"Virgil has no business disseminating information he knows nothing about. It is discomfiting for all of us, especially you, given all you have had to deal with these past few years."

He has you right where he wants . . .

"I want straight answers, not a vocabulary quiz. It is about time you let me determine what I can and cannot handle." I'm in no mood to sing to the tune of his Chaseisms while I walk a fine line between his compulsion to protect and his need to possess. Both assume I am as fragile as a child who must be shielded from the harsh realities of life.

He reaches out and massages my ear lobe, zooming in with that beautiful mouth to nuzzle my neck.

I swat his hand away. "Not happening." Control and tactile distractions in the bedroom invite liberating surrender and bliss. Use similar tactics during a crisis, and the results can be suffocating and demeaning. I shoot him a sharp eye. "Are you going to answer my questions or not, and if not, you better have a damn good reason why you won't."

He rubs the back of his neck. "I don't like when news travels through the grapevine this way. If Virgil overheard something, he should have asked Mac about it and not come to you for answers."

"You already said you don't like how this unfolded. There's no need to bring negative attention to Virgil. He's just as alarmed and confused as I am. Don't go on the attack against him, roping in Mac and Sammy and even Sunny in some joint effort to make sure he's silenced."

"Are you suggesting I'm going to trigger a kerfuffle?"

I whip out my phone and start tapping keys.

"What are you doing?"

"Consulting dictionary.com so we can finish this conversation."

"Okay, okay, I get it. You want answers." He reaches in and strokes my cheek. "I don't want you living in fear.

I lean into his touch. "I am afraid of what I don't know."

"You think having all the details makes you safer?"

"I'm not sure. I think not knowing gives my imagination license to conjure up all sorts of dreaded possibilities. It leaves me groping in the dark, searching for answers alone."

"You are not left in the dark and you sure as hell are not alone. We have Sammy and Mac and Sunny. You have me. Don't I make you feel safe?"

"Of course you do, but what about if I want to reestablish my career? That is going to require some travel. Do I take someone with me and live with the prospect that we face added danger because you are left shorthanded? We have three children to protect and there are Fiona and Liam to consider. Dimitri has threatened to kidnap Liam in the past. He tried to abort our children. I need to know what he might be up to next and how our problems may have escalated before I make any work-related decisions."

His silence rivals a graveyard at night.

"Then maybe it's best you stay local, grow your label here where it is safer."

Simple words, not any different from what I considered countless times. So why do I feel as if a dream has been drowned before it had a chance to float? I thought by now

I would have developed a namesake brand and a growing global enterprise that produced several collections a year. Instead, I'm shoehorned into a small namesake label constrained by my inability to take the necessary time needed to make it grow.

"I thought we could travel to Italy," he says. "With your practiced eye for quality and color, you could choose travertine from a quarry there to be used to panel the lobby walls in our new building."

I have helped select finishes before for new development projects and found the work satisfying. Now though, I have a different agenda. My gaze doesn't leave his.

"Tell me what's been happening and how this Buford person is involved," I murmur, clutching his hand.

His phone jingles from the night table. A quick peek reveals Buford is calling again. He reaches back and clicks it off. There is no way he wants me to hear his conversation with Buford and, given my demands for him to be transparent, he doesn't want to leave the room for a private conversation and deal with more probing questions afterwards.

"Go on." I clear my face of the fear I feel and wait.

"Buford operates a command center in Afghanistan. I reported to him after my rescue and then when I returned for my second debriefing."

"So why is he calling you now? I thought that assignment ended."

"It should have except for one lingering issue. Listen, this is going to sound crazy, but during my escape, I ran into Dimitri."

"You cannot be serious. In Afghanistan?"

"Yeah. He was *conducting business*. Dimitri always was a genius at knowing how to maximize misery for personal gain. It's no surprise that war is right up his alley." He blinks at me with slow unease as we embark on uncomfortable territory for him to talk about. The flashbacks and nightmares that rocked his body after he first returned still surface every now and again. I am going to have to tread lightly, but the subject cannot be avoided. I refuse to let concern hamper my right to know about the danger we all face. I reassuringly stroke his arm.

"I want to know. Believe me, I can take some hard knocks of truth. We're in this together. Now, what kind of business is Dimitri involved in?" Contrary to my bravado, a silent shiver creeps up my back. I have already begun conjuring all matter of ways that Dimitri has been sharpening his axe for the hit. Kidnapping, maiming, and killing are just a few of his tactics that stoke my anxieties.

"It seems Dimitri has graduated from drug trafficking to spearheading massive operations that sell munitions to enemy insurgents. My guess is he penetrated my target network and then made money off my kidnapping. Selling kidnap victims is a lucrative enterprise in Afghanistan. Ransom money paid to find and free hostages can be well into the millions."

The idea that our hard-earned money found its way into Dimitri's hands is sickening. The more I think about what Chase is saying, the more it makes perfect sense. Dimitri's fanatical obsession with vengeance, money, and power is limitless. Tons of cash can be made from arms and drug dealing, and lots of power gained from trading information to enemy governments and organizations.

The fact that this loathsome person has an even more powerful base and network of foot soldiers to do his bidding makes our situation even more precarious and uncertain. It's almost enough to make me long for the good old days when Dimitri and his small ring of thugs lopped off fingers.

"Do you think he stalked you on your assignment to ensure you were killed once he collected his millions?"

"At first, that's what I thought. I figured he wanted nothing more than to have my body as the bow on his gift-wrapped payday. But that wasn't the case. He may have tracked me there, but he didn't want me dead. He told me so himself."

If Dimitri had the opportunity to kill Chase and didn't, he must have used their meeting to make some kind of threat. Provoking Chase is Dimitri's specialty.

"What else did he say?"

Pain streaks across Chase's face. "Nothing. He was in a hurry to leave the compound, and I sure as hell wasn't going to hang around asking questions."

"I'm so grateful you made it home alive." I close my eyes and shut out the terrifying memories that stalked me when he was missing. Long, dark stretches of fear and loneliness that screamed inside my mind that he was lost forever.

Be brave, I remind myself. That was then. This is now. Demons from the past can shackle the mind to a chilling sameness that is done and gone. Dimitri's sexual assault and all the flashbacks I've suffered since have taught me that if you want to go to that dark space in your mind, bring a flashlight and a gun because there will be an all-consuming repetition of the worst.

Be brave . . .

"I still don't get why Buford is calling you," I nod toward his phone, "and contacting Mac."

"There's a silver lining to all of this."

I snort but give him my attention.

"Dimitri is a wanted man who is running out of options. He crossed the line when his weapons deals started interfering with US negotiations with the Taliban to end the war. Peace cannot be brokered if insurgents continue to get their hands on sophisticated weaponry to use against forces that are trying to stabilize the government. So now Dimitri is being sought by the US military and various allied intelligence organizations. Mac is being commissioned for routine digital surveillance and counterintelligence monitoring. His job will to be to provide tactical assistance from within the compound office. He won't be assigned to dangerous missions in enemy territory. He should be back in two weeks."

"And you? What's your part in all this?" I can barely get the words out.

He strokes my cheek with the cupped back of his hand. "Like I told you before, I'm off limits. My capture and escape more or less assures I won't be called back. You needn't worry. Dimitri will be apprehended soon. But we have to be careful." He pauses, and I study his face because I know there's more he's not telling.

"And why is that? We're always careful. What's changed that makes it more dangerous now than before?" I refuse to let him stop, even though I know there's more bad news to come.

He hesitates some more, hems and haws a bit, rubs the shadow on his chin with his fingers and then the back of his neck with his hand. He knows I will keep digging for information until I uncover the truth, so he goes against all his better instincts. "Buford's calling to follow up on a sighting. It seems the authorities identified the guy we saw at the rehab center as Dimitri's son, Yuri. They believe he can lead us to Dimitri's whereabouts."

"That's impossible. Yuri was killed in a gang war shootout in Moscow years ago. You told me so yourself."

"That is true. New intelligence indicates the egomaniac has several sons by different women in Russia, all named Yuri after Dimitri's father, who started the ring. *This* Yuri is quick with a gun and a knife, and he's smart. He holds advanced degrees in international politics and speaks several languages."

The terrorizing ramifications of this information race through my mind. Was Yuri there to hurt Juliette or kidnap Liam, then realized Chase was in pursuit with a gun and called it off? Either way, based on what I just heard, we are in a lot more danger than I realized. I can almost feel the noose tightening around our necks. Chase was especially concerned that Juliette was in danger that day, even though it was Liam who was missing. Apprehension stretches my nerves to the breaking point.

"Dimitri is coming after our children now, isn't he?" All had been quiet since that brute tried to abort the twins, so it was easy to assume that maybe, just maybe, this time it would all stop. I know Chase still hasn't told me everything. He never does, but right now I'm on overload. This is about all I can handle.

"Dimitri will never hurt our children, or any of us, for that matter."

"How can you be so sure?"

"Because organizations with powerful people are leaning on anyone who may know where he's hiding. They're tracking his sons, friends, family—anyone in his network who can lead to his whereabouts. Listen to me." He places his hands on either side of my face and makes me look him in the eye. "I will never let him hurt you or our children. We have crews and strategies in place that will prevent that from ever happening."

I wipe my eyes and firm up my backbone. I wanted the truth and now that I have it, it serves no purpose to unravel. If the *truth* be known, truth is not all it's cracked up to be. Right now, it seems to be kicking up a host of new problems that are out of my control to predict or solve.

I said I could handle knowing what has been happening, and I will, but not without formulating some offensive strategies of my own. Locking my trembling hands at my sides, I keep my voice from betraying my fear.

"I want to sign up for target practice and learn how to shoot." My tone is even and succinct. As expected, his response is incredulous and strained.

"That doesn't make sense. We have plenty of people here who have been trained to hit a target better than anyone you will ever know."

"I hear your confidence in yourself and those who protect our family. This will be for my benefit. A sort of just-in-case-all-else-fails approach. Dimitri communicates from either the barrel of a gun or the tip of a knife. I hate the idea of firing a gun, but I'm tired of feeling like I have no control over what may happen when it comes to dealing with Dimitri."

"I like when you lose control." He grazes his fingers across my breast and his mouth lingers near my ear. "All that recklessness released." Kisses rain down my neck. "So, if we're done with this conversation . . ."

He is distracting me while pretending he hasn't heard a word of what I've just said. Skillful tactic, but once again, it's time to reeducate. Lassoing my libido—no small feat with his lips nuzzling my neck—I take in a quick breath and get right to the point.

"I want to know that I can count on myself to protect our children if necessary. It wasn't so long ago that you, Sammy, and Mac were deployed at the same time. There are no guarantees that it will not happen again, and you know you all would report. I wouldn't expect anything less. So . . ." I ogle him with a fierce stare, "Are you going to teach me, or do I have to go to a shooting range and hire an instructor?"

"You are issuing lots of ultimatums tonight."

"I have no choice. It's the life we lead."

"It's the life I've led you to."

I hold my finger to his lips. It's not fair for him to carry a heavy residue of guilt for problems he did not cause. "Don't blame yourself for what's happened. I don't."

"It's because of me that you face this danger." Pain, regret, and doubt embed his gaze.

My heart squeezes so tight, it feels it might burst. "It's because of you that I feel alive and full of ideas. Before we met, it was like I was asleep, dreaming about what my life could be. You give me life-affirming adventures."

"More like life-jarring." His gaze is strong. "So much has happened that has gone wrong in my life, but you . . .

you were the one thing I got right." He cups my face with his hands, moves his lips to mine, and plants a searing kiss that weakens my knees and surrenders my resolve. Before we fall into bed, hurried and hungry for release, he says, "I'll teach you how to shoot." He may have added a *god help us all,* but passion grabs my senses, so I'm not sure.

I *am* sure, though, that the safety of children, home, and husband take precedence over job aspirations. There's time enough to recover the part of me that was on the path to a career as a designer and brand creator. I'll figure out where I want to be once this maniac is caught and jailed. Surrendering to his touch, thoughts evaporate from my mind like steam on a bathroom mirror. With every movement of his hands and mouth on my body, the weight of fear is replaced by a life so vibrant and so alive, it pulses with color.

CHAPTER 19

I wake to the loud clanging of pots and pans and the smell of fresh-brewed coffee. Slipping on my robe, I brush my teeth, then saunter toward the sounds of three high-pitched voices and one deep one issuing orders. Chase and the kids are cooking pancakes in a kitchen that looks like it's been burgled. A layer of flour dusts the countertops and floor. Pots and pans cover every inch of the tabletop, while spatulas, ladles, and wooden spoons streaked with batter lay abandoned on chairs and cabinet shelves. Teo, clad in an apron that reaches to his ankles, stirs a large bowl of pancake batter with a dipper the size of his head. Caroline demonstrates how it's done, oblivious to the white muck that dangles from her left ear. Juliette's duck barrette bobs haphazardly in Chase's hair as, hoisted atop his shoulders, she reaches for a sack of flour from the pantry shelf.

"Got it, Daddy," she huffs, but it's too heavy for her small hands and she's forced to let it drop. Chase thrusts out one hand to catch it while clasping Juliette's legs to his chest with his other. He places the flour onto the only remaining uncluttered section of countertop and slides Juliette off his shoulders.

"We're making pancakes, Mamma," Caroline calls out as she adds a cup of washed blueberries to the mix. There's enough stacked pancakes to feed a marine platoon, and still the mixing continues.

"That's some stack of delicious-looking pancakes you all have made."

"I couldn't have done it without the help of my mess hall squad. Right, soldiers?"

Caroline and Teo stand at attention and snap salutes. Juliette covers her mouth and giggles.

"Private Reardon," Chase stares down Juliette with one eye, the corner of his mouth quirking, "there is no laughing while saluting."

Eyes dancing with mirth, Juliette stifles a smile and offers a tepid salute that, if she wasn't so young, I would have thought mocking.

"Private," Chase repeats, "you are your mother's daughter."

Missing the innuendo, Juliette shrugs her shoulders and nods at the obvious before brandishing a spatula and climbing on top of the chair to flip a man-sized pancake. I cast my eye over the kitchen. Definitely a *mess* hall.

"How many pancakes have you made?" I start shelving the excess utensils and pans before Sunny sees what the *squad* has done to his meticulously-organized kitchen.

"Financial Management Analyst," Chase orders, "we need a tally." Everyone's confused, including me. "Who's our bean counter?" he clarifies, only to be greeted by more silence from the confused gaggle of kids. "I mean pancake counter," he adds.

Caroline squints and begins the slow count of piled pancakes, then shouts out, "Eighteen!"

Chase discreetly motions with his chin to the stove, causing Caroline to scamper onto a chair to include the additional pancakes stacked on the warming tray. "Twenty-four with those," she points to the just-cooked batch. The twins nod, making it official.

"Excellent job," he tells her, picking up the container of flour to mix yet another batch. She beams with pride.

I remove the flour from Chase's hands and the barrette dangling from his hair. "I think we're good."

His answer is to cut a piece of stacked blueberry pancakes dripping with maple syrup and slip it into my mouth.

"Mmm, they're delicious."

He kisses my sticky lips just as I swallow. "You're delicious," he whispers, cupping my ass and tugging me closer. A hair's breadth from my mouth, he palms my breast at an angle the children can't see, and we lock lips, tongue and all.

"Good morning," Sunny chirps, walking into the kitchen.

"I help Daddy make pancakes," Teo proudly tells Sunny.

"Your daddy is very busy this morning." Sunny eyes us with a straight face. He surveys his kitchen and starts stacking excess utensils, pots, pans, dishes, and cups to be put away.

My cheeks heat to deep pink as I escape from Chase's loosened arms and start clearing the table for breakfast.

Chase is undaunted. Giving me a disarming grin, he comes in for seconds, and it's not pancakes that he wants.

"Will you stop." I elbow his side. "We have an audience, for heaven's sake." I scrape off a small clump of pancake batter from the side of his neck. He uses the proximity to nuzzle my neck. "You're impossi—"

A loud crash steals our attention from each other.

"Shit!" Teo says, bending his head to survey the shattered bowl that spins and splatters batter across the kitchen floor. Caroline shakes her head and closes her eyes. Juliette becomes completely still. They know that, while accidents may happen, using that word spells trouble.

"Teo, you know you should not use that word and what happens when you do," Chase admonishes. He heads toward Teo's bedroom to fetch his piggy bank.

Teo's lips turn down and quiver. He has come to understand that every time he says an inappropriate word, he loses a nickel. He doesn't understand exactly what a nickel is or what it can buy. If he did, he probably would not mind if one was taken, but he is smart enough to know that he doesn't want to lose any when his sisters keep accumulating more.

Chase snaps off the plastic disc at the bottom of the bank and shakes out a nickel. When Teo sees it disappear into his father's pocket, he puts his head down and cries. It's pitiful to watch, but we've tried just about everything to get him to stop using swear words. We've ignored him, explained why he shouldn't say them, wagged our fingers, and told him no.

Nothing worked until Devie suggested a positive reinforcement method. She actually looked at us at the end of an overwhelming day with lots of crying, whining, and arguing and said, "Pay them all off." That's when Sunny suggested we use nickels. Devie had rolled her eyes at the stakes. "At least make it five bucks," but Chase and I agreed to the nickel because we saw it as more of a symbol of maintaining good behavior than an actual monetary bribe.

I pick up Teo and put him on my lap. "You know you are not supposed to say that word. It is not a nice word to use." He cries louder, burying his face into my chest, and I put my voice to his ear. "If you behave, later you can get your nickel back and maybe another one, too. Isn't that right, Daddy?" I look at Chase, widening my eyes and nodding, ready to say almost anything to silence Teo's wails.

Chase taps his pocket, "I'm keeping it safe right here for you to earn back later."

Teo turns his head and studies his father's face and then his pocket. "No spend it?"

"Nope. It's just for you, little man."

He quiets, then scoots off my lap to sit in his seat and eat his pancakes, the nickel forgotten while, I am fairly certain, the swear word stays etched in his mind.

"Mamma," Caroline interrupts the blissful silence and cup of iced espresso I had just started appreciating. "Did you make the bunny cake for school?"

Every year her pre-K runs a bake sale as part of their fundraising activities to raise scholarship funds for scholarship students. Last year, I baked and decorated a coconut vanilla crème cake in the shape of a rabbit that seemed to have been a hit.

Sh... I catch the word before it slips out of my mouth so all anyone hears is a lopsided sounding *shoot*. I had been so preoccupied with my meeting with Virgil and then my conversation with Chase that I forgot to buy the necessary ingredients.

"You promised," Caroline says. "Wilcox's mom even heard you say so. She wants to buy it because it's his favorite. She said we can have a playdate and eat some."

Chase's interest is piqued.

"Who's Wilcox?"

"My bestest friend. He's so funny. Sometimes he brings me a chocolate kiss for snack." She giggles into her hand. "He gave me a kiss once, too."

Chase shoots me a pointed stare. "Do you who know this kid is?" He pauses, and I know he's trying to place the name. "What does his father do for a living?"

"They are not even four years old, so I'm going to pretend you didn't ask me that."

"What's Wilcox's last name?" he asks Caroline, ignoring my comment.

"Peckard," Caroline pipes before turning to me with another request. "Don't forget to add chocolate kisses for the top of the cake. Wilcox really likes them."

Leaning into my ear, Chase whispers, "Wilcox Peckard?" That's like an invitation to be mocked."

I crook my finger at him and point to the hallway. Reluctantly, he follows.

"Here's the thing," I start once I know we can't be heard. "You are not going to inquire about what Wilcox Peckard Sr. does for a living." He bobs his head in reluctant acceptance. "There will be no snide comments about their names. It's a family name that they honor. And most of all, you are going to repeat to yourself that they are only three-and-a-half years old! Understood?"

"Yeah, I got it."

"Good. Now, I've got to run to the market. Can Sammy drop me off before taking you to your meeting? I'll wait for him to swing back and pick me up if I have to."

"No. Mac will take you. I'm already running behind schedule."

"Is Mac still available?"

"Yeah. He leaves tomorrow." He shoots off a quick text to Mac. "I should be home around eight. I know you're pressed for time, but don't forget to wait for Mac to drive you to the store. He said he'll be here in fifteen minutes."

"Of course." The reminder was not necessary, but I know he repeated it because he's worried. I am, too. We both need to reaffirm that we're following stringent safety measures.

"Mamma, I want to come with you," Juliette pouts. We haven't finished breakfast. She's still in her pajamas, and I've yet to shower. At this rate, I'll never leave.

"I'm in a hurry, sweetie. You can help me bake when I get back."

"No! I want to come." She starts to cry.

"You're such a mamma's girl," Caroline tells her between mouthfuls of pancakes.

Juliette cries louder, holding out her arms to me while Caroline singsongs, "Baby, baby, Juliette's a baby."

Before I can admonish Caroline, Chase returns to the kitchen. "We have told you again and again not to call your sister names. Now, go to your room for a thirty-minute time out."

I pick up Juliette, who continues to sob.

"No fair!" Caroline shouts, her mouth set in a straight

line that looks just like his when he's angry. "Teo says a bad word and only has to pay a dumb nickel. I say *mama's girl* and get sent to my room for THIRTY times." She means minutes but clearly, she understands the difference between the two punishments. "That is sexm, Daddy!"

My guess is she means sexist or sexism and must have heard Devie use the term. Devie often complains that the modeling culture treats females poorly. They are disrespected, and delayed salaries are expected negatives of the job. The fact that Caroline could apply the term to a life situation is impressive. I wouldn't say Chase is sexist, but the double-standard shoe fits him nicely.

"What you are trying to say, Caroline, is that Daddy is *sexist*," I clarify, hiding my smile and putting a placated Juliette down to climb into her seat and finish her pancakes. Caroline angrily crosses her arms and nods while I make a mental note to tell Devie to watch what she says now that we have three little mouthpieces listening and repeating.

Chase's answer is to point to her room and tell her to get going before he adds more time to her punishment for calling him names, too. Squinty-eyed, she snatches her plate of pancakes and a napkin from my outstretched hand and stomps off to her room. Once out of earshot, Chase shakes his head. "She may be just under four, but she mouths off like she's fourteen. Where are they learning these words?"

"They are quick studies. They hear something once, absorb it, then repeat it when it works to their advantage. Any one of them could be hired to work in sales. They are that good." I'm reminded of those occasions I gave in to their repeated whining for more cookies or a new toy just for some silence.

He seems befuddled until, in typical Chase fashion, he switches gears and strides toward me wearing a ridiculous grin. "So now you think I'm sexist, too?" he says, a warm, smooth timbre to his voice. Nuzzling my neck with his lips, he plants a maple-sweetened kiss on my lips, then one for each of the three tattooed stars that run down the side of my neck. My eyes involuntarily close and don't open again until that special place south of my waist pulses for more.

He scoops another forkful of pancakes into his mouth, then, plenty pleased with himself, scuttles through the door whistling. A split second later, he pops back his head. "Forget those chocolate kisses. *Wilcox Peckard* doesn't need more encouragement than he's already been given."

Clearly, Freud's psychosexual latency stage of childhood has never featured into his thinking. Whether his daughters are three or thirteen years old, the same prejudices hold. I would bet good money that his reaction would be different if Teo was the one who liked someone and did the kissing. I'm going to have to remind him to let go of this double standard. Good luck with *that*, I snort, stuffing my mouth with another bit of pancakes and rushing toward the bedroom to throw on some clothes.

• • •

The uncrowded supermarket allows me to scoot the shopping cart down the narrow aisles. Juliette, her hooded jacket unzipped over her pajamas, laughs in the child's seat as I run with the cart. Dressed in yoga pants and Chase's old sweatshirt, with my hair swept into a messy bun to match Juliette's uncombed ponytail, we could be billboard models for victims of a house heist.

I make a beeline toward the baking section and add sugar and baking powder to the cart. If I make it home in half an hour, I'll have just enough time to bake, cool, frost, and decorate the cake for the sale later this afternoon.

It's when I'm barreling down an aisle in search of vanilla that I spot Mimi Hardwick and Lily Michaels, two of Charlotte's cohorts, canvassing the shelves on the other side of the aisle. I push my cart into a U-turn getaway, but I'm not fast enough. Wearing smart business dresses, they beam matching shark smiles.

"Alicia, it's been a long time. How *nice* to see you again," Mimi says. It's no secret that Mimi turned against me after I gave my notice at Estelle Designs. She took every opportunity to insult my work, even sabotaged several of my pieces with crooked seams and mismatched corners. I'm guessing she felt slighted that Virgil and Charlotte chose me and not her to partner with. At the time, I couldn't give it much thought. Chase was deployed in Afghanistan and most of my energy was consumed with trying to get the funds to buy into the partnership. When Chase went missing, and I found out I was pregnant, everything fell apart. It's strange how life unexpectedly spins you in circles until every ounce of inner strength is needed just to remain upright.

I know Mimi and Charlotte still talk, and I think Charlotte periodically uses Mimi as a consultant. Lily, well, Lily is just plain lazy, averse to work and resistant to change. She still works at Estelle Designs, too,

"Hi, how are you, Mimi and . . . Lily, right?" I know Lily's name, but why reveal it is worth remembering? She nods. Stretching my lips back, I work hard to match their toothy grins when all I really want to do is buy what I need and get home to bake this damn cake.

Mimi's generally-flustered persona is cool and calm. Her once coiled and frizzy hair is coiffed into a smooth, highlighted bob. She eyes my clothes with a glint in her gaze that judges my shamble to her polish.

Gripping the handle of my cart, I meet her disapproving sneer with a calm assurance that refuses to apologize for my appearance. Inside I'm cringing, wishing I had a dimmer to tone down the glaring supermarket lights.

"We are well," Mimi answers for both of them, a clear indication that she's the one in charge. My guess is she was promoted after Charlotte, Virgil, and I left. Hence, the makeover and smug attitude. "We're here to pick up maraschino cherries for the Old Fashioned cocktails Charlotte's serving at the luncheon this afternoon."

"Will you be attending?" Lily asks, smiling indulgently. She knows full well I have not been invited. "Virgil will be there, along with other fashion industry aficionados." She scrutinizes my face for a read on my feelings. I blink and offer her nothing.

"No."

"How is Chase?" Mimi enthuses when I don't bite the bait. "I don't know if you remember," her eyes meet Lily's, "Alicia's husband, Chase, is who helped arrange for the jazz band that made our runway fashion show that year such a success."

Juliette hears Chase's name and looks up. "Daddy," she says smiling.

"That's right," Mimi beams close to Juliette's face.

"Chase is your Daddy."

Juliette nods, smiling. "Daddy sexme."

Holy Mother of God. My children are developing parrot mouths, tossing out versions of what they hear with no brain filter. I make my face go blank, pretending I didn't hear what Juliette clearly enunciated. Mimi, lips pursed like she's sucking Sour Nerds, darts a nervous glance at Lily, who is too busy skittering her thumbs across her phone to notice. She's probably Googling how to file a complaint with Child Services.

My mouth beams another false smile. "Uh, I've got to get going. It's good seeing you both."

"You, too," they chirp, two harmonized wind-up dolls droning in unison.

I head toward the checkout, snapping open a small box of animal crackers I grab from the shelf. This will keep Juliette's little mouth busy eating instead of talking. Realizing I have forgotten vanilla, I look heavenward and head back down the baking aisle, which is now empty. Tossing vanilla into the cart, I'm just about to head back to the cashier when Lily's high, pitchy voice from the next aisle pulls me up short.

"Oh my, how the mighty fall. That *was* Alicia Cesare, right? The designer who has that jacket line that is doing so well."

"That's her, alright. For a hot minute she had a promising partnership with Charlotte and Virgil."

"I remember she left Estelle Designs to pursue that prospect. She also was on the fast track at Estelle's, too. So, what happened to make her look a mess with a kid in tow and a cart full of baking supplies?"

"She chose the gilded life with that hot developer. Now she lives off of his dreams and money instead of fulfilling her own."

"You mean *that* Chase . . . Chase Reardon of Reardon Realty."

"The very same."

"Talk about fulfilling dreams. His must be worth close to half a billion. I noticed one of his properties going up on the corner of Eighty-Sixth and First. That massive footprint spans at least two city blocks. How did she snag that mogul?"

Silence, then snide laughter. "Babies and lots of them. Charlotte said she has one right after another. Wouldn't put it past her to be pregnant again."

"She's that desperate for a rich man that she'd compromise her career and her body. Who does that anymore?"

"Obviously, she does. Maybe that slew of staff Charlotte mentioned they employ makes it worth the trouble. She claims they even have a butler from Pakistan, of all places."

"She certainly doesn't dress the part. Did you see what she was wearing? She seemed so . . . blah. She looked boring. She sounded boring."

"I guess you can afford to be uninteresting when you have that kind of money."

Their voices waft down the aisle. Clamping down hard on the handle of the shopping cart, I take a deep breath. Their comments are especially hurtful, since they're steeped in the notion that I'm nothing more than a social climber whose sole purpose in life was to marry someone rich. They're like typical Park Avenue types who slap labels on people without knowing who they really are.

Did I just do the same?

I shake my head. At least I don't make a habit of trying to shove people into tidy little boxes without digging deeper.

Their petty insults that relegate our life to trite stereotypes smack of Charlotte's gossip. A hideous woman, with the sting of a scorpion, she always manages to hit a nerve.

The part about me being uninteresting and lackluster pushes all those old buttons I had when Chase and I first met. I saw then that my accomplishments did not compare to his. He was older. I had just graduated college. At some point, I figured I would fine-tune and expand my design abilities until I had a thriving brand. Now here I am, several years later, wedged between mediocrity and melodrama with only a minor brand to call my own and a maniac in pursuit of my family.

I rein in my temper, my mind drifting to when I worked with Mimi and Lily at Estelle Designs. Even then, when I was Charlotte and Virgil's junior assistant, I had little respect for Mimi and Lily's abilities. Mimi is a mediocre seamstress who creates by imitation and Lily's sole purpose is to pore through figures to search for ways why company changes are not cost-efficient. I don't need their approval to measure my successes or my shortcomings. Their gossip is mostly nonsense, anyway. To think that Sunny is our butler is as ridiculous as believing there is a cluster of staff on hand to serve our every whim. Those jabbering idiots have no idea of the gravity of the problems we deal with.

I maneuver the cart past bunches of flowers that cling to shelves in suffocating cellophane. Putting additional boxes of animal crackers for Caroline and Teo into the cart, I head toward the checkout counter. Juliette pokes through her box and selects a monkey. Turning it different ways, she chews off and swallows its head, laughing when she studies the headless cookie. Through all their supposed innocence, there is a frightening bent to children.

She gives me a disarming smile and rattles off again, "Daddy sex me."

"Is that right? Can you say, *Daddy is in jail*?"

She looks up, confused, and shakes her head no. Now, it's my turn to laugh. I give her tickling nibbles on her neck, and she bends it to her shoulder and giggles.

CHAPTER 20

I fall asleep wondering if I'll be able to start my own fashion house and wake up with myriad ideas on what would be needed to make it happen. For a long while, I stared at the ceiling in the dark, reevaluating my life's path while trying to invite sleep.

Chase and I have gotten so used to our current lives here at home. The part of his persona that frets about our safety remains in check because he knows that I'm at home with the children with Sunny here and Sammy or Mac standing guard and escorting us places.

Even the small factory I own is a family fortress. Built into the Apennines mountains near the Tuscan town of Romagna, it's where my extended family lives and operates a vineyard and winery. They have a huge presence in the town. Any strangers are noted and politely questioned. Even so, the few times I traveled there on business, Chase cleared his schedule and came. His concern is going to flash neon when I tell him what I'm planning to do.

My fingers itch for a cigarette. I fight the urge, and instead of a nicotine fix, the crisp texture of taffeta, the rustle of a chiffon evening dress, and the shimmer of a smoky black silk sequin dress floating down the runway during my own fashion show lull me to sleep.

With the early morning sun, I run my fingers through my hair, thinking about all the preparation that's required to expand. For starters, I'll have to find a larger factory, one that's capable of producing my jackets and fine-knit sweaters and dresses with precision and on a larger scale than the one I use now. I have a strong wholesale buy from my recent collection of jackets, but it's limited and contained to the US. I will need time to expand to designer crafting of dresses for both evening and daywear, along with skirts, blouses, pants, and coats. I'll make my sketchpad spring to life as a pre-collection that demonstrates superb craftsmanship and chic style.

The day feels charged with possibilities. I sketch a red rose with soft, vibrant curves for my visit to David, the tattooist in Williamsburg. Inked on the inside of my forearm, the rose will serve as a reminder of all I have to be grateful for. It was a small rosebush that a farmer carried to plant in a garden in Kabul that gave Chase the spark of hope he needed to safely get home. The rose and Chase survived a roadside bomb. The farmer did not. Chase carried the bush to the Kabul garden before he flew home. The tattoo, like the rose itself, will serve as a reminder that confidence and dreams pave paths to success.

Fueled with optimism, my mind whirls with ideas as I head to the kitchen to start a pot of coffee. With fewer bricks and mortar shops, I envision designs on an online platform with 3D views and iPads to place orders for delivery. A "see now, buy now" approach that allows customers to buy straight from the runway is a must.

I'll need a global presence and that would entail more travel and meetings in different time zones. A definite drawback to having three children. I consider how technology allows for efficient FaceTime and Zoom meetings with vendors and investors. This will limit the cost of travel while permitting more time for me to spend with family.

I want this, I tell myself, and I'm suddenly struck by this wild desire to grab all life has to offer with both hands. Travel, love, fashion, art, family. I need to find my place in this world with all of them there, not just fragments of some that lock me in one place. I can create a new journey, travel down different avenues, embrace other innovative and challenging prospects even if we are stalked by a vengeful maniac who wants me dead sooner rather than later.

My confidence sinks.

I swallow hard when I consider this obstacle. It is the major reason why Chase will object to my plan to grow a fashion house. Remembering what it was like when I worked full time in the industry, his voracious mind will calculate the amount of time and number of different places I will have to be as I move forward now. He will determine what is necessary to ensure I stay safe while pursuing that path again. It will all add up to fewer guarantees that my security can be maintained. He is going to become unhinged.

He will point out that my decision throws the safety of others into question. But then . . . I could mention how we could hire new help, someone with military experience who understands how to protect targets. Nope, that won't work either. I can hear his answer just as well as I can see the face he'll pull, along with strands of his hair. "That is out of the question." I mimic, deepening my voice. "Having a crew that knows and understands how Dimitri operates has kept us alive. Someone who doesn't understand the complexities of the problem would only be a liability." Ugh, damn it! This is going to be a hard sell. Sitting down, I rub my face and think some more.

If I take . . . No! *when* I take this risk, I'll just have to be careful and bring Sammy along. That will leave Mac, Sunny, and Eleanor here. There are no guarantees in life, so if the worst were to happen and Chase, Mac, and Sammy are deployed together again, I would operate out of Summit with Clyde helping just as he did before, and if Eleanor can wield a knife as forcefully as she does a needle, she'll be an added asset. That's what I'll tell him, and he's going to have to accept that taking a chance on building a successful enterprise while outwitting the devil, Dimitri, can work. My decision is final and starts this morning. Carpe diem. I plan to make each day of my future count, one moment at a time. There have already been too many detours and compromises. Enough of putting my professional life on hold because of Dimitri's threats.

It's early. The house is quiet. I pick up my sketchpad and, on its pages, I see myself sharper than ever before. My talent, guilt, shame, fear, love, insecurity, and conflict jump off the pages with each design. The violet-checked and backless floral silk dresses tell me Chase is safely home from his deployment. The pale cashmere coat signals Caroline's birth. The gauzy skirts in pale blue and lilac, worn with pastel bodysuits, tell the story of Teo and Juliette's healthy entry into the world. The black velvet and wool dresses, pants, and jackets, with hidden zippers and no buttons, speak of a dark period when Chase was missing. This sketchpad represents who I am and, even more so, who I'm yet to become. It affirms that I'm committed to live my life without being stifled by fear.

Now all that's left is convincing Chase that this is what I'm doing. Traveling to Paris with Virgil is where it begins.

I wipe my sweaty palms on my bathrobe. *He has you right where he wants you.* Virgil's words permeate my enthusiasm. I push them out of my mind and start drawing a plunging V-neck summer shift that flows dreamily to the ankle. *Everything about her is boring . . .* snippets of Mimi and Lily's conversation seep into my thinking and I add lively floral piping along the contours of the white dress to lessen the sting of their criticisms. Words can be thorns that prick in all the right places until your creativity drains and your imagination empties. I won't let that happen. Part of me, the part that was once a full-time fashion designer, feels right at home sketching in preparation for the Paris trip.

I hear the shower running in the master bedroom suite and know Chase is awake. I tiptoe into the children's rooms. They're still asleep. This should give us the chance to talk without the interruption of busy little hands and fast feet finding trouble.

Chase walks into the kitchen, shirtless, his chest rippling with muscle right down to his exposed navel.

My jaw drops, and I force my eyes back to my sketchpad. *Pay attention, Alicia. You've serious business to discuss with Mr. Perfect that he's not going to like.* Conscious of his eyes on me, I look up and meet his.

"You're up early." He bridges the distance between us in two large steps and kisses me hard, letting his teeth graze my lower lip while his hand goes in for my breast. As soon as it makes contact, I hear my sharp inhale of breath. This distraction is terrible to my cause. I tear my lips away, steady my breathing and give him a half smile.

"We need to talk."

He stops just short of coming in for a second round and straightens.

"Okay." He says it tentatively, watching my body tense before adding our go-to question when we're doubtful about how the other is feeling. "Is everything alright?" Three words we have gotten into the habit of asking given Dimitri's ongoing threats.

"Everything is fine." I blink nervously and force myself to keep from wringing my hands. "There is no easy way for me to say this after our last conversation about the danger we face, so I'm going to just spit it out." I lift my chin. "I'm returning to work full time."

Storm clouds cross his face. "You must be kidding. You have three young children, and we're dealing with serious threats made against our family. How do you propose to be able to return to a hectic work schedule, especially now that Mac is gone?"

"I've never been more serious about something, and . . . *we* have three children," I clarify, my eyes flashing. "That hasn't stopped you from building a real estate empire. Why do I have to be the one with the restrictions? You've known me long enough to understand that I define myself by creating. What is so hard to understand about the simple idea that I have dreams and aspirations just like you do?"

"So, now our marriage has become a competition . . . a race to see who can succeed more." He waves his hand, sputtering. "Your immature judgment about my business is making you view my success as a power play to limit yours. It's not!"

I see where this argument is headed and massage my temples to deal with what is becoming a drag-out, no-holds-barred fight. "I want to pursue my career."

He frowns, silently seething.

"I know this is a lot for you to digest after our lives have settled into a routine. I've considered that Mac will be gone and plan on having Sammy come with me to Paris."

"Paris!" he barks, self-control shattering. "Just the other night, you wanted to know all the details about Dimitri's threats. You even wanted to learn how to shoot, for Christ's sake. Now, you're talking about running off to jumpstart your career. You're all over the place." He points his forefinger in the air this way and that, then runs his fingers through his hair, spiking it in different directions. "When is this trip to France supposed to happen?" He hardens his jaw and pins me with a glare.

When surveying the chilly water of a swimming pool, I figure it's best to dive in and get the initial shock over with quickly, rather than lowering your body one torturous bit at a time.

"Next week. Thursday, to be exact. Like I was saying, Sammy can come with me to ensure my safety. That leaves Eleanor and Sunny here until Mac returns. You said yourself Mac's assignment is routine and that he'll be back in two weeks." I throw his nonchalant words about military missions back at him with just a tad of regret when I see the torn expression on his face. I don't mean for them to hurt him, just make him realize how serious I am about picking up my career where I left off before he went missing and the children were born. "As far as target practice goes, I'm as serious as ever about wanting to learn how to shoot. As soon as I return, you or any one of your marine buddies can teach me." I stare into his worried eyes and put my hands on either side of his face, forcing his eyes to meet mine. "We can do this. I'm not leaving the planet and . . . this is not a competition."

He looks at me skeptically.

"Okay, maybe I am a bit driven to achieve my goals. You've smashed through your pinnacle several times. You survived Afghanistan, then went on to graduate from Yale, and now you're acquiring one development project after another. You've achieved massive success. I've barely nicked my first. Besides, you know working in fashion design and creating and growing my own label are goals I've had since we first met. So, mostly I'm doing this for myself."

"Yeah, I get it." He pulls his face from my hands. "And you knew that marrying me came with dangerous caveats that required concessions."

I draw in a long, exasperated breath. "Don't you dare lecture me about concessions. I have spent the better part of our time together trying to figure out if I have the stamina to live the life we lead together. When you were missing, I had to draw on inner strength I didn't know I had just to survive day to day. I put my life on hold then, just as I've done now, to do what's needed to see that our lives run smoothly and safely." I stop to gather my thoughts and say what I've also been thinking. "I don't want to wake up one day and find I'm not where I expected myself to be."

"Not where you expected to be?" he hurls the words back in my face. "I thought you were happy being married. That our life together is the life you want to live. Are you saying I'm not enough for you . . . that our family is not enough to make you happy?" He gives me that look that oscillates between toughness and vulnerability, and I know my decision is taking him back to a past where control over his life slipped through his fingers every time he was forced to deal with Dimitri's vengeful tactics and his father's alcoholism.

"Of course, I'm happy being married. You and our children are my life, my loves, but . . ." Staring at the wall ahead, I swallow past my next words because I know how he's going to react.

"Go on. But what?"

I look him in the face. "My craft is a part of who I am, too."

He crosses his arms over his chest, struggling to rein in his temper.

"How long is this trip?"

I take another plunge into that icy pool. "Ten days."

"That's out of the question," he shouts, fear and frustration fusing into fury. "There is no way you can be that distant, for that length of time and stay safe."

"Shh, you'll wake the kids." I turn and step into the hallway to peek in the direction of their bedrooms. All is quiet.

"Why should that matter? Are you worried they'll overhear that you're planning to leave them for two weeks? How are they supposed to deal with you being gone that long? Juliette is still asking to nurse. You can't just ignore that they're still babies."

One-two-three, the guilt gun is fired into my back. I spin around so quickly, I nearly trip. He catches me by the elbow, and I wrench it away, refusing to put the brakes on my plan no matter what he says.

"It's ten days, not two weeks, and you are not fighting fair. The children will be fine for that length of time without me here. Juliette doesn't have to nurse. It's just something she feels she needs. I'll be sure to FaceTime with them every day. Eleanor and Sunny will hold things together here, and I won't be traveling alone. Virgil and Devie are coming, too. I plan on booking all of us on the same flight—"

"You'll do no such thing."

I grit my teeth. "Come again?"

"I can tell by the firm set of your jaw," he traces its line with his finger and cups my chin, "that you are hell-bent on doing this. It doesn't put me at ease that Devie will be there. She's as much of a target as you are." He switches gears, determined to get more information before he agrees to anything. "Why is Devie going to Paris?"

"She was offered jobs modeling new lines for Chanel and Hermes. She's beyond ecstatic. Dr. Stitcher has once again lived up to her reputation. The laser surgery on Devie's face was a huge success."

At the mention of the doctor, a frown creases his forehead, and he takes the palm of my hand in his and rubs his finger across the scar I have, compliments of Dimitri's sexual assault. Thanks to Dr. Stitcher, it fades more each year and I have full use of my hand.

"Just because Devie and Virgil are going doesn't mean I consent or approve of your decision."

I stiffen again at his choice of words.

He must be worried he crossed the line, because, massaging his neck, he adds, "I wasn't prepared for having you traipse around the world to grow a fashion house—at least not yet."

"Not ever, if you had your way," I mumble. He ignores me, rubbing his jaw and contemplating what he's going to say next.

"So, here's how this is all going to go down."

Do not punch the father of your children because of an asinine choice of words. I know him so well, I can actually see the wheels in his head turning as he weighs the options open to him.

"Go on. I'm all ears."

"Good," he says, ignoring the incredulous look I send his way. "*If,*" he lets the word hang for a bit then continues, "all is deemed safe, my pilot buddy will fly the four of you to Paris on his private jet. I'll make reservations at the George V Hotel. The security there is rock-solid. Sammy will stay there too and escort you where you have to go." Regaining control has made him calmer, but he still feels a need to add, "I have to know that you won't let your guard down and feel compelled to pursue an opportunity that suddenly presents itself without Sammy coming."

He issues his ideas as orders, indicating he doesn't completely trust the decisions I make. Hell, sometimes I don't even trust my choices, but this time my capacity for self-recrimination is less staggering than ever before. It's time to be kinder to myself and more in touch with what I want to accomplish. I'm determined to forget my mistakes and embrace my ambition. Quieting my umpteenth internal pep talk, I eye my challenger.

"Do not take me for a fool."

He looks back at me hard, waiting for an answer that directly address his concern.

"Of course, I'm not going to jeopardize my safety."

Light footsteps echo outside the kitchen. "Mamma."

I peek into the hallway and see Caroline standing there, sleep clouding her beautiful face, each tiny freckle splayed across her nose blessed by the sun.

"Good morning, Sweet Pea." I lift her and give her a kiss. "Do you want some breakfast?"

She nods and slides down, running over to Chase, who puts her on top of his shoulders.

"I heard your BIG voice, Daddy, and woke up," she says, laughing when he carries her over to the table and slides her into a chair.

I just can't help myself. Two opportunities in the span of two days to hit Mr. Perfect with less than stellar truths. "You mean you heard Daddy's BIG MOUTH," I pronounce, blinking rapidly with a false smile while I put the cereal bowl on the table.

He flashes me a grin, slipping his arm around my waist and tugging me into the shadow of the refrigerator and out of view. His voice growls quietly in my ear.

"Your trip to Paris is still on the table, but our conversation has not ended."

I tilt my head back and look him square in the eye. "I'll keep that in mind when I make sure we set aside quiet time to discuss what's involved *when* I leave for Paris."

He wraps his hand in my hair and pulls my head back.

"*If* you leave." His lips tickle my ear, but his tone is firm. "That determination depends on whether the conditions abroad are deemed stable after I carry out some investigations."

Winning this argument now is the kite that's not going to fly, especially since Dimitri has made several past attempts to hurt me and our family. However, I refuse to sit idly on the sidelines while he makes a unilateral final decision.

Feeling the tight tug of his hand in my hair, I rub my knee against his cock. "I understand and I agree. But . . ." I push harder with my knee and let the clarifying word hang for emphasis. "I must have access to all the information gathered with a say in evaluating the danger it presents or there's no deal. I will simply head off as planned."

"You have become quite the skilled negotiator, Mrs. Reardon."

"I have an accomplished teacher."

"It's agreed, then. We both review the assembled intel before any decision is made."

He doesn't wait for my answer before sealing our settlement with a searing kiss. The insufferable man does not cede control easily, and he fights dirty.

I open my mouth and slide in my tongue. *Deliciously dirty.*

CHAPTER 21

"I am actually flying on a private jet with my closest friend who has finally taken the plunge to launch a career after so many detours. Here's to you!" Beth reaches for her wine glass, her eyes lighting with mischief. "And here's to the amazing time we're going to have . . ."

I start to protest, but she stops me short. "In between those long hours you'll be working, of course."

I bury my head back into my laptop, making sure to add another talking point to my growing list of those I plan to discuss during the string of meetings Virgil has scheduled once we land.

"C'mon," Beth pokes me in the side, laughing. "Stop being so serious. How often do we get the opportunity to conduct business in Paris at the same time? We have to steal some time for ourselves."

Her enthusiasm is infectious, and I toast with the others. We clink, sip, and lower our glasses, but Beth's gaze remains fixed on mine. "I don't care what that alpha male husband of yours has to say about what you can and cannot safely do. These past few years, you have done enough 'adulting' to last a lifetime."

"I'll drink to that," Devie adds, emptying her glass.

"By the way, how did you ever manage to convince him to let you take this trip?"

Leaning back in my seat, I watch the pewter sky and floating clouds while I consider how to answer. I finally decide on the less-is-more response.

"I simply explained how important it was for me to go, and for the most part he was fine with my decision." I keep my best poker face, even though Chase's arguments replay in my mind.

Sammy's ears must still ring from them too, because he slides on his headphones and closes his eyes, making it obvious he has no desire to relive any parts of those *discussions* I choose to share. And who could blame him? Chase steadfastly repeated every conceivable worst-case scenario he could think of, stopping only long enough to support each one with facts about Dimitri's rising power status. One afternoon, he came home from work just to show me a computer-rendered map with Dimitri's global contact links. Paris shone as big and bold as a Forty-Second Street ad.

It seems Dimitri's power base is a well-oiled machine that churns out a steady stream of international arms and human-trafficking deals. This gives his army of thugs the necessary resources to track any one of us anywhere in the world. Another map with even more stars and arrows popped up with a few clicks of Chase's fingers. That one showed the places where Dimitri's sons maintain mercenary forces that shoot, beat, bomb, slaughter, or maim anyone who threatens their smuggling routes and weapons proliferation. "Soldiers" with code names like The Butcher and Scorcher lead hit teams that work with insurgents in unstable countries to destroy all adversaries, even whole villages if necessary.

Chase is convinced Dimitri or one of his sons are, at the very least, out to threaten me and at the worst . . . well, who needs to go there, especially since I'm expanding into new arenas.

Chase wouldn't let it go. During a particularly heated argument, he threatened to lock me in a room if I didn't see his reasons for not wanting me to leave. This was over-the-top behavior, even for him. He definitely knew something that he wasn't sharing, and I wasn't going to rile him or myself more by demanding to know what it was. As much as I want to know all the facts, I've come to realize that learned truths are like shouldered lead weights. The more you learn, the heavier they get. The sobering visuals of all the locations these gun-toting thugs operated from made me want to slip into hiding with Chase and the children.

No wonder Chase originally agreed to my terms. He must have realized that seeing and hearing all the details would shock me. He was right. I almost gave in and said I wouldn't go, especially after he mentioned that he had to travel to London on business on or around the same time. Then, I thought about how none of Chase's arguments included recent threats or attempts by Dimitri to harm us. In fact, Dimitri and his forces had been quiet since our last sighting of his son, Yuri, over two years ago, when we were visiting Fiona at the rehab center. It seems military intelligence was right when they determined that Dimitri and his army were being forced by several international agencies to suspend business and make themselves scarce.

This was the argument I used until Chase reluctantly agreed. But his doubt for my safety remained etched in his mind, carving frown lines into his forehead and the sides of his eyes. Our lovemaking that night was raw and consuming, his mouth and hands claiming every inch of my body. A mix of moving hands, mouths, and flexing bodies, we didn't stop until exhaustion collapsed our bodies into sweaty slumber.

Virgil looks up from his laptop and raises a skeptical brow. "Judging from the number of meetings Sammy attended at your place and Mac Skyped into from his assignment, it had to have been anything but fine. No doubt you were pressed into a hot seat and made to defend your ability to safely take this trip during each and every one of those conversations."

I take another sip of chardonnay. "We worked it all out like two consenting adults. Chase finally saw reason."

Virgil chuckles. Devie rolls her eyes. Beth points her finger. "I warned you about his bastard tendencies when you first hooked up with him in France. I can only imagine what he put you through."

I run my fingers through my hair, and that's when Beth sees the rose. She takes my arm in her hand for a closer look.

"It's stunning."

"Thanks."

Consumed with putting safety measures into place for me and the children, Chase's impeccable powers of observation took a hit. He never even noticed the tattoo. Just as well. We had enough to discuss before I left without adding this to the mix.

In fairness to him, his worry is justified. I wince when I think about how upset he was last night. I happened to walk in on him as he sat bent at his desk over some crumpled piece of paper, his face a study in torment. He forced a smile when he saw me, then folded it and shoved it in his pocket as if it was nothing important.

When curiosity got the best of me and I snooped around later, rifling through his pockets, it was gone.

Beth is silent for a few moments, then leans toward me and squeezes my hand. "You've been through a lot these last few years. I don't say that Chase is completely wrong in wanting to make sure that you stay safe. I remember what you looked like after your attack. I don't want to make you live through it again, but what kind of animal sends someone a severed finger in an envelope and then attacks her in a stairwell?"

It's hard to believe that, three years later, I'm still convinced that it was Fiona's ring on that bloody appendage. Yet she refuses to admit Dimitri had it stolen.

I've had this suspicion, call it an intuition, that there's a direct link between Dimitri's vengeance and Fiona's vulnerability. Her ring in his hands is not the only connection that supports my theory. Fiona was ten years old when Chase photographed Dimitri raping Devie, fourteen when he enlisted in the Marines. Chase denies that Fiona was affected, but how does he really know what happened after he left? He was gone for four years. That's a lot of time for a fiend like Dimitri to sink his fangs into someone. What made matters worse for Fiona was that Bill was still drinking heavily while Chase was gone. Grieving the loss of her mother and abandoned by an alcoholic father, it's no surprise that she started abusing drugs.

Beth shudders while I politely sip my wine in silence. I've learned from my attacks as well as Chase's sightings of Dimitri in Afghanistan that Dimitri has eyes and ears everywhere. I don't know who is part of his army of gangsters, but there's no way I'm putting anyone else in jeopardy by contributing inside information about Dimitri. There's enough of us already in his line of attack.

"All of that is history." I wave my hand. "Right now, I'm here and excited about what's next."

She gives me a slow smile. "You'll never guess who I've been seeing."

"What! You've been seeing someone that I don't know about?"

"Yeah."

"Is it serious?"

She shrugs. "Maybe."

"Well, do I know him?"

"Yeah."

I stare her down. "Don't even think about being coy with me, girl. Now, out with it. Who is he?"

"Andre."

"Andre? You mean the guy you met in Paris while we were traveling together?"

"Yep. Are you surprised?"

"A little. I knew you kept in touch, but I never thought you were seriously seeing each other. How's that long-distance relationship going?"

"It's not as hard as you would think. I travel a lot to London and Paris for business. His company has a New

York office, so we get together every chance we can." She flashes me a wide smile.

"I'm sure he's wild about you."

"How do you know that? You haven't seen him in over three years."

"That's true, but I do remember that he was never more than a few feet from you that entire trip. He took you on his motorcycle throughout the south of France and then followed you to Italy. Wait a minute." I stop for a second to stretch my memory. "I bet he even traveled with you to London after I flew home with Chase."

"He did."

"Will you be staying with him here in Paris?"

"I am." She shakes her head like she's surprising herself. "I'm crazy about him."

"That's fantastic." I give her a warm hug.

"Thanks. Hey, now that you know, we should all meet for dinner."

"I'd love to."

"Great. Oh, and Marcel would like to get together with us while we're in town. He suggested that we meet for drinks at Le Bar for old times' sake."

"Sure, why not. I'm staying at the George V, so it'll be easy enough to meet there for a quick cocktail." I throw my arm around her shoulder. "I'm so glad we'll have some time to spend together."

"Me too." Beth crooks her finger for me to join her in the seats away from the others. Once there, she hands me a long package wrapped in lavender wrapping paper. topped with the same color bow.

"What's this for?"

A mischievous smile edges across her pouty lips. "Just a *little* something to keep you company while you're away on business."

I tear off the paper and peek inside, my eyes bulging when I catch sight of what's inside. A neon-pink dildo measuring the length of my forearm stares up from the box.

I reach in and accidentally trigger a start button. It fires off like a rocket, nearly flying out of my hand.

"I figured it must be what you're used to." She flips it off when my nervous attempts to silence the damn contraption fail.

Dropping into a seat across from me, Devie steals a look at what's creating the ruckus. Her lively brows lift. "Is it a vibe or bomb?" she asks with a Russian bite to her words.

Beth throws her hands outward and makes an explosive sound. "Both. I've got one myself and can confirm firsthand that it gives the best orgasms." She turns it on full-speed. The pink extension, complete with painted veins, twists, wriggles, and hums.

"Will you turn that thing off," I say, laughing in spite of myself.

Handing it back to me, she and Devie return to their original seats, leaving me to gape at my present. *Okay, Rocket Man, time to put you to rest.* I gingerly place it in its box, making sure to hide it inside the large, zippered pocket of my travel bag.

I walk back to my seat and shift my focus back to business. "What's on the agenda after we land? You mentioned earlier that there were several meetings you set up to discuss the manufacturing and sales of our designs." I open my laptop, bringing up our schedule.

"That's right," Virgil says. "I'm thinking it's a good idea to draw up a specific agenda for that meeting."

"One major talking point we'll want to emphasize," I begin, typing as I speak, "concerns how we want to embrace our artisan roots, keeping the manufacturing and raw materials high-end, but the prices in the affordable range for a luxury brand."

"I agree. There's also the sales potential that will have to be focused on. Technology has caught on, with high-end buyers bringing the digital revolution to buyers of expensive items."

"Yes, absolutely. More people are shopping from their smartphones for these items. We need to be on board with this. The sales potential is enormous."

"I say we start with showing and promoting your jackets and those designs they complement."

There's a giant pause while I digest that Virgil wants to start by expanding my personal brand, and not one we have put together as a team.

"Don't look so surprised. I realize it's your exclusive design and brand. I don't mind initially climbing on board to help you expand its reach."

"Surprised is an understatement. I'm flabbergasted."

"Why? You've reinvented the classic jacket in every conceivable cut and color." He ticks off examples with his fingers. "You've got trendy leather, floral prints, smooth velvets, and your latest tweed wool design is showing signs of being a hit. Any or all are for any stage in life and they're a sellout success. What better place is there for me to start than by helping you use your brand as an offshoot to promote other designs? We can have the lawyers crunch out the details of my salary and entitled percentages from new creations once we launch." He studies me expectantly.

I've known Virgil since we first met at Villa Passalacqua when he was artistic director at Estelle Designs, and I was a fledgling designer with nothing more than a sketchpad of designs and a recent award for a jacket design I created at Parsons. He hired me after one interview despite Charlotte's protests that I was inexperienced. He offered me a promotion followed by a partnership deal not long after that. When I had to pull out at the last minute because Chase was missing and Dimitri was threatening the life of my unborn baby, he agreed, no questions asked, to disengage me from the partnership. He took a serious hit in one of our cars that was no doubt meant as a deadly message for our family and never uttered a word of complaint. He's Mac's lover and was instrumental in helping Mac, someone who doesn't let people in easily, discover a slice of happiness that comes from knowing who you are.

To this day, Virgil remains a trusted ally in a business that is cutthroat. Now, this talented and hardworking icon in the fashion industry has indicated he'll work under my umbrella. This technically makes him my employee with some shareholder rights.

Once I close my slack-jawed response, I reach out my hand without a second thought. "Robin Virgil May, you've got yourself a deal."

CHAPTER 22

I remove the towel from my wet hair, comb it through, then slip into my crème-colored silk chemise. Sitting on the toilet lid, I stretch out my legs and light up a cigarette, then hit Chase's cell number. It had been a long day of travel and meetings. I always figured Virgil knew lots of people who mattered in the fashion industry, but I never imagined how many that included. Chief executives, commercial and managing directors, wholesalers, retailers, investors, marketers, you name the category, and Virgil established a connection and set up a gathering of people who mattered.

At our last meeting, we sat around a conference table that stretched to the Seine River. Investors tossed around offers as if millions of euros were nothing more than bags of jellybeans. Their hardcore, aggressive approach caught me off guard. I had mostly prepared for meetings addressing the expansion of creative ideas and designs and how not to cross paths with a Mafia monster. I never anticipated investors would want to acquire my small label or toss additional money at me for parts of a business I had yet to develop.

Virgil said at meetings like this, you hum. I had no idea what he was talking about.

"When you're addressed, just press your lips together and go mmm or mmhmm."

So basically, I listened and kept my mouth shut while Virgil talked nonstop about our new venture. They hung on his words like they were promotional guarantees. Afterward, when I told him how in awe I was of his connections and abilities, he took my hand and shook his head. "Sweetie, I'm only the mouthpiece. You and your designs are what they want on board."

I wasn't convinced, so I told him he was more than a damn good spokesperson and that if I was there by myself, I would have been exposed as a clumsily ambitious newbie with passable talent and limited business sense.

He just stared ahead like a wise sage and shook his head.

Chase picks up on the third ring. I take a quiet drag of my cigarette and smile expectantly into the phone when I hear his deep, smooth voice answer. "Hey."

"Hi there, how's it going?"

"All good here. How about on your end?"

I miss him, and it's only a day since I've been gone. I sneak another puff before answering.

"It's been fine." My voice falters when I think about the pushy financiers who insisted they could boost my future endeavors threefold for a nice piece of the pie.

"What's wrong. Has anything happened to alarm you?" Chase's tone is clipped and demanding. He knows something is bothering me, and in typical Chase fashion thinks my life has been threatened.

"No, all has been quiet on that end. It's just that Virgil said he wanted to come work for me. Then I was approached by some investors—"

He skips over my mention of Virgil and targets what I didn't get a chance to finish. "Investors? What are you talking about? I thought this trip was all about boosting creative materials and designs."

"So did I, but a business meeting set up by one of Virgil's former business associates turned into an acquisition and financing discussion. I was getting some pressure to sell my small label. Then I was offered an investment sum for future endeavors."

His silence is short. His words that follow are sharp. "Absolutely not! From the way they bombarded you, my guess is they're looking for a piece of the action for much less than it's valued."

"Chase, they offered me fifteen million dollars for my Cesare label."

"What did you say?"

"I hummed."

His laughter crackles through the phone. Obviously, he's heard of that particular response when you have no idea what you're doing.

"Smart move for an initial meeting of that type. Keep in mind that for them those are very accessible price points."

"That may be true, but to me it's amazing. I don't have the defined brand identity and exposure to warrant that outlay of money. So why now? I've held onto my Cesare brand for the last three years. No one has ever approached me about selling it."

"It's all about timing. New York is well . . . New York,

but Paris is different. Seems to me that when you go through Paris, you're going global."

He's caught my ear. Even though he knows little about the fashion business, he does understand what makes an enterprise tick. He has this talent of taking a slice of information and using it to assess and analyze its overreaching ramifications. "And I disagree with your assessment of yourself," he says. "You do have a brand focus. Your DNA is already in place with your jacket creations. Your design talent embraces inclusivity. Anyone and everyone wears jackets. Investors understand that diversification is an essential element for growth. They figure they'll buy your name, then pay you as a lead player to help expand your line and increase your distribution network. Either that or they'll throw some money your way in exchange for a majority stake in your business. In either case, you cede control of your name and your label, something you don't want to do at this juncture of your career. You'd be accountable to them when making decisions you want to keep control of. It's like being a beginner pilot and handing over your wings before you get a chance to fly on your own."

Well said by the master of control. I take a last draw and stub out my cigarette in an ashtray that Parisian hotels blessedly still offer in guest bedrooms. "Well, it sounds like I'm going to have to mesh my creative vision with a solid business plan."

"I recommend you don't do anything until we have Lena look over the specifics of what you might be considering." He waits a bit then adds, "That includes your arrangement with Virgil. He's more like a trusted friend, but business is business. You want to take the time to be discerning so that any deal crafted represents your best interests." He pauses to garner the right words. "This is your project, but I suggest you wait until we can discuss the logistics of what moving forward entails."

"Sure. You're the financial genius. As for me, any further thinking about a course of action is going to have to be pushed to tomorrow. I'm exhausted." I pause a beat. "I'm sorry I didn't get to call earlier. Did everyone go off to sleep without too much of a fuss?"

"No more than the usual. Sunny bundled them up and took them to the park after their scheduled activities, so they were zonked when Eleanor took over the bedtime routine."

"I'm going to call first thing in the morning so I can speak to them. I miss you." I grasp my pack of cigarettes to light up just one more.

"Put away the cigarettes, Alicia."

My hand freezes. How the hell does he know?

He answers my question without my having to ask. "I can tell you're smoking by the quick inhale and exhale of your breathing earlier. It stopped for a bit and just now I caught the rustling sound of cellophane." He takes a Sherlock moment, most likely to build his case, then, just as I suspected, says, "Didn't you book a non-smoking room?"

That's two strikes against me in Mr. Perfect's rule book. One for smoking when I assured him I had quit, and the other for partaking where it's not allowed. I look out the open bathroom window and smile. Serves me right for marrying someone in military intelligence. Imagining his disapproving stare, I soak the cigarettes under the faucet and toss the pack into the wastepaper basket. Figuring his bionic ears would have heard the water running and the clatter when the wet cigarettes hit the bottom of the bin, I don't comment. I know I'm right when he drops the subject and moves onto the next topic.

"Before I forget, Mac's returning at the end of next week. He'd like to fly to Paris to spend some time with Virgil. I've got business to attend to in London, so we're going to need Sammy back here. That means you are going to have to sit tight next Friday night until Mac arrives. Will that work?"

"I think so. Give me a minute to check my schedule." I scroll through my calendar and see that the last meeting we have that Friday is at 10:00 a.m. Even if it continues through most of the day, I'll be finished by late afternoon. "That's no problem. Virgil is going to be so happy to see Mac." I offer a silent prayer of thanks to the higher power that protects soldiers.

"That's what I figured. And you? What do you have planned that night?"

"Nothing. It's my last day here, and if the week continues at the same work pace as today, I'll just crash in the hotel room, order room service, and pack."

"Okay. Good. Once you step on that private jet the next day, Virgil can spend all the time he wants with Mac."

"Mac is long overdue for some vacation time." Since Mac came out, he's more at ease with himself. He acts and moves like he fits into his own skin, but his core is no different. He's still the work machine he always was. He watches over our family, serves his country, and partners with Chase in various real estate ventures. He doesn't easily reveal what he's thinking or feeling and rarely complains. He's the rock-solid balance to Virgil's creative, off-beat energy.

Makes you realize that sexual preferences don't really change who a person is, but they sure as hell can affect how others perceive who they are. Virgil has shared stories about how he was bullied at school for the way he dressed and spoke. Doubtful anyone messed with Mac. His muscles are hard as steel, and he's fast, limber, and packs a punch that can knock a much larger person unconscious with one hit. Even so, he kept quiet about his sexuality for many years. It had to have been fear that silenced a truth he claims he knew since he was a kid.

I may be meandering off track, but a certain, singular-minded person is staying true to his core, which more or less proves my point.

"I plan on alerting hotel security to make sure there's someone who can be an extra pair of eyes during the change-over."

Still riding high on the prospect of my financial windfall, I try to lighten his worry. "How about if we FaceTime and I strip for *your* pair of eyes."

No such luck. His tone is brusque, clipped, and to the point.

"This is serious, Alicia. As long as Dimitri is at large, we're all in danger. I need to know you're on board with this plan."

Boarded and belted in, sir, I mouth silently while saluting into the phone. He's frantic and doesn't need to hear any wiseass comments, so I acquiesce, trying to keep any edge from my tone.

"Yes, I'm taking this seriously. I'm sorry if I came across as cavalier. I'll be sure to arrange for Virgil and Devie to have dinner with me in my room so I'm not alone. The suite has a dining table and plenty of space for us to enjoy a meal together."

It's irritating that I have to placate him when what I really want is to be expending energy on how to market my designs.

Then it hits. A knot of fear grips my stomach. Does he know something he's not sharing? Hearing him urgently reiterate that we're *all* facing trouble serves as a stark reminder that our children might be imminent targets. Now it's my turn to acquiesce to apprehension. "Were there any new actions against the children?" I close my eyes to shut out the guilt that creeps in when I think that mere seconds ago, all I was considering was my business venture.

"No, it's been quiet. I just like to be cautious."

"Even if you suspect something, you have to let me know. I'll take the next flight home." I eye the wet pack of cigarettes and could kick myself.

"We've got things under control. Just relax and do what you set out to accomplish."

"I'll relax once I know Sammy is back to help watch the children."

"Listen," he pauses, and I imagine him massaging the back of his neck. "I don't want to worry you. I just want to make sure you're being cautious and vigilant."

Knowing he's right about what I need to do doesn't prevent frustration from creeping back. I mean, what's wrong with wanting to grow a business, travel, and enjoy life without incessant reminders to be on guard for a potential catastrophe? I've not been gone for more than twenty-four hours, and already there's a chessboard of maneuvers in play to keep us safe. Coiled bands of obligations tighten around my head until all I want is to escape their bonds. Next, guilt marches in to excise its pound of flesh when I consider, yet again, it's resentment instead of gratitude I'm feeling for what I've been gifted with. My conscience wags its finger, rattling, *You've a husband who desires you, beautiful, healthy children, and a lucrative lifestyle. Stop being so selfish!* The internal clamor is as exhausting as it is deafening.

"Alicia, are you there?" His words tug me back to our current woes.

"I'm here."

"You sound upset."

How to say what's on my mind without offending? "I'm just a bit . . . um . . . overwhelmed."

"And aggravated, if I can guess by your tone." He knows me well.

"I just wish you would stop thinking that you have to always fix things, or that it's your responsibility to keep all of us safe all of the time. They're impossible tasks to assume."

He's silent. For. A. Long. Time.

Now it's my turn to wonder what's happened. "Hello, are you there?"

"I'm here." He sighs loudly.

"What's wrong? You sound weird."

"Everything's fine." *More silence.* "I'm just waiting."

What in heaven's name is he talking about?

"What do you mean? Waiting for what?" My senses fire alarm shots.

"I seem to recall that I was offered a striptease earlier."

His shift from unsurmountable concern to whimsy has my head spinning.

He taps his FaceTime button and switches to a video call. I accept, and there he is, leaning against fluffed pillows on our bed, waiting with hands behind his head and hiked brows.

He's made room for optimism, that feeling of energized, intuitive faith that goodness won't succumb to hate or well-being to harm in our war against a vengeful brute. It's infectious.

My slow, deliberate smile and cocked brow meet his hooded gaze.

"Well, I don't know. Let me check my Marine Military Code of Conduct to see if it's allowed." I lick my pointer finger and pretend to rifle through a pamphlet.

"Are you mocking me?"

"Moi? Never. Now, let's see . . . S for striptease. Hmm." I pause with the pretense of studying something closely. "The rulebook indicates that it's not only allowed. It's encouraged."

"Really?"

"Yeah. Seems it sharpens the eyesight of the spectator and boosts the heart rates of all involved."

"Are you sure?"

"Mmm hmm. Says it serves as a boot camp workout, too, *and* raises an essential appendage so it's aimed and ready to fire." My eyes travel toward his navel, where his cock is already lengthening in anticipation. "So, Marine Reardon,

Sir," I murmur coquettishly, tracing my moistened finger across my lower lip and letting a bit of my breast peek out from my lowered negligee. "Are you ready to let the show begin?"

"Baby, I am always ready for this."

I raise my finger, asking for a minute, and dart to the closet for my beige high-heeled pumps and cream-colored French lace thigh-highs. Sprinting toward the night table, I snatch my iPad for my song list and my special gift from Beth. I hit start and the vibrator roars to life, making me jump. Eyeing its contour, I switch it off. It may not be the real thing, but it sure as hell is a sizeable substitute.

Joe Cocker's "You Can Leave Your Hat On" is my first choice of music to work with. Placing the vibrator out of sight, I slip on my stockings and then my shoes. Standing in the doorway, my hands flattened against each side of its frame, my back facing the phone that's propped on a chair, I make sure I'm positioned in front of the propped phone. I'm about to start when, from the corner of the phone's screen, I spot a potential problem to our naughty plan.

"Close and lock the bedroom door," I mouth, pausing the song. I imagine nosy little eyes making their way into our bedroom after a nightmare and finding a worse one waiting when they see Daddy's eyes riveted on their mother dancing nude. That could make some therapist rich down the road.

Chase shoots off the bed, sticks his head out to scan the hallway, then shuts and locks the door. "All good. They're asleep."

I hit the start arrow. The beat strums. Keeping my arms raised and hands pressed against the inside of the doorway, my hips rock to the rhythm. Cocker's gravelly voice starts, "Baby take off your coat . . ." I lower my chemise one strap at a time. Shimmying my shoulders, I lean into Chase's image and reveal the tops of my breasts. A current of heat runs up my spine and circulates to the front. With an open smile, he bends forward for a better look, and I shake my hips to the rhythm with my hands behind my head to accommodate. "Take off your dress," Cocker drones, upping the stakes.

"Take it off," Chase mouths, swirling his finger. I ignore the request, because that would take the tease out of the strip and I'm hellbent on emphasizing the first while maybe or maybe not offering the second. It's time for the pupil to demonstrate to the teacher all that's been learned about delayed gratification. "Take off your shoes," Cocker croons.

I turn again. Massaging my thighs and slowly raising the hem of my chemise, I bend over, swaying, giving him just enough of a peek of my ass to stir his need for more. When I swivel my head, I see that he's lying on the bed, naked. My eyes follow his muscled chest down toward his ripped abs, where they lock on his Private Johnson standing rigid, red-faced, and ready to salute.

I have been in that position of need countless times. The switch is so empowering, I have to restrain a giggle, but that would only weaken my control that seems, after a view of his toned, naked body, to have slipped several notches. I moisten my lips and turn to meet his gaze head-on. Slowly, deliberately, I expose the tops of my breasts. I slide off one shoe, spin it on my finger and toss it in the direction of the phone. I repeat the maneuver with the other, making sure to show even more of my breasts. With his eyes glued on me and his penis aiming for the ceiling, I take pity and raise my hem, slowly sliding one stocking and then the other down my thighs and off my legs.

Swaying and lowering my body until I'm just about squatting, I nervously eye the contraption resting on the floor in front of me. I fire it up and insert its tip into my opening, and nearly soar through the ceiling with an orgasm.

Chase throws back his head and laughs. He knows as well as I do that the potential for this teaser to backfire can increase exponentially if I'm not careful.

Putting the rousing accoutrement down, I turn to the side and grip the doorway with both hands. Moving my head forward and back, I thrust out my ass and mouth for him to grab hold of his cock while I rock my bottom forward and backward. He's more than ready to agree and while his hand flies there, I grab my new friend and use it to get back to reaching for my own tender spots.

By the time the music ends he's flat on his back, satisfied, and I'm gasping from an orgasm. Chase and I never touched, but still, I feel the warmth of his body on mine. Winded and satiated, we lapse into silence.

"Good conversation."

"Yeah," he points at the floor where Beth's gift lies tossed. "That's some gizmo you wielded. Where did that come from?"

"Beth gifted it to me on the plane ride here. She thought it would be a good replacement for you while I was away."

"Not even on my best day. Just watch you don't rupture something."

I press the button and it rumbles to life again, making us both laugh.

"I miss you, baby," he says.

"I miss you, too. Let's 'catch up' again tomorrow."

"Yep. It's a date."

"Same time, same place?"

"Oh yeah. Give the kids kisses from me." Then I kiss my finger and touch the screen, just like I did countless times when he was deployed.

He does the same. "Until tomorrow."

"Until tomorrow," I repeat. We sign off.

Relaxed for the first time since I left, I slip on my nightgown and slide under the cool sheets, where I fall into a deep sleep. It will be the last good night's rest I get for a long while.

CHAPTER 23

"Is everything in place?" I study Devie with a critical eye just before she's about to stroll out for the catwalk show that is highlighting the bulk of my pre-collection designs. Parisian fashion is about lifestyle and attitude. It radiates a natural sophistication that emanates the idea of owning your body and your sexuality. I learned early that clothing design is a form of self-expression. Just like an author writes prose and an artist paints on a canvas, a designer converts cloth into art for the body. That said, I realize something is needed to complete her ensemble.

"Wait!" I stop her before she starts to walk down the runway on the fourth floor of the Musée d'Orsay. That I'm even here is a dream come true. Formerly a train station, the opulent building is a work of art in and of itself. High glass roof, arched halls, and huge, opulent clocks dress a structure that holds the world's largest collection of Impressionist paintings. Thanks to Virgil and that mega-wealthy investor hoping for a piece of my business, we were given a sought-after slot to showcase my designs.

I flick through the cart of my hanging garments and

grab a wispy fur stole to wrap around Devie's neck. It floats with her like the puff of a dark cloud. Paired with a black, sharply-cut jacket, black silk blouse, and flowing, black pleated pants, she resembles a stunning sliver of night. Her animal grace and dark hair coiffed to hit her chin at a razor angle telegraph chic glamour and confidence.

My remaining designs combine art with functionality. I eliminate anything boxy and focus on boot-length skinny skirts, sleek leather jackets, and silk cut-out blouses. To accommodate different body types and preferences, I highlight wide pants, silk tank tops, and free-flowing jackets that reach below the hip. Made from wrinkle-free fabrics, several of the outfits are serviceable for business travel and transformable from professional day wear to evening cocktails and dinner attire.

It wasn't easy to get everything in place for this pre-show. When I realized what would be needed, I had to hire an assistant back in New York to help me gather those garments I hadn't taken but were now necessary. Once again, Beth's contact list was a life saver. She recommended Clarisse, who was as efficient as she was experienced.

Together we spent hours FaceTiming so I could determine which of my designs in storage would show well. With little time to spare, I arranged to have them air shipped. I wasn't taking any chances on them getting lost or damaged, so Sammy drove me to the receiving station, where I personally picked up the boxes. I knew the drill well. Sammy stayed in the car guarding the entrance while I signed for the delivery, then carried the boxes from the repository to the trunk of the car. There was no way I was allowing Sammy to carry even one. He didn't care how many *Fragile-Handle with Care* labels were stamped on their surfaces. His eyes never traveled beyond a certain perimeter of where I was, so the likelihood of him becoming distracted by a potential threat and accidentally dropping, jostling, or overturning them was greater than if I was the one carefully carrying them to the car.

Even with all these precautions, there was a problem. The dress that was to be my finale did not arrive. It took hours of online tracking and phone calls to discover it had been shipped to a location on the other side of the city. Thank heavens it came early this morning.

"How do you stay so calm?" Virgil dabs his perspiring forehead with a handkerchief. I've slept only a handful of hours in the last seven days and haven't eaten a complete meal since we arrived. Even now, I'm too busy imagining what additions or takeaways are needed to answer Virgil's question. I've been living so much in my own head, contriving and changing designs, there's no space remaining to be flustered.

I sweep loose strands of hair away from my face and take a sip of iced espresso. "I don't know. We've been brainstorming and working round the clock for days to make sure everything is as perfect as possible; I just don't have any energy left to waste on being nervous."

"It seems to be going well," he adds, then swivels his head to observe a cluster of models getting ready to showcase Estelle Designs' most recent fashion line.

My eyes pop when I see one of their models wearing a gold lame mini tank dress embroidered with large silver and copper rings that jiggle every time she moves. If they were aiming for a fun piece, they overextended their reach.

Virgil lowers his voice to a near-whisper, "She sparkles like a disco diva on steroids." I've no time to comment because our last model gets ready to step out in my finale dress, a red beaded silk evening gown with a plunging neckline and enough of a side slit so the wearer can walk, dance, and move with ease. Like a flame dancing in the wind, the dress clings while still managing to flow with the body. It took me three weeks of steady close work to hand-sew the delicate crimson beading onto the entire surface of the dress. So much effort was put into the cut and form of its silhouette that it doesn't need an iota of tweaking.

I give her the sign to move along. Virgil's eyes remain glued to her back as she struts and turns for the judging spectators. Once she returns, the thunderous applause catches me by surprise. Devie pushes me and Virgil onto the carpet where, heart pounding, I begin my march in front of the large crowd. Cameras and phones extend toward us from all directions, and it's like I'm floating in a different universe where strangers clap while I smile and wave like I've known them my entire life.

"Ms. Cesare," someone shouts from the front row. It's the photographer who snapped the photograph of me and Juliette for Italian *Vogue*. When I look up, he follows me with his lens.

I can't help but compare the photographs he took over two years ago with those he's taking now. In the first set, I was bare from the waist up, but the contrast goes beyond nudity. Those photographs captured the magic of motherhood, while these will be a nod to designs born from my creative mind. In the frenzy of that moment, a question crystalizes. *How the hell am I going to manage both?* I have a family that needs to be kept safe. I crave a successful career. I can have them both as long as family is not sacrificed at the expense of business. The amount of time spent working during this trip has reminded me of the effort and energy that's going to be needed to build this business to my satisfaction. I thought I had it all figured out, but plotting logistics in your head is not the same as carrying them out in reality.

The resounding applause carries me from my ruminations to a bedazzled arena that the media, top designers, and Hollywood celebrities frequent. It's unbelievable that they are cheering me on. If I wasn't nervous before, I am now. Add a good-sized dose of self-consciousness to this whirling fifteen minutes of fame, and I'm spinning red-faced into what seems like someone else's reality. It's so foreign to my other life of babies and diapers and mobsters and bodyguards that, for the first time in a long while, my attention pivots from the past to a present that's as sweeping as it is surreal.

I round the curve toward the dressing room and catch a sudden movement from the corner of my eye. Something familiar glitters on one guy's wrist when his extended arm points an object in my direction. Just then, there's a loud pop. Something hits my temple, jarring me to a stop, and liquid splashes onto my face. I hit the floor of the stage facedown, my body pinned to the carpet by a weight that keeps me from shifting or getting up. From the distance, I hear Virgil's startled yelp and gasps from the audience. I try to raise my head to make out what's happening, but it's impossible to move even a muscle.

"Stay down," Sammy says from on top of my sprawled body. I catch a glimpse of Sammy's gun trained on a cluster of people who stand, stunned, in front of their seats. One celebrity type with cropped bangs peers through tinted aviator glasses with his hands raised like he's facing a firing squad. By now, my tongue tastes that the liquid splashed on my face is champagne. Some overzealous jerk must have popped a bottle of champagne to celebrate my success, and the cork hurled toward my head. This should go into the record books as one helluva fashion finale.

When Sammy helps me up, a quick glance in the direction of the bystanders shows me the champagne-toting reveler is gone. Sammy quickly guides me backstage, where clustering models gawk at us when we walk by. The glossy rings on the diva's dress swirl in hypnotic circles when she quickly steps back to give us space to pass.

Virgil, seeing that I'm fine, mops his brow yet again. "Trouble follows you . . ."

"Yeah, yeah, I know. Like a bridal train." My cheeks flush and I shake my head. Just when everything was going so well, I had to be attacked by a cork, soaked with champagne, and tackled by a bodyguard under the glare of hundreds of spectators.

Sammy could care less about my embarrassment. Ushering me into a back room, he looks both ways before shutting and locking the door. He wastes no time before pumping me for information. "Did you see the person who popped the bottle of champagne?"

Something familiar nudges my memory, but then fades. "I caught a glimpse of someone who was holding a bottle."

"Anyone you recognize?"

"No, I don't think so."

"What about you, Virgil?"

"From where I was standing, I couldn't see the person. All I know is that one minute Alicia and I were walking and the next there was this loud pop, and she was tackled to the floor like some linebacker." He studies me, concerned. "Are you okay?"

"I'm fine. Sammy monitored the force of the impact so it was swift and cushioned by his arms."

Sammy rivets his gaze back to me with business-like efficiency. "Is there anything else you recall?"

"I remember that he was male, and something shined from his wrist." I hesitate for a minute, still waiting for my heart to quit racing. If a hit to the front of the head after a loud pop isn't enough to trigger heart palpitations, a sudden takedown from behind will guarantee it.

Sammy drags over a chair, and I sit, brushing my hair back with my hand and sipping a cup of water Virgil hands me. Sammy waits patiently, and it's not long before another bit of my memory stirs to life. "I noticed he was wearing a navy blazer and a white shirt from the cuffs on his raised arms."

I slip off my shoes to ease my aching feet and stretch out my legs. In the distance I hear music and assume the show is continuing. In hindsight, everything that just happened seems blown out of proportion. "I think we can go back out and wrap things up," I suggest.

"Not yet."

"Sammy, it was just a bottle of champagne. Seems harmless enough. Don't you think?"

"Possibly." Sammy opens the door and peeks out at

the assembled audience for a last look around. Someone from security approaches. They talk for a bit, and after he leaves, Sammy stares into my face, his eyes showing determination.

"I'd like to know why he disappeared so fast, if his aim was to toast you and your show."

"I don't know. Maybe he got spooked by all the commotion."

Sammy looks skeptical. "Let's give it some more time. Bringing in outside alcohol is prohibited, so security is searching the premises for his whereabouts. Once they give the all-clear, you can be back to business as usual."

"Okay, I'll stay put for now. For the next two days, I'll even agree for you to accompany me and Virgil into the conference rooms for our meetings, but for now could we please keep this incident between us? No need for Chase to be alerted."

"That's not possible," Sammy says opening the door and peering once again into the crowd for some sign of the champagne culprit.

"Why not?" I try but fail to keep exasperation out of my tone. "He's worried enough as it is. Why give him more cause for concern when all that really happened was that some overzealous spectator popped a bottle of sparkling wine?" *And I don't need him insisting that I stay in my hotel room until the authorities get to the bottom of this fiasco.* I don't say that out loud, because I don't want to give Sammy any more ideas than he already has about how to handle the situation.

There's a knock on the door. Sammy unsheathes his gun from his shoulder holster. Placing it at his side, he cracks the door. With a wary eye, he opens it further when he spots who's standing outside the door.

From where I'm sitting, I catch a peek of a pale-looking attendant dressed in uniform. He was one of several in charge of seating guests.

"Yeah?" Sammy doesn't add *what the hell do you want, asshole?* but it sticks to the abruptness of his one-word greeting with the tenacity of chewing gum in hair.

"Bonjour, Monsieur." The conciliatory usher clears his throat. "I'm sorry to interrupt, but if all is well with Ms. Cesare, a reporter from *Le Monde* would like to interview her. Is she available?"

"Give us a minute." Sammy shuts the door in his face.

Just at that moment, my phone jingles. It's Chase, requesting a FaceTime chat. I glare at Sammy who shrugs his shoulders.

Chase knew I was having my show now, which leads me to believe he's calling because someone hit a red-light warning that signaled something was wrong. Since Sammy's right here in the thick of things, I have to believe he's the culprit. They must have devised some signal or button on their mobiles that alerts all of them to a potential problem. I don't fault them for that strategy. Dimitri can be ruthlessly quick with his attacks, so reaction time has to be fast and in sync. What does bother me is that, as usual, they failed to include me in the plan. I'm bristling at the thought of being left out of this strategizing. It's my life, damn it. I should at least have some say in what impacts it.

"Tell the assistant to give me five minutes. If you're able to clear the reporter's identity, he can interview me in here."

My tone is firm. "And Sammy . . ."

"Yeah."

"Put away the damn gun. You're going to give the Frenchman at the door a heart attack."

He holsters the gun and stares at the still-ringing phone. "I don't think Chase is going to like the idea of you granting that interview."

"I'll take care of Chase."

"Be sure to lock this door once I step outside." Sammy opens the door and cracks his knuckles. The waiting usher snaps to attention. "Tell the reporter to meet me at the east side of the runway," he says. The man's feet rapidly pound down the hallway toward the elevator.

"Good luck," Virgil mouths, making his getaway with Sammy and the usher. I lock the door and accept Chase's call, making sure to smile into the phone. No way am I letting him see I was in any way rattled by what just happened.

"Hi hon."

"Hey babe. Is everything alright?"

"Everything's fine. Just a small mishap."

"Mishap? What the hell does that mean?"

He's going to want the facts and then some, and I've got all of five minutes if I'm going to be able to be on time for this interview. *Le Monde* is an internationally recognized newspaper, comparable to *The New York Times* in the US. This type of opportunity doesn't happen easily, so I've got to take advantage of the timing.

"Some spectator popped a bottle of champagne, and the cork came flying in my direction." I see no reason to mention that it hit me in the head. It was just a cork, for heaven's sake.

"Were you hurt?"

"Just my pride. When it happened, Sammy hurled himself at me, and we both went crashing to the floor."

"He made a good call. It's best not to take anything for granted in these situations."

"I know."

"Where's Sammy now?"

"He just stepped into the hallway to clear someone who wants to interview me."

"Has the guy in the stands been apprehended and questioned?"

"Not yet, but security is working on it."

"Don't let anyone in until he's found. Reschedule the interview if you have to."

"I don't think that's going to be possible, but I'll try."

"You'll do more than try. We had an agreement, Alicia. You promised you wouldn't run off for an opportunity if it wasn't safe."

"I know. Sammy is vetting him first to make sure everything checks out. I promise I won't leave this room until I get the all-clear."

He rubs the back of his neck, but his hair remains in place, so I take that as a good sign.

There are footsteps in the hallway, and I hear Sammy telling the columnist to give me a few more minutes.

"I have to get going. Sammy's here. I promise I'll call as soon as the interview is over."

"Alright. Oh, and babe?"

"Yeah."

"You crushed it today."

"Thanks. How do you know how the show went?"

"Someone posted it on Instagram. You already have over ten thousand likes."

"You're kidding. I only just finished."

"Welcome to the information age, where global communication and visuals are just a click away from your fingertips."

"I'm flabbergasted." I swipe back my hair with my hands and shake my head. "Never in my wildest dreams did I anticipate this."

"Why not? You're the best at what you do. I know you've got to go, so promise me you'll take care of yourself. If you suspect any problems, tell Sammy and head straight back to the hotel."

"I will. I love you." I kiss my finger and press it to the screen, and watch as he does the same. Slipping my phone into my pocket, I hurriedly reach for a comb and lipstick. Peering into the small wall mirror, I put myself together the best I can on such short notice, then check my watch, worried I may have kept them waiting too long.

The simple movement triggers a memory. It was a watch that glimmered on the spectator's wrist. The person who opened the champagne was wearing an 18K Rolex Yacht-Master II watch, the same watch Yuri Ostopenko wore when I spotted him during our visit with Fiona.

I have a much bigger problem than I originally thought.

CHAPTER 24

"It's me," Virgil says from the other side of the door.

I let him in.

"What's wrong. You look like you've been spooked," he says.

I reach into the other pocket of my silk jacket and take out a cigarette. Flicking a lighter, I take a puff, then resume my pacing. "We have a problem, or I should say, I have a problem."

"What could be wrong? Sammy just cleared the reporter and the photographer who's accompanying him. They're on their way now."

I take a drag of my cigarette while continuing to walk.

"Well . . . are you going to tell me what's happened?"

I study his face. "I've figured out who it was that popped the bottle of champagne." I pause, wondering if I should share this information with Virgil. There is a grapevine from Virgil to Mac to Chase. And it's short and active.

"Well, who was this person?" he demands.

Oh, what the hell. Chase is going to find out sooner or later. "It was Dimitri's son, Yuri."

"Are you sure? It happened so quickly and—"

I cut him off. "He was standing in the front row. I couldn't catch his face, but it made it easy for me to see that he was wearing a Rolex. It was the same watch Yuri wore at the rehab facility. Also, his clothes were similar. I could tell he was wearing a navy jacket and a white shirt. That's what he was wearing then, too."

Virgil stays silent for a bit, and I know we're both contemplating the same dilemma. Do we take a chance and go ahead with this interview? He lets out an exasperated sigh. "We're just going to have to try and reschedule this interview until Yuri is found. Are you going to be the one to tell Sammy or do you want me to go out and tell them?"

I take a final drag and stub out my cigarette in an ashtray resting on the small end table. God bless the French.

"Neither. Sammy has already cleared both the interviewer and the photographer. He knows his business and would never be allowing either in if he had the least doubt of their authenticity. I say we go ahead with the interview. Then as soon as it's over, I'll tell Sammy what I know."

"I don't know about that. You might be putting yourself at unnecessary risk."

"I don't think so. Like I said before, both the reporter and the photographer will have been cleared. We're not leaving this room and for the duration of the interview, the door will stay locked with Sammy standing guard outside."

"Alright. Let's do this."

There's a rap on the door. "Who is it?" I put my ear close to the door and listen.

"It's me." Sammy's voice is clear and assured.

I open the door with a smile and let in a slender man

hauling a camera, and an older woman with a worn Italian leather satchel slung over her shoulder.

"Ms. Cesare, it's nice to meet you." She extends her hand. "I'm Sheila Foulquier from *Le Monde* and this is Jean Bisset."

"A pleasure to meet you both." I shake Sheila's hand, then smile at Jean. "It's good to see you again."

"You two know each other?"

"Yes, Ms. Cesare and I met when I was in Italy doing a shoot for Italian *Vogue*."

Virgil's eyes widen and he tips his head in my direction, but neither he or Jean comment about the photographs taken of me and Juliette.

"Please, call me Alicia." I introduce Virgil, and we both situate ourselves on the worn striped sofa squatting in the corner. Sheila takes a seat on a threadbare chair across from us. Only Jean remains standing, his camera clutched in his hands. Initial questions begin amicably about where I studied fashion and my first job at Estelle Designs. I skirt questions about my children, saying I have three but not sharing their names, ages, or where we live.

"What do you think women are looking for in your designs?" she asks, pen poised for my answer.

"I think most people are looking for fashions that are serviceable but make some sort of individualized statement about who they are and what they want from life. That's why I create designs that show confidence and inner strength."

Her next question catches me by surprise. "How do you feel about the criticism circulating that you've been neglecting your talent for design for the past several years?"

The question is loaded with subtle sexist overtones. I doubt that it will be asked of Virgil, who's also been on hiatus from full-time design since his injury.

My answer is simple. "There comes a time when you have to do and not just dream."

"So why now?"

I'm glad she didn't ask, *why not sooner?* This gives me the opportunity to focus on what I'm accomplishing in fashion and not on marriage and family. Given the current circumstances, I'd rather keep that aspect of my life quiet. I'm already feeling pangs of regret that Juliette's photo is out there, especially now that I see the global reach this photographer has, working for *Le Monde.*

"Virgil presented an amazing opportunity that I couldn't resist."

As I suspected, her next questions are directed toward Virgil. He confirms that he hired me in Lake Como straight out of college after I won a global contest for my jacket design. There's a few more questions, some photographs snapped, and it's over.

Virgil attempts to excuse himself, mumbling that he's got some loose ends to tie up after the show. I take hold of the back of his jacket. "Oh no you don't. You're not leaving me here to face the music alone with Sammy and Chase. We're in this together. Besides, I need you to confirm that you thought it was safe, too."

"Are you kidding me? That means I have to admit I knew. Mac is going to give me a hard time."

"Don't be such a coward. You need to stand firm if you want us both to attend the final string of meetings you put together to help launch our fall line. Sammy, Mac, and

Chase already have a tremendous advantage."

"How so?"

"They'll have acquired prior information leading up to this incident that we know nothing about."

"What do you mean? It just happened."

"They're in intelligence, Virgil. That's what they do. They gather evidence about an enemy in record time, and they don't share that info with anyone outside their network. How long do you have to be with Mac before you get that?"

"Obviously longer than I have been."

"They're going to band together and present a convincing case as to why we should head home. And it won't be tomorrow or the next day. Chase is going to want it to be now. So, buck up and be ready."

Virgil buffs the perspiration from his top lip with his handkerchief.

"Relax and take deep breaths. It's all going to be fine. Besides I'm going to be the one to take the brunt of it once Chase finds out I knew it was Yuri."

"I'm telling you now, there's no way I'm going to be in the room when you share that tidbit of info."

"I'll be sure to speak to him first to smooth things over. I need to make sure everything is quiet at home and that my kids are safe. Then we'll have a joint discussion so we're privy to all the facts."

"Oh, so you think that's going to be a discussion."

"Yeah. What are you imagining?"

"What am I imagining?" He looks heavenward and shakes his head. "I'm thinking it's going to be an all-out, knock-'em-down, last-man-standing argument." He dabs his brow.

There's some tapping at the door, and a few quick words tells us Sammy's back.

I point my finger at Virgil. "Stay strong."

He answers with a high-pitched moan.

I let Sammy in, and he quickly shuts and locks the door.

"Still no sign of party boy. He's probably long gone by now."

There's a beat of silence that I let hang in the air while I think of the best way to answer. I decide a short and non-committal reply is a good start.

"Maybe."

Sammy looks at me, concerned. "You think he's still in the vicinity?"

"He might be."

"C'mon, Alicia. Don't make me fish for answers. What do you know about this person?"

"I'm fairly certain it was Yuri."

Sammy's expression goes blank. Chase does that too, right before he's about to get red-cheeked, pop-eyed angry. It must be in the Marine guidebook for the face to pull when you don't want your adversary to know what you're going to do next.

"Why didn't you say something sooner?"

"I only figured it out a few minutes before the reporter arrived."

"You knew, too?" Sammy glowers at Virgil.

"I told Virgil at the last minute."

Virgil stands up straight as if reporting to a drill sergeant. "I knew and agreed with Alicia that we should go ahead and grant the interview. We were in a locked room with you guarding the door. You had already questioned the newspaper employees and determined they were legit. We made the adult decision that as long as those safety measures were in place it was safe."

"And there's no reason to squirrel away to a hidden spot to call Chase or give him some sign that there's real trouble." I look Sammy square in the eye, "Because I'm calling him now to explain everything, including that you didn't learn what I figured out until just now. Then we'll all go on speaker phone and discuss what should happen next."

Sammy tenses slightly.

"Just give me a few minutes to talk to him alone first," I add. Best to have him vent at me before we discuss viable options as a group. I'll put up with his anger because I wasn't immediately forthright about our agreement to share information, but I refuse to tolerate any decisions made about my life without my feedback.

As soon as Sammy and Virgil step out of the room, I hit his number. He answers quickly.

"Hi, it's me. Did I get you at a bad time?" He had let me know during our previous conversation that he had a string of meetings scheduled to discuss a new development project on Eighty-Sixth and First.

"No. I'm in between meetings. What about you? How'd the interview go?"

"It was fine. How are things at home?"

"They're good."

"And the kids, what have they been up to?"

"The usual. Teo refuses to go to sleep until you call and sing him that song. You didn't call last night, and we couldn't reach you." His tone is not accusatory, just matter-of-fact.

"I've been singing *Everything is Gonna be Alright* to him over the phone almost every night since I left. I was so busy with the show yesterday that I didn't get a chance to call or check my phone. How was bedtime?"

"Brutal. Teo threw a tantrum. Juliette started howling, and Caroline ran screaming from the room. It was a one-on-one-man job just to gather them together. Eleanor searched for Caroline. I stood watch over Teo until he stopped kicking his feet against the floor, and Sunny consoled Juliette."

"Oh no." I look heavenward and chastise myself for being forgetful. I should have known that changing the routine would be upsetting to all three and they'd resist bedtime even more than usual. It's like they want to hang onto every bit of life without letting go until they collapse from exhaustion. It doesn't help that they're so close in age so what one does, the others imitate, especially if it's something they don't like doing.

"I'll be sure to call tonight."

"I get it. You have a lot on your plate."

"So . . . other than that, everything has been quiet?" We both know that this type of question refers to only one aspect of our lives: Dimitri's cutthroat threats.

"Yeah. How about with you? Any new developments?" The pause of silence that bought me time with Sammy doesn't work with Chase. "What happened?" he demands.

"I'm fine. I . . . well . . . I figured out that it was Yuri who was in the stands. I didn't see his face but could tell it was him by the watch he was wearing and the length of his arms."

"You knew it was him because you recognized the size of his arms?"

"Yeah. I remembered from the first time I saw him that they're extra long."

"When did you determine it was Yuri?" His tone gets a serious edge and I know my answer is not going to be appreciated.

"Just before the reporter and photographer came to conduct the interview."

"Did you share this with Sammy?" Another question whose answer is going to land me in trouble.

"No, not then. I told him afterwards."

"I need to talk to Sammy," he says, brusquely dismissing me and anything else I might have to add.

"I was hoping we could all talk on speaker phone to put together a plan about what should happen next."

"Oh, so now you want to discuss a strategy for moving forward. You didn't seem to want to talk when you first identified Yuri as the culprit. You just went ahead on your own and held your interview," he barks, making me flinch and extend the clutched phone away from my ear. "Where's Sammy now?" he demands.

"In the hallway with Virgil. I'll go tell them to come inside." I walk toward the door, happy to put a pause on his tirade. "He's furious," I mouth to both. No one bats an eye. Once they're inside, I calmly announce, "Chase and I thought we should all discuss the best course of action to take next."

Virgil looks queasy.

"I think he wants to talk to you first, Sammy," I add.

Virgil visibly relaxes.

I hit speaker and set the phone on the table.

"Sammy here."

Chase's terse reply is firm and to the point. "Sammy, Alicia is fairly certain that it was Yuri who aimed the bottle in her direction. Has security made any progress tracking him down?"

"No, it's like he's vanished into thin air."

"That fits in with what my intel is reporting. He had been living in London. Then about ten days ago he traveled to Cassis."

I shoot Virgil a knowing glance, and he gives a slight nod in agreement.

"Given that he got this close to Alicia, the fact that he's gone is irrelevant. It's important that you escort her home today."

I feel the beginning of a small headache that I'm sure will be a cluster migraine by the time this conversation ends.

"I'm right here, Chase. You can speak to me, too."

He lets out an exasperated sigh but doesn't disagree.

"What is it you'd like to *discuss*?" I ask, pretending to have no idea that he's still hell-bent on ordering me to fly home today, not caring how many cancelled meetings or pieces of business I'll leave unfinished and unattended.

"It's in your best interest and our family's to head home now." Before I can answer, he adds, "Sammy, what's your opinion on this?"

That's like asking a duck to quack.

"It might be the best way to go since we no longer have eyes on Yuri, and his behavior is unpredictable."

No longer have eyes on Yuri. Does that mean that they

had been tracking him and knew he was in Paris before this incident occurred? Come to think of it, Chase didn't seem that surprised when I indicated it was Yuri who was the cork popper. They must have informants everywhere helping to track down Dimitri.

With that, Sammy's phone chimes and the name Buford pops up. He quickly declines the call and silences his phone.

"I haven't ruled out returning home before the trip is scheduled to end, but . . . did I confirm that you and Sammy already knew about Yuri's whereabouts?"

Sammy thinks for a moment. Chase is silent. Both behaviors tell me they know more than they're sharing.

It's hard to keep annoyance from my tone. "Virgil and I were hoping you could share what info you have on Yuri. It would help us determine what to do next." I let the comment slide into the conversation so both Chase and Sammy understand that I'm not just packing up and fleeing without more information.

Virgil tugs on the collar of his shirt now that his name has been dropped into the conversation.

More silence follows. I don't budge. Virgil sweats more. A loud sigh from Chase follows. "As usual you're digging in your heels instead of following ord . . ." He stops and corrects orders to, *"recommendations,"* making sure to drag out the latter's pronunciation for exaggerated emphasis. If the sarcasm is eliminated, the verbal change is a step in the right direction. Still, it's not enough for me to give in to their pact to keep relevant information a secret.

"Are you or aren't you going to answer my question?"

"We *suspected* Yuri was somewhere in Paris. What we

didn't know was that he'd show up at your fashion show. Like Sammy says, his behavior has become erratic. We never know what he's up to next."

Something in my brain clicks. Both Sammy and Chase have indicated that Yuri's behavior has become unpredictable. I also noticed that there was an oddness to how Yuri was acting. It was in the way he extended his hands and shook the bottle and then there was a sound. He whistled through his teeth like he was genuinely pleased with my show. Could Dimitri's son Yuri have attended my show to demonstrate his support for my work? Now that's a crazy assumption. But still, it's the gut feeling I get.

Virgil follows my train of thought. "I heard a loud whistle coming from the direction of the spray of the bottle. It was a sound of approval, not a catcall. There was nothing that jumped out at me as being nasty or disapproving the entire time we were out there walking."

That's the spirit, Virgil. I smile my appreciation.

"This may sound strange, but I think Yuri was displaying appreciation for my show. The clapping, the whistle, the champagne, all indicate that he meant no harm to me or Virgil. If he really wanted to hurt us, he was so close, he could have done serious damage."

Sammy fixes me with a stare. His face is expressionless, but I can tell he's assessing the situation.

Once again, Chase answers first. I realize that since I'm involved, Sammy is conceding to Chase for any reactions.

"Recent intel indicates that Yuri had a falling-out with his father. He's not too keen on Dimitri's business dealings in the Middle East. It's not surprising. Outcomes can be murky when an Oxford education clashes with one earned from hard knocks on the streets," Chase says.

"It makes sense," I say to the room. "An international education at an Ivy League school would have taught Yuri that interfering in the messy politics of war-torn countries is a fool's mission. Why would he want to follow in his father's footsteps if he disagrees with the arms deals Dimitri continues to broker in the Middle East?"

"Ease up, Alicia. This is all speculation. We still don't know for sure why Yuri got so close to you." Chase is not accepting my rationale as fact. But I'm surer than ever that it's what happened.

"Is there any intel indicating that Dimitri is in the vicinity?"

"Would you be in Paris if there was?" He's being testy because he realizes I'm questioning his belief that I should leave Paris today.

"I'm not doubting your surveillance capabilities—"

He cuts me off. "We need to talk privately."

"Alright." I look toward Sammy and Virgil.

Sammy is already reaching for the doorknob.

"Are you going to be okay?" Virgil mouths.

I nod assent, holding up five fingers for the time I think I'll need before helping him wrap up here. Once they're out the door, I steel myself for what Chase is going to share. Even though I don't know exactly what it is, I know it's bad. Otherwise, he would have shared it during our countless discussions before I left for Paris. I click the lock and give him my full attention, feeling my heart start to race in anticipation.

"Chase, I'm back." I collapse into a chair and let out a deep breath, the residual effects of a very long and tiring day hitting me like a brick.

"You seem exhausted. Have you been getting any sleep?"

"It's been hectic. My mind has been on overload, so falling and staying asleep is hard." Imagining his arms around me, I'm stricken with longing. "I miss having you next to me in bed."

"Me too. The phone sex was good, but I like the feel of your body next to mine." He's quiet and I notice he's running his hand through his hair but decide to give him time to say what's on his mind. "I'm going to let my common sense prevail here. I think you're right in assuming that Yuri meant you no harm. Still, that doesn't mean he's not working with or for someone who deals with his father's underworld network. We know he and his father have broken off contact with each other, but not the reason why. What worries me," he continues, his voice becoming softer, which scares the crap out of me, "is that if Yuri knows where you are, Dimitri might too, especially if he's keeping tabs on his son. We can't assume that all of a sudden Yuri wishes you well because he had a difference of opinion with his father."

"I hear you, but I still don't get why Yuri chose to do nothing to hurt me when he was so close to where I was walking."

"Maybe it's to sow doubt in our minds about Dimitri's real intent, so we let our guard down."

"I hadn't considered that Yuri's presence could be a distraction from something that could happen that's far worse than what we've already been dealing with." I rub my temples, worrying that fatigue is clouding my judgment, then sit there, stunned, for a moment before finding my voice again. "Do you think Dimitri is planning to," I nearly choke on the word but force it out, "*kill* our children?" As the words escape my mouth. I ask myself how it's possible for someone to lose all humanity and seek to harm innocent children.

"I won't let that happen." He sounds grave.

"But you think he's planning to. Is that what you're saying?"

Silence.

A dark cloud falls over me as I consider what could happen. "I'm taking the next flight home."

"No, wait. It's *you* I'm worried about. The children are safe here."

"You're concerned that it's me who Dimitri wants to attack? How is that anything new?" Seconds tick by. There is something else, something darker that he's not sharing.

His tone grows harsh. "Dimitri's a psychopath who's being hunted down by multiple global agencies. He's running out of options and desperate people are apt to commit desperate acts. All I'm saying is that you have to watch your back."

"You think it's a good idea for me to stay in Paris to complete the job?"

"I don't think it's a *good* idea. But if you stay vigilant and close to Sammy, you should be able to safely finish what you set out to accomplish."

I get up and start to pace.

"I don't want you worrying about the children. I have that covered."

This calms me a little, but fear and doubt still chew at my insides. "You know how much I want this, but not at the expense of our family. You have to let me know if the danger back home has gotten worse."

"It hasn't. All I'm asking is that you exercise extra caution now that you've identified Yuri as having been at your show. I'm especially concerned about what can happen after Sammy leaves to replace Mac here. I'm thinking Sammy should stay and fly back with you on Saturday."

"Absolutely not." Panic settles into my voice. "I want Sammy with the children as quickly as possible after Mac leaves, and please don't insist that Mac cancel his trip to Paris. Virgil hasn't seen him for several weeks and Mac needs some vacation time after his deployment. I'll be fine. I've already arranged for Devie and Virgil to have dinner in my suite on Friday night. Sammy is going to order room service while we're at our meeting and have it delivered before he leaves for the airport. After I'm done, I'm heading straight back to the hotel in the private car we've been using since we arrived. Sammy has already cleared the driver. It's a good plan, Chase."

"I'll go along with it, but you can't hold back if you suspect something's wrong. Mac and Virgil can always go to Paris together at another time."

I force a smile and an even tone, more to convince myself that everything is going to be alright than to keep Chase from knowing that I figured out what he's holding back.

"Don't worry. I'll be fine."

There's a rap at the door and Virgil walks in, pointing to his watch.

"I've got to go. They're wrapping up here, and I have a ton of outfits to pack up before we leave for our meeting."

"Stay safe." He kisses his fingers and touches the screen.

"You too. I love you." And I do the same. Staring at the dark screen, I dig into my pocket and fish out a cigarette and my lighter. My first drag calms a bit of my frayed nerves.

"That bad?" Virgil inquires.

"It could be better, but I am here for the duration of our trip."

"That's good news. Sammy's waiting just outside the door. I'm going to head toward the staging area and start gathering our merchandise."

"I'll be there shortly." Holding the cigarette to my lips with a shaking hand, I search the white, blank wall ahead for some clue about what to do next to thwart this maniac's moves. Instead of crafting a plan, all my mind conjures is the shadow of a serpent, head raised, fangs bloodied and bared. The image blends human hatred with bestial force. I close my eyes to shut out the haunting sight, but the reality of its intentional brutality won't quit. Dimitri wasn't just out to torment us as he'd done so often in the past. Somehow, he had gotten the message across to Chase that he was going to kill me and our children.

I know that when Dimitri had that fawn shot, he meant it as a threat to Caroline, just like I know that when he attempted to force me to abort both pregnancies, he was determined to keep Chase from having a family. Since he holds Chase accountable for his eldest son's death, and his wife and children being placed in the witness protection program when Chase had him incarcerated, he covets our family. Simply put, if he can't have his family, Chase can't have one either.

But why wait so long before setting out to hunt and kill me and our children? Dimitri hasn't made any attempts to hurt us since the twins were born. Even when his son Yuri stalked us to the rehab center while we were visiting Fiona, he didn't harm anyone. Dimitri had the same mad motivation to murder me and the children after the twins were born as he did before. So why not even try? This waiting game gets me to thinking that maybe he's hungry for something else. Something he feels he needs to have to tie up loose ends before he destroys our lives.

Dimitri always grabs what he wants when he wants it, using devious strategies to accomplish his goals. He didn't just assault me by overpowering me in the mailroom of my building. He needed to show he could get hold of something personal and meaningful, something that was directly connected to our family. That's why he stole Fiona's ring and placed it on a severed finger as a lure to get me alone. The same type of personalized threat was employed when he left Caroline's mangled car seat outside our apartment door. Besides these, what other trophies does he crave from us before he plans his attack?

I take a final drag, stub out the cigarette, and head for the door. Without more information, I can't make sense of why Dimitri has chosen now to transform from a tormentor to a premeditated murderer. Maybe it's simply because, as Chase says, international intelligence agencies are closing in on his whereabouts and he knows his time for seeking revenge is running out.

There isn't anything I can do about these unanswered questions now, but once I'm back home, I plan on demanding more information from Chase about when he discovered Dimitri decided to go for the kill. Maybe then we can use the information to stop him from putting his heinous actions in motion.

CHAPTER 25

The rain pelts our faces as Virgil and I dart from our final meeting to the car. Back in my hotel room, I toss off my wet heels and slide down damp stockings that are soaked at the toes.

Our final meeting lasted several more hours than anticipated and emphasized the mounting demands of incoming orders for this year's line. The requests were flattering but invited a staggering number of details, paramount being where to secure adequate space for my growing enterprise. I know I want to have work areas where everything can be made under one roof. Crafting a sustainable element behind my luxury brand requires making products on site within the New York City area. The problem is going to be keeping my high-end designs in the affordable range for the growing upper-middle-class. This means I need to find reasonably-priced rental space, an impossible task in the city. Even the rents in the outer boroughs have become prohibitive.

I can always ask Chase. That would be the easiest path to take. He is in real estate, owns multiple buildings, and would have no doubts about giving my business the space it needs. But would it be mine, or would he, in typical Chase fashion, want to dictate where it should be and whether it was sheltered enough, and close enough to home and our protective network over the more pressing problems of productivity, revenue, and profits? As a businessman, and a damn good one at that, those priorities would normally come first, but where I'm concerned, he cares less about commerce and more about my safety. The more I think about it, the more I come to believe that this is something I have to do on my own.

My brain throbs with work-related issues. Time to take a break before a migraine sets in. I scrub my hands and face, slip into sweats and a cropped tee, and sweep my rain-soaked hair into a ponytail, then hit the mini-bar. As planned, Sammy arranged for dinners to be placed in the room on warming trays before he left. They must have just arrived, because each covered platter is hot to the touch. I mix a gin and tonic, stirring it with my finger, and lift the domed silver lids, smelling herbal fragrances of Sole Meunière and Duck l'Orange. Roasted baby carrots and asparagus dress each of the plates. I dab my pinky finger in the dark, rich sauce that's drizzled over the vegetables and pop it into my mouth. Scrumptious.

If I thought sipping a drink would loosen my limbs and ease my fear, I was wrong. Alone in my hotel room with silent walls, lots of *what ifs* clamor to be heard. *What if* Yuri *was* sent as a diversion so another attack could happen? If that's the case, how do we determine where or who Dimitri will strike? Speculative notions spin into horrific scenarios. *What if* Dimitri kills Chase or discovers from

Yuri where I'm staying in Paris and, like an animal drawn to its prey for sport, finds and murders me in my hotel room? Worse still, *what if* he succeeds in harming my children while I am away?

What started as routine worries about work accelerates into increasing layers of angst about our safety. The air becomes so close, so smothering, that I feel I need to find a place just to be able to breathe. Do I run? Stay? Scream? Bolt the door to shut out the horrible thoughts? Dread swells in the pit of my stomach as images of my children, hurt or worse, flood my thinking. I take a long breath and let it out, slow and even, to try to escape the dark walls of my thoughts. Sitting on the edge of the bed, I take a swig of my drink. My heart hammers in my chest. *Calm down*, an internal voice hums, but clouds of uncertainty and responsibility are too strong for me to let go of. Questions worm into my anxiety, carving a path like snails inching along sand.

How did I get here? It seems as if one minute Chase and I were on a whirlwind trip of passion through Europe, and the next we were peering into the jaws of death, with me attacked by a Mafia boss and he a prisoner of the Taliban in Afghanistan. Three children followed in quick succession. More obligations with more that could go wrong. It's like every which way I turn, there is a repeat of the sameness of worry. Where does it stop?

My phone jingles. I look up swiftly, welcoming the distraction. It's Chase, and the relief when his face shows on my phone's screen is like seeing life replace death. I'm not alone in this never-ending fiasco of fear and danger.

"Hello."

"Hey, it's me."

As if I didn't know. "How's it going? Are you in London yet?"

"I've just landed. I wanted you to know that everything is fine at home. My buddy just radioed that Sammy's flight landed at JFK. He's driving to be with the kids as we speak. I gave the okay for Mac to leave. He's scheduled to land at Orly in about five hours."

"That's good." I can only imagine the cost of all these private flights, but it's the only way for Chase to keep control of the times everyone leaves and arrives. "And the kids, what have they been up to?"

"Since we were left shorthanded, all three are being kept busy playing games indoors with Sunny and Eleanor."

It warms me that he's calling to put me at ease when he's worked so hard to keep things together at home. "I'm going to call once we hang up."

"That's good, because Caroline wanted to know exactly when you were coming home tomorrow. She even carried her play clock to me and made me move the hands to show how many hours it would be. Said she would never have let you go if she knew it was going to be for this long."

"I miss the little rascals. Have they been behaving?"

Pause.

"For the most part, they've been good."

"That does not sound good. What did they do now?

"I was told that early this morning they crept into the kitchen to surprise Sunny and Eleanor with homemade pancakes. Caroline dragged over the chair and used it to climb onto the counter to reach the glass mixing bowls, but she couldn't handle their weight. They crashed down, shattering into a thousand pieces around her chair. Some shards shot into her and the twins' hair."

"Oh no. Any blood? Stitches?"

"Surprisingly, no. Eleanor and Sammy removed pieces from Teo and Juliette's heads with tweezers, but Caroline ran and hid. It took them close to half an hour to find where she was hiding."

"And where, pray tell, was that this time?"

"Somehow she managed to scrunch herself on a low shelf in the back of your walk-in storage closet."

"How in god's name did she find that shelf? It's buried in the back of that huge closet and the bulbs have all gone out. It's completely dark. I kept meaning to have them replaced but was distracted by this trip."

"I have no idea how she found that spot. Sunny needed his military night-vision goggles to finally find her. It was so dark, and she hid herself under so many dresses, that a simple flashlight wasn't enough."

I slap my hand across my mouth. I don't know whether to laugh or be concerned. "You're kidding, right?"

"Nope. Our kids now require military-grade equipment to be kept in line." We both laugh at the same time.

"I think we have to give Eleanor and Sunny a raise."

"There might not be enough money to offer, especially when so many of us are traveling." He's quiet. Then, as suspected, his voice tenses. "What are your plans for the rest of the day?"

"I think I might take a nap before Devie and Virgil come up to the room. I'm exhausted."

"Still not sleeping well?"

"No, there's so much to digest that my head keeps

spinning." The truth is, I miss the press of his body next to mine and those breathing noises he makes that are not quite snores but heavier than regular breaths. If I wake during the night, they lull me back to sleep.

"How did your last set of meetings go?" He jumps in with a question about my business concerns while thoughts about him still circulate. There's an ache reminiscent of the time I thought he might be dead that still lingers when we're apart.

"They went well. I'm going to need to find space sooner rather than later to meet the demand of all the incoming orders. I was thinking of renting space in the Garment District to keep everything under one roof. It will be good to try and enliven the area again with some clothing manufacturing."

"There's no need to rent space when we own a five-story building in the vicinity that's currently empty. I can have it gutted and designed to your specifications. The cost-effectiveness of this move will be in everyone's best interest."

Here he goes again, assuming control and dictating terms. "I thought it would be easier to just rent space using the money I have set aside from my small brand. Time is of the essence here and well this way, it would be mi—"

"It would be solely yours either way. Look, I get your need for independence, but you're letting emotions dictate where business sense should prevail."

"What do you mean? All I plan on doing is renting space in midtown. Once I'm approved, the move should be quick and efficient."

"It might happen quickly—you have good credit and

some cash set aside—but it won't be cost-effective. All business owners below Ninety-Sixth Street must give the city 3.9 percent of what they pay in rent if that rent exceeds $250,000 a year."

I sweep back my hair and start to pace with the phone held to my ear. I know nothing about this tax.

"And . . ." he drives his point home, "this commercial rent tax is increased by a real-estate tax if the tenant occupies the ground floor, which I assume you will want to do for your retail shop."

Mr. Perfect is 100 percent on target, and he's still not done with his argument, so I jump in quickly to make my point, show that I'm not financially ignorant of the problems and potential solutions. "I plan to keep the manufacturing and design under one roof. That cuts out the thousands of air travel miles clothing made out of the US and sold here uses. Now it can take anywhere from four to twenty-four weeks for items to be produced and delivered. That wasted time costs money and leaves a detrimental carbon footprint. With localized fashion, items usually take as little as three days to be made and be ready to sell. Won't capitalizing on that efficiency offset those costs?"

His answer is swift. "No."

We're both silent.

I cave first. "Why not?"

"You say you're working to sustain local garment manufacturing, making what you design in New York rather than China or Vietnam."

He stops, waiting for my confirmation.

"That's right."

"Well, this tax is especially prohibitive for you. It could

crush your business before it gets off the ground."

"So, what do you suggest?"

"Exactly what I said earlier. Take one of the buildings we own. That way you'll have a vertical business where you own and manage every aspect of design, manufacturing, retail, and real estate. There won't be any middlemen. Everything will be completely self-financed."

"With your money and your investments." Once again, my distinctiveness is lost in his achievements.

"With *our* money. We invest in each other. That's how this works. I believe in your talent. Why can't you trust and believe in my decisions?"

Trust. The word snaps the wind from my sails. It's hard to believe you are succeeding when so much of your identity is buoyed and defined by another, more powerful, figure. You can weave, bob, and dart but no matter how hard you try to pull ahead, you never quite escape the shadow of the titan's touch.

"You have an identity, *Alicia*, and it extends beyond me, if that's what you're worried about."

It's unsettling to be read like an open book, so I don't answer.

He doesn't stop. "It's on the pages of your sketchpad. You took blank pieces of paper and turned them into extensions of yourself. Now, all you need to do is bring them to life. They're yours. You own them. I'm only here to help by sharing what I know about business growth and development."

I open my mouth to disagree, then shut it, wondering if it's ever a problem for him not to have to struggle to be perfect. There's absolutely nothing to take issue with here. Only an idiot would disagree. Besides, it feels good to be talking about business matters instead of being vanquished by vindictiveness.

"You make a good point. When I get home, will you take me to see the property you have in mind?"

His tone brightens. "Sure. And if it's not suitable, we'll look for another."

"Okay, it all sounds good."

That done, the lightened mood fades. I circle my finger along the rim of my glass, waiting for him to get to the point still pressing on his nerves.

"So, everything is set for tonight?"

"Yep, food's already here. It must have been delivered when I was en route. Virgil's coming before Devie so we can meet to tie up some loose ends before our planned dinner. I'm guessing Mac will be here before they both leave. If not, I'll bolt myself in my room and wait for Mac's knock."

"Good. Stay in and get some rest."

"That's the plan. Take care of yourself, too. Can't wait to see you again."

"I'm going to try and finish up tomorrow night so I can fly back home first thing the following morning."

"Are we going to be London homeowners?"

"If I can negotiate 13 percent off the asking price. With the current strong dollar and weaker pound, it's a good buying opportunity. We can rent it for a nice sum until housing prices increase."

"Well, you are definitely the expert in negotiating."

"Except when I'm dealing with you. Your stubbornness tops my ability any day."

"Not true. I respect your thinking. You're Mr. Perfect."

"How comforting to know I've nothing to live up to or improve."

"On second thought, maybe 'perfect' is a stretch."

"Really. And why is that?"

"Well, your ears stick out a tad."

He laughs. "Well, yours are perfect. They're, uh, *blush pink*."

I laugh, knowing he's heard me use that color to describe some of my designs.

"I can't wait to nibble them with kisses."

I stop smiling and listen to his husky-sounding words.

"Before I move my lips down your perfect neck, all the way to your perfect breasts and nipples." The words of his playful, sexy chatter shoot through my body. "I love you, baby. Stay safe," he says.

"I love you too. See you soon."

I hit the red disconnect button and quickly phone home. First, I apologize to Sunny, then move along to Eleanor with basically the same speech, explaining how Chase and I are going to have a serious talk about safety dos and don'ts with all three children. It's wonderful to hear their little voices piping with enthusiasm as they fumble with each other for the phone.

"Come home now, Mamma," Teo demands. I snort at his tone because of who it reminds me of and give him assurances I'll be back after he goes to sleep, wakes up, and comes home from gymnasium class. Caroline tells me she's going to Wilcox's house for a playdate tomorrow but wants me home today. Juliette says she's made me a card with rainbows and *come home soon* in "big words" that she asked Eleanor to write. Missing from the conversation is any mention of the pancake debacle. Stupid, they're not. When Sunny takes back the phone to say good-bye, all three are either whining or crying that they want me home now.

After the call, I finish my drink and push down the comforter and sheet, hoping for some serious shut-eye before Virgil arrives. Hovering on the edge of sleep without being able to succumb to its release, time crawls. Crowded thoughts about the tasks waiting for me once I'm home bombard my mind. I make a mental note to download that sleep app Beth is always raving about, then will myself to take deep breaths, hold, and slowly release each. I close my eyes.

It seems like only minutes have ticked by when I notice thin light escaping from the slats in the shuttered window, basking the room in a late-afternoon winter haze. There's a tapping sound. First, one thump. Then, lots more, until the pounding can't be ignored. A blankness swims in my sluggish consciousness. It takes me a while to figure out that it's coming from outside the door of my suite.

The glowing digital clock on the end table shows it's 3:11 p.m. Mac's not expected for another four or five hours. It's still too early for my meeting with Virgil, and Devie is at a modeling gig for Estée Lauder. I stumble from the bed and make my way toward the intermittent banging, not realizing until I'm at the door that my heart is pounding in sync with the knocking.

In the hallway, someone is talking. It's a raspy voice but too low-toned to make out. I hold my ear to the door and another louder and deep, guttural voice asks, "You sure she's in her room?"

I look through the peephole and a head of dark soft waves fills the view. It's Beth, getting ready to pound her hand against the door again. Standing next to her is a thuggish-looking man I've never seen before.

"Ali, are you in there? It's me, Beth." More loud knocking.

I don't open the door. I need to know who she's with first. If someone is using her to get to me then we're both in trouble, and it helps neither of us if I open this door. She must realize my situation, because she adds, "The person with me is a bodyguard I trust. I know you're alone so I thought he could help until Mac gets here. If you're in your room, please open the door. I'm starting to get worried."

I didn't think it possible, but she bangs her open palm even louder against the door. I look through the peephole again and note that she seems at ease with whomever she's with.

"You think I should break through the door?" he asks. "If she's in trouble, I will help."

"No, if she doesn't answer, I'm going to phone her husband. He can try calling. If he can't reach her," Beth's voice quavers then firms, "we'll have to get the manager or call the police. I've already tried phoning her several times. I also called her friends who are traveling with her here in Paris. No one is answering."

A quick glance at my phone shows I have four missed calls. I had silenced it when I was trying to fall asleep and mustn't have heard it vibrating. I watch Beth scroll through her phone searching for Chase's number. This tells me she and her friend's visit is legit.

Beth's face beams relief when she sees me in the

doorway. "Thank god you're alright." She gives me a giant hug. Stepping back, she flips her thumb toward her companion. "This is Luis, but everyone calls him 'El Árbol.'"

One glance at El Árbol reduces me to slack-jawed silence. The man standing in the hallway easily stretches to seven feet. His broad nose is flattened flush to his face. He strides toward me, his smile flashing two gold-tipped incisors.

"Ms. Cesare, you have NO problems when El Árbol is here."

I smile thinly and look toward Beth. "What's this all about?"

"I'll explain in a minute. Can we come in?"

"Yeah, sure."

El Árbol ushers Beth in first, then ducks his length under the door frame.

"You have a few hours before Virgil and Devie get here, right?"

I nod. "So? Do you want to join us here for dinner?" I glance back at the warming trays with several covered dishes. "We've plenty of food."

"Maybe later. Right now, I am so stoked. I managed to get us both hair appointments with Jean Louis David, who is only the most sought-after hair stylist in Paris."

I start to protest, but she cuts me off.

"Just hear me out. El Árbol will accompany us in a private car with the driver Sammy hired."

"Yeah, but I planned to stay here and—"

"I get how you must have promised Chase you'd stay put until Mac got here, but I've covered all bases to ensure that no thugs or henchmen will get anywhere close to where you'll be tonight."

At the mention of thugs and henchmen, El Árbol's bushy eyebrows go up. He scoops two large walnuts from his pocket and crushes them against each other in one bare hand. Tossing pieces of nut and shells into his mouth, he sets his eighteen-karat choppers to work while his eyes remain riveted in my direction. He's already on the job, and I haven't even left my room.

Beth looks at me with devilish merriment. "Let's grab some Parisian moments shopping for lingerie and getting haircuts and makeovers. Afterward, we can meet for a drink at Le Bar. Uh-uh," she wags her finger to silence my protest. "Le Bar is right here in your hotel, and El Árbol will be with us the whole time. We'll even invite Virgil and Devie to join our party. I know Marcel is coming and so is Andre. Besides," she studies my tangled bedhead and wrinkled shirt, "you are in serious need of some fun."

I bite my bottom lip, worrying a piece of skin that's struggling to break free.

"You're right. What's so terrible about a bit of free time to shop and groom in Paris?"

All of a sudden, I realize how tired I am of being so doom-laden. I need . . . no, I *crave* a release to silence the commotion rattling inside my head. My gaze snags on the height and girth of El Árbol. As far as safety goes, my new bodyguard seems more than up to the task of taking on an adversary or two. Now if only I could convince Chase that everything is under control. I glance at my watch. If we leave quickly, I can be back in time for dinner with Virgil and Devie here in the room. Afterward, we could all go downstairs to Le Bar for a quick drink. Mac should be here by then and could come, too. I'll give Chase a call as soon as Mac arrives.

"Give me five minutes to change."

"Take all the time you need," Beth calls out to my retreating back.

Jeez, I really must look bad.

CHAPTER 26

"I love this city." Beth inhales the cold, crisp air when we step out of the hired car and onto the outdoor plush carpet of the George V Hotel. A doorman, dressed in top hat and vested suit, immediately heads toward the trunk of our limo and removes our bags from our shopping spree at Cadolle.

"Please *mademoiselles*. I will take your coats, too." We hand them over and drain the crystal flutes of champagne we carried out from the car.

"I've just purchased enough new lingerie and underwear to last a lifetime."

"Not after Chase tears them from your body, including that Leavers lace black corset you just bought."

I shake my head and roll my eyes. "I can't believe you talked me into wearing it now along with all this." I circle my free hand around the newly-purchased ivory pleated chiffon blouse and tapered black silk skirt. The sales attendant couldn't have been more accommodating, removing the tickets and labels and steaming out wrinkles from the skirt so I looked *parfaite*. I wouldn't let her touch the blouse with a hot steamer, lest she ruin the pleats.

"And why not? You look fantastic."

"It seems very chic for a quiet dinner in my room and a quick drink afterwards." Absently, my finger slides up the sheer sleeve of my blouse that's slipped off my shoulder.

"Oh no you don't." Beth stares me down under the hazy beam of light above the hotel entrance. "That's half the beauty of the look." She slips the edge of the sleeve off my shoulder, making sure the black silk strap of the corset shows. "Think of this as a dress rehearsal for when you're with Chase. In fact, you can pretend he's watching you when you're wearing it tonight."

"Okay, but Andre *is* seeing you later. Talk about tearing off someone's clothing. I can't wait to watch him try to keep his hands from stripping off that black silk bustier you're wearing." It's hard to believe, but she blushes, which makes me laugh and nudge her with my elbow.

"Alicia?" Devie strides up to the hotel's entrance and studies my new look. "You have a new hairstyle."

"It's just a trim and some highlights."

She takes my arms and holds me at a distance. "Cool, very cool. I mean you always look good in your designs but now, ooh la la, you have that sexy French look."

This is a real compliment coming from Devie, who wears glamour like a pair of walking shoes. Devie could don a black silk-and-sheen pantsuit like she's wearing now or a long, print prairie dress and carry both with the same ambiance of mystical allure.

What started as a reassuring shopping spree and make-over morphs again into thoughts about the safety of Chase and my children. I fish for my phone. "I should call Chase."

"That's your decision to make, but we're already back at the hotel and you're not leaving the premises again."

Beth studies my worried expression. "He's going to be difficult about this, isn't he?"

I don't answer, mostly because I'm already thinking about how to approach the topic of my change of plans when we speak tonight.

"Well, if he's anything like my father, he'll distance himself rather than yell as a reaction."

I shake my head. "Nope. He'll do both. First the yelling about how I don't know how to stick to decisions made as partners in a commitment. Then he'll distance himself, freeze me right out."

"It's those bastard tendencies I warned you about," Beth points her finger at me, lips compressed. "You shouldn't let the tantrum he has when he finds out he wasn't the one in control tonight interfere with your fun today. You've earned this reprieve."

I look past her and into the hotel, thinking about the several conversations Chase and I had concerning my being on my own tonight.

"It's not just that. We have this whole trust issue going on, and I promised to stay in. I should at least call and tell him my plans."

Before I can use my phone, Devie swipes it from my hand. "That is not good idea. You look great with all those long beach waves," her hand swirls around my head for effect. Raising an inquisitive brow, she turns and studies El Árbol, who hovers over me like a secret service agent.

"Devie, this is El Árbol, who has been hired to protect Alicia. El Árbol, meet our friend Devie," Beth says. El

Árbol grunts a hello, and Devie raises her chin in greeting before turning her attention back my way.

"El Árbol seems like diligent bodyguard, and you don't plan to leave the hotel tonight. Why call. Besides, do you know where he is right now?"

"Of course I do. He's in London."

Devie throws up her hands. "We all know he's in London, but do you know *exactly*," she emphasizes the word as if speaking to a thick-skulled child, "where he is or what he's planned for the night?"

I don't, but if I had to guess, I'd say Mr. Perfect is either holed up in his hotel room preparing for a host of meetings the following day or completing a workout routine that rivals boot camp.

Devie does make a valid point, though. I've made no demands on Chase about his schedule or his whereabouts.

"You're all the time working or with children or with Chase and his buddies. You walk a straight line. Now is your time to break free and celebrate the success of your fashion show."

Did she just hint that I'm *boring*?

An internal force surfaces that's determined to show her she's wrong, that I can be impetuous, that I am spontaneous, but I push it back down again, reminding myself of my promise to Chase.

"You of all people should understand Dimitri's nefarious motives are what worries Chase," I tell her pointedly.

"Nefarious motives? That sounds like Chase's big Ivy League degree talking. Me? I like to say Dimitri's fucked us over one too many times and needs to be taken out. But tonight is not the time to be thinking about all that."

"Devie's right," Beth chimes in. "Call Chase later when you're back in your room. Explain about El Árbol and all of us hanging out together. He'll eventually see he has nothing to worry about."

I shift uneasily. Something inside tells me it's not going to be that simple. Devie knows the battle I have in store, too, because she swirls her finger toward my chest. "Show him that black lacy get-up you're wearing under your clothes. You'll have hot makeup sex and all will be forgiven. Now, let's get going," she winces, rubbing her temples. "I need a wind-me-down drink just thinking about all this commitment, trust shit."

It's coming over loud and clear. I need to let my guard down, go out, clown around with friends, not be afraid to celebrate a good time after a long and tiring business trip. There are no guarantees that stopping in my tracks will keep Dimitri from the destruction he's determined to cause. What harm is there in going for a cocktail in a ritzy bar in my hotel where there are hordes of employees and doormen close by, and I'm surrounded by trusted friends?

A crack, several crackles, and more crunching stalk me into the hotel lobby. I put my phone back in my purse and add one nut-chomping hulk of a bodyguard to the list.

• • •

"Here's to Cesare Designs going global and setting the bar for where fashion is going," Beth toasts.

"*A votre santé*," Andre says, and he and Marcel second in unison. We all clink glasses. Marcel's mane of wavy, dark hair is shorter than I remember from when we first met here in this very bar. With his skinny trousers, tan suede shoes, and tailored jacket, he cuts a sharp Parisian look.

It feels good to be sipping a martini in the splendor of Louis XVI furniture, swag curtains, and crystal chandeliers. Very adult. Professional. Independent. Like being in a time machine and traveling back to a period before marriage, children, and death threats sent me hurtling into my present life.

El Árbol's heavy shadow hovers near the doorway, his broad back in contrast to the elegant fixtures and flickering table candles. Well, maybe this hiatus hasn't completely removed me from my current life, but it does show that I'm not taking any chances while Mac is delayed in transit.

"One more for my talented friend here," Virgil points his finger toward the top of my head, "who happens to be the newest rising star in the fashion industry." He leans in, eyes glossy from his third George Fizz champagne concoction. "It's amazing how you glammed up our fashion show with winning styles."

Staring at the recessed, wood-paneled bar, I figure, what's one more drink in such opulence especially since all that stretches ahead are hours of sleepless tossing and turning? When the waiter brings my drink, I raise my glass to the table. "Here's to Virgil, who gave an inexperienced upstart her first opportunity to be part of the world of fashion design. Thanks for trusting my ability."

Andre nuzzles Beth's neck, and once again it's like I've traveled back in time.

"It's been a long time." Marcel swivels a bit and places his arm around my shoulder. Shifting my body from his arm, I smile. "You look good, Marcel."

I'm not just making polite small talk. He really does

look good. There's this lively sparkle to his eyes and when he smiles, his soft lips reveal perfectly straight, small teeth. I vaguely remember how soft his lips were from the kiss he stole when we were dancing at some downtown New York City club. It was uneventful except for the outcome it produced. Chase and I were dating then, and let's just say he was less than thrilled when he saw the photos of me with Marcel that Beth posted on several social media sites. At the time, we had been arguing. His sister was missing. He was stressed and made nasty comments to me that he didn't mean. I got angry, thought he was not calling because he was with someone else. Blah blah blah.

"No, it is you who looks good. Very beautiful." Marcel sidles closer, squeezing my shoulder. "I seenk the last time we saw each other was at the Christmas party you had at your apartment. Do you remember?"

How could I forget? It was right before Chase left for Afghanistan, where he would be captured and tortured for months. So many memories that strain my heart.

"Have I made you sad?"

I take a long sip of my drink. "No. You've made me grateful."

Now, if only I could have a cigarette, I'd feel less sad that Chase isn't here. I miss him. Some more sips of gin, along with a firm reminder to Marcel to behave when he leans in too close, earn me a mischievous smile from him and the surprised realization that I've emptied my second martini glass.

Without asking, another follows, this time from Beth, who insists on showing a video playback of Sammy's defensive acrobatic leap at the end of my show.

"It's like watching a takedown in wrestling match," Devie says.

"More like a mismatch. Look at that size difference." Beth plays it again, and sure enough, one second I'm upright and smiling and the next I'm lying face down under Sammy's mass of muscles with not so much as a stray hair visible. "Paying homage to both Virgil and Ali," Beth adds, "I want to present highlights from her fashion presentation."

My eyes dart upward, and I can feel my cheeks reddening. "It's really not necessary. I mean—"

"Nonsense. You were amazing." And over more cocktails, I watch the screen of her phone. When the red gown wafts down the carpet, there's relevance in its brightness, meaning in its sheen and elegance in its flow that surpasses just any formal item of clothing. It reflects my awareness that creativity pushes life forward. For the first time in a long time, I'm taking an unflinching journey into myself, exploring who I am, what I want and where I want to be. People are viewing it and talking about my show in a way I never imagined possible. It's a wonderful feeling that fills me with confidence. My world becomes a less formidable place. Goodbye anxiety, fretful anticipation, and family pressures. The weight of doom lifts from my head. leaving just me, my friends, and another martini to celebrate the launch of a successful project. I unleash a piece of myself that believes ambition is limitless and mine alone to determine.

Somewhere along the course of the night, someone suggests we go dancing at a club. Le Bound is mentioned, and within the next several minutes our tab is paid, and we're on our way in the limo. It feels good to be part of plans that change in the moment based on a whim, instead of having to adhere to planned schedules based on who's available to escort me somewhere.

I slide into the back seat, while El Árbol sits vigilantly next to the driver. I may be caught up in a wave of optimism, but I'm not naive about the importance of keeping certain elements in place for safety.

Once in the club, the music, a cross between rock and jazz with some Buddha Bar tunes thrown into the mix, pushes me to move to its beat. We're shown to a table and Marcel slips me what looks like a cross between a cigarette and small cigar.

"Take one hit. It'll relax you." I do and when I hand it back, he slides a pack of them into an outside pocket of my purse. "For later," he says. "It will make your worries disappear so you can sleep." He tosses a side glance toward El Árbol, who's searching for a spot in a corner where he can watch the entrance as well as the bar. I know those moves as well as the ones that rollick on the dance floor.

"Thanks, but it's not necessary." I try to hand it back. He ignores my outstretched hand, calling over the waiter to order a bottle of champagne for the table. I discreetly take a hit before putting it out and sliding it and the pack into my purse.

As soon as our coats are checked, Virgil nods his chin toward the dance floor, a deep and broad section at the back of the club. He moves his body to the beat. Marcel follows and I melt into the music with them, my feet moving lightly across the floor while my body sways to the rhythm. Andre roves Beth's waist with his hands while his eyes never leave her face. Go-go dancers jiggle and shimmer on top of the bar, bathed in the glow of flashing lights.

I experience a rush of exuberance. I am young and alive, with no responsibilities except for what this particular night in this particular club holds for me at this particular moment. Rising, locking arms with Virgil, then Marcel, we turn to the rhythm, then separate to raise our hands and shake to the beat. I playfully but firmly wag my finger when Marcel comes in for a nibble on the tattooed stars on my neck. The clock moves with the speed of my dancing feet as, sucked into the revelry, I shed the tedium of work and the worry of motherhood. One song turns into two, then three, until, too winded for another, I head back to the table for something to drink. This goes on several more times: the music beckoning, the chilled champagne refreshing, and the pangs of concern wilting away.

Somewhere in the distance, Devie calls out, "Mamma gone wild. It's about time!"

I'm exploding with a rush of freedom until I spot Virgil standing by our table, waving my purse in the air.

"Your phone hasn't stopped vibrating," he says when I collapse in my chair. Sipping some ice water, I reach for it and, sure enough, feel it vibrating in my hands. Unlocked, it glares 3:00 a.m. and seventeen missed calls.

I had no idea it was this late. I scroll through my countless texts. *Just tried calling. r u okay?*

Twenty minutes later there's another. *Getting worried. Call me* ASAP

I skip through the rest to the last. *Where the hell r u? On my way!*

Virgil sees my look of concern. "They're from the

Chaser, right?"

"Yeah. Did he try phoning or texting you?"

"Who knows. Who can hear anything with all this loud music?"

He checks his phone and grimaces. "He called a bunch of times over the last several hours."

I close my eyes. "How many?"

"At least ten."

I immediately hit Chase's number, but it goes straight to voicemail. I'm about to leave a message when Marcel catches me off guard.

Flush with pleasure from dancing and one too many cocktails, he slips a lit joint between my lips, sweeps my hair away and tries to place a playful kiss on my neck.

I'm just about to shove him away when I look up and catch sight of someone at the entrance. My outstretched arm freezes on Marcel's shoulder as blue eyes search and lock on mine, snapping into focus my hair, my outfit, the pot-infused cigarillo hanging from my lips and, last but not least, Marcel's lips inches from my neck. It's Chase. With mussed hair, the shadow of a beard, and an unzipped bomber jacket revealing a black t-shirt stretched across broad shoulders, he looks out of character and smokin' hot.

For the briefest moment an expression of enormous relief flickers across his face. It doesn't take long for that moment to pass. Hand thrust into his jacket pocket and moving with a singular purpose, he strides toward me, mad as all hell.

I take a quick hit of the joint and give Marcel a sharp shove. He sways toward me again, a sloppy smile tugging his lips as he maneuvers for more nuzzling.

"Chase," I smile, dropping then squashing the joint under my foot. "What are you doing here? I was just about to call." Surprised as I am to see him here, I'm genuinely pleased.

He, on the other hand, looks less than thrilled. He eyes me, then Marcel, with an inscrutable look that on someone else would indicate nothing out of the ordinary is about to happen. I'm not fooled. Sure enough, just as Marcel makes the mistake of coming toward my neck for another playful snuggle, Chase hauls off and lands him a left hook. Marcel topples to the floor.

"You've changed your hair," he says, impervious to Marcel who, down for the count, looks up dazed.

"Yeah. About tonight. Let me explain," I suggest, peering over Chase's shoulder to sneak a peek at Marcel. Marcel, too tipsy to gather the needed momentum to struggle to his feet, stares vacantly ahead, rubbing his jaw.

"Let's go," Chase takes my hand. "Not to worry. I only clipped the Frenchman's jaw."

I pull back a bit. "Okay, but first I want to tell Virgil I'm leaving and say goodbye to Beth and Devie."

"You'll call them once we're back at the hotel. Now let's go." He gives my hand another tug. Why is he in such a rush? He's here. I'm here alive and well. Why not say hello to everyone or at least let me tell them that I'm heading back to the hotel?

And then a realization crystalizes. He doesn't think I can be trusted, so he's making me leave the club, the way a recalcitrant child is led away from a troubling situation. The thought prickles in my mind that it wasn't only Chase's concern about the menace of Dimitri that made him travel from London to Paris unannounced and angry as all hell. Betray trust in someone you love once, and suspicion will stalk you for a lifetime.

I try but fail to shut out the painful memory of my past actions, but know to the depths of my core that I would never violate our marriage vows again. Marcel may have been out of line, but I would never let him cross that line of propriety. Somehow, I will get Chase to believe that, too. But for now, he needs to know that I never let my guard down tonight. I traveled in a hired car with a trusted driver, and El Árbol was at my side to offer protection at all times. I dig in my heels.

"Listen, Chase, there's someone I'd like you to meet." I smile and extend my arm toward El Árbol, who steps over Marcel's outstretched legs and warily studies Chase even as he starts to hold out his hand.

Meeting El Árbol should have been the end of any misunderstanding about my safety, but Chase's agitation has shifted to high gear. "Not now. You can tell me everything back at the hotel," he snaps, ignoring El Árbol's attempt to shake his hand.

My growing frustration is all the fuel El Árbol needs to assume a bodyguard persona with the vigor of a lion protecting a member of its pride. Stepping between us, he glowers at Chase. "Ms. Cesare wants to say something, and she wants to say it NOW."

Chase eyes El Árbol from head to toe, then back up again. I can hear the drumbeat in Chase's mind, pounding with doubt as to whether this giant of a stranger can be trusted.

"Who the hell are you?"

El Árbol hits two pointer fingers into the front of his shoulders. "El Árbol, and Ms. Cesare goes nowhere without me."

Chase's internal rhythm becomes louder and swifter, pulsing through his squinting eye and tight jaw. Hoping to diffuse a situation that threatens to snap into a scene, I try to explain, yet again, who El Árbol is, but Chase has seen enough to tell him that the situation has spun out of his control. With the snap of a finger, my view shifts from wall to floor. I'm tossed over his shoulder, and his arm clasps my legs like a vise as he strides toward the exit. I don't want to shout because at the moment the music and revelry on the dance floor are drowning out our personal drama. Floor and feet whiz by as he purposely strides toward the door.

"Put me down now," I say through gritted teeth. I catch a fleeting glimpse of El Árbol advancing, his gold choppers pulled into a steely grimace. Before I know what's happening, I'm sliding down Chase's chest and spun into a steel chest of muscles. It's Mac. Call it an occupational hazard that my eyes block out the mayhem and note his simple white Prada shirt, black Burberry trousers, gray tailored jacket by Dries Van Noten, and a Rolex watch peeking out from the cuff of his shirt. Mac always did know how to sport designer dress discreetly.

"Mac, when did you get here?" Without answering, he whips me behind his body, then dodges El Árbol's swinging fist. The force of Mac's shove topples me to the floor where, legs splayed, I land unceremoniously on my backside. I shake it off and watch as Mac ducks, weaves, and whirls out of El Árbol's reach. Seems El Árbol has shifted his ire from Chase to Mac in some mad attempt to keep me safe from both. Swinging fists every which way, my giant of a bodyguard teeters then totters so close to where I'm plopped on the floor, his booted foot nearly crushes my head. Shrieking, I slide out of its path. El Árbol randomly shifts his focus from trying to tackle Mac to attempting a right hook at Chase. Chase deftly dodges his beefy fist while Mac hoists me up by the hand and moves me out of the way of all the bedlam.

"All of you, cut it out," I yell, trying to get as close as I can without getting clobbered. My words vanish into flashes of flying fists. Bouncing like boxers dodging an opponent in a ring, Chase shifts his body to the right of El Árbol while Mac steers to the left. All muscle but no speed, El Árbol spins in sluggish confusion, unsure of where his clouts should strike next. His attempted left jab is easily deflected by Chase's forearm. His tries to renew his momentum with several more punches that Chase deflects with quick ducks and side-to-side shifts. Torso and feet spinning into what looks like a move from Extreme Championship Wrestling, Chase presses his head and shoulder into the muscled giant's body. Several seconds and multiple grunts later, El Árbol is felled like an oak run through by a chainsaw. The place shudders to its beams.

"Her name is Mrs. Reardon, asshole," Chase sneers, looking down at the sprawled giant.

I brush off the back of my dress and direct a hard stare at Mac. "Will you please talk some sense into him? Somewhere buried inside his crazy tonight is the rationale of a Yale honor graduate."

Mac shrugs.

"Nothing wrong with being a scholar who can take down someone in a bar fight."

Ugh. I should have known he'd take Chase's side. Reigning in my outrage, I point my finger at both of them and then toward El Árbol who remains spreadeagled on the floor.

"There was not one good reason to fight El Árbol. He was hired as my bodyguard, for heaven's sake!"

Mac looks at Chase. Chase lifts a shoulder, then lets it drop. Both look down at El Árbol. El Árbol nods in agreement, and just like that, giant bodyguard vs. black ops fighters is settled.

Mac reaches out a hand and helps a befuddled El Árbol to his feet, then rights the table and chairs knocked over with the takedown. The immediate area remains empty, with everyone either on the dance floor or at the bar for a last round of drinks before the club closes.

Not wanting to raise Chase's hackles further, I grab my purse and take his arm. "Let's go. I'll explain everything in the car."

Devie saunters over, her only sign of concern showing in the hitch of a brow. "Did you forget your club?" She must have caught the over-the-shoulder debacle, and I wonder who else may have seen what happened.

"I should have known you'd be in on this. I thought you were going to have a quiet dinner together." Chase laces into her with a squinty-eyed stare.

"We changed our minds," she glares back, both of them holding their ground like they must have done countless times when quarrelling as children. Devie looks away first just as Beth heads in our direction, her brow furrowed with worry. By now our antics have caught the attention of some hefty club employee. Flanked by a smaller man with slicked-back hair, both head our way. They do not look like the sensible management types.

With my coat slung across his arm, Mac holds open the door and points his chin toward the street, a silent reminder to Chase that we should leave before we're tossed out on our asses or hauled off by the police.

"I'll catch you later," Chase tells Mac, an indication that Mac is off for the night.

"Is she going to be alright?" Beth asks Devie.

"All good," Devie responds, "unless you think a fuck-fest after a marital tiff is a bad thing."

I close my eyes, embarrassed to the tips of my toes by the scene we created.

CHAPTER 27

Stony silence follows me onto the street.

Chase stops at the curb, his silhouette lit under a lamppost as he bends toward a motorcycle and hands me a helmet that could pass for a superhero mask.

"You rented a motorcycle?"

"No."

I pinch the bridge of my nose in an attempt to deal with his icy, monosyllabic response. "Then why are we getting ready to take off on one?"

"Because," his voice slices across mine, "I bought it." He pauses then adds tersely, "You've got some explaining to do once we get to the hotel."

My mouth flaps open. "You went out and *bought* a motorcycle without so much as a mention, and I'm the only one who has explaining to do?"

"Let's get going. It's too cold to stand on the street talking." He eyes my clothing, focusing on my high-heeled shoes and long coat. "You're not exactly dressed for this kind of ride, but there was no time to change vehicles once I got to Paris. Hang on tight, and you'll be alright."

I ignore his reference to how I'm not dressed appropriately for a motorcycle ride, mostly because I'm having a hard time processing how he rode here from London on a vehicle I didn't know he knew how to drive, or, for that matter, was licensed to drive. And yes, I'm sure he's duly certified. Mr. Perfect would never operate one unless qualified and accredited.

"When did you learn how to ride a motorcycle?"

"It's a BMW R1250. I was born to ride this beauty. Now get on," he commands and stares ahead wordlessly.

"Good to know anger hasn't leveled that cockiness." I slip on the helmet, hitch up my coat and skirt, and ease onto the rear seat. He's angry, worried, and jealous, a trifecta of triggers for him to haul and me to have to deal with. Best to enjoy the emotional freeze-out because when the words come, they'll be raw and piercing.

Rocketing down a quiet Avenue George V, turns and curves are made at breakneck speed. Who is this person that sits in front gripping the bars, working their mechanisms, maneuvering the wheels so that at times we're flying forward and at other times bending into a turn nearly level with the narrow empty road? Earlier tonight, I felt a refreshed spirit, an energized weightlessness when I tossed aside worry and family responsibilities. Now, on this motorcycle, speeding along with Chase in control, the world slips to a distance where all that remains are the two of us racing inside a dimension all our own. Adrenaline pumps through my veins. The ability to relinquish control to someone I trust with my life gives me a defining rush. My hair whips into my neck under the helmet, the icy-wet wind bites my cheeks and, laughing, I screech out loud. He knows exactly what he's doing, exactly how far he can push it before I can no longer maintain my balance on the seat, and even though he's furious, he would never test that limit.

I'm breathless when we finally pull up to the curb in front of the hotel. Maneuvering off the seat, I remove my helmet. Chase hands it and the cycle to an all-too-eager attendant who, wide-eyed and open-jawed, jumps forward as if he's just been handed the Holy Grail.

He spots me and does a double take. "You're that designer who models, right?"

I hesitate, then clarify, "I am a fashion designer, but I don't model."

He grunts, forgetting I exist when he takes full command of the cycle. "*Monsieur*, I will take good care of it."

Chase dismisses him with a wave of his hand, then precipitously heads toward the door. Determined this time to keep my feet firmly planted on the ground, I jog after him, deciding that if he tries that over-the-shoulder stunt again, I might have to hit him in the head with my stiletto. I immediately disregard the thought. I'd never jeopardize a pair of Valentino Rockstud pumps by knocking them over his hard noggin.

Inside the elevator, tension crackles in the air and follows us into the hotel room. From the corner of my eye, I see his tight-lipped scowl. I open my mouth to tell him how the evening innocently unfolded, then snap it shut when I realize I don't know where to start. I did agree to follow a designated plan and then did everything but what I said I would do. It may not be a good excuse given the promise I made, but I did take every precaution possible to ensure safety. I was with a large group of close friends. I had a hired car and a trusted driver at my disposal. El Árbol remained diligently by my side. All went well. I stifle an exasperated sigh.

How do I explain that if we are out of touch for a bit, it doesn't mean catastrophe has hit, when time after time that's exactly what it meant when he was growing up? If his father didn't return from work he *was* incapacitated, lying drunk and unconscious somewhere in the street or on a neighbor's lawn. If his friend didn't answer the door when he called on the way to school, she was not just running late. She was being raped by her mother's boyfriend, a Russian mob king. Or if his mother was not there when he returned home from school, she was not out shopping and running late from work. She was in the hospital, fighting killer cancer cells that hijacked her body. These were his teachers, the masters who showed him time and time again that if someone was not where he or she should be, disaster was to blame. There's no way I can undo that type of worst-case scenario training.

Granted, I should have called, but in deference to my decision not to, it would have meant a blowout argument, and he probably still would have showed up in a tizzy. I slide off my heels and, wincing, rub an aching foot against my leg. Hours of dancing in high heels have crimped my toes. I steal a glance at him, hoping his mood has calmed.

Nope. Same scowl is stuck in place. Hoping he'll say something first starts to feel like waiting for the sun to explode in an apocalypse.

"I'm sorry you were worried. Everything was fine. El Árbol was hired . . ." Stopping midsentence, I track his widened eyes toward the top of the polished table.

"What the hell . . ." He steps toward it, leaving the unfinished comment to hang between us.

Oh no! I swallow hard. Near a vase of fresh flowers are the early editions of several newspapers, arranged in a half-open fan. Several photos showcase at a glance what is to be found in the fashion and entertainment section.

"From Motherhood to Design Celebrity," the headline boasts in bold print, and there I am, bare-breasted, a sheer ivory wrap revealing rather than covering skin, while Juliette wistfully stares from my arms into the camera.

The second shot has me striding down the runway after my show, wearing a look of disbelieving triumph. My eyes snap from the photos to his gaze, which seems to turn in slow motion from the newspaper toward where I remain rooted to the carpet.

I had no idea this article and those photos were going to be featured today. Hence, no time to prepare Chase for their impact on our lives, especially since he had no idea that the first photo was ever taken.

He becomes still. *Very* still.

I beeline it toward the bathroom, where a locked door between us will allow me to gather my thoughts and him to calm down. A definite win-win, if only my reflexes were a match for his quickness.

Within the span of two swift strides, he snakes his arm around my waist and lifts me off my feet, tugging me snugly against his body. "You've been very busy, Mzzz Cesare," he says in a voice that caresses my ear. He lifts my arm to study the tattoo of the rose that's inked there.

"I . . . I," the words lodge in my throat because one

second my back is flush against his stomach and the next I'm spun so that we're face to face. His lips capture mine in a kiss where an equal measure of pressure and warmth swallows my surprise. Running a hand over my breast, then down my spine to my bottom, he firmly squeezes and pulls me closer. When his lips separate from mine, my brain is hobbled and my heart skips beats here and there.

He studies my face with a look that pierces my soul. "You can always run toward me, baby, not away." Keeping one arm around me, he extends the other to hold up the newspaper. When he looks back, his expression makes me feel more naked and more vulnerable than that damn photo ever could.

"Why didn't you tell me you and Juliette modeled for this photograph?"

I have no easy answer to his question. Telling myself that it would only appear in Italian *Vogue* was just a convenient excuse for keeping it quiet when I knew it should have been discussed.

It's hard to explain the wild openness I craved after marrying and giving birth to three children in two years. When this modeling request unexpectedly presented itself, I saw it as an opportunity to express the vibrant part of me that thrived in my role as a mother. I had been so worried about the health of the twins. Then there were Dimitri's threats and Chase's constant concerns, all issues that he deftly dealt with while building a lucrative real estate empire. But for me, well . . . it was as if I was evaporating into him and our children. It was as if my form, my mind, my creativity were nothing but bits and pieces of *their* lives.

The more Chase focused on and grew his empire, the

more I felt myself disappearing. That photograph became the narrative that spoke of who I was and who I was yet to become: Alicia Cesare Reardon, wife, mother, and fashion design icon. The fact that it was to appear in a top fashion magazine made it all the more enticing as a first attempt toward my ultimate professional objective. But now, it doesn't make me feel more magnetic. Instead, vanity and selfishness vie for position in my head when I consider its ramifications. I wonder if all I managed to do with this stroke of reckless decision-making was deceive Chase and hand over a photo of Juliette to Dimitri.

He cuts into my thoughts. "You could have told me. I don't bite."

"I know, but your bark does," I say softly.

He studies the photo in awe. "It's beautiful. The two of you look beautiful."

Okay, then.

This is a switch I can deal with. There's no wrath or recriminations. Instead, he's letting his heart overpower his fury. I shouldn't be surprised. He's done it before, when I did the unthinkable and violated our marriage vows.

I grasp the back of his head, pulling his mouth toward mine in a hungry kiss that unleashes the passion I've held inside since I've been away. Pressing my body toward his, the palm of my hand travels to massage his thickening bulge. A deep rumble escapes from his throat and I thrust my tongue into his mouth and press my hand even harder against his cock.

He tears his lips from mine and lets his fingers travel to my breast, where he squeezes my nipple until his touch and the friction of fabric make it pucker. He reaches for the bottom of my sheer blouse and gently tugs it over my head, before letting it drop onto the chair. I sigh into his mouth when his lips seize mine in another kiss. Without breaking contact, his hand slips toward my back, where nimble fingers unbutton then unzip my skirt until it slides to a heap at my feet. When his mouth finally tears itself from mine, I'm wearing nothing but my corset and stockings. Hooded eyes travel from my stocking feet to the top of my uplifted breasts.

"You look very enticing for your night out on the town," he tells me, his voice hot in my ear.

"They're for you. Only for you," I say, dragging his lips back to mine. From the moment I selected the items, I imagined Chase removing each piece from my body. He's not disappointing my imagination. He clasps his hand under my legs and lifts me from my skirt, letting me down onto the floor near the bed.

"Do you want to try something new tonight, Mzzz Cesare?" he asks, the edgy dare in his tone sending a shiver of anticipation up my spine.

"Whaddya mean?

"Are you thinking about a visit from a strange man?" he asks.

My brain moves my mouth to clarify while the rest of my body sends out an automatic *yes* message. Strange man is our code name for kinky sex, thanks to an explanation I gave my mother about what *S & M* meant. This unlikely conversation took place several chapters into what I refer to as "book one" of my adult life. It reads somewhat like this: I start a torrid relationship with Chase in Europe. Massimo discovers us making out in the corridor of my new apartment. He reminds Chase of the oath they swore years ago that made sexual relationships with each other's sisters taboo. A fistfight breaks out. We tumble into the apartment, where we spot Antonio and Fiona *sans* clothing having an S & M romp in what they assumed was an empty apartment. She's tied to a chair blindfolded. He's standing nearby in his underwear. All former sworn pledges have vacated the vicinity.

Chase goes into a tizzy. He shouts, "We swore an oath, you kinky S & M bastard." Another brawl erupts, this time between Antonio and Chase. As arranged beforehand, my mother arrives to help with my move and return Liam, who she is babysitting. She demands an explanation from me as to exactly what 'S & M' and 'kinky' mean. I say I think the former refers to a *strange man*. The rest is ancient history, except for right now, when 'strange man' might be making a comeback.

"You won't be disappointed. Do you trust me with this choice?" There's that word trust again, and once more my mind waffles while my libido shouts *yes, we do*. In the end, the two shout out a *let's-go-for-it, hooray*. I may have defied him tonight, but I trust him with my heart and soul, so why not with my body. It's not like we just met. We're married with three children, for heaven's sake. I take in his expressively large hands with their long, dexterous fingers. Then search the curve of his lips and remind myself of his talent for using all to get my body thrumming for more.

"Yes." My answer comes out as a nervous hush. *Not where I promised to be, out on the town, Marcel's mouth near my neck, the tattoo, the sexy new clothes, the pot, his worry,* all of them incriminating realities that indicate maybe we should talk this through first.

The hesitant tenor of my assent doesn't go unnoticed. "We can stop at any time if you're uncomfortable, but I don't think you will be."

"Okay." I stare into his eyes, stroking his face. "I missed you." We float together in a dreamlike quiet that serves as a stark reminder of how little time alone we've had since we married.

He cocks his head to the side, studying my corset and lace-top silk stockings. "Really?"

"Yes." This time my answer is direct and decisive. "I missed having you next to me in bed. I even missed the orders you snap while pretending they're suggestions."

"How can they be orders if they're never obeyed." The slow roll of his voice washes over me.

Oh no, here we go. Me and my big mouth. "Erm, I wouldn't say, *never.*"

"How about . . ." His mouth carves a trail of kisses down the small stars tattooed on that titillating area of my neck behind my ear. I bend to give him more access, and his kisses move toward my shoulder. "Tonight . . ." his kisses travel toward my breast and my breath hitches in anticipation.

"Tonight," I repeat, looking for the words my passion is stealing. "Wasn't planned. It . . ." His mouth moves toward my breast and all thoughts scatter when his teeth nip at my nipple through the fabric of my corset.

"Go on." He lifts his head, taking my mind back to the topic.

"Just happened." I push his head back toward my breast. He raises it again and reaches into the back pocket of his jeans.

"I see. Now, I just *happen* to have something for us to use tonight." He dangles a pair of handcuffs from his finger.

Strange man is definitely making an appearance.

Chewing on the inside of my mouth, I study the restraints.

"I also have this," he adds, holding out the palm of his hand to reveal a key. "You can keep it in your hand while wearing the cuffs, so you know where it is, but I don't recommend it."

"Why not?" I ask, studying the key and wondering how all this is going to go down.

"It's very easy to drop and lose when you're lost in the heat of the moment. Then we'll have to search the area when we're finished. Instead, I can place the key on the table where you can get it at any time, but I don't think you're going to want to use it until we're done." He's sounding too much like a practiced pro for my liking. We may have used simple restraints during sex before, but never handcuffs. He waits a beat. "You look . . . confused."

"Well, Mist*errr* Reardon, since when have you have become such an expert with this particular type of paraphernalia?" I wave my hand in a circle around the cuffs and key.

He wags his brows and shoots me a smile that stretches the width of his face, providing all that's needed to remind me of the robust sex life he had before we met. His numerous girlfriends and affairs painted a colorful sexual portrait next to my empty canvas.

"Sure. I'm in. When do you want to be handcuffed?" I cavalierly smirk. The question is worth the incredulous look his face assumes. "Just kidding. This time I'll go firs—"

He seizes my mouth with a kiss that blasts me with a driving force that begs for more. His tongue tangles with mine, while the pressure of his lips against mine strengthens. He knows his kisses disarm me, and tonight he's using them to his advantage. His hands slide down my sides, then toward my back, where he deftly loosens and lowers my corset, exposing my breasts for the taking. The tip of his tongue glides over my nipple in a silken caress, and I melt into his body. Lowering my hand, I cup his groin and massage, but he returns it to my side, using his strength to keep it pressed to my side while his tongue continues to work its magic across my nipples. Instinctively, my body leans toward his mouth while my other hand reaches down toward his lengthening bulk. Again, he takes it by the wrist and presses it against my thigh. Trying to free either of my hands would be a useless waste of energy.

He grazes his teeth along the soft flesh of my lower belly, inching the corset down until it drops to the floor. He softly kisses my C-section scar, then lets his mouth travel with moist kisses to that nub which can easily send me skyrocketing. He moves slowly, deliberately, with forward-and-away motions that are just enough to keep me wanting. "Baby," he whispers huskily.

"Yeah," my voice is drugged with longing.

"Are you okay with me handcuffing you now?"

I figure what the hell. I already can't move them.

"Almost."

He loosens his grip on my hands. I grasp the sides of his arms and softly kiss every scar that mars his chest and back, each one a reminder of the pain he endured serving his country and the way I let him down at the time. I can't undo the past, nor can I completely forget that it happened. All I can do now is realize my mistakes, accept my shortcomings, and move on, knowing that I will never repeat it again.

"I'm ready now."

"You won't be disappointed. I promise you." He turns my body so my tummy presses against a low-backed upholstered chair. Taking one arm and then the other, he gently places each behind my back and fastens the cuffs onto my wrists. When I turn, desire flames in his eyes.

"Do you still want this?" he asks, his voice quiet.

"Yes," I answer, wondering what he has in mind next.

I don't have long to wait before he scoops his arm around my waist and gently bends me over the back of the chair. The smooth, soft fabric of its pillowed surface presses into my stomach while my cool buttocks are uplifted and exposed for him to squeeze and mold any way he wants. After what happened tonight, I know that what he wants to do to my ass doesn't only include soft kisses, at least not at first. I also know what happens when I agree to a visit from a strange man. That's why I'm not surprised by the first crack of his palm against my backside. He rubs it while whispering in my ear. "After spending lots of time tracking you down earlier, it's good to see you anchored in one place." The second strike comes before I can answer and, pressing my feet into the carpet, I balance as best as I can while I brace for another. Only this time, he bends and kisses my bottom. "You put yourself in harm's way tonight.

I pause for a bit to gather my thoughts. Then I answer with the truth as I see it before passion restrains my tongue along with my arms.

"I didn't feel like I was in danger."

There's waiting silence before he answers with a slight sigh, and I ready myself for another hit, but it never comes. Instead, he leaves me waiting while he unzips and steps out of his pants and underwear. I'm tempted to raise my stomach from the back of the chair, but the sudden small nibbles of his mouth across my ass and his open palm cradling my breast keep me in place. I drop my head with a murmuring sigh. My nipple tightens with his light touch, then hardens and puckers when he takes it between his finger and thumb. With my head hanging down the front of the chair and my hands restrained, I'm at the mercy of what he wants to do next, and he knows exactly where to go to make me beg for more. I automatically spread my thighs when two fingers of his other hand massage that erogenous zone that's throbbing for his touch. He circles and presses them inside and my moan stretches raw with achy longing. Splayed and wanting, I draw in a slow, easy breath. I know he's not one to rush, especially when begged, so even though I'm famished for his penetration, I lean into his fingers and say nothing.

"Well, Mrs. Reardon, you are just about ready to be fucked until you scream," and wrapping his arms around my waist, he firmly tugs me back toward his hard cock. I'm more than ready when he enters from behind, his girth going so deep I take the biggest inhale of my life. It almost hurts. Almost, but not quite because, with his arm wrapped around my middle for balance, his plunges are like being swept to the top of a tsunami of pleasure. Head hanging down, arms restrained in cuffs, I lose the ability to see or hear.

His breaths are short and sharp, his pumps inside me hard and quick.

With every charge into me, my legs shake, my body spasms until I explode with pleasure. And still, there's more. My brain hums with short-circuited bliss and I scream as his gyrating climax has me peaking one last wave of bliss.

"Yeah, baby. That's how it's done after being apart."

And before I know what's happening, my hands are freed. Exhausted and sheened with sweat, we collapse onto the carpet.

CHAPTER 28

"Why don't you think El Árbol was right for the job?"

Naked, in the dimly-lit room, we sit on top of a towel spread across the carpeted floor. Chase lights one of the joints from my pack, hands it to me, then leans back against the chair with his arms folded behind his head.

I inhale, pressing my lips together to hold in the hit.

"Aside from being brainless and slow as a snail, he's okay."

"Well, he *is* trustworthy. He never left my side the whole night, and he was paid for his loyalty with a punch."

At the mention of loyalty, he raises my hand and rubs his thumb along my wedding band.

"You wore it tonight?"

"Of course. Why wouldn't I?"

Joint pressed between two fingers, he inhales, leans his head back, and waits before exhaling.

Mr. Perfect has done this before.

I've never seen him smoke so much as a cigarette, so any pot smoking must have been done during the wild stints of adolescence, before he morphed into Mr. Perfect. He reaches out to hand it back.

I shake my head no, thinking how Juliette may still want to nurse when I get back tomorrow. I've been expressing a bit of breast milk each day just in case she's needy after I've been away for so long. My mind shifts to how Caroline and Teo are also going to react once I'm back. This separation couldn't have been easy for them. And that's when I start to really think about my actions tonight. I know I craved something different, and I know what that was.

Tonight, I exiled any thoughts about family. I shed motherhood like a skin left behind during some animal molting process. My children didn't exist. I was just an ordinary twenty-seven-year-old celebrating with friends in Paris without a care in the world. However, not once during the entire evening did I forget I was married. This detail doesn't make me feel any better, but judging from Chase's comment about my wedding band, bears mentioning.

There is nothing careless about Chase. Both in his private and business life, he is fantastically thorough. He can calculate and recall the measurements of a development property the size of a city block to the nearest square foot. He isolates and analyzes problems and comes up with viable solutions that take into account each aspect of a negotiation. It's the same with words. If he says something, it's full of all matter of meaning and substance.

I look him straight in the eye. "I would never go out and deliberately not wear my wedding band. I'm not frivolous about my marriage vows." I take the sides of his face in my palms and pull his lips to mine, relishing the tenderness of a post-coital kiss. "My commitment to you is *forever*," I murmur, my lips inches from his.

He offers me another hit and I shake my head, feeling tears pool when I think of Juliette's neediness and Caroline and Teo's pleas for me to come home when we last spoke.

"I did something awful tonight, and I did it deliberately. I actually *set out* to do it before the evening started."

Chase wraps his arm around me, and I can tell he's stifling a grin. "You mean like premeditated murder?"

I jab his ribs with my elbow. I'm contained and warm snuggled next to him, but it doesn't stop the knot in my throat from tightening.

"I'm a terrible mamma." Pressed against his dense chest, I look up at his face. "I went out tonight determined to forget I had children. Poof." I throw both hands out from the sides of my forehead. "They just disappeared from my mind. What kind of mother does that?" I remember how throughout the course of the evening, I refused to even talk about my children. When Andre asked me how they were, I pretended I didn't hear what he was asking. And when Devi shouted out that I was a mom gone wild, I was convinced that my friends and associates thought I'd compromised my creativity and stifled my independence when I gave birth to three children instead of pursuing my career.

"I felt like I had so much lost time to make up. It was as if everyone else was swimming laps and I was just treading water." I wipe my eyes before going on. "Even Mimi was moving up the professional ladder."

He hasn't a clue who Mimi is, but he doesn't interrupt. "And I . . ." my sentence staggers, but I pull myself together, determined to continue with my saga. "I was stuck with a small label and the demands of three children. I needed an escape, somewhere I could celebrate an advancing career that didn't just include having children, but that doesn't mean I ever forgot you, not during your deployments, not last night, not *ever*." I'm admitting my shortcomings and my loyalty and love for him, but I still don't feel any better. I go on, closing my eyes and letting myself drown in self-deprecation. "I was determined to show everyone tonight that I was Alicia Cesare, independent woman, rising business star, fashionista extraordinaire, not the complacent stay-at-home mom Mimi and Lily labeled me behind my back. I drank, danced, laughed until my responsibilities faded into nothingness."

What juvenile behavior. Tonight, I became a stranger even to myself. I detangle myself from Chase's arms and rest my forehead against my raised knees.

"Here's how I see it . . ." he says, then quickly adds, "that is, if you are interested in hearing what I want to share."

I raise my head and give him my full attention. Lighting the joint again, he inhales before passing it along. I take it this time, but don't take a hit, which, given an arrest for smoking pot and a continued slew of appointments with a hypnotist for cigarette addiction, shows how upset I am.

"I get what you were trying to convey tonight, but I wouldn't say you ever let yourself get locked in somewhere. You're too forward-thinking and energetic to remain in one place. But I see how you may have thought you were idling on the side of the road, when you really wanted to speed away. You needed to carve out your own space, have some separateness in our togetherness as a couple and as a mother.

"Despite what you may be feeling now," he takes the cigarette back, "you are a great mother. For the record," he circles the joint around my breast area, "it's time you reclaim that territory as yours and yours alone." He pauses, pulling a serious face. "Except for my stake in the region."

In spite of myself, I feel a bubble of laughter rising.

"Really? And what exactly does *your* share involve?" I pluck the joint from his fingers and take a hit, then go for another.

He deftly removes it from my hand before it reaches my mouth and snuffs it out with two fingers.

"Squatter's rights. I come and go as you like, but I'm guessing more often than not, you'll be wanting me to stay. No, I take that back."

I raise an inquisitive brow.

"You'll be *begging* me to stay." He eyes the remnant of a hickey on my neck and the red chafing on my wrists from the handcuffs.

Straddling his lap, I nip his nose. "A little overconfident but on target."

I'm grinning too, but I haven't forgotten all that happened or why it happened. How could I? He traveled three hundred miles like a madman in the dead of the night to make sure I was alright. Why all the panic, I'm still not completely sure. All I can do is continue to determine why it was so important for me to escape my life without letting him know.

"Do you think I'm boring?" The words slide out of my mouth unintentionally. I bite my lip and wait.

"What?" He seems confused.

"You know, ordinary, unexciting, bland."

He studies the opened pack of joints, my black corset, the empty champagne bottles, the newspaper photo of me nude, then sends an unblinking gaze my way. "Baby, you are hard-wired for trouble."

"I wasn't the only one who forgot who she was. Your behavior was not exactly stellar either."

"That damn Frenchman had it coming. He was acting like an asshole."

"So, you decided to offer him competition."

"I may have been a little out of line."

"A *little*? You leveled him and El Árbol without giving anyone a chance to explain. You tossed me over your shoulder like I was a sack of potatoes."

"I had little choice in the matter. I had to get you out of there."

"Let me tell you something." I squint my eyes and shake my head for emphasis. "Unless I'm unconscious inside a burning building, you are never to do that again. Understand?"

"I admit it may have been over the top."

"You are not even a *little* funny."

"What did you expect me to do? I saw this monster of a guy I never met sticking to you like glue. How the hell was I supposed to know he was your bodyguard? I thought he bullied you into letting him come along."

"Well, he didn't. Beth hired him based on a strong recommendation from a trusted source."

"Noted. I'll reach out to El Árbol to pay him for his services. I value loyalty, and he stood by your side throughout the course of the day and night. Given his size, he was a deterrent to anyone who may have considered harming you. As far as the motorcycle goes, it was the best way I knew of to get to Paris."

"You have been busy too, *Monopoly Man*. Purchasing property in London, buying a motorcycle with helmets that look like props from Iron Man. I don't know how you pulled off such a quick purchase, but there's no way any of the kids are going to see you riding that vehicle. Teo, especially. He already repeats everything you say and do."

"Agreed." It's a short and sweet answer that makes me think he's not so enthused about owning a motorcycle, which is weird given he just bought one. "But . . ." He thrusts out his bottom lip and stops.

I wait. He says nothing.

"But what?" I finally ask, both hands extended.

"Since I seem to have slipped from Mr. Perfect to Monopoly Man in such a short span of time, I'm wondering what I have to do to regain my former status."

"Well . . ." I tap my lips with my finger and study the ceiling. "I never thought I'd live to see the day, so I'm going to need time to give the decline some consideration before advising on a course of correction."

"Perfectly understandable." He leans back. I eye his torso, long and muscled down to his navel, and then lower, with all exposed for the taking. Resting my hand on his chest, I trace my finger across his bare shoulder.

"Off the top of my head, though, it could involve some more of this," I lock my lips on his with a forceful tongue thrust. Before he can catch his breath, I take his forefinger in my mouth and suck, then slowly remove it and place it between the folds of my vagina. "And a bit more of that."

Round two starts with his mouth descending between

my legs. It's so sudden it catches me by surprise. I slide down onto the carpet, giving a sharp inhale at the moist warmth of his flicking tongue perfectly placed *there*. I lose control of my legs, while my fingers futilely try to grip hold of the tight weave of carpet.

He stops what he's doing, rises up on one elbow, and grins. "Is that going perfectly for you?"

"Yeah, but more would be even better."

He grins wider and gets back to business, only to stop again, leaving my body splayed with longing. He stares at me. "Will more of this get me back my title of Mr. Perfect?"

"Possibly."

He remains still. "I'm going to require some assurances before I can continue."

"Yes," I tell him impatiently.

He lowers his head.

I feel it again, that sensation of bliss that starts to peak. Further up I climb until I'm swallowed by sensations of pleasure. My legs stiffen. I can't see or hear anything, and just as I reach the point of more becoming most, he stops.

"How about now?" he grins. "Am I Mr. Perfect again?"

I grit my teeth with frustration. "Yes."

"Yes, what?"

The bastard is not going to continue until he hears the exact words from my mouth. So, what do I do? I lift my head, look him straight in the eye and tell him that he's Mr. Perfect. I have no shame when being undone by his tongue.

He flattens his hand on my chest and pushes me back down. By the time I orgasm, my heart is racing like I ran a mile-long sprint, and my skull feels like it's exploding.

"That was amazing," I say, once I'm coherent again.

He disappears into the bathroom, and from my vantage point I watch him rinse his face and wet his hair back. The playful grin is gone, replaced by clenched lips. The change is so sudden I have to restrain myself from getting up and taking him in my arms. He doesn't know I'm watching, or he would never have let his face show what he's feeling. Despite all the fun we just had, he's worried. The only explanation I can come up with is that I put him in a panic when I disappeared from his radar screen.

Relaxed expression back in place, he returns with a warm cloth for me to sponge myself with. Then, wrapped in a towel, he sits on the carpet by my side. I study his chiseled features.

"Are you still angry with me?"

He doesn't give me a yes or no answer, and I hold off opening my mouth first. Last thing I want is to offer another litany of excuses. I cringe when I think about how I couldn't be reached because I was too busy celebrating the notion that I didn't have children to hear my phone. What I'm going to do now is listen to what *he* has to say.

He rubs the underside of his chin. "It's simple. You have this edgy energy that craves a creative outlet. Your current label is too narrow for your level of talent. You need to expand, and you are off to a great start. Don't get distracted by what other people think, and—"

I don't let him finish. "I know. I know. I should have told you I changed my plans."

His face grows weary with tension. Bracing for a chastising lecture about the importance of remaining in touch and staying true to our word, I'm surprised when he pulls me to him and kisses my forehead. "I'm glad that you're not afraid to go after what it is you want in spite of the obstacles in your way."

"You didn't seem to think it was such a sterling quality earlier."

"Well, I do now," he nibbles each tattooed star on my neck.

"Oh yeah, and why is that?"

"Because," his lips travel down the breadth of my neck, "you and I are alike in that way. We understand each other *and . . .*"

I wait for him to finish, eager to hear what he has left to say.

"If you weren't courageous, you would never have chosen me to marry."

The heat of his breath warms my neck.

Oh boy. Any more sex tonight, and I will need a hospital stay to recover.

I shrug sleepily. "It does take courage to deal with you." Yawning, I rest my head on his shoulder and murmur, "But all in all, you'll do."

He pulls me toward him and knuckles my head, then gets to his feet and reaches out his hand to help me up. I latch onto it, hoist myself to my feet, and kiss his nose. "I'm glad you're here," I tell him.

"Me too. Before I forget, I have something for you." He strides over to the chair where his leather jacket hangs and fishes inside its left pocket, taking out a small, wrapped box. He walks over and hands it to me. "Congratulations, baby. You really did wow Paris with your talent."

It's a box from Cartier. I untie the ribbon and inside the

box is a pair of diamond stud earrings, each stone so perfectly clear, so luminously bright, they glimmer flawlessly.

"Thank you. They're beautiful. I wasn't expecting such a lavish gift."

"You never do, which is why it's so easy to shower you with them. Now time for some shut-eye." He takes the box from my hands and leads me to the bed.

Weariness rattles down on me like a shutter slamming against a window. I melt into the soft coverlet.

"Sleep," he says, kissing my forehead.

My eyes won't stay open, but my mind keeps racing. I feel myself drifting into that space between wakefulness and sleep where thoughts become a slide show of past events: the fashion show, Le Bar, Le Bound, Chase storming in looking rattled, fists flying, a mad-dash motorcycle ride. It's hard to hold onto one thought at a time and the conjoint memories slowly slip away except for one. It's when I first spot Chase, nervously scanning the dance floor for me, his hand jammed inside the right pocket of his jacket. Once our eyes meet, he purposely strides in my direction, but his hand never leaves his pocket, even when he reaches where I'm standing.

There's a light shuffling sound. My eyes open into narrow slits. It's dark, but I can still make out the shadow of Chase as he buries his hand into that same pocket of his leather jacket that now hangs on the back of the desk chair. He's all business when he pulls out a revolver and checks that it's loaded. Without a whisper of a sound, he strides toward the bed in his bare feet and secures the loaded weapon under the mattress within arm's reach of his right hand. He gets into bed and pulls me close, wrapping his arm protectively around my body.

Apprehension rear-ends fatigue when a knife-sharp realization crystalizes.

I never saw the danger I was in tonight.

Too tired to confront him now for answers, I slide into sleep, safely cocooned in the crook of his body.

CHAPTER 29

Ensconced in a cozy hotel bathrobe, shampooed hair wrapped in a towel, I lounge in a chair and stare at the morning sun through the balcony window. Last night was fraught with self-discovery and unknown menace. The first I've started to come to grips with and the latter . . . well, that remains to be revealed once Chase and I talk. The loaded gun he furtively placed under the mattress nudges me to get to the bottom of it all sooner rather than later.

I pop a plump strawberry from the breakfast tray into my mouth and plunk myself down on Chase's lap, sliding the damp towel from my head. How do I find the right words to encourage him to open up about why he rushed all the way from London to Paris to find me? He wraps his arms around me, then reaches for a strawberry and places it in his mouth. I eye him carefully, thinking there's no better time than now to get answers to the pressing questions that weigh on my mind.

"I want to know what really happened last night that made you rush to find me in Paris."

His face darkens for the briefest moment before it evens into a matter-of-fact expression. "What exactly do you want to know?"

A question to answer a question. Evasive, elusive, and clever. Only it's not going to work this time. I'm onto his cagey tactics and won't, as he hopes, run out of steam before I get the concise information I want.

I slide off his lap and stare at him in astonishment. "It's incredible how you know what I'm asking for yet pretend that you don't. I want to know *exactly* why you rode a motorcycle in the middle of the night to a different country with no advance warning that you were coming."

"I couldn't reach you, and I was worried, and . . . you were gone a long time. I figured we were so close, why not ride to you so we could spend some quality time together."

"Did you pick that up from Mount Bullshit on your way here?"

"I already told you why. You hadn't called. You weren't answering your phone or responding to my texts. I had no idea where you were." He's hedging, hoping to redirect any blows the truth wields my way.

It's as if he was trained to answer questions without disclosing crucial details. Then I remember that he was an operator in military intelligence, so technically he's a spy, and if there's one thing a spy understands, it's how to deflect questions. That gets me thinking back to last night. I recall the gun, the motorcycle, the leather jacket and jeans he wore. These are not the clothes a businessman packs to negotiate the purchase of large swaths of development properties. Chase always dresses in a suit and tie during these types of meetings. In fact, that and workout clothes are all he ever packs when traveling for business. If buying properties was not the primary reason he was traveling, then why was he really in London? My mind summons a truth I'm unable to understand, while at the same time unable to *not* understand.

He was on some sort of mission.

But how could that be? His last deployment was almost three years ago. The reason hits me like a sledgehammer. He must still be active in military intelligence. If this is true, then Sammy and Mac must be involved too.

Chase's expression doesn't change, but he keeps his eyes on me as if sees what my mind is registering.

Still unable to parse what this all means, I steel my eyes on his. "I'll be more precise. Were you in London on some sort of assignment that involved Dimitri?"

He snorts in disgust at the mention of Dimitri's name, then folds his arms and studies the wall ahead. His body language is all I need to understand that he *was* working undercover, and he doesn't plan to reveal the details. Maybe military orders indicate that he can't talk about his operation. I get that, but he sure as hell can tell me if Dimitri or any of his army of thugs were in the vicinity with the intent to have me killed. He's going to have to learn that keeping *everything* from me serves no purpose. It doesn't protect me emotionally or physically. I give him one more chance to say something, anything, that reveals more about what really happened these past few days.

No reply.

Inside, a lever is pushed that releases a flood of frustration and anger. I meander over to the mattress, reach down, and pull out the gun. Waving it this way and that, I walk back to where he's sitting—or was sitting. He's definitely standing now, with arms outstretched and hands palms up.

"Now baby, I need you to relax, and give me the gun." He slowly reaches out his palm.

My answer is to aim first at the ceiling, then in his direction. He ducks, then pops back up, his eyes riveted on my hand. I bite back a smile. Is it even acceptable to see humor in this situation?

My answer is a resounding, *Yes*.

"Whoa now. That's a loaded gun." He changes tack, sounding more like a ranch hand trying to calm a restive horse than a husband trying to reason with his wife. What he doesn't know, and what I have no intention of telling him at this particular moment, is that I unloaded the revolver this morning while he was sleeping.

A few weeks ago, I had convinced Sammy to show me how to load and unload the gun we had in the apartment just in case I needed to use it to protect myself and my children. He agreed only because he knew Chase planned to teach me how to shoot.

He studies me for a bit, then shrugs his shoulders. "I knew Yuri was in Paris. You told me so yourself. When I couldn't reach you, I became convinced he hurt you, so I set out to find you myself."

"You're offering a haircut to a bald man. I want answers, Reardon, and I want them now, or I might be forced to see if my beginner's aim will help me hit that light bulb." I point the gun just shy of his left ear toward the lamp and watch his composure slacken. See how he likes not knowing the truth when he thinks his safety is at risk. I'm tired of him having more knowledge about the danger I face than I do.

"Okay, okay. I hear you. You want more details."

His loosened bathrobe, revealing his muscled chest and tight abs, entices me to envision what lies below. I dig deeper for resolve, mostly because I am now worried by two things: The shrinking length of time I have to pull off this charade and the very real possibility that I won't be able to keep my mind off other matters so I can get what I want before he calls my bluff and wrestles the gun from my hands.

"That's right. I want specifics, not just pieces of the truth." I give him my fiercest glare, which is not easy, given how tired my extended arms are getting. "I'll make it easy for you. Why don't you explain why you are carrying a gun, then shift to the motorcycle purchase and the speedy ride to Paris when you should have been locking up a development deal."

I know him well enough to see the sweep of disturbance that crosses his face before he becomes weighted with seriousness.

"You were so confident, so poised and deliberate during your show, and the people there loved your fashions. I didn't want to be a klaxon of doom who broke your streak of success with bad news."

If he hurls an SAT test at me in lieu of definitive details, I may just have to reload and take aim. "I can handle the nasty grit of what you have to say." Not letting him off the hook, I am explicit about the answers I want by going back to the source of his *business venture*. "I'll make it simpler for you. How about giving me a *bullet* list of the real reasons you took this trip to London."

He regards me steadily, a tug of a smile pulling up his lips. He eyes my shaking arms, then saunters toward me and removes the gun from my grip.

Goodness, that's a relief.

Muzzle aimed away from both of us, he opens the cylinder and sees that it's empty.

"As if!" I shake my head in disgust. It was ludicrous of him to think I'd wave a loaded gun willy-nilly around the room like some harebrained child.

"You seem to be inventing new ways of being a pain in the ass on this trip."

Now it's my turn to grin, because it's true. I've kept him hopping since I first told him I was seizing this business opportunity.

He rests the gun on top of the table and studies me with a combination of vulnerability, resilience, and authority. It's an expression he allows only me to see. It gets me thinking about his unwavering and ever-constant determination to keep those he loves safe. Its far-reaching sweep includes family, friends, and country. On all these fronts, he commandeers battles that would topple the most steadfast soldier.

"I never planned to give you a reason to worry."

Wrapping my arms around his neck, I am more determined than ever to make my point. "But you can't make yourself the gatekeeper to the truth because you think it keeps me from worrying. I'm not fragile. I won't break."

His thumb strokes my jawline. "I like how you raise your chin like some bantamweight fighter when you're determined to make a point. I don't think of you as being fragile. You're strong. You weren't afraid to leave the country to grow your business even though you knew Dimitri's intentions. You did a great job with your fashion show despite living under a cloud of threats; but this hasn't been an easy life for you. You shouldn't have to spend your life worrying that you're going to die or someone you love is going to be hurt."

He looks straight into my eyes. "I keep the whole truth from you to keep you brave. What good is it if you go through life afraid to leave the house? What example would that set for our children, seeing their mother scared all the time? You should be bold and plucky. Those are needed to succeed in business, but what you did last night was reckless. Instead of gliding into the limelight like we planned, you lurched without the benefit of a discussion." Wistfully, he strokes the side of my cheek with his thumb. "I thought time would heal all wounds, but now I see it's a misconception. Some things just remain hurtful problems that refuse to be fixed."

Oh god, where is he going with this?

My brain vibrates with concern as it hopscotches to another thought. If he's going to tell me I can't be trusted, he's right. How can you trust someone who doesn't keep her word? What I did last night was inexcusable. I not only worried him. I put myself in unnecessary danger. He's wrong to withhold information, but I'm at fault here, too. I allowed myself to forget that my behavior endangered Chase's life and could have affected the mental well-being of my children. If anything happened to me, they would be without a mother, and if both Chase and I succumbed to Dimitri's deadly plots because of my recklessness, they would be left orphaned and far less protected.

And there it is again, flashing in neon-lit letters across my mind.

Guilt.

He must see the distress in my eyes, because he pulls me closer. His warm breath caresses my ear, and the unease that casts a cold shadow over my heart lifts.

"The sad truth is that I haven't been able to stop this maniac. I couldn't protect you from his attack. I couldn't keep Devie safe. No matter how hard I struggle to stop him, I can't. It would kill me if I couldn't keep him from hurting you or our children." He clutches me as if to prove that he will never let that happen. The words are not necessary because I already trust him with my life and the lives of our children. "Just knowing I haven't been able to fix this is ripping me to shreds."

More than ever, I feel the load of pain and worry he's borne since this all began over twenty years ago.

"Don't. Don't do this to yourself. You shouldn't have to carry this burden alone. I can help. I want to help, but I can't if you don't tell me what's happening. I admit I behaved rashly last night, and I have a feeling that once we talk, I'm going to regret it more than I do now, but you have to understand that it's not healthy for you or me or our relationship if you don't share the problems that affect our lives. I need you to be more transparent."

He stares ahead, his face hard with determination. When he looks back at me, I know he's ready to explain details that are going to colossally disrupt my peace of mind. I see that he's been hiding clusters of facts since he returned from his last deployment. One reason he would do that is that there are components that are top secret. Another is to shield me from information he feels is too horrific to share. Reaching into the pocket of my robe, I take out two cigarettes from my pack and light them for us both. Surprisingly, he takes one. Once lit, a searing stench hits my nose, telling me the hypnosis treatments are having an effect on my habit. I let the smell penetrate, until it can be ignored. Chase holds his to his mouth, inhales, letting the smoke escape from his nose. His eyes slide toward mine.

"You were right to assume I was on a mission in London." Every inch of my being stills. "When it came to my attention that Dimitri's ties had a global reach, I wasn't surprised. I saw first-hand that he was selling illegal arms and acting as a cohort with enemies of the state in Afghanistan." He takes a long pull at the cigarette. I wait. "It seems Dimitri now heads a Mafia gang with links to senior officials in Russia. His influence is enormous."

"How was it possible for him to gain that kind of power?"

Chase doesn't have to think long before rattling off an answer rife with specifics.

"Corruption is rife in Russia. Dimitri is cunning and ruthless. He knows how to optimize a situation in his favor. Once the Soviet Union collapsed, he used the resulting chaos to his benefit. He closed deals for weapons that were sold by the government and passed along in the black market. He maintained and grew his influence by organizing Mafia-style hits against his opponents. With this newfound power, he sold missile technology to Iran and has smuggled weapons to insurgents, warlords, and just about anyone who has the money to pay. It has helped arm a two-thousand-man Taliban militia. They, in turn, assist him by protecting his drug and human trafficking routes, using IEDs, assassinations, car bombs, torture . . . anything and everything that will ensure Dimitri's smuggling routes remain operative."

"Doesn't that keep him busy enough? It certainly sounds like it's keeping him rich enough. Why still come after our family? We're nothing but peons in the whole scheme of his operations."

"Dimitri is driven by bloody vengeance. His hatred is like a virus that invades his body cell by cell until the only recourse left for us is to kill him to destroy the infection."

"Devie says he needs to be taken out." I watch him closely. When he doesn't answer, I add, "Is that why you were in London?"

"Not exactly."

Silence.

Yet again, he's making me work for answers. I take several long drags of my cigarette, pacing and smoking in silence. When it's finished, my hand automatically reaches for another. He snaps it from my fingers and deftly removes the pack from my pocket.

"I was there to follow up on a truck full of human bodies that was discovered on a deserted street. They were illegal immigrants, mostly Afghans and Syrians who died a gruesome death locked inside the truck's trailer after the driver left the engine running and disappeared. All of them were female, some of them children under the age of five."

"That's horrifying!" I pause, confused. "But I don't understand what that has to do with you. You're not a homicide detective."

"The activity involved more than smuggling illegal immigrants from war-torn countries. Turns out most had been sold, including the children, as part of a sex slave trade. Further investigations led to exposure of a wider ring of international sex traffickers led by none other than Dimitri."

"So, he was in London."

"Yeah."

"Were you assigned by . . ." I struggle to recall the name I first heard from Virgil, but Chase quickly fills the void. He knows I'll figure it out sooner or later.

"His name is Buford. We've been in communication."

"Why are you still involved in military affairs? I understand your personal connection to Dimitri, but this seems to be official business and you're a civilian now."

"I'm still involved because I asked to be. Military intelligence provides classified information that allows me to track Dimitri's whereabouts. These reports keep me apprised of what he and his army of thugs may be plotting and where he might strike against us next."

If I thought the man I married was strictly a business tycoon, I was sorely mistaken. Chase accepted a mission to bring down an international crime syndicate. As hard as this information is to digest, it takes even more courage to ask my next question. The bravado that had me wielding a gun and demanding answers earlier evaporates as fear creeps across my skin.

"Was Dimitri coming to kidnap me to add to the lot of those poor victims?" My briar-sharp gaze refuses to let him off the hook.

His answer is simple and honest. "There was evidence

indicating that was his intention." He takes my hand and kisses its palm. "I would never let that happen." The warmth of his touch gives me the strength to ask my next question.

"Do you know where he is now?"

"The driver of the truck was caught, along with several other members of this particular ring, but Dimitri escaped."

Chase's look is that of a tortured man, someone who time and time again tries to defeat a deadly nemesis only to be forced to watch it rise up again even stronger. My anger flares.

Enough of this anguish and turmoil. The ubiquity of Dimitri's decades of terrorizing abuse and relentless stalking have to end. There are too many forces looking to bring down his underground network for him to continue to succeed. Until that time comes, we can't allow his threats to cripple our ability to move through life. We will be cautious, but not stifled.

"Well, I won't let him be the impetus who turns our happiness into fear and bitterness."

"Yeah . . . I know." His tone is hesitant, frayed with doubt and concern.

"Is there something else you're not saying?"

Looking pale and troubled, he gazes out the window.

I stare at a silent room that stares back, and wait, anticipating particulars to follow that will be infinitely worse than what I've already been told. Chase's heightened distress is alarming, but I refuse to let fear keep me from learning the truth. Denial is not an option when you know the person who is after you also kidnaps children to sell as sex slaves.

A thin funnel of morning light filters through the blinds, illuminating a sinister shadow of a thought. My throat clutches. Icy fear drives through my chest and into my stomach. Anger transforms into terror, sparking my brain to freeze on one thought and one thought only.

You've got to get home, now.

"Oh my God," I shout, throwing my hand over my mouth. My head swivels from side to side as a giant wave of primal rage drives my limbs into motion. Grabbing clothes from hangers and shoes from shelves, I stuff them haphazardly into my suitcase. Once I start shouting, I can't stop. "Who is that monster after now? Tell me! Has he tried to take Caroline?" I don't wait for his answer, because I already know that an attempt has been made or at the very least was planned. Then, mercifully uncovered and stopped.

"What are you doing?" Chase's voice sounds muffled, like an echo that reverberates from the end of a long, dark tunnel. It's not until he circles his arms around mine that I let myself disintegrate into the thousand small pieces of someone so mutilated by horror she can't see reason.

"Please," I beg, my eyes stinging from unshed tears. "We have to head back now. Call and get one of your pilot buddies to fly us home."

His arms tighten around my shoulders until my ragged breathing slows.

"I'm so sorry." I choke out. "I didn't know, or I would never have left for Paris. How could I have been so selfish?"

"Shh," he soothes. "It's going to be alright." But inside me, everything has been turned upside down. Any sense of security, peace, and even hope that our family could enjoy a normal life is shattered. The brutal and unvarnished truth I asked for is too much to bear. I want nothing more than to take immediate action and go to my children. His arms continue to wrap me in a silent cocoon, and that's how we stay until, finally, I'm calmer.

My self-centered behavior from last night prickles, but I know I have to keep my wits about me or Dimitri wins. This is not easy because in the short span of time between my conversation with Chase and my meltdown, I am able to figure out Dimitri's menacing scheme. Craving sadistic revenge, he planned to hold me in captivity until he eventually kidnapped Caroline. Then, he would make me watch as Caroline was sold to the highest bidder. Seeing a mother suffer such cruelty, such devastation, would give him the grim satisfaction he craves to avenge the loss of his wife and children. There is no other explanation for why an arms smuggler worth half a billion dollars was overseeing such a small sex-slave operation. Dimitri could easily have ordered a group of his goons to implement his plot. The thought tears the breath from my mouth, and I actually flinch as if Dimitri were right here in this room with a knife to my neck.

Focus on solutions. You are in charge of your life.

Somehow, I muster the courage and calm to cling to those beliefs. Hysteria and ill-thought-out reactions put me at the mercy of Dimitri's sinister plots. We've won the battles so far because we've remained strong and in control.

I watch Chase walk an information tightrope, deciding what to say and what to keep quiet. In the end, there's only silence. I decide against asking any follow-up questions.

He didn't deny what I just uncovered and revealed. For now, that has to be enough. I square my shoulders and in a strained, hoarse whisper, apologize again.

He puts a hand on either side of my face and lifts it up so our eyes meet. "None of this is your fault. You have nothing to be sorry for," he tells me gently.

I drop my gaze. "Don't I?" My behavior last night remains a hallmark of my guilt.

He shakes his head. "You should not have to apologize for wanting to celebrate an accomplishment." He looks all torn up, like once again, he's let me down.

Now, it's my turn to tighten my arms around him, help him see that he's not at fault either. "That disgusting excuse of a man is not going to ruin our lives. You need to put the blame for what's happening behind you."

We both fall silent.

I watch him closely, waiting for some kind of response.

He looks down and shakes his head, his expression one of complete despair. "My God, Alicia. He could have gotten you and . . ." His voice cracks when he tries to say Caroline's name. "And all because of his hatred for me. It's personal for him, and I'm the one he wants to punish."

"You weren't the one to plan and execute these terrible plots. Dimitri was. Nothing you've ever done deserves that kind of retribution."

"Tell that to Devie, who's scarred for life, or to Virgil who walks with a cane . . . and you." He chokes up again. "You still have nightmares about his attack and the times he tried to get you to abort our babies. I'm not sure I can put that kind of guilt behind me." His tired voice is like a boulder on my chest.

"Yes, you can." I stroke the side of his cheek. "If you remain blinded by guilt, Dimitri wins on two fronts. One, he's crawled inside your brain, so he gets personal satisfaction from the torment that wreaks, and two, he keeps you from thinking straight. If you're not on top of your game, you can't track him down. It's a win-win for him. It's what he's depending on."

"I know that."

"So don't let him have that satisfaction."

"That's easier said than done." This comes across loud and clear. Unlike Dimitri who feels nothing, Chase *feels*. Hurt, guilt, and worry for the well-being of those he loves are vulnerabilities that Dimitri can transform into weapons to strike out and destroy us.

"Not for someone with your abilities. You've survived two deployments in Afghanistan, imprisonment by the Taliban, and multiple attacks by Dimitri. You can get this bastard." I pause to gather inner strength. "Especially if we work together." I know we have no other choice. Chase can't let remorse prevent him from stopping Dimitri. I can't allow myself to unravel each time Dimitri attempts another atrocity. If we let raw emotion replace strategic planning, Dimitri succeeds. Chase has known this all along. That's why he tells me just enough to keep me level-headed and aware. It does no one any good if I'm so fearful, I act impulsively or irrationally.

"Why aren't you arranging to get us back sooner rather than later?" I'm calmer but still emphatic that we have to leave now. He may know our children are safe, but I want to hold them close and feel their physical presence.

"We can't return yet."

I shake my head, indicating that there's no way we can stay in Paris any longer. "I need to talk to them now."

"It's too early in the morning there for you to phone now. They'll still be sleeping. I'm telling you, the kids are safe. They're in Summit tobogganing, ice skating, taking horse-drawn sleigh rides; Sammy even bought them all skis and is giving them beginner ski lessons and . . . before you interrupt that going off to a ski lodge is not safe"—that's exactly what I was going to do—"all their activities are being done on our property with Clyde, Sammy, and Eleanor taking turns guarding the perimeter. Sammy even arranged for Sandy to come and stay for more hands on deck. She brought a litter of puppies with her for the kids to play with."

I haven't seen Sandy for some time and remember her as a kind and soft-spoken woman who breeds golden retrievers in a tiny hamlet at the base of Summit. She and Sammy have been seeing one another for several years. All of this is fine except for one fact that sticks in my craw.

"How long have the kids been in Summit?"

"For about a week."

"I'm their mother. I should have been told where they were staying."

"It happened so fast. As soon as I confirmed that Dimitri was active again, Sammy got everyone out of town."

I'm guessing Chase didn't give Sammy or Sunny a choice and told them to get their asses moving. When it comes to dealing with Dimitri, you don't score points for diplomacy.

"What about Fiona and Liam?" The fear that Dimitri will hurt Liam never drifts far from my thinking.

"Everyone is fine. They're in Summit, too," he says, his face creased with concern for me, and the terror he knows I feel. "I didn't say anything because I didn't want you to worry. You would have figured out something was wrong if you knew they were plucked from their school programs and shuttled off to the country. I was going to tell you last night, but certain points of interest swung me in a different direction." He presses his mouth to the side of my neck and kisses each tattooed star.

Blinking slowly, I murmur, "I seem to remember, swinging fists also kept you busy last night."

His lips leave my neck. "That's another reason we can't leave yet."

I eye the gun resting on top of the table. "Last night is over and done with."

"It won't be over until I make amends." He fixes me with a canny eye. "What's with that weird look?"

"You're going to *apologize*?"

"Yeah. I know how to admit when I'm wrong."

I almost laugh outright, but he's being so earnest, I pull a straight face and wait for him to finish.

"I invited everyone you were with last night to lunch at Hotel Costes. A buddy of mine will fly us home first thing tomorrow morning. Sammy is driving the kids to the airport to meet our flight." While I slept, in typical Chase fashion, he went to work, calling friends, gathering information, making reservations and keeping us safe.

It's hard to stay angry when you're married to Mr. Perfect. Yet, I can't shake the dread that gnaws at my stomach. By coming after me and then Caroline in the cruelest of ways, Dimitri not only seeks to crush Chase's dreams;

he wants to obliterate his soul, too.

Chase's anxious face studies mine. He's worried about how I'm taking all this new information.

I tip my head up. "We need a plan. I'll feel better if we've decided where we should live while Dimitri is on the loose. I think Summit is best. It's remote. Clyde is there to offer more protection. The children will be safer and there's all sorts of activities they can have fun with to replace their programs in the city. There's plenty of room for Fiona and Liam to stay with us. Liam can transfer to a school there or he can be homeschooled."

"And you?" he says. Two short words that take me by surprise.

"What do you mean, *and me*? I'll be there too. Do you think I would just go on my merry way somewhere else when all of this is happening?"

"No."

"Are we back to speaking in single syllables now? Swinging from yesterday's optimism to today's anxiety while fishing for answers all morning has been exhausting. I just want to get home, see with my own eyes that my children are safe, and then move us all to Summit."

"We already have a plan in play, and it's about growing your business. You initiated it, and if I remember, you were very firm about accomplishing your goals."

"That was then. This is now." I can't help but think that the rock-hard reality of Dimitri's plan to abduct Caroline puts a lifetime of change in between both. "I can't risk anything happening to our children. My business is secondary. It has waited this long. It can wait a bit longer." The anticipation of someone deliberately wanting to hurt my children releases a dread so powerful it deadens my desire to fulfill a career.

"I know you're worried, but think about it for a moment. Has anything *really* changed since you left?" He moves along to his next point without giving me space to answer. "You may not have known the exact details, but you understood from what happened before that Dimitri presented a serious threat to us. Yet you still mustered the courage to move on."

He's right. I'm not so naive that I can't see the force of a tidal wave headed in my direction, but having it barrel toward one of my children is different. That would be a blow I'd never recover from.

"Look." He raises his palm before I can respond with what I think is my only recourse. "We would never put our children at risk. We've always taken every precaution, and we'll continue to make sure they stay safe." He tightens his fist. His eyes darken, transformed by a resolve so weighty it masks any specks of softness. It's a fearsome look I haven't seen before and leaves once he reaches out his palm to caress my face. "It helped that you were traveling and away from the children. It made it harder for Dimitri to have access to both you and Caroline at the same time. You've got serious momentum going now. I say we don't stop here."

I like how he uses the word *we*, like he's all on board with my career choices, but fear has a hold on my psyche, and I can't stop shaking.

"For you, work is a healthy outlet," he says, seeing that I'm not convinced. "When you sketch, you slip into another world. You have a gift for creating designs that people want. They were a huge success on this trip." He's smiling now. His hand cupping my chin is solid, warm, and a bit of my terror ebbs.

"There's hardly a day that passes that I don't think about that heinous bastard." I say it bitterly, wishing I could just wake up from this never-ending nightmare.

"I know. But that's not such a bad thing. It keeps you on your guard until he's caught or . . ."

Killed.

The unspoken word is not shared, for fear it might not happen. Dimitri has succeeded in bringing us down to his level. We now believe the death of another human being is warranted for our survival. A death in exchange for a life. For me, it's an old story. My first breath of life had death at its exhale.

"We'll go on with our lives, you with your business, me with mine. We'll tweak and change course if necessary, make sure we're canny and resourceful. What we won't do is crouch, hands over heads, just waiting for Dimitri to attack. I need you to be on board with this, because it's harder to do alone. Of course, I'll support whatever decision you make. This is your life, and you have to be the one who is in charge of the course you take."

I try to puzzle things out through the clamor of a question that repeats in my head. Can I safely balance motherhood and a career under the weight of this burden? I hope so, because our lives may damn well depend on it.

Chase eyes me critically, weighing the impact of my reaction. I feel my chest rise and fall as I'm thrust into the harsh reality of my mother's look of distress every time she watched me reach a milestone. I knew she yearned for the shadow of someone who should have been present but never would be. I didn't want to go through my life longing for what could have been. I wanted and deserved success for my talent and hard work.

"Okay. I'll stay on this career track, and we'll continue to live in the city."

"Good. Oh, and you have one, no two"—he glances at his phone for clarification—"appointments to add to your calendar before you get too busy." He hands me my phone.

Taking it, I eye him cautiously.

"Target practice Thursday morning at nine. Dr. Alexander, Friday afternoon at four." He loops the crumpled pack of cigarettes into the waste bin, where it spins into the can like a basketball along the rim of a hoop before a score. So much for being in charge of my life.

CHAPTER 30

C hase clears his throat before beginning. "I want to thank you all for joining me and Alicia today. It means a lot to us both." He glances up at the large table of guests assembled for our luncheon. Sitting in the Hotel Costes restaurant is like visiting a sliver of old-world Europe—polished paneled walls, mounted brass light fixtures that mimic candle-lit sconces, and a hand-painted ceiling, boasting clusters of crystal chandeliers that present a stylish ambience.

The tables are full, each diner sitting on plush, red cushioned chairs, eating with fine French flatware, while a pianist plays soft music in the background. Despite the opulence, the atmosphere is warm and cozy. It's almost enough to make a person believe there was never any lurking danger.

The champagne, like the décor, is impeccable. I take a sip, then two, grateful for the warm buzz the alcohol brings after what I learned last night.

Beth leans into my ear and whispers, "It appears that your man is going to make some sort of announcement."

She looks at my stomach and her eyes widen with surprise. "You're not . . ."

I don't give her a spare second to finish. "Have you lost your mind? Of course not. Chase had a vasectomy."

"I seem to remember he had one before you became pregnant with twins."

"Yeah, well, this last one did the trick."

"Those earrings are gorgeous, by the way," Beth sweeps back my hair for a closer look. "They're Cartier, right?

I nod and she adds, "Chase always did know how to present spectacular gifts. Now if only he was as good at making speeches."

We both focus on Chase, who looks like he's about to swallow a slug.

"He's going to apologize for how he acted last night," I tell her.

Beth's usually bright and avid expression appears skeptical. "He keeps looking in your direction. Maybe he'd do better if you left for a few minutes. You could excuse yourself and go to the restroom."

"Leave? Not in this lifetime. I'd pay good money to hear Mr. Perfect say he was sorry." I think about this expensive, fancy lunch and figure that we are already paying a hefty sum. Definitely worth every penny. I shoot Chase an expectant look to encourage him to move it along.

He scratches behind his ear, pauses, then frowns, but says nothing.

Devie leans her bare, pale face in my direction. She's going for a less-is-more look today. Her red-painted lips are the only splash of color applied to her face. The contrast between her glossy lips and ink-black hair is striking.

In fact, the entire elegance of the place makes me glad I chose to wear a short, off-the-shoulder, black crepe dress, and my t-strapped heels with sapphire clasps. A gift from Chase, they're still my favorite pair.

"If this wasn't so painful to watch, I'd be laughing out loud or at least trying to make him laugh." She says this with a cool directness that's not without fondness.

Beth flashes Chase a smile that would encourage the most reluctant public speaker.

"He is a man of action, not a poet. We must be patient," Andre comments while continuing to stare at Chase with pure admiration, as if he was getting ready to give a presidential speech instead of a few, warbled words of apology.

"I just want to . . . I mean I . . ." Chase sputters, studying me with a serious expression.

Widening my eyes, I purse my lips and slowly nod my head like I do when I'm giving one of the twins my firm, *you know what you have to do* look before they apologize for a wrongdoing.

Chase stops cold, waits a beat, then blurts, "Oh, what the hell . . ." Striding toward me with a strong sense of purpose, he thrusts out his hand. When I take it, he hoists me out of my chair. Before I know what's happening, I'm spun and bent back over his arm. He leans in and plants a long, deep kiss on my lips. Popping his head back up, he matter-of-factly says to everyone, "About last night . . . What can I say? A beautiful woman makes a man do things he shouldn't." The kiss wrinkles my thoughts, but I'm not so moony that I don't hear the whistles, mad clapping, and guffaws that follow.

"Nice rally, bro," Mac calls out.

As I'm placed upright, something pokes my ribs. It's the handle of the gun from our bedroom, packed in the waistband of his pants and covered by his jacket. Pressing his hand into mine, he pulls me past the row of chairs to where Marcel is sitting. Marcel smiles up at us through a swollen cheek, and Chase gives him a friendly pat on the back. I was surprised to hear that Marcel accepted Chase's invitation, and when I mentioned it to Beth earlier, she said Marcel never hesitated. He told her he had it coming after getting so drunk and behaving badly toward a married woman. Not letting go of my hand, Chase leads us toward El Árbol.

"Thank you," he says, holding out his hand. El Árbol freezes, his eyes shifting uneasily. Then, gold tooth flashing, he shoves forward his right hand for Chase's handshake. "You filled in when we were down a man," Chase continues. "And you did a damn good job."

El Árbol's bruised eye crinkles from his grin, which even stretches wider when Chase hands him an envelope full of cash for his protective service yesterday. Chase escorts me to my chair, then adjusts himself in a seat across from mine and gives me a practiced look of innocence. "You see how easy it is for me to apologize."

"In what universe was that an apology?"

He cocks his head in a way that signals he's perplexed. "What do you mean? I admitted I was wrong and paid you a compliment." Admiring the cleavage peeking out from the black, lace bustier I'm wearing under my dress, he grazes my lips with a kiss. "You can thank me in the bedroom later," he whispers, the hot rush of his breath still lingering on my mouth when he sits back in his chair. I tilt my head and eye his quirking brows.

"You're hopeless."

"Four bottles of Petrus Pommerol, 2009 for the table, please," he calls out to the waiter, ignoring my comment.

I want to give him a piece of my mind about how he cleverly dragged me into his supposed apology, but the spread of food that's just arrived smells too appetizing for me to think of anything more than eating. After our morning discussion, I was too upset to eat any breakfast other than a couple of strawberries. Now, all of a sudden, I'm famished. The array of fusion dishes spread out on the table catches my eye: crispy chicken rolls, marinated steak, pan-seared tuna. Then, there's *Niçoise* salad, succulent and tangy with green beans, baby potatoes, cucumbers, olives, capers, and more fresh tuna.

I'm readying my fork to pierce this assortment of freshness when I notice Chase's demeanor suddenly change. My eyes follow his and rest on a clean-shaven, fit man with neatly parted hair and the commanding posture of a military officer. Chase's left eye squints appraisingly in his direction. His jaw and shoulders tighten. He does not trust this man. The stranger heads our way, stopping first to speak to Mac, who's seated at the end of our table. Virgil, glancing up, raises a single brow, then reaches out his hand when introductions are made. My ears strain to hear what they're saying, but the din of restaurant conversation doesn't allow me to make out their words.

I needn't have tried, because he immediately strides toward Chase with a firm sense of purpose. Chase gets up and meets him halfway down the length of the table. Unlike Mac's inclusion of Virgil, Chase makes no attempt to involve me in any introductions, nor does he shake this person's hand. It's only when the man notices me watching them that Chase invites me with a smile and the wave of his hand to join their conversation. From the corner of my eye, I catch Virgil's lips silently blowing together like a fish's.

Buford. The name comes across as clearly as if he had shouted it out.

I walk over, smiling but cautious, the designation of military intelligence resonating loudly and clearly.

"George, this is my wife, Alicia." Chase says it half-heartedly, like it's an obligation, not anything he wants to do.

I extend my hand to meet Buford's for a handshake. Instead, he bends and kisses the top of my hand. This rankles Chase. I get the impression that Buford knew it would, and that's why he did it.

"It's a pleasure to make your acquaintance. I understand you had quite a successful show here in Paris. I thought I'd come here personally to extend my congratulations." He smiles above his tightly-knotted tie, but his eyes don't seem to get the message. Their cool indifference tells me this visit is not really for my benefit.

I can't let go of the fact that Chase deliberately left out George's last name. It irritates me that he wants to delay my finding out that George is in fact Buford. There could be many reasons for this and none of them are good.

"Thank you for your kind words." I smile, then innocently add, "How do the two of you know each other?"

"We served in Afghanistan together," Chase answers, his tone clipped.

Buford smoothly switches the conversation from Afghanistan and keeps some small talk flowing for a bit before asking Chase for "a minute of his time."

"I'll be right back," Chase says. He follows Buford to the entrance of the restaurant. As promised, their conversation is brief. When they return to the table, Buford makes no attempt to leave, so Chase requests an extra chair and seats him next to Mac and Virgil. Several times during the course of our lunch, I look across the table to study Buford. He seems to fit in nicely. He talks but not too much, sips his wine in moderation, and remains in constant control. His posture is erect. There's not a hair out of place nor the shadow of a whisker visible. He's more than satisfied to let those around him steer the conversation. There is no doubt in my mind that Buford is making a business call and the recipient is Chase.

As the head of an intelligence operation in Afghanistan, he was the one who demanded Chase return for a final debriefing. I later discovered that this quizzing involved details from Chase about Dimitri's illegal arms deals with insurgents. Could Buford be here because of Dimitri? Chase indicated Dimitri was looking to kidnap me and Caroline. Caroline is safe in Summit, but I'm still here in Paris, protected, yes, but freely out and about conducting business and socializing with friends.

I look for some signs of concern from Chase, but just like Buford, he acts bland and at ease. Hand thrown casually around my shoulder, he enjoys everyone's stories and jokes, chiming in every now and again with one of his own. Mac, too, is calm and relaxed, sharing *foie gras* with Virgil and laughing at all the appropriate times. I'm not fooled for a minute. Something's up or Buford would not be here.

The rest of our lunch continues uneventfully. Toasts are made. More congratulations are sent my way, and the great food and expensive wines keep coming. Through it all, there's no clarification from Chase about who George really is. The more time that passes, the more imperative it becomes for me to hear it directly from Chase's mouth that George is in fact Buford. I lean into his ear and whisper "Is that Bufo—?" but the rest of my question is interrupted when Virgil raises his glass for a toast.

"Here's to Alicia. May this be only the beginning of many more successes for you . . . and for us." There's a round of clapping, leaving me no choice but to replace my uneasy question with a forced smile for my guests.

"Why don't you say a few words," Chase suggests and, nodding, I stand to make a small speech of thanks.

"It seems we keep celebrating the success of my fashion show, but I assure you it never gets old. Thanks to my husband for his ceaseless love and encouragement. I couldn't have done this without your support." I turn to him and smile, and this time it's genuine. I may be peeved by his secrecy, but it doesn't change the fact that he's my rock, my anchor, and the force of a wind that steers me in the right direction. My attention shifts to the others.

"Thank you, Virgil, for your expertise and help. And a big thank-you to all my friends who support me and my success. Here's to love, life, and good health."

And to everyone remaining well and alive after this day is done.

I don't say those last words, but I'm damn well thinking them when I raise my glass in a toast. It's become more obvious than before that Dimitri is in the vicinity, scheming, plotting, and planning evil with no apparent end in sight.

Everyone cheers, clinks glasses, and drinks. I wash my panic down with several swigs of wine.

"Is everything alright?" Beth asks.

"Fine. Everything is fine," I squeeze her hand and force another smile, or maybe it's the same one that's stayed stuck to my face all afternoon to keep everyone calm. "Thanks for all you did to help Chase pull this together."

"I enjoyed every minute of it." She squeezes my hand back. "Let me know if you need anything. *Anything,*" she reiterates, her eyes earnestly studying mine.

My face smooths to a blank serenity. I find this easy to do now that I've had Chase, Mac, and Sammy as teachers in this department. Sunny's pretty damn good at it too.

The rest of the luncheon is uneventful. Buford is the first to leave, with the others following shortly after.

As soon as we settle back into our suite, Chase disappears into the bedroom. When he reappears, he's wearing the pants, shirt, and leather jacket he had on last night.

"I have to leave for a bit," he says, tucking in his t-shirt.

A sudden chill covers the room, stealing any lingering warmth from the shared luncheon with friends. "Where are you going?" My eyes don't leave his face while I try to steady my nerves.

Silence.

"Are you going after Dimitri again? Is that why Buford showed up before?" Three questions fired in a row, demanding to be answered.

Stepping forward, he strokes the side of my cheek with

the back of his hand, and it's like he's touched a vein that goes straight to my heart.

"A business problem came up that I have to deal with. Don't worry. I'll be fine. It's imperative you stay here with Mac. I'll see you soon." A veil descends over his eyes, and it's like he's already someplace else, somewhere dark and dangerous. Before I can answer, Mac knocks and Chase quickly ushers him into our room. "I explained to Alicia that I have to leave to take care of a business matter." Mac's expression doesn't waver for a second, and no further comments are exchanged.

I run my fingers through my hair and look up at the ceiling. Neither are going to share where Chase is going. Given our harrowing reality, it's not hard for me to piece together what's happening. Chase is assigned to a mission that involves Dimitri, which makes it a dangerous one.

And judging by his outfit, he's taking that damn motorcycle.

I reach out my hand and grasp his, feeling that familiar pull that's like an invisible cord linking my heart to his. "Go. I'll be waiting here with Mac. Text me when you're on your way back." I kiss him lightly. "Be careful."

He holds my gaze for a moment before looking away and heading toward the door. Stone-faced, his resolve is palpable when he closes it tightly behind him.

A fearful silence follows. It's a silence that runs so deep, so sharp, it slices into me, peeling away layers that leave me exposed and chilled. When I finally find my voice, I look at Mac. "Do you think he's going to be alright? Maybe he needs you as backup if the problem gets out of hand. I can bolt myself in here while you're gone and be perfectly safe."

"Trust him to know what he's doing. He'll be fine,"

Mac says, double-locking the door. "Now, what will it be?" he grins, holding up a deck of cards. "Gin rummy, poker, or hearts?"

Mac's here to stay and that's that. I walk over to the mini bar and bend to peer inside.

"Rummy. How about you?" I squint up at him. "Gin, vodka, or wine?"

He shakes his head. He's not going to have a drink while on the job, but since I've nothing to do but watch the clock and worry, I grab two mini-bottles of gin and a can of tonic water.

Quiet hangs heavily in the room. We both know that any assignment involving Dimitri is life-threatening and since no one has denied that Dimitri is the one compelling Chase to leave, it's accepted that it is now common knowledge among the three of us.

I escape into the bedroom and quickly change into slouchy pants and a cropped sweatshirt, then sit down to begin my vigil with some mindless card playing. "Do you think Virgil wants to join us? Where is he anyway?" I ask, wondering if we should be concerned about his safety, too.

"He's sitting tight in our room, relaxing and watching some TV. He's good where he is." Mac wants to keep his protection concentrated, more one-on-one and without any distractions that might slow his response time or add another chess piece for Dimitri to use to his advantage. Dimitri already dragged Virgil into his web of vengeance when he had a car slam into one of our vehicles that Virgil happened to be driving that day. Mac also knows that this time, it's me Dimitri is after. The air gets close, and I feel bile rising into my throat when my mind shifts to my children.

And Caroline. He's after her, too.

No! I won't let fear and panic take over. I paint a picture in my mind that shows Caroline safe in Summit, sledding and sipping hot cocoa with her brother and sister. The thought is comforting.

Two hours and several hands in with no word from Chase has my hand trembling when it's my turn to deal. I check my phone again.

"Take a deep breath, Alicia," Mac says, placing his hand on top of mine. "Just because there's no word from Chase, doesn't mean that something's wrong." He picks a card from the pile and tosses another down. "Your move."

I force myself to concentrate, throw a random card down, then forget to pick up. I look up at Mac.

"Check your phone again, Mac. Please. Maybe he emailed you." I know it's ridiculous. Who would take the time to compose an email in the middle of a dangerous assignment? But I need to be certain that Chase hasn't tried to make some contact.

Mac scrolls through his phone and shakes his head. Too edgy to sit any longer, I pace the length of the room. My fingers itch for a cigarette, but when I eye the waste bin where Chase had tossed them earlier, it's empty. "You think he's alright," I say, lowering myself back into my chair. "I have the same feeling I did when he was missing in Afghanistan." My voice cracks, so I take some more sips of my drink to calm my nerves, if only for a few passing moments.

"This is different, Alicia. He's operating in a friendly country with plenty of resources and backup." Mac is at least admitting that Chase is on a mission. What would be the use of maintaining the pretense that nothing serious is happening? He knows I've figured out the gist of the situation.

Late-afternoon light fades through the window, making me wonder if it's easier to win a fight under the cover of night. In my mind's eye, Chase's encounter with Dimitri will be nothing short of a fierce battle fought in an ongoing war. Dimitri is powerful, ruthless, and relentless with an army of thugs and rogue governments at his disposal.

Mac pours me a second drink and continues our card game as if everything is normal. His calmness steadies my jitteriness. I take another large swallow and another deep breath. Watching me from the corner of his eye, Mac suggests we play poker just to change it up. After each hand, he calls out different wild cards, while sharing humorous stories about his antics in the military.

"Chase told me that you all had your share of experiences serving together." I study him seriously. "He said you and Sammy rode shotgun for him."

Mac nods but seems to be totally engaged in his cards. He knows I had hoped he and Sammy could be with Chase now, but somehow that wasn't the plan, and since I wasn't privy to the strategy they engineered to capture Dimitri, I had no say in the matter. I rub my palms along the top of my jeans to ease their trembling and sweatiness and pick up my cards, forcing myself to focus on yet another round. Somewhere during our third round, Mac stills and glances toward the door.

"What's wrong?" He holds a finger to his lips, and my mouth clamps shut. Pointing to the bedroom, he gestures that I should go inside and lock the door. That's when I finally hear it, too. A muffled, shuffling thud coming from the hallway just outside our door. For one awful moment, I imagine Dimitri with one of his strongmen, armed and ready to kidnap me after having just killed Chase.

I duck toward the bedroom as silently as I can. Something clicks against the door, and I freeze. Mac pulls a gun from the back of his waistband and steps toward the door, pointing again toward the bedroom. I swallow hard and walk toward the bedroom. With his back flush against the wall closest to the door, Mac holds his gun with both hands and listens.

My ears perk, hoping to hear something besides my tortured breath. Sure enough, there it is again, the same shuffling noise. Someone is definitely in the corridor outside our room. Peeking through a crack in the bedroom door, I watch as Mac slips off the security chain and stands to the side. Slowly, he reaches out and grips the knob. He waits a bit, then throws the door open and charges through the opening, swinging his gun to the left then to the right. There's a screech, bang, and some swearing.

"What the hell?" Mac says. "I could have fucking killed you. What were you thinking, coming here?"

I recognize that tone because I've heard it so many times before from Chase.

"Oh, calm down. I was worried. I thought I'd listen outside the door to make sure everything was alright."

I let out a breath I didn't realize I was holding when I recognize Virgil's voice.

"Really, and if it wasn't, what the hell were you going to do?" Mac says, fury whipping across his face.

Stepping into the living area of our suite, Virgil stands in the doorway, leaning on his cane with one hand and brandishing a large vase he swiped from his room in the other.

"Forget I even asked," Mac says. "And give me that damn thing." He grabs the urn from Virgil's tight grip and rests it on an end table.

"Hi Virgil." I wiggle my fingers, smiling.

"Thank god you're okay," he calls out, clutching his heart. "Any word yet?"

I shake my head.

"Don't just stand there. Come inside," Mac barks, sticking his head out to check both ends of the hallway. Once Virgil's inside, he bolts the door and returns the gun to his back waistband.

"Let me make you a drink," I offer while an ashen-faced Virgil mops his brow with his handkerchief.

"A scotch on the rocks would be great," he says, then, without missing a beat, turns to Mac and remarks, "Those frowns are going to prematurely wrinkle your face. You can't blame me for wanting to make sure you were okay." Virgil takes the drink I poured, then reaches out and kisses me on both cheeks.

"You look worried."

"I'm fine," I lie.

"What have you been doing to pass the time?" Virgil asks, eyeing our card game and fishing for an invite. He takes a large swig of his drink, hoping to calm nerves that are as tattered as mine.

"Cards." This clipped, curt response shows Mac's not ready to let go of his anger yet.

"Why don't you pull up a chair and join us," I suggest.

"Sure. It'll be a relief to pass the time doing something instead of being cooped up in our room with only my awful imaginings to keep me company."

Mac softens when he hears this and carries over a chair for Virgil to take. For the most part, Virgil's leg has healed nicely. It's mostly at the end of a long day that the pain kicks up, and he needs to use his cane. How he thought he could balance a heavy vase for protection while leaning on a walking stick is beyond me, but I'm the last person to judge someone's actions during a challenging time. I probably would be trying to track down Chase tonight if Mac wasn't here to stop me.

The card game drags on. Even the slightest concentration requires an effort I'm unable to muster. It's no surprise I'm losing badly. Organizing my cards and forcing myself to focus, I jump, then freeze, when Mac's phone twitches on the table. He picks it up.

"Mac here." I can hear a man speaking on the other end, but it doesn't sound like Chase's voice. "No, Buford. He's not here yet," Mac says.

Virgil nervously glances my way, removes his handkerchief from his pocket, and dabs perspiration from his brow.

I lean forward in my chair and steeple my hands, hoping to hear more. Mac listens and, as unflappable as ever, answers, "That's a negative. No word, either."

Virgil takes another slug of his drink and offers me mine. I shake my head. My heart is thumping too hard in my chest for me to do anything but listen. I have questions to ask, but I don't dare open my mouth for fear I'll miss something. Then the level, clear voice on the other end says, "It just came through. He's heading back as we speak."

"Chase is on his way," Mac says, sitting back and looking relieved. I don't have a chance to ask for details because my phone interrupts with its familiar jingle. It's Chase. I snatch it from the table and answer the call.

"We got him, baby. We got him." I hear the rush of traffic in the background with a smattering of horns blowing and the repetitive one-two screech of a European emergency siren racing down the street.

"You caught Dimitri?" I ask, dumbfounded, quickly adding, "Are you okay?" I stand and start to pace.

"I'm fine. Dimitri's in police custody." There's a loud revving noise, then a smoother but just as noisy accelerating sound. "I'm on my way back now," he shouts above the gunning motor. Worry has my patience slipping a notch, then two, when I realize what he's doing.

"Are you using your phone while riding that motorcycle?" I ask, hand on hip, ready to square off with him.

"Chill, Alicia," he says.

Mouth open, I stare ahead, at a loss for words. Did he just tell *me* to chill?

"I love you, baby," he adds, laughing out loud, then signs off.

Who is this person? I walk back to my chair mumbling to myself. "He survived that murderous thug, and now he's looking to kill himself on that damn motorcycle." The last several hours have been fraught, and even though the worst seems to be over, it's hard for me to calm down.

"You're a fine one to be complaining about him taking risks. You drive him crazy with all your spicy, spur-of-the-moment recklessness," Virgil says. He hands me my drink to cool me down.

I take a long pull of my gin and tonic, then smile as wide as I can. It seems to hit us all at once.

"We got him!" Mac booms, taking me in a hug. His overt enthusiasm is so out of character that it has me shouting out, too.

"We got him. We got him!" Three simple words that mean the difference between dealing with deadly plots or enjoying smooth sailing without headwinds of chaos and panic. Rubbing the top of his cleanly-shaved head, Mac looks relieved.

"Why don't you both go back to your room and rest. I'll be fine," I tell both of them. Since Mac arrived in Paris, most of his time has been spent working for us when I know he and Virgil want nothing more than to spend time together.

"I'll wait until Chase gets here. He won't be long," Mac says.

"Can you at least tell me where he's coming from?"

"It's nearby."

"How near?"

"Less than a mile from the hotel," he answers, finding it hard to look me in the eye.

Virgil blows out a long whistle. "Talk about being too close for comfort."

Virgil's right. For all I know, Dimitri had me under surveillance the entire time I was in Paris, just waiting for the best time to strike. My recklessness last night could have delivered me straight into the belly of the beast. Consistently having to confront a reality that is fraught with peril scars your psyche because so much time is spent trying to figure out if someone you love will encounter a terrifying calamity. Even though we can take solace in the fact that Dimitri is out of commission, the lingering shadow of his actions still exists. He was incarcerated and still managed to get paroled before he served his complete sentence. That's why Chase makes a point of keeping anything to do with Dimitri on an even keel. We don't wildly celebrate our successes, nor do we overstate our worries. Level—always level—and that's how it's going to have to be now, except for the fact that my seesawing emotions refuse to settle down. I'm too wired up from waiting.

I open the door and step onto the terrace for some air. Mac gets as close as he can without intruding, his eyes scoping the surrounding perimeter.

"I'm glad you were here to help. Right now, I just need a few minutes to myself to gather my thoughts before Chase returns."

Mac nods and turns back inside.

An icy wind threads through my hair, my arms, around my chest, and down my legs. *He is alive*, it whirs. *All is well*, it repeats. I don't know how long I stare into the distance on the balcony—it can't have been long—because I'm not too chilled despite the wind. It's his hands that I feel first when he steps onto the balcony behind where I'm standing. Hands that slowly and methodically massage my shoulders while lips graze the length of my neck. I bend it to the side to give the warmth of their touch more access.

"Are you okay?" he asks.

I close my eyes and breathe in relief. "I'm fine," I say, looking over my shoulder and smiling to put him at ease. When I turn to face him, I see that he's tired but calm.

There's a brightness to his gaze, and a lightness to his bearing. It's as if, with the press of a button, the brutal press of his past has lifted. My fingers touch his hair. "I should be the one asking if you're alright. How did it go?"

"All good," he says, taking my hands and pulling me inside. "It's freezing out here." Under the glare of the hotel lamp, I give him a searching look, then moisten my thumb with my tongue and use it to remove a fleck of dried blood from his jaw.

"Liar," I say softly, lifting the bruised knuckles of his right hand to my lips for light kisses. We press our foreheads together. I lace my fingers through his, feeling the warmth of their grasp. Slowly, relief replaces the tension that imprisoned me earlier.

He pulls his head back and massages the crease between my brows with the pad of his thumb. "There's no need to worry, now. He's gone. I personally watched as agents dragged him away in handcuffs."

"That's good to hear. Where did you finally find him?"

"With the help of Interpol, we learned he was holed up in a small, seedy hotel not too far from here."

"Did he put up much of a fight?"

"A bit. I knew I had to bring him in alive. We needed to find out how far up the Russian chain of command his operation extended."

"And how far up do you think that reach goes?" I can feel the prickle of fear inching back up my spine.

Chase pauses, his expression intense. "Just like we thought, it could be all the way to the Kremlin."

I study his face and notice another smudge of blood on his cheek. "With contacts that high up, he must have had lots of protection. How were you able to get to him?"

"Canvassed the building and found a way I could climb up to the window of his room."

I check the raw, scraped palms of his hands and kiss both. "How high up was that?"

"Ten floors."

My eyes widen.

"But there were ridges outside each window and I had a rope."

He had a rope, I mumble, shaking my head. "Well, I'm glad you're back alive and in one piece."

"It helped that Dimitri was caught off guard. He wasn't expecting a raid, and he especially wasn't expecting me. Once he was cuffed, I could see the arsenal of weapons he had stored in his room. You'd think he was staying in a war zone instead of on a sleepy street in Paris. There were also several passports from different countries and under various aliases. Lots of euros too. Our friend had big plans."

"He was alone?"

"Surprisingly, yes. I would have thought he'd have at least one bodyguard. The only thing I can think of is that getting to us was his 'pet project,' something he wanted to do all on his own. He probably had one or two other men out there keeping us under surveillance."

"You mean me. You can say it. He had people watching me."

He bobs and weaves a bit, not wanting to cause me further worry, then flatly says, "Yes. You. But before you go beating up on yourself again about the other night, you need to realize how smart you were to hire El Árbol. He was a deterrent to anyone who wanted to harm you that day."

"I know, but I promise it will be a long time before I do anything like that again."

He lightly kisses my lips. "Don't make promises you can't keep." He knows me better than I know myself.

"Why did Buford choose you to be the one to go after Dimitri?"

"He knows I've been dealing with Dimitri for a long time. I know his moves, how he thinks."

"And you wanted to be the one to gain the satisfaction of a capture." I say.

At first, he doesn't answer. Then, sighing, he nods a yes. "I'm sorry I had to leave again without saying anything. I know how hard this is for you. You shouldn't have to continue to wait, worrying about serious unknowns. You've been dragged into my brutal battles since the start of our relationship."

"I knew what I was getting myself into." I rest the palm of my hand on his cheek. "I will always wait for you. I made that promise after your last deployment, and I plan to keep it." I smile and pause for a second. "Besides, I wasn't all that worried."

"Liar," he smirks, cupping my chin.

I burrow my head in his shoulder and soak up scents of sandalwood soap coupled with sweat. When I raise my head, he strokes my lips with his thumb. "It's over," he says. "Dimitri will never see the light of day again."

"What about the rest of his stone-cold assassins?"

"My contacts at the CIA, MI-6, and General Directorate for External Security are all clamoring to grill Dimitri for info about who he's been working with. Even the GRU wants him for questioning. The people who work for Dimitri have scattered into crevices like scared rats."

The way he rattles off this alphabet soup of what I assume are international intelligence agencies makes me think he's been engaging with them for some time now. I've obviously heard of the CIA, but any information I have about its operation comes from Netflix. I'm clueless about those other organizations. I start to wonder about what clandestine geopolitical operations Chase might be part of, ones that not only include Dimitri, but also involve finding out about others who support his underground network's sphere of influence. There's a yawning gap between going on one mission to take down a personal nemesis and navigating through others that aim to expose complicit governments and countries. The extent of Chase's involvement in all this and how long it is expected to continue remain a mystery.

I swallow hard and ask, "Is this the end of the spy business for you now?"

He studies me intently. He knows that the thought he could be called away at any given moment is a burden that haunts my days and dreams.

"I have no reason to actively participate in any new assignments."

Lead weights drop from my shoulders. Dimitri is in custody *and* Chase is done with the military spy business.

I say nothing. Like so many times before, I work hard to keep my excitement contained. The motto Chase lives by is *never get too overwhelmed or too over-exuberant with news concerning Dimitri.* That changes when he quickly grabs my hand and calls out to Mac and Virgil, who are sipping cocktails and recapping details in the sitting room of the suite. "How about we all go out tonight and celebrate. Give Beth a call and ask her to see if the luncheon group is available to come along."

Mac, who's been waiting to wrap things up, nods and pulls out his phone.

I call out Beth's phone number, but Chase says, "Not necessary."

Of course, Mac already has Beth's number and most likely the cell numbers of everyone I have been with since I arrived in Paris.

Chase scoops me up from under my knees and lifts me off my feet, making me squeal with surprise. "I'll need some time to . . . er. . . brief Alicia on the finer details of what's happening," he says, striding toward the bedroom.

"Just don't let those *particulars* keep you both up all night," Virgil calls out, thrusting his chin in our direction. "Remember, Alicia, we have an agreement. I'm going to be blatantly blunt. You already have three kids, and this is the third deal we've tried to seal."

There's a beat of a pause. "What?" Virgil adds in a softer voice, obviously to Mac. "He's a special ops marksman. The man always hits his target."

I blush to the roots of my hair as Chase shoves the door closed with the heel of his shoe.

CHAPTER 31

"Mamma, Mamma, Mamma." Misty-eyed, I watch as whole parts of my life run toward my open arms. Caroline's longer legs propel her to me first. I pick her up and press her face to my neck. I kiss her hair, her cheeks, her temple, the former pain of fear for her safety still a dull ache in my stomach.

"Mamma, you're squeezing me *soo* tight," she laughs, hugging me back.

"I missed you, Sweet Pea," I tell her, loosening my grip but still not letting go.

"Me. Me. Me," Teo says, jumping up and down and raising his arms to be lifted. I let Caroline slide down, and scooping him up, I smother his face with kisses while Juliette wraps her arms around my legs. I try to put Teo down so I can lift Juliette for her turn, but he tucks his face into my neck, pops his thumb into his mouth, and refuses to let go. I bend as best I can and wrap my free arm around Juliette's tiny shoulders, then kiss the top of her head. She turns a delighted face upward, then thrusts out her lower lip.

"You away fourteen hundred years, Mamma."

"I know. I was gone for a while," I tell her, smiling, "But I'm home now. I missed you all so much."

Fiona and Antonio wear welcoming smiles while Liam wildly waves his hands and runs toward us. Flying private, we breezed through customs. Now, in a quieter part of JFK close to where aircrafts are permitted to land, our loved ones can meet us in an arrivals terminal. I had shipped home my luggage with all the carefully packed outfits from the show and now only carry a small bag of clothing. Chase arranged for the same, since he obviously could not have hauled his suitcases on the back of a motorcycle. This allows us free arms to hug, cuddle, kiss, and hold our children.

"Hi there," Fiona says, kissing my cheek." She leans back and studies my face. "You. Look. Fantastic! I love your hair. Very classy."

"Thanks." I ruffle Liam's hair. "Hi, buddy." He reaches up and gives me a kiss.

"Hey sis. How've you been?" Antonio steps in next and wraps me in a big hug. After all the hard work, the worry, Chase's leaving, Dimitri's capture, I finally let myself relax in the comfort and warmth of family.

"I'm good." Getting crunched from all the embraces, Teo wiggles out of my arms and runs to hop onto Chase's shoulders. Sammy brings up the rear of the group. His protective presence doesn't go unnoticed. Clasping Teo's ankles close to his chest, Chase gives Sammy a one-armed hug. I follow with an even bigger one. "Thank you for keeping my babies safe," I say close to his ear.

"It wasn't hard. Eleanor and Sunny offered good

backup.”

“Everyone’s help is so appreciated. Where are they now?”

“They’re at the apartment, stocking up on food and supplies and preparing for everyone’s return.”

Sammy quickly swivels from me and follows Caroline, who has bolted from the pack.

“Look, Mamma. It’s Daddy. Over there.” Caroline says, pointing to a rack of newspapers stacked to meet her lower eye level. My eyes follow her outstretched finger, and my hand flies toward my open mouth.

Chase sees my startled gaze. “It can’t be,” I tell him, blinking rapidly, hoping my eyes are playing tricks on me.

He moves toward the stand for a closer look, with me not far behind. Sure enough, there we both are, staring out from the front page of *Gossip* magazine. I should say it’s Chase who’s glaring wide-eyed into the camera. Tossed over his shoulder, it’s my ass that greets the camera. How anyone took that photo is beyond me. I was sure no one in the place saw the fiasco Chase created when he arrived. Welcome to the world of social media, where everyone is a fingertip away from connecting to the rest of the world.

I glance around the large arrivals area. It’s empty except for a harried couple briskly walking toward the exit. My relief is short-lived because one second, Liam is walking alongside us, and the next he runs, pointing, toward another stand where the same photo glares from a different newspaper.

Liam grabs one from the rack and studies the page. “Bottoms up to a great show!” reads the boldly-printed headline on the cover of the racy newspaper, *Scandal*.

A long, embarrassing silence follows.

"Well, look at that," Fiona finally says, snapping the newspaper from Liam's hands and placing its cover face-down on the shelf. "Uncle Chase and Aunt Alicia are having fun playing a game."

"What game?" Liam asks.

"Yeah, I'd like to know about this game, too. We might want to play it later." Antonio looks at Fiona and wiggles his brows.

Awesome. Just Awesome.

Even my own brother is laughing at us.

Four little faces stare expectantly at Fiona. She shoots Antonio the stink eye, then opens her mouth to speak, shuts it, then opens it again. "It's called . . . um . . . Rescue," she says, nodding and smiling as if she's known it all along.

Blank stares.

"It's when you pretend aliens are invading and someone needs to be saved," Fiona quickly adds.

Caroline looks back at the magazine rack, scrunches up her face and shakes her head. "No, Aunt Fiona. When Daddy makes this face," she thrusts out her chin, tightens her jaw, and except for her auburn pigtails, looks exactly like Chase when he's angry, "he's not playing a game. He's *really* mad. Mommy," Caroline looks up at me expectantly, "was Daddy mad because of that Frenchman?"

A frown pinches together Teo's small, feathery brows. "Goddamn Fwenchman," he says as if on cue. Antonio laughs out loud.

"Teo!" I call out firmly. His face gets very still. "Those are not nice words to say about someone. Where did you ever hear such a thing?"

"Daddy said it when he was on FaceTime with Uncle

Sammy," Caroline clarifies.

I narrow my eyes at Chase, who seems to be at a loss for words. He rubs his chin and shoots me a sheepish look. "I may have said it," he admits through the side of his mouth so only I can hear, "but only that one time. That kid's a swear sponge. He hears one once and it sticks like metal to a magnet."

Chase is just about to speak to Teo about his choice of language when something catches his eye. "You stay right there, buddy," he says, pointing his finger at the spot where Teo is standing. Teo's lip quivers like he's going to cry, so Fiona lifts him into her arms while Chase drifts toward a particular newspaper rack.

"What are you looking at?" I hit the branded newsstand hot on Chase's heels, and reel back from the onslaught that glares at me from the racks. Clustered against a wall are several newspapers with their front pages suggestively exposed. "Rear Up Over and Done" screams a tagline under an enlarged close-up of my butt. Another photo shows Chase taking down a bewildered El Árbol. "Tycoon fuels fight in Paris Club" reads that bolded caption.

I close my eyes and tell myself to stop reading, but some obsessive force keeps my eyes moving from one to another. "Stunned and Bummed" a British tabloid flashes. At least that one shows me upright and face front. Snapped after my fashion show, it captures how astonished and humbled I was by the audience's enthusiastic response. The best-selling magazine *Crowd* displays a wild-eyed Chase on its glossy cover with the caption, "Angry Chase Reardon Sweeps Away Fashion-Design Sensation, Alicia Cesare."

"Nice plug," Chase says, pointing to *Crowd* magazine.

If he feels any awkwardness, he's not letting it show. For a brief second, I'm proud of the accolade despite its shady source.

"It's not too shabby," I say, feigning indifference. But the hyperbolic flair of the headlines tapping into our personal life is derogatory and humiliating. Embarrassment doesn't even begin to describe how I'm feeling.

Chase slides his arm around me. "It's all recycled news that will be forgotten tomorrow," he says. Then in typical Chase fashion, the articles are dismissed, and he moves toward what must have initially captured his attention. A light-speed calculus flicks across his gaze when he studies one particular photo. "Focus over here," he tells me, circling his finger on a section where a wide camera angle captured the entire front and inside of the club that night. I don't know how the photographer escaped Chase and Mac's notice but then again, both were in a big hurry to get us away from there. I peer closer but see nothing out of the ordinary. Once again, he outlines a specific section. Sure enough, there it is! A shadowy form that looks to be the shape of a person watching us from a dark corner of the club. I didn't remember seeing anyone in our vicinity at the time, but I didn't have the best view with my head hanging down. Chase wouldn't have seen the person either, because he was rushing toward the exit.

He edges closer to the stand, while I proceed to scan our immediate surroundings, looking for people who might recognize us from the photos peppering the newsstands. There doesn't appear to be any need for concern. The terminal remains relatively empty. In an effort to identify who the skulking form might be, Chase picks up the newspaper and we hunch over it head-to-head.

Fiona hands Teo to Sammy and saunters over to us. "What's wrong?" she asks, excusing herself before stepping in front of me so she can see what has us so concerned.

"Chase spotted someone hiding in the background of the club," I tell her, studying the photo over her shoulder. All I see is the outline of a person lurking in the far end of the bar. "It's too dark. I can't make out who the person is," I say, giving up. Chase leans his head to one side and then the other trying to decipher the image, before he shakes his head. "I can't either. It's not someone I recognize."

"That's Yuri," Fiona says.

Chase flicks a surprised gaze at her.

"At least I think it's him," she adds.

"What makes you say it's Yuri?" Chase says.

"See the chin and the sharp line of a jaw." She traces a specific area. "And look at those tall, slender legs." She points to a lower part of the form, then traces her finger upwards to show the length. "Also, right here," again her fingers swirl across the shape, "you can see the slouchy and relaxed posture of a man leaning his hip against a wall while his arm rests on a tall corner table. I remember this particular height, form, and features from all the photos you shared of Yuri when you were trying to figure out if he was the one who spoke to Liam at the rehab center."

When I think about it, it's not surprising that Fiona is such a quick study on the nuances of photographic depictions. A keen recognition of form, shape, and silhouette help professional photographers capture their subjects.

Chase looks stunned. "You're right." He pauses a moment, then adds more to himself than to us, "What the hell was he doing there?"

"Why *was* Penko there?" Fiona's voice trails off in a low, hushed whisper.

My ears perk at the mention of the name, and something stirs in my memory. Chase, standing furthest from her, shows no sign that he registered what Fiona just said. Both stare at the photograph, wondering, just as I am, what Yuri was plotting, with or without his father's blessing. This incident makes it a total of three times that Yuri was in the same place I was. First, at the drug rehab center, then at my show, and now at Le Bound. This last time, he was within ten feet of us, and we never saw him. It's still a puzzle, but lots of thoughts jostle around in my head. Was Yuri the one wielding the net that was closing in on me? Chase labored under the assumption that Yuri was out to harm me. Yet, all three times I didn't come close to being hurt or threatened.

"I could be wrong," Chase says, "but I don't think it was a coincidence that Yuri was there. I also don't think he planned to hurt anyone." Chase looks in my direction. "My guess is you had two bodyguards that night."

"Two? What are you talking about?"

"I think that Yuri was there to make sure nothing happened to you," he answers.

"Why would Yuri be there to protect *me*?"

Chase's lips form a tight line. He's reluctant to share more but all at once, it's not necessary because I figure it out.

"Yuri was at the club because he knew his father had people there planning to kidnap me, right?"

"Yeah. That's what it's beginning to look like. Seems

the falling-out he's had with his father is greater than we thought."

I'm studying the photo of the dark interior of the club when I suddenly remember Penko was the name Fiona used when Liam was missing at the rehab center. "It might be Penko," she had said. When I tried to get more information out of her, she was evasive. Come to think of it, she also mentioned someone with a name that sounded like Penko when Devi and I found her weak and high on heroin at Four Freedoms Park. Originally, we thought this Penko guy was someone she owed money to, but now I'm not so sure. Could Penko and Yuri be the same person? If that's the case, why would Yuri show up at The Four Freedoms Park?

I observe Chase to see if he sees that something is off here, but he just keeps staring at the photo, giving no indication that he's making any new connections. I'm not surprised. Chase's belief held that Dimitri's eye-for-an-eye was only directed against me and our children as revenge for the wife and children Dimitri felt he lost because of Chase. He firmly believed Fiona and his father were spared. Denial runs deep when dealing with loved ones.

Absently twirling her hair, Fiona studies the photo from all angles. She turns my way when she realizes I'm staring at her and shrugs. "Nothing else is decipherable."

I think back to the club, the music, the dance floor, but I can't think of one thing that presented even a sliver of danger. Yet it's apparent that Dimitri had people embedded there ready to pounce the moment they had a chance. El Árbol, Yuri, and then Chase and Mac prevented that from happening.

Chase hooks his arm with mine. "Let's gather the troops and get out of here. We'll figure all this out later."

"Did the Frenchman do something bad, Daddy?" Caroline asks when we join the rest of the group. She doesn't seem to want to let go of what she's seen and heard. Continuing to hold onto her hand, Sammy smirks but says nothing.

Chase slips back into Daddy mode and starts with Teo first. He scoops him in his arms and looks him full in the face. "Your mamma's right. We shouldn't talk about people like that. It's not nice. It makes them feel sad."

"Teo didn't mean to say those bad words, Daddy," Juliette explains. Teo nods and says he's sorry. I pick up Juliette, who always seems ready to step in to protect her twin when he's in trouble, and hold her close, giving her the hugs she missed before.

"What about the bad Frenchman?" Caroline asks again.

Chase lowers Teo and studies all four children. "We should never judge or say bad things about a person because of where they come from. That is not fair, and this particular Frenchman wasn't really a bad man." He stops for a beat and widens his eyes, "Except for the GIANT roving eye he had *smackaroo* on his forehead." Chase slaps the palm of his hand against the center of his forehead. Juliette gasps. Teo's mouth opens and Liam stares wordlessly at Chase waiting for his next words. Chase doesn't disappoint. "This eye would pop open," he continues, "And move all around like a giant telescope." He juts out his head and moves his neck in slow circles, zooming in on each of them with bulging eyes. "But instead of studying the stars and the planets in the sky, do you know what it did?" Four heads shake no. "It searched for a beautiful person for him to be with."

"Chase," I warn. "End the story, now."

Fiona looks down to try and hide her smirk.

"Did you blind him with a sword like Odysseus did with the Cyclops?" Liam asks, encouraging Chase to continue.

"No. You never want to use a weapon to solve a problem when words will work. I just reminded him . . ." Chase tightens his fist and studies Liam with mock seriousness, "that he needed a rest from all that prowling."

Caroline ponders this, the wheels in her young mind turning as she processes what she just heard and how it fits into her life. She stares up at me and Chase. "Then, who's the bad man that wants to hurt us?" Innocent words that pull us up short in our tracks.

Chase looks like he just took a punch to the gut while my stomach clenches into a knot. To say we are shocked is an understatement. We did everything as parents to shelter our children from Dimitri's threats and attacks. We didn't even think they knew he existed. He was never mentioned in their presence. There was always someone around to take them from the room if there was just an iota of talk about imminent danger. Yet none of us can deny that Dimitri occupies a fierce place in our fears. Who's to say that Caroline didn't overhear us talking from behind a closed door?

I can't dismiss all the phone conversations spoken in hushed, coded words that we mistakenly believed she wasn't hearing—but in fact, she was not only listening to but absorbing what was being said. One in particular comes to mind. It was when we thought Dimitri had people watching Liam and Teo playing in the park. I was home that morning helping Eleanor with the girls, who were struggling with colds and feverish coughs, when Sunny called my cell.

"We need to get home now. We're being followed," he had said.

"Is it *him*?" My voice must have sounded panicky, because even now I can feel what it felt like when I thought the children might be in danger.

"No, not Dimitri," he answered and explained that two men and a woman had been following them since they arrived in the park. He didn't want to walk down any of the deserted paths to get to the street without an extra pair of hands.

"I'm on my way now," I said, running to grab my purse.

"No!" his normally even tone bellowed. "Send Eleanor. She'll know what to do and can be here in five minutes by foot.

"Sunny needs you by the Alice in Wonderland statue," I called out to Eleanor. I remember her sharp, knowing gaze as she wordlessly threw on her coat and ran for the door. It was Caroline's stillness that first captured my attention. That and the knowing look she gave me when she wordlessly held out her doll for me to hold.

So . . . If there's one thing I've learned about children, it's that they read our thoughts, like images staring at them from a canvas. They observe our facial expressions and study our reactions to what's being said or done. They absorb our fears and concerns along with our displays of love and affection. Long and short of it: children are clairvoyant when it comes to knowing their parents' thoughts, so how would they not know that evil stalked our family?

Chase manages to smile when he lifts Caroline into his arms. "Here's the thing, Sweet Pea," he says keeping close eye contact. "In this world, most people are good. They play nicely, they share their toys with others without fighting and they just flat-out want to help you."

"Like me. I'm good."

"Yes, you are." He gives her a squeeze and her face lights with a smile. "Like I said, most people are good, but sometimes a person comes along who can't be trusted."

"What happens then?"

"Well, you try to talk to that person. You explain how it's better to be kind to other people than it is to hurt them."

"Did you talk to the bad man? Is he going to stop?" Caroline asks, and my heart cracks a bit that she should have to be thinking about this at such a young age.

"I tried, but he didn't listen, so I had to do something else."

"Did you fight him and then throw him in a dungeon?" Liam asks, raising his hand as if he's wielding a sword. Lately he's obsessed with reading stories about Greek heroes and King Arthur's Knights of the Round Table.

"I helped the police capture him," Chase answers. "Now he's locked up in jail where he will never hurt anyone again."

Chase's talk seems to have altered the grim turn Caroline's mind took. Satisfied for the moment, she gets antsy in Chase's arms and squirrels down to join her cousin and siblings who are locked into an imaginary swordfight. Gathering everyone together, we head toward the exit of the arrivals terminal and make our way to the parking lot.

Sammy spots him first, a tall, gawky fellow hauling a suitcase on wheels. "That's Sean Marlowe from the online magazine, *Rag*," Sammy says. As soon as the words are out of Sammy's mouth, we realize we're being followed. When Sean realizes he's been spotted, he melts into the opening of the washroom. Even though he seems to be gone now, it's only a matter of time before photos he's secretly taken of us appear in *Rag*.

Chase squints in the photographer's direction and mulls over our dilemma. "Oh, why not," he says to me, a smirk playing across his lips.

"I don't follow," I answer. "Why not, what?"

"Let's give them their money's worth." And, just like in the restaurant the other day, he bends me over his arm and plants a long, lingering kiss on my lips. As soon as I'm upright again, I smooth over my hair, straighten my shirt, and swallow my angry retort. Best to just smile for the camera.

"Daddy kiss Mamma smackaroo on the lips," Teo calls out, tapping his lips with the palm of his hand. Caroline rolls her eyes while Juliette covers her mouth and giggles. Talk about getting their money's worth. We've provided enough fodder for the tabloid press to devour for some time to come.

CHAPTER 32

The space that I choose for my atelier and business offices is in a gleaming new high rise on Sixty-Fifth and Lexington. A&C Reardon House is one of several buildings Chase developed in the area. Comprised of ten high-ceilinged, spacious rooms with lots of natural light and panoramic views of the East River, Alicia Cesare Enterprises occupies the entire penthouse level. A private elevator goes from both the lobby and the parking garage straight to my office with just one swipe of an identity card.

We never did figure out exactly why Yuri was following me in Paris, nor did Fiona provide any additional information about who Penko was, other than to say that he was someone from her past who was now out of the picture and best forgotten. With so many unanswered questions, Chase is not taking any chances. Surveillance cameras have been installed in the main lobby and in all hallways and stairwells. One camera in particular is so tiny, it records facial features without anyone knowing. Added to this mix of devices are Mac and Sammy. One or the other is always somewhere in the vicinity, supervising security guards in the lobby or observing arrivals who pass through security scans and bag checks on their way into the building. The last security measure is more a result of the 9/11 terrorist attack than Dimitri. Nevertheless, it makes us all breathe easier.

At first, I thought the space was too extravagant, too much square footage for a starter company, but Chase insisted, explaining that I had already established myself with a successful label. It was time to move on and move up, he had said. And so I did, all the way to the thirtieth floor.

Virgil and I settle in nicely. He assumes one corner office. I take the other, and in between there is ample space for our employees to sketch, design, assemble, style, model, curate, and ready our merchandise for delivery. Technically, I own ACE. It bears my name and logo, a display of three jade-tinted block letters configured on a diagonal with a tan background and a narrow ginger stripe woven through each letter. However, when I suggested Lena draw up a contract for Virgil, I made sure the financial benefits were too generous for him to turn down.

Together, we extend the momentum of the Paris trip by creating and unveiling blockbuster winter and spring lines, and the upcoming year looks to be even better. Not only has ACE doubled turnover from the previous year, it is set to double that turnover next year.

It helps that we're located in A&C Reardon House, because all the brand's offices are consolidated into one single New York office that Chase and I own outright. Rent is not paid by us but collected from other lessees in the building. All manufacturing is absorbed into the company and no fees are paid for outside licensing. This helps control costs and any subsequent debt. We've increased our marketing budget, which has allowed us to use social media to expand quickly in Asia.

Since you are only as good as your next bestselling design in the competitive fashion world, designers must consistently work hard to innovate if they want to grow and prosper. That's why it helps that Virgil and I share a similar fashion philosophy. We understand that the critical core of fashion is to allow the wearer to feel both comfortable and empowered. When evaluating the nature of a particular design, beauty is not only in the eyes of the beholder. It's embedded in the viewpoint of the wearers, who are envisioning how they appear to themselves and to others. That notion, that perception, is key to the success of fashion. We create fashion to satisfy the demands of the purchaser, not the critic sitting in the stands at a show.

Our goal is to put the needs of regular people first. To do that, different body sizes and shapes must be taken into consideration. A tapered dress with a cinched waist would not work on a rounded figure. I make sure to add designs to my collection that drape as well as cling. Creating an array of different designs that look good on different figures is not easy. Designs should have attitude, but if you strain too hard to accomplish this, the result can be gaudy and amateurish. It takes lots of hours of work with lots of help on hand to fit all the pieces needed to complete a specific design.

My jackets remain my personal style signifiers. Using different fabrics and different cuts, I keep them sleek, timeless, and multi-purpose. Most can be worn with mini or maxi skirts and all different styles of pants. My current favorite, a cropped tweed beauty with a candy-pink silk lining, is crafted from organic cotton from Swiss mills. Inside one of the spacious well-lit areas adjacent to my office, I study the jacket's drape and cut and imagine the finishing touches needed to get it perfect: maybe a sharper line or a shorter collar and a flatter pocket.

Virgil stops by and steps alongside me to study its contour on the dress form. "How about if we highlight the line on top and define the waist just a bit here." He pins that section, and all at once the jacket form pops into a multifaceted concept that's pleasing to the eye. It can be worn with jeans, different length skirts, or straight leg or flared pants. He leans back, studies the jacket and nods.

"I think it works, except for . . ." I loosen the waist and smooth the shoulders a tad so it's not so retro, 1930s-looking, with its padded shoulders and cinched waist. Virgil nods, accepting the modification, but still I'm not 100 percent satisfied.

"Tear your eyes away from that jacket for a moment. I have news to share."

I stop, straight pin in hand, and turn in his direction.

"Have you seen the article in the *Times* on your last live-streamed show?"

"Our show," I correct.

"Our show," he repeats, grinning.

"Yes. Chase emailed me the link and had someone drop off a stack of newspapers. They're over there." I point to the worktable adjacent to several dress forms holding different outfits waiting to be tweaked.

"You are a one-of-a-kind," he says, eyeing the newspapers

on my desk.

"I sure hope so. You can't excel in this business if you don't create unique designs." I eye the jacket critically.

"I'm not referring to your work." He raises his eyes and shakes his head. "It's impeccable. I just can't believe you haven't read the article yet. You are more captivated by design than fame."

That's not entirely true. I had skimmed the article, saw that it was mostly positive, then gave into the demands of the jacket that beckoned from the mannequin to be finished.

"I've mostly read it. It's encouraging."

"Well, it's about time you hear it in its entirety." He scoops up a newspaper and flicks through its large, thin pages until he finds the right one. One or two minutes in, he looks up and turns his attention toward me. "Listen to this," he says.

"'ACE's eye-popping, live-streamed, and live-tweeted show was a sensation second to none. The runway show held in a Brooklyn warehouse combined art and functionality, merging the unseen parts of nature with beautiful designs. There were smart skirt suits, richly-painted silks and a sharp working wardrobe with super-chic leather jackets. Liquid silk black dresses, fluid charcoal-colored trousers, and tweed jackets crafted with leather pannier pockets stole the show. The privately owned company ACE . . .'" Here Virgil exercises his usual dramatic streak by extending a long pause before continuing, "'is owned by the *brilliant* designer, Alicia Cesare, and commandeered by the talented . . .'" another dramatic pause, "'Virgil May as chief executive. ACE continues to push forward and has emerged as a global luxury brand. With its jacket and perfume divisions soaring, it reported a healthy rise in earnings. Net profit increased 18 percent to $800 million in the first half of the year. Profitability reached an all-time high of 35.3 percent of sales.'" Virgil stops reading and waves the newspaper like a banner.

"I know. It's amazing. I'm grateful we've been so successful. Now, we have to keep the momentum going," I answer, before slipping back into designer mode to make yet another change to the jacket's cut.

"Does part of your plan to keep the *momentum* going still involve a trip into Afghanistan so you can meet with whoever it was that helped Chase when he was held hostage there?" It's clear by Virgil's expression that he doesn't approve of my plans. The fact that he knows about them at all only came about because he overheard me on the phone when I was inquiring about transport to Afghanistan. Gifted with some kind of radar-like sight and supersonic hearing when it comes to office gossip, there is little that escapes Virgil's attention.

"Yes, it is. Ashraf wasn't much older than a boy when he risked his life to help Chase." Like some monster woken from a deep slumber, the past roars back when I'm reminded of that dark period of time in our lives. I swallow past a stone of sorrow that lodges in my throat and my voice sounds more ragged than I would like. "If it wasn't for Ashraf's help and those in his family who sheltered him, Chase would have been killed."

Virgil reaches out and touches my arm. It's a sympathetic gesture, but the words that follow are brutally honest.

"I realize there's good everywhere and it's to your credit that you recognize it, but may I remind you that there were also many people there who tortured him and wanted him dead."

"I understand that. I'm not planning to travel to any dangerous areas. There's a garden in Kabul that I'd like to contribute to in Ashraf's name. The garden meant a lot to Chase during his deployment. He said he carried a small rose bush there on behalf of a local who was killed by a roadside bomb before he could complete the trip. Now that ACE's foray into the fragrance arena with its rose-and-sage scent is such a winner, I'd like to give back to those who got Chase to safety. My plan is to have one of Chase's military pilot buddies fly me into Kabul. A representative from the garden will meet me at the airport to receive the contribution. I already spoke to her, and she sounds lovely. After that, I immediately fly back."

I don't say that this is my way of trying to lay to rest the trove of shame I still carry from what I did during that period of time. I hate how I wasn't able to muster the courage to navigate through life without wallowing in self-misery. I hate how my weakness sullied Chase's honor and the bravery of those who helped save his life. I hate how—no matter how successful I am in fashion—I'm unable to bury my betrayal deep enough to forget. Traveling to Afghanistan is a mission, a personal quest that will allow me to replace dishonor with thriving flora that symbolize the heroism of those who risk their lives to save others. I need to create beauty that visually shows my gratitude and appreciation for this valor.

How can I explain to Virgil—to anyone for that

matter—my internal need to supplant betrayal with honor, weakness with courage, and immaturity with wisdom? Good, bad or indifferent, personally presenting a gift that adds to the life-affirming beauty of a garden in a war-torn country is the best way I know of achieving this.

Virgil looks at me with a puzzled and disapproving expression. "It's an absurd idea, Alicia. I can't believe Chase agreed to it."

I maintain eye contact and don't answer, pretending to wait for him to say more. He sees right through the cloak of my silence. "Jesus, Alicia! You're planning on leaving next week, and you haven't told him yet. What are you waiting for? You need to sit down and have a constructive conversation with him about your plans."

I want to tell him that I'm waiting to tell Chase because it's hard for me to explain how I'm feeling without dredging up a past incident that's best forgotten. Only I can't seem to forget what I did.

"Look, I give up trying to convince you what you should do. I don't understand what's motivating you to traipse off to Afghanistan, but I can guess there's something you hope to get from it that includes more than honoring bravery by promoting a perfume. It's one thing to be vigilant in your principles and quite another to risk your life to prove they exist."

He knows more about me than I give him credit for. I look up at him and let him know that I know what I need to do, and the sooner the better. There's word of a US military withdrawal from the area, so this trip cannot be delayed.

"I plan on having a conversation with Chase about my

plans tonight." I try to sound calm, but my palms have already started to sweat in anticipation of the *discussion* that waits to be had.

"That's good, because you will need to focus a lot of your attention on what needs to be done here, given what's been requested of you."

"What are you talking about? What request?"

Virgil waits a beat, then shakes his head. I know he can't believe that I have no idea about the important matter that's on his mind. It's also sad to say that I can't tear my eyes away from that jacket that seems to need just one more snip to its length. I reach for the area, armed with a few pins.

"The pressure is on," Virgil enunciates in a loud tone to make sure I'm listening while I work, "because you have been invited to design the outfit for Lady Farrah to wear to the MET gala event."

I stop what I'm doing. "What!" The honor of being chosen to be the designer to dress someone that famous for an event that is world-renowned in the fashion world has surprise, awe, and a fair share of trepidation ringing through my mind. How am I going to pull this off? As it is, I don't have time to pay as much attention to the business end of ACE as I should.

"You didn't read that part?"

"No. I didn't get that far. How does the newspaper have that information before we do?"

"Just out of curiosity, Alicia," Virgil queries, "have you bothered to check your messages lately?"

I say nothing at first because the honest answer is *No, I haven't,* but now I don't want to appear even more irresponsible, so I say, "Heather brought them to my attention, and I glanced through one or two of them."

Mirrored in his face is the same skepticism I'm feeling. "When? Last week? Two weeks ago?"

Again, I'm mum because, other than making sure I spend time at home with my children and Chase, the only items commanding my attention are my new line of jacket designs, the launch of our new fragrance, and target practice. True to his word, Chase has been taking me to the shooting range to sharpen my aim. Seems like I'm not only good wielding a needle and thread. My hand-eye coordination, steady hold, and accurate aim allow me to hit the target with consistent accuracy. At least that's what Chase has been telling me I have. It's not my favorite pastime, but it's a skill I still feel I should hone, given what's happened in our lives up to this point.

"It's just as I thought," Virgil says. "You don't have a clue what's going on. He shakes his head and flicks a finger toward the mannequins. "Those passion projects compel all of your creative energy and interest. It doesn't help that you're obsessed with developing our new fragrance line."

I stop what I'm doing and give him my full attention.

"Tell me what you know about this MET gala event."

"All I know so far is it's in May and the theme is Ode to Painted Nature."

"You mean like creating designs that bridge nature and art."

"Yes, that is exactly what I mean, and it's right up your alley. I think there's going to be elements of going green needed in the design, which should make you enjoy it even more."

He's right. It's already hard to contain my enthusiasm. It will not be easy work, because the design will have to incorporate drama in epic proportions as well as originality, superlative fit, and unique materials. Like finding and crafting a perfect diamond, flaws in fabric and design will have to be shaved away until the resulting product is a design never seen before. Another challenge will be working with a mega-star like Lady Farrah, a vain, sumptuous type with set ideas on what she wants and doesn't want in a dress design. Something akin to the gravitational pull of the moon to the sea draws my attention toward fashioning a design that could become a narrative of future possibilities.

I envision a dress fashioned using a unique white fabric manufactured from wood pulp, harvested from sustainable forests in Northern Europe. This fabric caught my attention the last time Chase and I were in Europe. We had just purchased manufacturing space in Umbria that would afford me a coveted made-in-Italy label when we decided to celebrate by traveling to Austria and Finland. It was there that I saw the fabric that I am considering now. What caught my eye was how breathable and soft on the skin it was. There was no illegal deforestations or harmful chemicals used in its production, and it was the perfect weight for draping.

My mind is wrestled from its musings when Heather, one of my young team of assistants stands in front of me, looking out of sorts. "Is Mercury in retrograde?" she asks.

Virgil's eyes peek out from above the wide-open newspaper he's reading. In typical Heather fashion, she watches us both, waiting for an answer.

Finally, Virgil says, "I don't know, Heather, did the planet happen to indicate what's happened to Alicia's unread messages?"

Poor Heather looks confused. As a transplant from Los Angeles, she operates under the assumption that everyone understands how the mystery of life's complexities can be explained through planetary flotation.

"I have no idea," I tell her. "Why are you asking?"

"Because I'm having real communication issues today. Someone insists on seeing you right now. I made it clear that she needs to make an appointment, but it was as if she wasn't understanding my words. Says she knows you both well and is on her way up. She sounded very stressed."

"Did she give her name?"

"I asked, but she was so adamant about seeing you, she hung up before telling me who she was."

I stop to think who might want to urgently see me and start to wonder if everything is alright at home. Just as I'm grabbing for my cell, Virgil checks his phone.

He looks vexed. "Charlotte is here. Let's all try to contain our delight." He yanks an unlit pipe from his jacket pocket and clamps it in his mouth. He would never light it inside. I have strict rules about smoking and food smells anywhere near our floor. There's no way I want our designs to absorb those odors. He asks Heather if she could please bring him a double espresso. "I'd prefer a scotch on the rocks, but I need to fire up my brain cells to be able to deal with what she might have to say."

"What can she possibly want?" I ask.

"Who knows, but it can't be good. It never is."

"You both seem super stressed," Heather says, tucking

her hair around her ears. "Mercury is definitely in retrograde. My body is tense, too. The usual adaptogens are not helping. My matcha-and-mushroom drink flat out did not work this morning." She lets out a sigh. "I'm going to need my chaga to pull its weight."

Virgil and I fall silent.

"It's a macadamia nut latte with a triple shot." Heather beams with toothy pleasure. "One double espresso coming up, Virgil. Can I get you anything, Alicia?"

"A double espresso over ice would be great. Thanks."

With a robust bounce to her step, she turns and leaves.

"That must be L.A. speak for god knows what," Virgil mutters once she's out of earshot. "How long has she been working here?"

"Over a year and despite her choice of words and lifestyle, she's good at what she does. She's punctual and organized. She's got an eye for glamour, too."

"She sure does. That Valentino taffeta skirt she's wearing is gorgeous. She even knows how to pair it with one of your sharp little jackets. How much are we paying her?"

"Stop being a New York snob, Virgil. They were samples left from last year's show. She spotted them on the rack and asked if I could set them aside for her until she could pay them off."

"So, you gave them to her," he says, giving me a knowing look.

"Absolutely. They looked gorgeous on her, and what were we going to do with them, anyway?"

"You're too—" Virgil doesn't get to finish because in the distance, a high-pitched call that could pass for a crow's caw echoes through the offices.

"Hellooo," Charlotte's voice rings out, the rhythm of her stilettos slamming against the polished wooden floor as she approaches. She strides past us, then whips her head around when she realizes she's gone too far.

"Oh, there you are," she says, lips pursed. "I need a word with Alicia."

Virgil studies her with a direct, frank gaze. "Hello, Charlotte. How are youuuu? Or are you too busy these days to be bothered with polite pleasantries?"

"Not at all. I'm fine. How are you?" Before he can reply, her gaze snaps back to me.

"My . . . my . . ." she studies me all the way down to my Prada shoes and back again. "The upstart who wanted to please everyone has ascended in the fashion world. I read the article in the *Times*. Congratulations." Her beatific smile drips with poisoned honey.

My eyes hold steady on her face.

"Thank you, Charlotte. I'm assuming you didn't come here unannounced just to applaud my talents. What can I do for you?"

Chilly eyes take in my worktable, the mannequins, the view of the river, and the jacket design I'd been working on. Even her regular Botox treatments can't keep the scowl from creasing her forehead.

"I thought you and I could speak in private."

I'm ready to singularly take her on, but not at the expense of Virgil's feelings and input. He's indispensable to ACE's success, and any conversation about it should include both of us. "Anything you have to say to me can be said with Virgil here."

She looks stonily through me, but I don't give her the

benefit of adding to what I've already said. In the end, it's Virgil who extricates himself, with some lame excuse that he has a call to return to one of our buyers. Once we're alone, she makes herself comfortable in one of the office chairs.

"Why don't you have a seat while we chat," she says. The fact that she is inviting me to sit in my office as if she's the one in charge is galling, but I don't let on. Spiked, reactionary anger during a business conflict is the enemy of victory and success.

"How thoughtful of you to offer me a seat in one of my own chairs, but I'm comfortable standing, thank you." I stare down at her, marking my territorial attack from a higher vantage point. "What is it you want to talk about?"

"I think you know me well enough by now to understand that I don't mince words. I say what's on my mind, and I stand by what I say."

"I'm still in the weeds here," I tell her. "Why exactly are you here, Charlotte?" I repeat.

"Let me make myself clearer." She stands and pushes herself a little more into my space. "We can start with that jacket you're working on."

I remain impassive even as I'm starting to grasp what she's getting at. My eyes lock on hers as I prepare myself for battle.

"The question that begs to be answered is: would you have been able to accomplish all this," she waves her hand around the office space, the expansive views of river and skyscrapers, then stops and points a red-tipped finger at the jacket that hangs on the mannequin, "if you didn't have the help of Estelle Designs?" Her question holds the unmistakable edge of a threat.

"I have no idea what you're talking about. Why don't you just get to the point or get out."

She eyes me with arrogance and contempt. "You designed many of these jackets while employed at Estelle Designs under my tutelage. Technically the company rightfully deserves, if not outright owns, a piece of the pie." She stares nobly through the big window and watches the river snake past. "I just want to do what's right for Estelle Designs."

It's hard to keep from laughing out loud.

All Charlotte has ever wanted was to satisfy her own ruthless ambition. Now she's found a way to weaponize my jacket designs to win an attention war and a chunk of cash, hoping that both will elevate her position at Estelle Designs.

"I'm sure you do. However, despite your good intentions to gain Estelle Designs its rightful due, my jacket designs were crafted before I became an employee there and the launch of ACE followed several years after I resigned."

"Our legal team disagrees. We have proof that several jackets were designed and perfected by you while you were still under contract at Estelle Designs." Charlotte's voice swells with righteous conviction. She actually believes these fabrications.

"That couldn't be further from the truth. Minor additions may have been added during that time, but the jackets were from the original designs created before I started to work at Estelle Designs."

"I came here as a matter of courtesy, thinking we could come to an agreement. I wanted to be fair about this dilemma. We've worked together in the past," she studies her fingernails. "So, I thought you should know what to expect. Now I see that this is all over your head. I want to see who's really in charge here," she says, not bothering to hide her impatience.

I raise a quizzical brow as the tension between us mounts. "Really, and who do you think that might be?"

"You may have expanded your horizons since you worked as my assistant at Estelle Designs, but it's obvious Chase is the brains and money behind this operation. Without him, you're just a simple wannabe grasping for fame." She says this without batting an eye.

I stare at her with any icy calm that forces any inner turmoil to settle before I answer. "I could care less who you think runs ACE, Charlotte. This meeting is over. It's time for you to leave."

But instead of leaving she narrows her eyes in appraisal and hisses, "You're already on your way to being a has-been. I look forward to our day in court."

When she still makes no attempt to leave, I turn my back on her and buzz security. Within seconds Mac appears. "Mac, could you please escort Charlotte out of the building."

He edges closer to her, and she takes a step back.

"It's good to see you, Mac," she says, as if they shared a friendship instead of a bodyguard vs. intruder connection. When he stares back, dead-faced, and doesn't answer, she turns and totters on her heels toward the elevator. Mac follows at a close enough distance to make sure she knows she's being watched until she leaves the premises.

My hand shakes when I reach for my cell to phone

Chase, but once his number pops up, I stop. Like the painful sting of a scorpion, Charlotte's words keep my hand from doing what my mind willed it to. It's the *without him you'd be a nothing* part that freezes me in place. Old wounds about my self-worth and dependency surface. I can't help but wonder how many others think ACE thrives only as an appendage of Chase's achievements. Any talent I offer is buried under their belief that my brand is well-known because his real estate business supports and boosts its growth.

This is ridiculous, I tell myself. I'm letting a jealous competitor dictate how I think. I stretch my thumb to finish the call, but, at the last second, pull it back. Instead, I phone our attorney, Lena. I'll make the time later to talk to Chase about the lawsuit and my plans to travel to Afghanistan.

CHAPTER 33

The painful grip of my headache tightens, making me wonder how things could have deteriorated so quickly. The evening began simply enough. I got home well before Chase did, helped Eleanor round up all three children to take baths and change into their pajamas. This process is akin to being in a football scrimmage once the ball is snapped. Sunny jumped into the fray, making the process a one-on-one "tackle and tickle." Without him, it would have taken the two of us double time to get the first down. Once they were in bed and had their favorite stories read aloud, twice, I chilled a bottle of chardonnay and took out two wine glasses in preparation for my discussion with Chase. I wanted to discuss Charlotte's visit but, more importantly, I wanted to explain to Chase why it was important for me to take this trip to Afghanistan.

I had already taken steps to make it happen. After Charlotte left, or I should say *was thrown out*, I arranged to meet the pilot who Chase had used several times to fly us to Europe. He agreed to fly me to Kabul Thursday of next week unless of course—as he put it—unforeseen obstacles intervened. This I understood to mean the possibility of car bombings, kidnappings, or any combination of the two. I had assumed he agreed because he surmised I had discussed it with Chase. I didn't outright lie and tell him Chase knew, but I may have intimated it when he indicated Chase probably thought it best that I not stay for any length of time, and I nodded my head and said, "That's right."

Now, sitting across from Chase at the dining room table, I take a sip of wine and look directly into his eyes. We just finished a delicious dinner of shrimp scampi over wild rice, and I watch as he leans back in his chair and pours himself another glass of wine. *Drink as much wine as you want*, I think, *because what I tell you next is not going to go over as well as hearing about Charlotte's threat of a lawsuit did.*

"I can tell," Chase interrupts my thoughts and takes hold of my hand that's resting on the table, "that you're still concerned about this lawsuit. Like I said before, I had documents drawn up about your rightful ownership of your jacket designs just as you started to work at Estelle Designs."

"I vaguely remember signing them, but we weren't even engaged to be married at that point. How did you know I would need that kind of protection?"

"Call it business intuition."

I nod, thinking once again he's one step ahead of me concerning affairs that I should be on top of myself. I look up and smile, not wanting to seem ungrateful. Actually, I'm relieved. Thanks to him, it's one less problem I have to consider.

"My guess is Charlotte is still going to proceed with the suit, but our documentation will slow the process to a grind. Eventually it's going to get too costly to proceed. No need to keep worrying." He strokes the top of my hand with his thumb.

"That's a relief . . . uh . . . Chase?"

"Yeah." He looks me straight in the eye.

"I . . . um . . . I had an idea concerning ACE's new fragrance line."

"It's doing really well. I understand sales are soaring."

"That's right. I thought of a way I could give back, show some gratitude for its success. You know I based the scent on the story you told me about the garden in Kabul. Well, I've gotten in touch with Ashraf, and we arranged to have a representative from the garden meet me in Kabul to receive a contribution in Ashraf's name."

At first, he says nothing. He just keeps staring at my face, which is wearing an absurd grin.

"You must be joking."

"No, I'm not."

"You want to go to Afghanistan to promote your rose sage scent?"

"No, not promote it. I want to personally offer a contribution in the name of the person who helped save your life. I already spoke to your pilot buddy, and he said he'd fly me into Kabul . . ." I don't finish because one look at him makes me think my request is going to induce a seizure.

"Absolutely not! Of all your crazy ideas in the past, this is by far the most insane and reckless. There was a suicide bombing in a police station outside of Kabul just last week and," he pushes both hands through his already-spiked hair, looking as if he's ready to tear it out, "there's serious talks being conducted about an American force withdrawal. It is not safe to go now and conditions will only worsen when and if that happens."

I run my fingertips over my forehead to loosen the knot of my migraine. This is not going as planned. Time for me to placate his jittery nerves.

"I get how you might think that this is not the best time for that *quick* trip to Kabul I was *considering*. So, if not now, when do you think it might be safer? It would just be for the day. I've read peace negotiations are underway with the Taliban."

"When?" he snaps back. "I'm thinking the month of not happening between the two days of never."

His door-slammed, subject-closed attitude irks, and I can't resist a smart-ass retort. "So that's a no?"

He throws me a dark look I don't want to trifle with, and I clamp my mouth shut.

"What I can't believe, most of all, is that you went ahead and arranged these plans with a buddy of mine without first discussing them with me."

"Nothing is definitive. I would never go without talking about it with you first."

"When were you planning on leaving?"

Guilt grumbles inside me, but I won't hide the truth. "Next Thursday."

"That's only a week away. You had to have been planning this for a while."

I look away, finding it hard to meet his eye. I had been corresponding with the facilitator of the garden for months. She helped me name the scent, Lillia Sage, after the flowers in the lily and sage families that are indigenous to Afghanistan.

"I was only planning on staying for a day."

"You do realize it's at least an eighteen-hour flight from New York to Kabul and that it requires a stop for refueling. There and back is impossible for one pilot to accomplish in a day."

"I know. I was going to stop in Turkey for a night on the way back."

He stares at me without blinking. Now that he knows I acted on going to Afghanistan without discussing it with him first, his gaze shifts from anger to detachment then to stoic stone. Scraping back his chair, he gets up to leave.

"We're done here," he says flatly.

"Can't we at least discuss this further?"

He doesn't even slow down his exit from the room.

"Where are you going?"

Abruptly, he stops. He turns and walks back to where I'm seated. Planting each hand on either side of my chair, he leans toward my face and glares. "Not the fuck to Kabul or Istanbul, that's for sure, and if," he lets the word hang ominously, "you even attempt to set out on this hapless venture, I will personally handcuff you to a chair until you see reason." His tone doesn't move above a low, calibrated delivery, which is more unsettling than if he had shouted his words out in a fury.

I flinch, then jump, when he slams the bedroom door.

So much for *constructive conversations*.

• • •

Later that night, I take my time getting into bed, sketching some ideas for Lady Farrah's dress until I'm bleary-eyed and then lighting some candles and soaking in a warm bath to try and decompress. Watching the flickering flame, I start to probe why I felt so compelled to plan this trip.

The idea first took root once Dimitri was locked behind bars. With him out of the picture, I felt safer than I had in a long time. I now had the time to manage and address those parts of my life that I considered essential. I could concentrate on growing my business, raising my children, and strengthening my marriage without worrying when the next ominous threat or fatal blow might strike. These holes of additional time begged to be filled. They gave me the chance to examine personal vulnerabilities I'd struggled with, those weaknesses that drove me to compulsively smoke, to unravel when Chase was called away on business or missions, or to worry incessantly about my children's health and safety. Now, I want to seize the power to conquer them and, in the process, lighten a blemish that, in my mind, continues to stain my honor and integrity.

This itch or need to step into the lion's den, the very place where Chase was held hostage, would be a way for me to stand up to my fear of loneliness and abandonment. Time has made me see what I was willing to trade to loosen their grip when the uncertainty of loss had no end in sight. It wasn't some need to satisfy a forbidden desire that pushed me toward Thomas's advances. Fear is what drove me to have sex with a man I didn't love while I was married to a man I loved with all my heart and soul. That's a misstep a person doesn't easily back out of. I knew then that what I was doing was wrong. Yet, I allowed weakness to tarnish my honor. It's a shortcoming that continues to scar my conscience.

So, no longer having to dodge a killer maniac, I thought I could lighten my burden of shame, look Ashraf in the eye in his war-torn homeland, and tell him how thankful I was for all he did to save Chase's life. The only problem is that I didn't see the blistering impact it could have on Chase's peace of mind. I sought to replace self-centered fear with self-centered redemption. How could that ever strengthen a relationship?

A heaviness pushes on my chest. I hate when we have these types of arguments. They tend to last days, sometimes weeks, because one or the other of us can't let go of our anger. My head spins in different directions, but the reason for my thinking becomes clear. My motive was never to hurt or worry him or put myself at risk. It was to take a journey as a quest to find enlightenment and courage so I wouldn't be driven to do something I didn't want to because of fear.

Wrapping myself in a towel, I make a promise to talk to Chase about how I'm feeling first thing in the morning. Maybe if he heard why I wanted to do this, he would understand that my behavior was more a desire for improvement than a betrayal of trust.

I slide under the covers, snuggle close to him and attempt to wrap my arm around his. He yanks it away and turns to his other side. Tomorrow. Tomorrow, I'll explain everything.

The first awareness I get that something is wrong is when I'm awakened by a sharp poke from Chase's elbow.

Rubbing my chest with the palm of my hand, I watch him toss and turn in our bed. Not wanting to frighten him any more than he already is, I quietly wait, but his thrashing only accelerates. Terror flies from him in guttural shouts as if he's trying to crawl out of his skin. He jumps from the bed and, with arms raised, stares at the ceiling and turns in slow circles.

"Incoming, incoming. Shake and bake," he cries out. By now, I know he's spun hard and fast into a combat flashback. He had them after he first returned, but this particular one seems especially bad. Wild-eyed and sweaty, he stands and shouts like he's about to implode from dread and tension.

I'm finding it hard to watch without doing something, anything to help. I slowly approach him, hoping I can stop him from hurting himself, but he lashes out with his arm and clips the side of my head. I hit the floor hard.

Hearing the ruckus, Sunny steps into our bedroom. He helps me up and walks me to a safe distance. "It is best to stand by the bedroom door until he comes out of this," he whispers.

I want so badly to gather Chase into my arms, rock him, and offer him the comfort of knowing he's safe, but I can't. He's so caught up in the horror of his past, he wouldn't recognize the overture.

Eventually, his terrified chattering, shouting, ducking, and pacing stop. I watch the panic drain from his face.

He blinks at me, confused, then his attention swings to Sunny. "It's over," I tell him softly. "You're safe."

He stares at me with an expression I've never seen from him before. It's a cross between sadness, vulnerability, and relief.

I walk toward him, wanting to rest his head on my shoulder, but Sunny holds me back and presses a wet towel into my hand. I look at the towel, not knowing what to do with it. Sunny takes it from my shaking hand and holds it gently to the side of my forehead. Only then do I realize I'm bleeding. By now, Chase is calm enough to take in his surroundings. He studies me and his face becomes sharp and tight. I know he's remembering our argument. Tears sting my eyes. It's because of me and what I had planned that he suffered this horrific flashback.

"I'm fine," he says, his tone low and clipped. He shoots me a glance, his eye catching the blood that seeps into the towel from the gash on my head. "I think it's best if I sleep in the guest room," he adds, taking his pillow and walking out of the bedroom without once looking back. I can tell he's shutting down, slipping into that distant, angry place where he slams and locks the door to his feelings. It's a place he refuses to let me enter.

The following night, I try again to explain my motives for the trip. I had a long day at the office, planning for the MET gala, conferring with Lena and our legal team regarding Estelle Designs' lawsuit, and finishing the jacket line we were about to release. Then putting the three kids to sleep was the usual clamorous exercise. Plenty of screeching, stomping, running, and hiding kept me and Sunny in constant motion until all three were tucked in and asleep.

When Chase finally gets home from the office, it's late and he looks beat. The second he spies me, he turns away as if I'm not there.

I approach him with wary reserve.

"Hi." I give him a small smile.

He nods his head in greeting.

"How did it go today? I note the dark circles that ring his eyes. "Looks like you had a busy day at the office." Or a terrible night of tossing and turning in the throes of another flashback, I think, while helping him remove his coat.

"It was fine."

"That's good." I pause a bit. "How are you feeling?"

"I'm fine."

Fine seems to be the operative word in his repertoire of monosyllables tonight. We're anything but *fine*. "Any more . . . episodes?" I tentatively add, hoping for some clarification about how he's really feeling.

"I said I was fine."

"Can we talk?"

"About what?"

"You know what."

"I've nothing to say when you stream a recipe for crazy."

"I never said I was definitely going to Afghanistan. I only inquired about the possibility of making the trip."

"You advanced your plans to the point of talking to a friend of mine and scheduling a date on one of his planes." He laser-drills me with cold eyes. "Then you contacted my former asset in Afghanistan and reached out to an administrator at The Garden of Babur, both of whom you planned to meet. You did all this without discussing it with me first."

I shoot him an uneasy look. "A *tentative* date. Nothing was finalized."

He stares back, his eyes an arctic blue, but says nothing.

"Are you hungry? I kept a plate warm from dinner for

you."

"I'm fine." He walks into our bedroom, reaches into the closet, and grabs his overnight bag from a top shelf.

"Where are you going?"

"To our hotel suite," he says in a serrated tone. "I plan on finalizing the contracts for the Henderson, Foster, and Zilson developments in the upcoming week. I'll be here until nine, if you need me." He finishes in the cool, practiced voice of someone relaying his whereabouts to a business assistant.

What about us? I say to myself. *You forgot to include our talk in your plans.*

"Won't you at least give me a chance to explain?"

"I already heard all I want to know. There's no point in talking about this further."

"I'm so sorry. I never meant to hurt you," I say, on the verge of tears. "When you're ready to talk, I'll be here."

He leaves later just as the clock strikes nine.

I'm hurt. I'm sad. But I owe him some patience. Looking back, I regret that I overlooked how much this trip would affect him. My actions pushed him into the throes of a flashback. I've had enough of them to know that, like roaches, once one crawls into your space you can damn well be sure more will follow. The need to explain myself is strong, but seeing the fatigue that lines his face from lack of sleep undoes me. Any discussion will have to wait.

When I walk into our empty bedroom, it's no surprise that echoes of silence charged with pain are waiting. If I dig deep, it's the charred feelings of aloneness I had as a child that haunt me now. When my mother, too depressed to talk or eat, took to her bed for weeks at a time, I blamed myself. It didn't help that these episodes coincided with special events in my life, events that should have been shared with another child if only he had the weight and strength at birth that I had. Seems like I excel in causing loved ones bouts of sadness that force them to emotionally and physically detach from me.

My survival response to the dejection: round-the-clock working interrupted only by quality time with my children and the occasional smoking break on our rooftop. I figure, what the hell, two out of three positives are not bad, given the current situation.

The dress I'm making for Lady Farrah's appearance at the MET gala comes together artfully and beautifully. The layered, cream-colored fabric of the gown is crafted into two tapered tiers, with a draped flow that accents Lady Farrah's tall frame without clinging to her hips and backside. Underneath, I sew a built-in brassiere that will make her feel that she's held together while having freedom of movement. From the back of the waist, I design a train that fans out to reveal a handcrafted tapestry of flowers to match the floral piece she will wear in her hair. Since the theme is an ode to nature, I sketch a dramatic headpiece that offers a contrast to her long, jet-black hair. It will be fashioned on one side with a real bird of paradise flower, along with a red amaryllis, a fuchsia orchid, and two gilded peony leaves.

In a workshop at my office, I'm putting the finishing touches on my design for this floral touch, when my cell chimes. Hoping it's Chase, I eagerly fish in my pocket for my phone. He told me he was coming home early tonight to spend time with the kids and help put them to bed. I figure it will be a great time to corner him for our long-overdue talk before he takes off again. Our argument has boiled over into a cold war that has gone on long enough.

The caller isn't Chase. It's Beth, her smoky voice upbeat as usual.

"Hi there! It's me. I've come to rescue you from your never-ending grind of work and take you out for drinks and a late lunch." She doesn't give me a chance to say anything before moving right along. "I'm in the lobby of your office, which, by the way, has more security than the White House and Pentagon combined. They won't let me up because I'm not listed on some registry. I've asked for Mac or Sammy, but they're not here."

"We're short-staffed today so security is tight. I'll arrange to have them send you up. We can chat over coffee in my office. The view is great."

"Oh no you don't. You're not blowing me off, Alicia. I ran into Fiona outside the park, and she's confirmed that you're working non-stop. She was coming up to see how you were doing, too. C'mon," she coaxes. "It's the start of the weekend. Let's have a boozy Friday lunch at The Mark."

I eye the dress I wanted to get to next. "I don't think—"

"I refuse to take no for an answer. You deserve some time out."

When Beth is this insistent, it's impossible to get her to back down. I also know that if I'm going to have that needed conversation with Chase, tonight is the night to corner him alone right after we put the kids to sleep.

Eleanor is visiting her ailing mom in Michigan and not due back until tomorrow. Sunny has the flu. Sammy is in Summit taking some time off to spend with Sandy, and Mac will be on duty in the car watching the entrance. It will be just the two of us in a quiet apartment. I'm bleary-eyed with exhaustion from the hours of detailed sewing I've been putting in to complete the gown. I'm even returning during the early hours of the morning when the children are asleep to continue sewing every stitch and seam myself. I refuse to let my assistants lay even one finger on the fabric. This break might help me free my mind and rest my eyes so I can get a good night's rest and a fresh start in the morning.

"Okay, okay. But I can't stay long," I say, making a mental note that I'm going to have to be cool-headed and sober for my talk with Chase. One glass of wine will be my limit. "I'll meet you in the lobby in five." I brush my hair until it shines, put on under-eye concealer to hide the dark circles, and refresh my lipstick. Grabbing my purse and jacket, I head for the elevator while thumbing a text to Chase.

OMW *to The Mark for lunch with Beth. cu soon.*

He may not be speaking to me, but it's doubtful he'd ignore one of my texts.

Standing near the front desk, I spot Beth. She's wearing wide movie-star shades on top of her long, wavy hair and a clingy print dress and matching heels. She looks every bit the successful PR executive she's worked hard to become. She spots me and waves. Standing next to her is Fiona, wearing one of my insignia jackets that I designed expressly for her diminutive body size. Because I created it while employed at Estelle Designs, it remains a disputed argument in the lawsuit. The fact that it's my original design—the only difference being it was crafted in leather instead of fabric—doesn't appear to be relevant to Estelle Designs' legal team. Nor do they care that I constructed it at home on my own time.

Fiona's eyes dart toward the entrance before shifting my way. A look of relief crosses her face, then swings to a composed expression once I approach.

"Okay, friend," Beth gives me a once-over, then a fierce hug. "I'm buying you a drink to help wipe that tired and sad look from your face." I've known Beth since first grade, so her perception of what I am feeling is generally razor-sharp. What she doesn't know is why I look depressed. Finding out will be her primary mission during cocktails.

"Hey there, Fiona. What a nice surprise." I kiss her cheek without addressing Beth's assessment. Lots of time during lunch to get into the specifics.

"I hope you don't mind if I join you and Beth. I happened to be photographing in the park and ran into Beth on the street when she said she was on her way here to talk you into a late lunch."

I give her a hug. "Happy to have you along. Now we can both consider ourselves rescued by Beth for some adult time."

"That's exactly what I thought. Dad is picking up Liam from school and taking him to chess club. Then we're driving to the beach house for the weekend."

I loop her arm and Beth's and off we go toward Mac, who's waiting to drive us to the posh hotel on Seventy-Seventh and Madison.

• • •

Perfect hair, taut faces and butt cheeks, and scads of Louis Vuitton purses fill the Mark Hotel Bar to capacity. Malt scotch for the few scattered men and chardonnay for the female majority are the favored drinks. As expected, there's a reserved sign perched on top of a corner table with three cushioned chairs, just waiting for us to be seated. No doubt Beth used one of her contacts to secure the coveted table.

Fiona offers to squeeze into the seat that presses against the wall. "I have the shortest legs of the three of us," she laughs. "I have no problem sitting here."

A hostess appears, places menus on the table, and asks to take our drink order. I decide to stick to my plan to keep it light.

"I'll have a glass of chardonnay, please."

Beth groans. "I think you need a cocktail, if for no other reason than to keep the mixologist from putting his head through the mirrored wall if he has to pour another glass of house wine."

A guy in a butler suit stares aimlessly into space from behind the bar.

"Alright, you win." I switch to an Old Fashioned, then ask for a bottle of sparkling water to stay hydrated. A quick glance at my phone shows me Chase has yet to answer my text.

Beth orders a dirty Stoli martini with exactly three olives speared horizontally. The waitress, who is writing none of this down, quickly turns her attention to Fiona, who sticks to a spicy Bloody Mary, sans alcohol.

Two sips into my drink and my arms feel numb. One more and it seeps into my legs. I haven't slept through the night since my argument with Chase or eaten a full hot meal since I started working on Lady Farrah's dress. I push the cocktail glass aside and take a large swallow of club soda. No way I'm getting plastered during this lunch. There's too much at stake later. I pick up my phone and check the screen just in case I didn't hear the ping of his incoming text.

Nada.

"I'm thinking your sad, pinched face has something to do with checking your phone for messages," Beth says once my attention reverts back to the table. She reaches for my hand and gives it a squeeze. "What's wrong?"

"It's nothing." I wave my hand in the air and shake my head. "Chase and I had a disagreement that we need to talk about tonight." My phone pings with an incoming text. I eagerly tap on Chase's message, and the screen lights up. *Ok.* One word, but at least he responded.

"Let me guess, that was Chase, right?" Beth says. When I don't answer, she ploughs ahead. "That's what I thought. For you to look this upset, you both had more than just an ordinary argument. What happened?" Beth looks earnest and Fiona finally turns from watching the entrance to studying me, too.

"Nothing really *happened*. I mean, no one was hurt. Well, not physically injured," I stammer. Both stare and wait. "I considered traveling to Kabul to make a donation to a garden there in the name of someone who helped Chase escape." The words escape in a rush and are answered by silence.

"Not your brightest lightbulb moment," Beth finally says, "even though your heart was in the right place."

Fiona looks shell-shocked. "Let me get this straight. You were planning to fly to Afghanistan?"

"I was considering it," I clarify.

"Now listen to me carefully," she says, looking me square in the eye. "That trip is never going to happen." I've never heard Fiona sound so definite, so determined, and so simultaneously pissed off; and she's not done. "I don't care how beneficial you may think it is to the people who helped Chase. It's not worth sacrificing your life. You have three children who depend on you and a husband who doesn't need to be reminded about what happened to him while he was a prisoner there." Fiona studies me as if watching someone who might need to be carted off to a mental institution. Presumably, in a straitjacket.

"Okay, I get the picture. I didn't go, and I don't plan on ever going."

"Have you said that to Chase?"

I shake my head, tears starting to prickle.

"Why the hell not?" Beth demands.

"He refuses to speak to me about it . . . about anything for that matter."

"He's that angry at you just because you *thought* about going to Afghanistan?"

I start to squirm. "He's angry because I contacted the person he once told me had helped him escape. Then, I reached out to a proprietor of a famous garden in Kabul that Chase said gave him hope during his first deployment. We were all scheduled to meet a few weeks ago. I also spoke to one of Chase's pilot buddies. He was going to fly me to Kabul in a private jet, then back again with a stopover in Istanbul."

"Let me guess," Beth says, "You didn't share any of these plans with Chase."

I shake my head.

"And when were you thinking of telling him? Never?" Fiona snaps. "Every other week, there are terrorist explosions near the airport. Just a few weeks ago a car bomb killed ten civilians." She's on a tear and she has every right to be angry. I had planned to go somewhere that was a source of her brother's suffering as well as months of worry for all of us who feared the worst.

Her agitation sets me on edge. I'm tired, overworked, and agitated. My private life is in tatters, and with the MET Gala less than three weeks away, my nerves won't stop jangling.

"I thought the trip would prove that I was up to a challenge that showed gratitude and good will." I manage to hold a steady gaze, but inside I'm unraveling. I don't share how I was hoping it would undo a wrong, that, in my mind, continues to tarnish my integrity.

"Looking backward to that painful time in your life and hoping to do something about it . . . that's positive and takes courage," Beth says, putting her arm around my shoulders.

Jaw set, eyes fixed on mine, Fiona ignores Beth's reference to my attributes.

"You will not give us one more thing to worry about. Is that understood?"

I clasp her hand in mine. "I won't. I promise," I say, then call for the check before Beth orders another round. Grabbing my purse and coat, I plop down two fifties. "Drinks are on me." I give Beth a hug and reach over and kiss Fiona on the cheek. "Thanks for the rescue," I say in a clear, firm voice. I'm already shifting gears in preparation for my conversation with Chase.

"Where are you going?" Fiona asks. There's a tense lilt to her voice.

"Home." Chase has pressed down his off switch long enough. Time to talk and resolve issues. I can't go on like this.

"Wait," Fiona says. "I'm coming, too. We'll share a cab home."

Beth blows me a kiss, then holds up a finger to catch the bartender's attention. "Another, please," she says, smiling the five-hundred-watt smile and giving him a wink.

CHAPTER 34

I walk through the door of the apartment to a volley of screeches and running feet. Caroline and Juliette chase each other, like miniature greyhounds racing for a win. Teo munches from a large bag of popcorn, and every now and again he tosses a handful at his sisters' heads. Once they spot me, they run, laughing, and jump into my arms. Their hugs are welcomed. The mess is not. Legos, puzzle pieces, stuffed animals, plastic dinosaurs, and colored tiles of all sizes and shapes lay scattered across the floor.

In the kitchen, an even larger clutter waits. Frying pans litter the stove, spilled puddles of milk stain the table, and several yellow globs of what seems to be melted cheese cling to the countertops.

"Chase," I call out, trying to keep my voice from sounding too tight. Last thing I want is to set the wrong tone before we even start to talk.

He appears looking like he's just stepped from a men's fashion shoot: sharp-looking dark suit, crisp white shirt, silk tie, and Italian leather shoes polished to a glow.

"Did you just get home?" I ask.

"No, I've been home for a while. I'm on my way out, now."

My jaw drops.

"I fed and played with the kids so they should be good and tired. Sunny is still in bed with a fever and Eleanor will be back from visiting her mother in the morning. "

"I know all this. I thought you were going to help me put the kids to bed."

"Sorry, but I have a business meeting to attend followed by dinner. No way out of it." It's a lame apology, and he knows it.

I stare up at the ceiling and take a long, quiet breath. "Are you coming home tonight?"

"Probably. I'll text you if I'm not."

Then, without looking back, he kisses the kids and leaves me to fight the battle of bedtime alone.

I hustle into the bedroom and quickly change into jeans and a t-shirt, then grab a copy of the picture book, *Click, Clack, Moo,* from their playroom. "Who's ready for a story?" I call out. They clamor around me and we all plop cross-legged onto the floor. The story takes all of six minutes to read out loud and not a one of them appears even a little bit drowsy once it's done.

"Okay, you all know what this means. You've had a story and now it's bath time," I chirp, making it sound like fun, when they all know bedtime follows. I lock eyeballs with Teo first. He squints one eye. The apple doesn't fall far . . .

"No jammies," he shouts, crossing his arms in defiance.

I wrap my arm around his middle and scoop him up to start our march to the bathroom, but he has other ideas. Kicking and screaming, he stiffens his legs and slams his head into my lip.

Once I lower him to the floor, my hand flies to my mouth where I begin to taste blood. "Shi…" I stop myself mid-word, and muttering, head to the bathroom for a tissue. Holding the tissue to my mouth, I sail back into the playroom, a captain determined to wrestle back control of her mutinous sailors. Unfazed by the mess that surrounds him, Teo sits in a sea of popcorn, stuffing handfuls into his mouth.

"I want some," Juliette says, her lip quivering into a pout.

"Teo, that's enough popcorn," I say, reaching for the bag. "No! Mine."

"Mamma, Teo's not sharing," Juliette whines.

"Juliette's a tattle teller. Juliette's a mamma's girl," Caroline sings, imitating Juliette's stretched-out voice.

An uncontrollable intake of air escapes from Juliette as the touted label finally registers as an insult. "No Mamma's girl," she shouts and wallops Caroline on the side of her head with her fist. Caroline's look of shock precedes the sharp shove she gives Juliette, who promptly lands hard on her bottom. With bared teeth, Juliette swivels toward Teo and bites his arm as he clutches his bag of popcorn.

Screaming, Teo throws the bag and clutches his arm. The bag slams into Caroline's face, sending popcorn flying into the air like snowflakes in a storm. Her face, now as red as her hair, scrunches with fury. She swings back her leg and slams her foot into Teo's stomach as if punting a football. He flops down into the sea of popcorn. Wailing, he springs back up, lowers his head and readies himself for what looks to be another head slam, this time into Caroline.

We have slid into some unknown but no less terrifying chapter of *Lord of the Flies*.

"That's it," I shout over the ruckus. It's baths and bed-time, NOW!" Three shrieking children take frenetic flight in opposite directions. Sunny emerges from his room, glassy-eyed and flushed with fever.

"Is everything alright?" he asks.

"Everything is fine. You need to go back to bed. I'll heat you some chicken soup once the children are asleep."

He nods, sneezes into a bunch of tissues, and shuts his bedroom door.

Outnumbered and too weary to fight anymore, I do what I only hope countless other parents have done in these situations. I bribe them. "There's milk and cookies to whomever marches into the bathroom for baths."

Caroline is the first to stop short in her tracks and backtrack to where I'm standing. "I want hot chocolate... please."

Since I'd rather stick a needle in my eye than let a drop of caffeine cross their lips, I stare her down and make my final offer. "Warm milk with honey and vanilla."

She nods, then holds up two fingers, "We would like two cookies, not one."

Definitely her father's daughter. "Agreed," I answer, not too proud to admit defeat. With smiles stuck to their faces, they celebrate their victory by marching into the bathroom for baths.

Watching Caroline and Juliette play with the bubbles in their bath, and Teo dance under the shower spray wearing a snorkel and mask, I decide they're too cute not to photograph. I snap them splashing, singing, and laughing.

Once they're dried, in pajamas, and have had their milk and cookies, they brush their teeth, and I walk them into their bedrooms. By now they're tired, and I'm worn to a frazzle.

Snug under the covers, Teo reaches out his finger and lightly touches my lip.

"How did you get that boo-boo, Mamma?"

"You know how, young man. You cannot yell and scream like that at bedtime. Understood?" He nods his head, yes.

"I kiss and make it all better," he says and places a gentle kiss on my sore lip. More hugs follow from Caroline and Juliette when I walk into their rooms. "I love you," both say before I turn on their night lights.

"I love you more," I answer.

And then . . . blissful silence.

Everyone has made it through the sleep skirmish with no visits to the ER, but the frontline bears the brunt of the battle. Legos, dolls, board game pieces, and popcorn kernels litter the floors of the playroom and living area. Water has puddled on the bathroom floor from all the splashing, and tub toys are scattered about in the bathtub, shower, and tiled floor. I start with the mess in the kitchen first. No way I am leaving it like that for Sunny to deal with should he be up and about tomorrow morning.

I rummage in the fridge for the container of leftover chicken soup I made two days ago when Caroline had the sniffles. While it heats and the kettle boils for tea, I put on a pot of espresso for myself. Sipping the strong brew, I load the dishwasher and scrub down the counters, sink, and table. Once the soup simmers to a boil, I ladle it into a bowl. In a large mug, I pour boiling water over chamomile tea, then add honey and a squeeze of lemon. I put it all on a tray with decongestant tablets and a large glass of water and carry it to Sunny's room.

He calls out on my first light knock. "Please leave the tray outside the door. I'll get it once you leave. No need for you to get sick, too."

"Okay," I answer, and lower the tray to the floor. "How are you feeling?"

"Better. Fever's gone."

"Good. Let me know if you need anything else."

"Thank you. Get some rest," he adds. "I'll be okay."

I toggle my head back and forth to iron out the kinks from the long day and head toward the bathroom to mop up the floor. Dizziness from fatigue stops me from finishing the job. I have got to get some sleep.

The empty, perfectly-made king-size bed stretches before my eyes. It's a painful reminder that I'll be sleeping in it alone yet again. Inside the nightstand drawer, I rummage for my pack of cigarettes, tap one out, and light it. God, I need a drink. I grab the ashtray resting next to the secret stash and head toward the liquor cabinet.

Massive lawsuit pending, absent husband, kids on a rampage. Yep, it's safe to say I'm having a bad week. I grab the first bottle my hand touches. Slipping the ashtray under my arm, I remove the cigarette from my mouth, tear off the bottle's seal, and pull out the cork with my teeth. The first swig goes down smoothly. I hold up the bottle to see what I'm drinking. Scotch. Not my first choice, but why not. I swallow several more generous mouthfuls without there being any backburn. When I take a drag of my cigarette, though, it's like inhaling fumes from the busted tailpipe of a car. I have no desire to finish it.

"Congratulations, Dr. Alexander," I say out loud to the empty room and stub it out.

Fatigue weighs on every bone and muscle in my body. I place the ashtray and liquor bottle on the nightstand, spread my arms, and collapse face first onto the bed, not even bothering to take off my shoes.

A screech, slam, crash, and shout jolt me from a deep sleep. "Son of a bitch," Chase's cry comes from across the hall.

I stagger, heavy with sleep, from the bed into the hallway and see him sprawled on his ass on the bathroom floor, spiffed shoes pointing upright. He pops back onto his feet and rubs his back, wincing. No need for the ER. All is good.

I walk back into the bedroom and let my head crash back onto the pillow. A bit later, a presence hovers over my side of the bed. I force my eyes open.

"What the hell happened to your lip?" he asks, reaching down to slip off my shoes.

"Head butt," I slur, sleepily.

"The place looks like a tsunami hit," he adds, unbuttoning and sliding down my jeans.

"Couldn't be helped, heaps of screaming, hitting, biting, name-calling, and, psfh," I throw my hands in the air, "a popcorn explosion." I snuggle under the fold of the covers. The last thing I remember is the cold press of an ice pack held to my lip.

• • •

S lashed sunlight shifts through the blinds. I feel for my phone and hit the side button. 8:30 lights up below the lock symbol.

The first thing I notice is silence. It's an unusual quiet, different from the normal rambunctious morning routine. I hoist my feet over the side of the bed and force my eyes to remain open. Grabbing my robe, I head for the bathroom to take care of business, brush my teeth, and take a quick shower. My stomach rumbles with hunger, but instead of heading to the kitchen, I follow the silence to all the suspect places where trouble could be brewing. Playroom: empty and looking pristine. Someone cleaned up this morning. Den: Unoccupied and just as tidy as the playroom. I head toward the study, and hear Chase's voice, heavy with authority. Standing out of view, I watch him don his most serious expression: tight lips, hard stare, clenched jaw.

Caroline, Juliette, and Teo sit upright on the sofa, legs stretched out and still, hands folded in their laps, solemn expressions on their faces.

"We are here to talk about bedtime protocol," Chase says.

Not a one of them says a word or makes a move. They may not understand what a protocol is, but bedtime sure as hell is heavy with meaning.

"I have heard, *and* I have seen firsthand that the three of you do not listen when it is time for bed. This behavior will stop, NOW. Is that understood?"

Three heads nod yes. "If anyone runs, hits, hollers, hides, kicks, bites or otherwise refuses to take a bath and put on their pajamas she," Chase looks at Caroline and

Juliette, "and he," Teo gets a firm stare next, "will get a spanking. Period. Full stop. Does anyone here want a spanking?"

Silence.

As if they answered, Chase goes on. "That's what I thought. So, at exactly nineteen hundred hours every night you will all go for baths and then put on your pajamas and get into bed. Is that clear?" Juliette slowly raises her hand. "What is it, Juliette?"

She hesitates, pops her thumb in her mouth, takes it out, then says, "I dunno nine hund teen hours."

"Very good point," Chase says. "Caroline, go get your large clock with the moveable hands."

Caroline springs to her feet and dashes to her room as if following instructions is what she lives for. She returns with the clock and Chase moves the hands to demonstrate to all three what nineteen hundred hours looks like. Then he shifts the settings on his watch and shows them what seven o'clock looks like digitally. "Now that you understand, let's review the terms. At nineteen hundred hours you're all going to get into?" he cups his ear to listen.

"Jammies and bed," they say as a rehearsed chorus.

"And Caroline, what are you going to remember?"

"No name calling," she says, loud and clear. Chase points to Juliette.

"No hitting or biting," she answers. His finger swings toward Teo.

"Share my COCKPORN," he shouts, beaming.

I cup my hand over my mouth and stifle a laugh. Chase struggles to keep a straight face.

"Very good, troops. Now, attention!" he commands.

They jump off the sofa and stand tall, arms glued to their sides. Obedience rules. Threats work.

"Left face!" Chase orders. Some head bumping and body banging follow, mostly because the twins have yet to master the difference between left and right. Eventually, they get the idea and march toward the kitchen, where Eleanor has returned this morning and will give them breakfast.

Once they're gone, Chase finally cracks a smile. Our eyes meet. The smile turns wintry. With a tilt of his jaw, he says, "A word in the bedroom, please."

Uh-oh. Polite chilliness. I'm in for it now. Must have something to do with the cigarette I lit inside the house. The soppy bathroom tumble he took is not helping either. I follow him into the bedroom, where he doesn't waste a spare second to lace into me with blistering criticism. "So, now you're smoking and swigging scotch in front of our children?" His eyes smolder at me accusingly, but I've had enough of his harsh judgments, stretched silences, and long absences. These past few weeks have made me realize more than ever that who I am is not how other people see me or how they expect me to behave.

I step closer to him but refuse to answer. Beneath the band of his jeans, I eye that seam of hair from his navel to below, and I'm almost tempted to trace its path with my finger.

"That was a fifty-thousand-dollar bottle of Macallan Scotch from 1937 you opened," he remonstrates, cutting through my silence.

What the fuck?

I fight to keep my face expressionless and move so close

to where he's standing, our lips almost touch.

"That's one helluva hefty price for a distilled spirit," I whisper, then suck on my forefinger and run it slowly across my lips. "I think I need a spanking and . . . bed."

His face splits into an unholy grin. It vanishes the instant I smile back, and the air between us becomes leaden with silence. It lasts so long that I think I struck out in getting him to respond.

"First, we are going to talk," he finally says. My relief is absolute.

"Sure. I want to—"

He cuts me off midsentence. "Let me rephrase that. I'm going to talk and you are going to listen."

His face, weary from lack of sleep and tension, unleashes a torrent of self-blame and guilt inside me. I am an idiot. I never should have gone behind his back and planned that trip to Afghanistan. The least I can do is hear what he has to say without first giving any self-serving explanations. Besides, I have had enough of defining myself by how other people see me and then fighting to prove otherwise. It's time to accept my decisions as my own and my mistakes as part of a learning curve.

A series of emotions play across his face. He rubs the scruffiness of his morning beard with the palm of his hand while he grasps for the right words. "I know it's hard for you to understand what I'm about to say; it wouldn't be easy for anyone who hasn't fought in war to get. What I saw . . . What I did . . ." He seems to gulp for air while swallowing grief. "I saw people, innocent young Afghans, with their whole lives still ahead of them, leave their families in the morning only to be brought back in coffins several hours later, blown to pieces from roadside bombs or suicide bombers. With the snap of a finger, a generation worth of dreams, gone. I watched as the lives of fellow soldiers who covered my back in tight spots ended in the split second it took for someone to pull a trigger or launch a rocket grenade." He looks down and rubs his neck with his palm.

"When I was held in Afghanistan, I had the choice of going mad or accepting defeat and death. I chose neither and used every moment crafting a plan of escape. All I needed was a window and a drone attack offered me one. Once I was free and back home, the real hard part began. The only way I knew how to survive was compartmentalizing my life. Afghanistan was the past; you and our children, the present. I assured myself that the two were distinct entities that need never cross. This gave me the strength to move forward.

"After you said you were going to Afghanistan, the line I had drawn between the two was crossed. My coping mechanism took a hit." He looks at me with an expression stripped bare of defenses. Gone is the anger and steely ambivalence of the past several weeks. "I started having dreams that I was in a slaughter block drowning in my own blood, then . . ." he struggles for a beat, "in your blood."

I rest my palm against his cheek and, fighting tears, stare into a mesmerizing contrast of blue eyes and dark lashes.

"I promise I will never blur that line again." Each word leaches out of me like a sworn oath of allegiance. He has suffered enough. Dimitri and his linchpins, terrorist armies, capture and torture, these pieces from his past are over. Best to let them stay where they belong, and that includes those who helped Chase survive. Time to stay in the present, where we can watch our children grow up and our businesses thrive.

He strokes his thumb across my cheek and grazes my lips with a kiss.

The funny thing about a thawing ice wall is that once one crack forms, there's no stopping more from following until a thunderous collapse follows. The weights of anger and fear kept us apart for weeks with little talking and even less touching. The heady combination of physical desire and a sexual reconciliation after no sensual contact for several weeks draws us together. Without breaking eye contact, I undo my robe and let it slide off my shoulders. The edge of his fingertips skims up the bare flesh of my sides.

His next move takes me by surprise. To say he pushes me up against the wall is an understatement. It's more of a slam.

I love it. It affirms that I am alive. No. It saturates me with life. It ignites a passion that sparks self-sustaining energy and vigor.

Wrists fisted in his hand and held above my head, his body presses against mine. His tongue pries open my lips, and, arms raised, eyes closed, my body responds as if magnetized to his. Chase has the long, slender fingers of a piano player, deliberate with their reach and calculating with their touch.

He slides his hand under my t-shirt and caresses my breast, and my nipple puckers. When he uses thumb and finger to twirl its surface, then lowers his mouth and grazes it with his teeth, it flames. His hand drops my wrists and travels between my legs so fast, my mind races with anticipation. Deft, diabolical fingers swirl and press and flick in time to a rhythm that has my body craving to be turned inside out with pleasure. With a soft moan, my head sinks against his chest.

Deprived of touch and conversation for weeks and fraught with guilt and self-blame, submission of my body to his touch is my gift to myself and to him for the pain my foolishness inflicted on us both. With every kiss and erotic touch showered onto my body, I kiss the recriminations goodbye. It's release that I want, knowing full well it will come in the liberation inherent in surrender of my body.

He spins me around and, with the flattened palm of his hand, pushes on my back until my breasts and stomach are flush with the wall. I flatten both palms against it and thrust my backside toward his lengthened member. He slaps my ass hard, and before I rebound from the blow, he lowers his jeans and drives his penis inside. The surprise triggers a hedonistic craving that holds my body captive. Hard stabs delve toward that special spot that brings me to the brink of orgasm. Biting my lip to stifle the needy moan that escapes anyway, I climb an ever-building wave of bliss. Just as I'm about to reach my peak, his body stiffens and, legs shaking, body strumming, he spills his pleasure inside me. Satiated and satisfied, his body rests against mine while I'm left hanging.

I huff a frustrated breath and my hand automatically drifts toward the throbbing below. He takes my wrist and shifts it away from an area that screams for release, then wags his finger. Resting his hand on the back of my head, he pushes my face toward his penis. After spending weeks dragged through drowning-dreams that took him to a place where delusions became reality, he's going to seize control of our lovemaking, and why not? He knows I never objected to it before.

I kneel and, with each push and pull of my lips, marvel at how his penis strengthens again. Hard and full, he pushes me back by my shoulders. I clasp my hands in his hair and pull him toward my belly, arching my back when his lowered tongue presses into a place, burning with need, that sends me skyrocketing. He stops just shy of my release. Only this time, he drives his penis inside and plunges with a force that sends my body soaring. I drop into an abyss with an explosion of jubilation that makes it feel like the world is shaking. We collapse onto the bed, our bodies damp from the exertion. Coils of tight tension unwind, and we lie, hearts pounding, bodies satiated.

He grabs for the bottle of scotch, pops off the cork, and takes a four-thousand-dollar swig before passing it to me as a peace offering. I take a generous swallow and pass it back.

"You were saving that bottle for someone, right?" I ask, wiping my mouth with the back of my hand.

"It was for one of my clients who collects rare bottles of scotch."

"I'm sorry. I didn't know." Any more fuckups, and I'll need an autocorrect implant to get back on track. Propped on an elbow, I stroke his chest with my finger. "Are you still angry at me?"

"Nah. What's done is done. This made it worth it."

"Really?" I can't help but think that a fifty-thousand-dollar lay is plenty expensive even if the pleasure points are off the charts.

"Yeah. Makeup sex is sex therapy."

"What do you mean?" I know sex is generally better after an argument, but I want to know the specifics of how it's different in his mind.

"You let me take over your whole body with complete trust. It's like the first time all over again."

Wow.

"And you make all these little sighs when you're trying not to beg for more," he teases, imitating my mews and moans. I don't even bother denying it, but I do start to think about the noise level during this robust morning tryst.

"I hope we weren't too loud." I feel my neck get hot. I made sure to shut and lock the bedroom door, but it's hard to keep lustful exclamations and squeaking bedsprings from seeping through walls, doors, and floors.

"No, it was fine. Eleanor said she was planning to play their favorite songs and have a sing-along. You're blushing. Here, take a few more swigs. It'll make you not give a damn."

I swallow some more and smack my lips. "Damn good stuff," I tell him, smiling.

"I need to tell you something, but I don't want you to worry."

I look at him, surprised.

"What is it? What's wrong?" I'm not completely freaking out because we are all here safe, and I know for a fact that Fiona and Liam are on Long Island, spending time with Chase's father.

"Military intelligence picked up some troubling online

chatter." He stops and studies my expression.

"You mean from Dimitri."

"Yeah. He might be galvanizing his forces for some kind of attack."

"From prison?"

"Could be. We're watching it."

"How can he be plotting anything? I thought he was in solitary."

"He was until a few days ago. His lawyer was able to have him released into the general prison population."

If Chase is sharing this information with me, it's been confirmed, and it's serious. I guzzle some more hefty mouthfuls of the liquid gold. "So, when does target practice start again?" I say between swallows.

"I'll clear my schedule for tomorrow afternoon, but for now," he runs his gaze down my body, "I owe you one." My hands melt back behind my head, and I draw in a long breath as his mouth starts to work its magic.

CHAPTER 35

The day of the MET gala approaches slowly, then all at once, with an urgency that has me rattled. I nail down the form, fit, and design of Lady's Farrah's dress, but still my brain is rife with anxieties. Any number of uncontrollable mishaps could happen. A wardrobe malfunction, an accidental spill, a tear, a fall, a sudden illness, the ever-growing list rocks my mind. When I'm not working to prepare for the event, I'm thinking about it.

In between these thoughts, the possibility of another attack by Dimitri invades my peace of mind. Our initial euphoria after his capture has been doused by "chatter" intelligence organizations have picked up. They may not know exactly what this information indicates, but it's concerning enough to be presumed dangerous.

Being incarcerated has never stopped Dimitri from trying to hurt us. With Dimitri it's never *if*, but *when*. His assaults are often cloaked in trickery, a tactic he refers to as *maskirovka*. *Maskirovka* is a hoax designed to manipulate a target into doing something that facilitates a surprise attack. Packaging and sending a severed finger wearing

Fiona's ring was a tactic he used to manipulate me into believing that he had harmed Fiona, when in fact she was safe at home. I let my guard down, thinking I needed to help, and that's when the *maskirovka* master struck.

Consistent target practice eases my worry a bit. My skill improves to the point where I can hit the target I'm aiming for with consistent accuracy.

Chase says my skill is innate, given I've had so little time to perfect my aim.

Virgil claims our children have the genetic tools to become super-snipers.

I tell him he's not funny, and I don't want to hear it again. Eyes bright with laughter, he puffs on his pipe and stays quiet.

Everyone knows I'm on edge, but I push aside my fears, and on this early Sunday morning, the day before the MET gala, I prepare to head to my office for last-minute tweaks on Lady Farrah's gown. Once done, my plan is to personally drive it to her townhouse on Sixty-Fifth and Park for a final fitting.

The sun is just starting to rise on this mild and breezy April day when I tiptoe out of the apartment. Chase left hours ago to address an emergency at one of his new construction sites in Brooklyn where sometime during the night, an elevated crane sprung loose from its hold. Dangling precariously from the building's rooftop, it poses a serious threat to other buildings in the vicinity and any pedestrians walking on the street below. His phone call about an hour ago assured me it was under control, and he would be home shortly to help me in any way he could. By the time I reach the sidewalk in front of our building, Mac is already waiting to drive me to the office.

"Big day tomorrow. How are you holding up?"

"I'm good. I just need a few hours to make some final changes," I answer, biting my lower lip when I think about the need to take in a seam in the chest area.

He studies my feet and looks skeptical.

When I look down, I notice I'm wearing different-colored sneakers. "It's official. I'm being driven over the edge by this event."

"Relax. You're going to be fine." We pull into the garage adjacent to the building, and Mac escorts me to the private elevator. He takes a quick look around and, satisfied, tells me he'll be waiting in the car in front of the building. "Text me when you're finished and on your way down," he says. It's how it's always done, but somehow Mac thinks it's worth repeating this morning. This could have something to do with the shoe mix-up.

"Will do. I won't be any more than a couple of hours."

"No rush. Best to get everything just right."

I give a quick nod and step into the elevator, my mind already shifting to the work that still needs to be done.

Midway up to the penthouse level, the elevator jerks to a stop. The lights flicker and suddenly go out, enveloping me in inky blackness. I grope in my purse for my phone, but before I can find its flashlight, the cab's backup lights go on. I hit the emergency button and wait a few seconds before poking it again.

"Hello, hello," I announce a bit too loudly. "Is anyone there?"

Finally, a voice answers. I respond to the elevator repair center with my location. She assures me someone will be out to address the problem shortly. Their definition of soon and mine are not in sync. With my mind in sensory overload planning all that needs to be done before tomorrow night's event, I can't get out of this confined space fast enough.

A wise inner voice tells me to buck up and hold onto my composure. I try to call Mac to see if he has any idea what's happening, but there's not enough bars on my phone to get through from inside the elevator. Minutes tick by until finally, the numbers designating each floor light indicating the elevator is in motion. Reaching the penthouse, I step out and walk toward my work room.

A spooky, weird kind of silence permeates the space. I stop and stiffen my shoulders for several moments, then pick up my stride, assuring myself any uneasiness stems from not being in the habit of showing up to work at 6:00 a.m. on a Sunday. I slip into my workroom and shut and lock the door.

What I see catches me by surprise. Sitting and gazing through the wall of windows, like she owns the place, is Charlotte. As usual, she looks good even from behind: tailored white jacket, wide, matching belt and skirt. Hair tied back in an elegant chignon that's neatly tucked under a snappy, brimmed hat.

"Charlotte. What are you doing here?" Accusing silence answers, and I can just picture her smug smile when she deigns me worthy enough to swivel in her seat and meet my gaze head-on. To be here this early on a Sunday morning, she must have a walloping chunk of incriminating evidence about the lawsuit to wave in my face.

Taking measured steps closer, I study her with

unconcealed irritation and then anger. Enough is enough. I lean forward and swivel the chair in my direction. A shudder of cold horror whips through my body when my eyes fix on her face. Charlotte's carefully lipsticked mouth hangs open in a silent scream of unabating panic. Empty, unblinking eyes stare ahead. A trickle of blood oozes from her left ear and stains her neck.

I yank myself backward as if shoved, my heart pumping in overdrive. Panic drives me into the hallway, where I freeze in terror when the grind of opening and closing elevator doors sounds in the distance. The tap, tap, tap of footsteps from the vestibule follows. I flatten myself against the wall and listen. The steps get closer. The urge to flee is overpowering, but any flight toward the exit would put me in direct contact with the intruder. Holding my breath, I slowly backtrack into my workspace. *Do not lose your nerve,* I tell myself, avoiding the grim sight sitting in my chair. *The dead can't harm you, but the living can.* I lock the door and wildly search for my purse. I spot it resting against the leg of the worktable and reach inside for my phone. Outside, the footsteps quicken.

One swift kick opens the door. I scream and drop my phone, certain that death waits to take me as it did Charlotte.

"Are you alright?" Mac says, clutching his gun.

I barely have the chance to nod and pick up my phone, before he clutches my arm and spins into motion. "We have to get out of here."

We charge through the hallway and into the closest stairwell, leaping two steps at a time past several landings. I'm no match for Mac's speed, and he's forced to slow down and catch me when I flounder. We're making good progress toward the first floor when the electricity goes out again. The emergency lights swathe the corridor in eerie shadows of red. Mac stops, glances down at me, then at the ceiling. Faint footsteps echo from above. Someone is fooling with the electrical circuits to slow us down.

"Listen to me, Alicia," he says, clutching my arm. "We have to split up. I want you to continue heading down to the lobby. There's no time to wait for help to get here, not with several people on the loose in the building."

I've no idea what sixth sense Mac has that allows him to discern that there are multiple players in pursuit, but I have no doubt about his abilities.

"Okay," I whisper. Swallowing hard, I add, "How many do you think there are?"

"Five, maybe six," he says. His gaze blazes when he presses something hard into my hand. It's the pistol Chase carried when we were in Paris. It doesn't make me feel better to have to carry a weapon that can be used to kill another human being, but I take it anyway. Better to have some means of self-defense than be at the mercy of people who want you dead. I sense Mac's eyes boring into my back, as I sprint down the stairs. When I stop to look back, he's gone. I hurl myself down with reckless speed, slowing on every landing to make sure any pursuing footsteps remain far enough away.

I'm somewhere close to the twentieth floor when the lights flicker then go back on. I lean my palm against the rough concrete wall of the stairwell and fight to catch my breath. Silence surrounds me. I have no idea how long the muted taps of footsteps from the floor above have been gone. It's unlikely Mac has overtaken all the culprits because if he had, he would have called to make sure I was alright. That can only mean . . . Terror rockets me to reverse course and charge back up the stairs. I know I've been overtaken and those in pursuit have outrun me and are now ready to pounce the second I come barreling down to where they wait on both stairwells.

I pull out my phone, then dismiss the idea to phone Chase for help. I work my bottom lip, racking my brain for ideas. When one forms, I know I have to act quickly. Sprinting up the stairs, I skirt through the door of the nearest floor, not surprised to see that this early on a Sunday morning, it's empty of office workers. I stay there ten, maybe fifteen minutes, hoping to give Mac and the police more time to get here. I think I hear some scraping and grunting noises coming from the rear stairwell, but they quickly fade into the distance. I know that if I stay in one place for too long, I'll be found. Chase has often explained that mobile targets tended to survive.

Off the main vestibule, I spot a large storage closet shoehorned into a corner between the architectural designers' and aesthetic surgeons' offices.

I hide my phone inside under the dust cloths, broom, and tools that clutter the lower shelf. If my phone is being traced, I could gain valuable minutes by throwing my pursuers off track. My rear flank remains a worry. Some of my attackers could have fanned out before Mac got to them. Six-to-two odds are not favorable. Still, I have no choice but to backtrack. It's a move they'd least expect from a novice. Taking two steps at a time, I head back to my office. My gut tightens when I hear voices coming from the penthouse workspace Mac and I fled a short time ago. I duck back into the shadows.

"We waste precious time so, as you Americans say, chop-chop, or my *partner* shoots you, and I slice off your sister's head."

Dimitri. How the hell did he get out of jail?

There's some whimpering that sounds like it could be Fiona, but from where I'm standing, it's hard to tell for sure. I slide my hand over the butt of the blue-plated .38 inside my jacket and slip it out. My finger moves to the trigger guard and then to the trigger. I nudge off the safety and wait.

A voice stops me in my tracks.

"Let Fiona go, Dimitri," Chase says. "It's not too late for you to walk out of here a free man. I'm sure your loyal followers are waiting close by. If they were clever enough to dig a tunnel equipped with a motorbike to help you escape from your jail cell, they can land a helicopter on this rooftop to help you get away before the authorities get here. You're a marked man, Dimitri. Wasting time accumulating bodies won't help."

"So, you heard about my prison escape. That's the beauty of military intelligence, there are no secrets. Too bad it didn't give you enough time to get help before I got here. It was good trick to loosen crane in one of your buildings to get you away from your home. One less guard there makes my job easier. And as far as accumulating bodies . . . well. . . everything was going according to plan, until that woman showed up. What's her name?" he queries.

"Charlotte," a voice that sounds familiar answers, making me wonder how many more are still at large, ready to strike. This was a plan that was in the making for weeks, if not months. Someone must have been tracking me, just waiting for the right opportunity to get me alone. What better time than to trap me at my office early on a Sunday morning when the building is empty and there's less surveillance.

"I had no intention of killing *Charlotte,* until she waved those sewing scissors in my face," Dimitri says. "Judging from their size and her proximity to your wife's workroom on a Sunday morning, I think they were going to be used to destroy the dress Alicia's been working on for so long." He stops and slowly shakes his head. "You and your wife seem very good at stockpiling enemies."

"She's dead, Dimitri. Whether you meant to kill her or not is irrelevant. With your criminal record, you could be looking at spending the rest of your life in prison if you're caught, maybe even extradited to face the death penalty. This is your chance to escape a free man."

Chase has to know he's wasting words on a psychopath whose sole purpose in life is to retaliate against those he thinks wronged him. He must be stalling for time, waiting for Mac to surface. Where the hell is Mac anyway? A deep-throated moan answers my question. The stretched groan repeats, sounding like someone fighting to push limbs into motion that won't obey.

"Your friend seems to be waking up. Welcome back, Mac." Dimitri says, his tone dripping with derision. I contemplate the disquieting fact that those I thought could save me are now Dimitri's captives. Dimitri had to have had several men as front and rear guards to overpower Mac so quickly and keep Chase from bringing him down.

Stealthily approaching the doorway that leads to my workspace, I shrink to one side and hug the shadow of the wall. A chilling scene unfolds before my eyes. Dimitri's eel-like lips slither across his face in a grin while he holds a knife to Fiona's throat. Hands tied behind his back with a zip-tie, face covered with blood, Mac lies crumpled on the floor. He must have given several of Dimitri's soldiers the fight of their lives before being overpowered.

Chase's glance flickers toward me then quickly away.

"Let go of the knife, Dimitri, and call off your masked goon, and I'll drop my weapon." Chase's pistol points at Dimitri while someone shrouded in a black balaclava aims a gun at Chase. Despite being outnumbered, Chase does not sound panicked. "We can all walk out of here alive if you and your friend leave now."

Dimitri's knife moves across Fiona's neck. A tiny trail of blood follows in its wake. She sobs silently as droplets of her blood splash onto the floor.

"Drop your weapon now, or next time I cut deeper," Dimitri shouts, bits of spittle whitening the corners of his mouth.

Chase's gun clatters to the floor

Dimitri bows his head as if contemplating an unknown dilemma that only he can fathom. "This is what you don't understand," he says, raising livid eyes toward Chase. "I am a businessman, a family man just like you are. I have no intention of killing anyone. I love Fiona." He stretches his insolent mouth to her face and kisses her cheek. "She is the mother of my grandson."

Chase ices him with a glare but says nothing.

"She raised Liam well. Now, he needs men in his life.

Liam will become another Yuri," Dimitri says with an oily trace of a proud smile. "He will be well-trained in Russia to be proud of his Ostopenko roots. He will learn how to fight for his family's honor. So, my offer is," he flaps his lank hair, greasy with prison grime, from his forehead and gives Chase an unblinking stare. "I take Liam, Caroline and Alicia, and you and the rest of your family are free of me for good. Is a fair swap, no? Your nephew, daughter, and wife in exchange for the loss of my children and wife."

"Mamma, Daddy." Caroline's cries ring in my ears, and it's as if the breath is torn from my mouth. I think back to waking up this morning with the notion that I had nothing more to be concerned about than Lady Farrah's dress. I can't work out how on earth I got from there to here, trapped beneath the iron fist of a psychopathic mobster.

The steel blade Dimitri holds to Fiona's neck glistens in the shaded room. I step into the light and angle myself so Dimitri can see me from the corner of his eye. His lips peel back into a smile.

"How accommodating of you to show up, Alicia." His tone holds affected surprise. "It saves us the unnecessary time and effort of tracking your phone."

For a second, I stand there stunned, my heart beating so furiously I'm sure Dimitri can hear it. A split second later, my reflexes spin into action when the second-in-command tears off his mask. I point my gun toward his head.

"Let Fiona go, Papa," a stone-faced Yuri says to his father. "It's time you left. I'll cover for you—make sure everyone stays put. The chopper is coming."

If Chase is surprised that it's Yuri who's pressing a gun muzzle to his head, he doesn't show it.

Dimitri's eyes feverishly glitter, his knife tickling Fiona's trembling carotid. I scan the periphery and spot Liam curled asleep in the far corner of my workspace. There's no sign of Caroline. I glance at Chase, a question in my eye. I need some guidance here. Do I try and shoot Dimitri for the kill or keep my eye on Yuri, whose gun still points toward Chase's head?

Every cell in Chase's body stays fixed on Yuri. I can hear his gears grinding, his mind working on two tracks. He's thinking Dimitri's vengeful intent is set in stone. Dimitri can easily kill Fiona, but at the moment he hasn't done so. He's also not wielding a gun. Yuri, on the other hand, has proven to be ambivalent about doing any of us harm, but he can easily shoot me then Chase before I figure out what's happened and pull the trigger. Yuri is the wild card in this Mexican standoff.

"Drop your gun, Alicia *or* watch your husband be crushed by one of Yuri's bullets," Dimitri says. Malice rages through his words. "Shoot him, Yuri. One hit to the spine is enough to keep him strapped to a wheelchair for the rest of his life."

I force out a hard breath. "Or, fuckwit," I shout, keeping my eyes fixed on Yuri's waist. "I can shoot your son, so he doesn't ever have to worry about adjusting his balls inside those Gucci pants he fancies."

Arms rigidly stretched, my aim remains set toward Yuri.

"Where's my daughter? Caroline, Caroline," I screech. The walls echo silence.

Reflexively, Dimitri glances at Yuri, but his words are directed toward me. "All in good time, you will see your daughter." Cocking his head, he swivels his reedy neck toward Fiona and licks the inside of her ear, then stares back at us with perverse gratification.

"Let Fiona go," Yuri repeats, his voice low. A new urgency hunches his shoulders forward.

"Yuri always have soft spot for Fiona," he says looking Chase square in the eye. "He even pay me so he can fuck her good and hard," Dimitri taunts Chase. "I sold your sister to my son for ten grand. It was good deal. By that time, she so high on drugs I force on her she would screw anyone for her next hit. Is right, Fiona?"

Chase's jaw tightens but not another muscle in his body moves. It's hard to digest the horror of how Dimitri ravaged Fiona, but I take my cue from Chase seeing firsthand that raw emotion cannot be allowed to mar rational thinking in this life death tango.

"It's you who is the addict, Papa. Rabid vengeance is the drug you crave. No matter how much time passes, you redouble your drive to destroy one person. I am tired of this death match you fight with an enemy that lives only in your mind. Put down the knife. My son belongs with his mother. He. . . they are the best I will ever do," Yuri says, his gun wavering with the emotion of his words.

Dimitri makes a ferocious noise, more feral than human. "He killed your older brother, and you say I don't have the right to destroy him and his family. You are useless and weak, nothing more than a shell of a man. Now shoot him or I slice Fiona's throat."

The room rocks with silence. Yuri stays still, finger held near the trigger. A slow smile spreads across Dimitri's face. Right before he raises his knife for the kill, I pivot and fire. The mid-section of his arm jerks then flaps, revealing a bloody pulp of bone and flesh that was once his elbow. The clang of his knife hitting the floor ricochets through the room.

Fiona, on all fours, scurries away, but Dimitri still has enough life, or maybe it's hate, left to grab her back by her hair with his other arm.

"Shoot him," he shrieks at Yuri, his ropy neck protruding above his shirt collar. Wrapping his good arm around Fiona's neck, he presses until she gurgles for air.

I aim my gun, looking for a clean hit to Dimitri's head, banking on the fact that, if Yuri had any mind to, he would have taken his shot at Chase by now.

Dimitri licks his lips, his face twisted with pain, and still his arm tightens around Fiona's neck.

"You have no room for anything but hate. It crowds out all healthy human emotion. That's bad for my son, and that's bad for business," Yuri says.

Dimitri hesitates for the briefest second, giving Fiona a small window of opportunity.

"Fuck you," she screams, thrusting the heel of her foot into Dimitri's groin.

Doubling over, he folds to his knees and Fiona scuttles out of his reach. My finger freezes on the trigger. Dimitri lifts his head. Eyes flare into mine, the same color as Liam's only stone-cold. I waver, watching him on his knees, a look of defeat claiming his face.

A moment later, Dimitri transforms into a flash of fury, grabbing at the back of his waist with his good arm.

Shots blister the air. A hole opens in Dimitri's forehead.

My limbs lock. My hand remains curled around the butt of the gun I was unable to fire for the kill. Motionless, we watch Dimitri die. His eyes stare, pupils fixed, mouth gaping.

Yuri slides the weapon he used to kill his father across the floor and raises his hands in surrender.

"Where's my daughter?" Chase asks, his voice low and tight. Dangerously tight.

"Your daughter is safe at home. I have no gripe with you or your family," Yuri says.

"Don't bullshit me. I heard her voice."

"It was a recording my father set to play at certain intervals. He wanted to make Alicia believe he already had Caroline. That way, she'd be more willing to come with us. Once he had Alicia, he was going to use every power he had to kidnap Caroline before we left for Russia."

Chase leaps toward him and topples him to the floor. His hands tighten around Yuri's throat, the torment from the past decade-and-a-half seeping into the coiled strength of his grasp.

"Stop," Fiona pleads. "What good does it do if someone else is killed?"

The force of Chase's stranglehold presses on. The hate-filled vengeance of a relentless predator has spilled into him, inciting him to kill an unarmed man with his bare hands.

"Mommy, Mommy." Low wails drift from the small, crumpled form cowering in the corner of the room.

It is his nephew's beseeching voice that helps Chase loosen his murderous hold on Yuri's throat. The next instant, Fiona is at Liam's side, cradling his drowsy body in her arms. I watch it all as if looking through the lens of someone else's camera: Chase standing, head bowed, hands resting at his sides, Liam, nestled in his mother's arms, eyes fluttering, struggling to stay awake, Fiona, rocking him, soothing them both with the motion and Yuri . . . gaze flashing from Chase to me and then to his son, where it lingers, soft and smiling, eliciting the comfort one feels from a breeze that ruffles hair on a hot day.

A voice comes from far away. "Baby, it's okay. It's over."

The voice becomes louder, firmer. "Move your finger away from the trigger, Alicia." It takes a bit for me to realize I'm being coaxed to let go of the gun; I had no idea I was still aiming to shoot. Police sirens shriek from the street below. The loud noise of a helicopter's whirling blades slice through the room.

"That would be my ride," Yuri says, staring upwards. He strides through the doorway, stopping only for one last glance at Liam and Fiona.

Our eyes remain riveted on Fiona, who has been to hell and back. She nods a tight goodbye to Yuri.

My thoughts tumble in the quiet that follows. It's as if the tumultuous truth of what we just witnessed has turned me inside out, exposing fear, disbelief, and dismay.

Chase wraps his arms around me, and I drift into the scent of his suit. Sandalwood and soap. He ignores the buzz of his phone and lets me linger there until my shaking stops. The warmth of his touch and the smell of his essence keep me from collapsing.

"We have to leave. Now," he emphasizes, turning me away from Charlotte and Dimitri's corpses.

Fiona nods, stands, and grasps Liam under his arms.

Mac struggles to his feet, kicking away the tranquilizing dart that brought him down. Liam is so groggy, he needs help staying upright. There's no doubt he was also drugged.

Chase scoops up Dimitri's knife and slices through Mac's restraints.

Shaking off his fatigue, Mac hurries toward Fiona and lifts Liam from her arms.

Wordlessly, Chase takes my hand and hurries me through the office doors, then motions for the others to follow.

When his phone screeches with an accompaniment of angry buzzing, he doesn't even slow down to see who's calling.

I hustle toward the elevators.

"No," Chase says and guides me and the others toward the stairwell. Hitting the steps at a rapid pace, we head down with Chase in the lead. Gun drawn, his head moves in every direction. Mac brings up the rear. About fifteen floors down, Chase stops and guides us toward the wall while Mac leaps ahead two steps at a time.

Fiona covers Liam's eyes with her hand and pulls him to her chest. Three bodies lay strewn across the landing, one with a cracked skull resting in a puddle of blood and the other two with legs and necks bent at odd angles. These must be the men Mac took down before he was hit by the tranquilizing gun.

As we race down the steps, buzzes and jingles continue in rapid succession from Chase's phone. It's not until we're in the garage that he whips it from his pocket.

"Reardon," he barks and waits, tension tightening his jaw with every passing second that he listens to whomever is on the other end.

"Over my dead body," he finally shouts. "She already has a job. The only thing I want out of you is this crime scene processed and swept clean. She was never here today, Buford. You got that?" He hits end, pops the phone into his pocket, and clasps my hand.

"Let's go home."

How Buford knew what had happened here is anyone's guess. The thought that my office may have been bugged is unsettling.

Even more perturbing is Chase's comment that won't stop buzzing in my head.

Did Buford just offer me a job?

CHAPTER 36

A chain is only as strong as its weakest link. Fiona's life had been mutilated by Dimitri. We never stood a chance of defeating Dimitri as long as he had this hold on Fiona. Back at our apartment, with all the children safe and playing together in the other room, Fiona wordlessly sips tea. The only indications of her ordeal are the bandage that covers the side of her stitched neck and the slight tremble of her hand when she brings the cup to her mouth. Once she starts to talk, words tumble out in clusters of horrific happenings that spelled the course of her life for over a decade.

"From the day you left for your enlistment, Dimitri used me as a tool to drive his vengeance into our family. It started when I was grabbed on my way to school and thrown in the back of a van. Some thugs brought me to some deserted restaurant, where I was tied to a chair in the basement. They stuck a syringe in my arm. A rush of euphoria hit followed by a feeling of numbed bliss that I had never felt before. It was the first day of ninth grade and instead of opening a book, I was learning how to get high.

I was told if I didn't cooperate, Dad would be tortured and killed."

She throws a worried look at Chase. "All the times you were beaten. I also knew what that bastard did to Devie. I figured if I cooperated, he would eventually stop, but that was only the beginning of relentless abductions where syringes filled with drugs would be injected into my arm. No matter how hard I fought, I was unable to lessen the craving for the high they brought. With time, Dimitri used my fear of withdrawals to keep me dependent on him as much as the drugs.

"After you returned from Afghanistan, Dimitri said you and Dad would stay safe as long as I obeyed. I was a useless mess by then, unable to concentrate, failing most subjects at school, living from one high to the next. That's when Dimitri turned me over to Yuri. He figured it would be easy for Yuri to keep me under control. Instead, Yuri helped me turn my life around. He weaned me off drugs, then became my lover. It wasn't until later that I realized Dimitri had sold me to his son. Once Liam was born—and yes, Yuri is Liam's father—" she adds, without any trace of doubt, "Dimitri started taking a renewed interest in me and his grandson. He demanded visits once a year on Liam's birthday. When Liam was a baby, it was easy to do. I'd let that bastard hold Liam for a bit, but when Liam got older, I started to resist. I didn't want to expose my son to his ruthlessness. Dimitri became enraged when I would show up without Liam. In a tirade, he'd shoot me up with drugs, or beat me and threaten to kidnap Liam."

Chase squints. "Why didn't you tell me this was happening?"

"So many times I tried, but in the end I was too ashamed to say what I had done." She lowers her head. "I was afraid of what you'd all think of me . . . of how you'd feel about Liam. How could you respect someone who did what I had done? Worse still, how could you possibly love someone related to such an evil sadist? Oh God," she sobs into her hands, then raises her head and sucks in a breath. "I made a deal with the devil to protect my family and my son," she says, her chest heaving with every breath. "Now I have to live with my ghosts."

All the scenes of this tragedy unfold in my mind in rapid sequence: Fiona's unexplained bouts of drug addiction, her disappearances on Liam's birthday, her ring on a severed finger sent to me, the name Penko, a shortened version of Dimitri's surname, Ostopenko, uttered by Fiona at Roosevelt's Four Freedoms Park and again at the rehab center, Yuri's appearances at the rehab center and again at my show. All attacks orchestrated by Dimitri as a way to punish Chase with Yuri in the background, attempting to moderate his father's wrath. Dimitri was the vengeful predator who permanently changed the landscape of Fiona's life. Seems to me that good and evil are powers that cross over even as one defeats the other. We had become irrevocably cojoined with our enemy with no one to blame for the resulting hardships except Dimitri.

"You did nothing wrong." I stroke her hair. "You sacrificed yourself for our well-being."

"They're my ghosts too," Chase says, and takes Fiona in a hug. "How could you ever think I would stop loving you or Liam?"

"Because," Fiona lifts her head, her gaze penetrating his.

"People die but ghosts linger. They keep you from shedding the past."

"You're not the only one haunted by ghosts," he says. "There were times and places where I couldn't believe what I was doing . . . what I was capable of doing. I've learned that it's not about how many regrets you shoulder, but how capable you are of forgiving yourself for accumulating them. Once you absolve yourself, the ghosts dwindle into nothing more than surface scars."

"Does that include forgiving the Ostopenko family?" Fiona asks, deliberately including the surname that would have been Liam's had she documented Yuri as Liam's father. The Ostopenko bloodline runs through Liam and as his mother, she wants to be assured that any lingering rage will not be directed at her son.

"Forgiveness? That's a tall order. What I can assure you is that I will never visit the sins of the father against the son. No one understands that more than I do."

A knot forms in my throat. I remember all too well the teenager with the floppy-soled sneakers who would lift his drunken father over his shoulder and carry him home past the school bus of jeering students. I remember, as a second grader, how I would smile and wave to that blue-eyed, handsome boy from my seat on the bus. I admired him even then.

Fiona rests the teacup in her saucer, closes her eyes, and expels a sigh of relief. Standing, she takes her brother's face in both palms and smiles.

"It's over," he says.

She nods, kisses him on the cheek, then looks at me. "I owe Antonio an explanation. I'm meeting him for dinner tonight and plan on telling him everything. With a bit of luck, he'll forgive me."

"My brother will understand," I tell her, assured of Antonio's easy and flexible nature.

"I hope so. I've kept far too many secrets while masquerading as someone who had none. 'You're only as sick as the secrets you keep.' I've heard that in just about every treatment program I was in, and each time it was said, I nodded and pretended to agree while my lies kept accumulating. No more. My healing starts with telling the truth regardless of the consequences. I owe that to myself and to my family." She leans one hip on the doorframe and peeks her head into the playroom, becoming wistful when she focuses on Liam. "Thank goodness the emergency room doctor cleared him to leave. I had no idea what the long-term effects of the drug he was given would be."

"It may not be any of my business," Chase says, "but I think Liam's a little young to shoulder so many truths about his father and his father's family."

Fiona glances up at Chase. "Liam will be told the truth when he's old enough to figure out what it all means. Will you both support me on this?"

Chase and I nod in agreement.

"You'll be the judge of when that should be," he tells her. "In the meantime, he'll hear nothing about it from us. I don't think he even remembers what happened earlier, he was so drugged."

"I went wild when one of Dimitri's thugs injected Liam. Screaming, kicking, I jumped on his back, gave it all I had." Fiona shakes her head. "That ended when some guy with Incredible Hulk arms and a massive overbite pried me off his friend with one arm while he stuffed a sock into my mouth with the other. Liam was scooped up in a blanket," Fiona continues, her voice pale, "while I was pushed through the hallway and down the rear stairwell. The doorman and handyman were too preoccupied calling the police and dealing with the bloodied and unconscious guys Sammy was dropping outside the lobby to notice us being led through the service entrance. They would have done the same to Caroline, only Sammy was back on the job before they could get to her." Fiona stops and draws in a long breath. "Thank you," she says, expelling it in a rush, "for everything you've done for me and Liam."

I wave my hand, indicating no thanks are needed. "Why don't you let Liam spend the night with us while you're out to dinner with my brother?"

Before Fiona can object, Chase says, "We've a full staff here tonight. Liam will be safe."

I watch Caroline scoot for a ball that runs through her legs and worry my bottom lip.

Chase wraps his hand around my waist. "All the children are safe now."

• • •

"I don't know whether to get seriously buzzed or not drink at all." I reach for the bottle of champagne tucked inside the bar of the limo that's driving us to the MET gala. Jittery nerves from yesterday's mix of murder, mayhem, and hair-raising revelations have left me unhinged.

Chase slides the bottle from my hands. "I'd say the latter, at least until Lady Farrah appears in your dress, and you've given your interview."

"Charlotte should have been here," I whisper, shaking my head. "She may have set out to destroy my success tonight, but she didn't deserve to be murdered. How was she able to get past security?"

"She showed some bogus document that indicated she was on a list to assist for the MET gala. Security remembered her from a former visit and allowed her to go up."

Chase looks grim. Yesterday is as vivid in his mind as it is in mine. We have no idea if the weight of Fiona's revelations will make each day heavier to bear than the next. We can only hope that the pangs of pain will eventually quiet. Right now, the hurt is as raw and tattered as a torn seam in an otherwise beautiful cloak.

Chase reaches in and smooths between my brows with the pad of his thumb. "It's your night, your time to be celebrated and enjoyed. Why the worry?"

"This is probably not the right time or place to ask this question, but I've been bothered by how Buford knew what happened in my office before anyone had the chance to call it in. Is my office bugged?"

"No." His answer is swift and definitive. "Buford knew what was happening because Mac was wearing a wire. After Intelligence indicated Dimitri was planning something, Mac and Sammy started wearing wires while on duty. The details were too sketchy to know a specific location or time, so the only recourse we had was to be on constant alert."

"If Buford knew what was happening that morning, why not send help sooner?"

"Putting together a team and strategizing skilled action

takes time, especially when hostages are involved. A plan of attack was being put in place, but after you shot Dimitri, the odds shifted in our favor and the raid was put on hold."

"I couldn't kill him. I just couldn't shoot someone unarmed and on his knees. I could have gotten us all killed, because I didn't have the courage to pull the trigger."

Chase raises both my hands to his lips and kisses their palms. "These hands create. They don't destroy." His eyes pierce mine. "Kill someone and you carry that person's ghost for the rest of your life. You did a good job. You incapacitated Dimitri just enough to keep him from killing Fiona."

"Is that why Buford wanted to hire me?"

Chase doesn't even pretend to be surprised that I know.

"He appreciated how you kept a cool head in a heated situation. You didn't shoot for the kill. If Dimitri had been brought in alive, there would have been a greater chance of eliminating his murderous organization. My guess is Yuri knew that, too. Dimitri had become a liability to the family business."

"You don't think Yuri shot his father to protect Fiona and his son."

"I don't know. On one hand Yuri safeguarded Fiona and Liam, and on the other, he put them in constant danger. There's no doubt he was a contributor to Fiona's problems."

"Is Buford planning to track down and arrest Yuri?"

Chase remains silent, which is all the answer I need.

"Why did you let him escape if you knew he would be a wanted man?"

He studies me, with a ragged look that's tired of the hate, the fighting, and the relentless rage.

"Fiona has suffered enough. Her youth and innocence were mutilated by a psychopath who held them hostage as retaliation against me and my actions. Why lay another death at her feet?"

I take his head and pull it to mine, capturing his lips in a kiss that tightens with the push and pull of our passion. When we separate, I stroke his hair. "I love you with every breath of my life. There will never be any man who means as much to me as you do."

I reach for the bottle of champagne and hand it to Chase. He pops the cork, and when I hold out two flutes, he fills both.

"To happiness and love," I say. We clink glasses and drink. Afterwards, he reaches into his pocket for his handkerchief and smooths my smeared lipstick.

"We can't let the cameras know what we've been up to on the way here."

I take it from his hand and wipe creases of color from his lips, too.

The car pulls to the curb adjacent to the majestic stretch of granite steps that lead to the entrance of the Metropolitan Museum of Art.

Chase opens the car door and steps out, standing tall and erect in his tuxedo. He bends and reaches out his hand to help me out of the car.

"Well, Mzzz Cesare," he drops his voice a decibel. "This is a well-heeled group that's come to applaud your fashion empire." Glitz and glamor parade up the steps. Cameras flash, phones are raised, and people from behind police barricades wave and shout.

"Ms. Cesare, Mr. Reardon, over here," they call out,

hoping to capture us on camera. We stop and smile in unison, allowing them to get their shots. My eyes sweep across the lined crowds, the lights, the colorful banner that swings from the museum's rooftop announcing the event, then back to Chase. I lean into the comfort of his arm and, gripping his hand, whisper, "This is all very exciting, but my real empire is with you and our children. It's all I want and need."

"Baby, I've never wanted anything more than us. Everything I do is for us."

He reaches in and brushes my lips with a kiss.

My knees wobble, my breath hitches.

After a beat, he takes my hand. "Onward and upward," he says and, one concrete stair at a time, we climb toward the museum's entrance.

END

www.ingramcontent.com/pod-product-compliance
Lightning Source LLC
Chambersburg PA
CBHW070729120726
47910CB00001B/38